RESISTANT

A WORLD DIVIDED

ERIKA MODRAK

Black Rose Writing | Texas

ISBN: 978-1-68433-393-6
PUBLISHED BY BLACK ROSE WRITING
www.blackrosewriting.com

Printed in the United States of America
Suggested Retail Price (SRP) $19.95

Resistant is printed in Calluna

*The final word count for this book may not match your standard expectation versus
the final page count. In an effort to reduce paper usage and energy costs, Black Rose
Writing, as a planet-friendly publisher, does its best to eliminate unnecessary waste
without lessening your reading experience.

For Payton,
Holden,
& Rylan
who first gave me inspiration and then gave me the room to write
and for all my students past, present, & future who appreciate the written
word as much as I do—
You are why I write.

RESISTANT

"And now was acknowledged the presence of the Red Death. He had come like a thief in the night. And one by one dropped the revellers in the blood-bedewed halls of their revel, and died each in the despairing posture of his fall."

"The Masque of the Red Death"
~Edgar Allan Poe

PART I

1: CAT

The sun is setting on The Community when I find myself at last on the way home from clinical. The sky, a perfect blend of hazy pinks and oranges, does its best to mock me and my contradictory somber mood. I climb the steps of the rowhouse slowly, the muscles in my legs exhausted from the long hours of standing hovered around microscopes and lab results, the medicinal smell of the building wafting from seemingly every fiber of my jeans and snug, white T-shirt. Pungent. I wrinkle my nose.

I am glad that at the close of each school day, at least my lab coat stays behind to be bleached. It's the little things I am thankful for these days. *A new start for a new day*, I think wearily as I scan my identification bracelet across the small glowing screen above the door handle. Though the daily smell of defeat isn't ever washed out.

Hearing the anticipated click, I turn the knob and enter the shadowy hallway of the two-story house I share with my mother and her part-time nurse, Rhema. I don't bother to turn on the lights as I head toward the rear of the house, old wooden floorboards creaking with a sad familiarity. This evening darkness feels like a friend.

At the end of the narrow hallway, I pause, leaning my shoulder into the wall, a sudden dizziness clouding my vision. Closing my eyes as tightly as I can, I hold this pose for a couple minutes, bright stars streaking across the backs of each eyelid. It's as if I believe that by shutting my eyes, the harsh realities of the remaining world can be willed away. That I can shut out the agony of another failed day in clinical.

Because today marks yet another day where we hadn't found a cure. Another prominent red X on the calendar in my mind. Another setback that I will be forced to dismiss tomorrow and the next day and the one after that.

Forge ahead.

My breathing slows. My heartbeat settles. And as I count each inhale and exhale of my lungs, each time filling them entirely and holding onto the oxygen for as long as I can, my body gradually relaxes, and the dizziness subsides. I am fortunate to have a healthy pair of lungs; I realize this. I also realize that I can't afford to fall apart because I'm suddenly overcome with the raw emotion of the moment.

Still, I can't ignore just how long and challenging today had, in fact, been for me and the dwindling class of 2085, what's left of Generation R as we are called. Not one but two of our schoolmates failed to show up this morning, which usually means one of two things: they are sick with the Virus, or someone close to them is.

It also means the remaining students—me included—were made to suffer through the rest of the day's requirements with heavy hearts and two fewer able minds and bodies to do the work.

Never a day off. Not from clinical and not from the reminders of how bad things in The Community have actually become.

Gathering my strength, I bypass the cramped kitchen, deciding I'm not at all hungry despite my rumbling stomach, and make my way instead to the far back of the house where I find a handwritten note from Rhema pin cushioned to the communication board just outside my mother's small room: *Your mother is resting. Last intravenous bag @ 4:00.* I twist my arm, look to the bracelet encircling my wrist that immediately illuminates: 7:30. There is still time.

I take the note from the board, fold it, place it in my pocket, and make my way into the sitting area that Rhema and I attempted only a few short weeks ago to transform into a makeshift bedroom for my mother. The word *hospice* worms its way into my thoughts for what's probably the millionth time, but I dismiss it quickly because upon entering my mother's pathetic excuse for a bedroom there's soft music playing, a beautiful Old-World album that my mother has refused to throw out. I smile, in spite of the grim situation, and stand motionlessly in the doorway listening to the quiet instrumental that brings me a sudden sense of peace.

It's just like her, my mother. Listening to something so beautiful, so full of life, when she, in fact, is dying. She isn't like the rest of The Community members who have been conditioned to forget. She instead chooses to remember.

"Always remember, Cat."

And for a second I can't tell if this is her speaking now or just a memory, floating alongside the crescendoing music. I walk to the old disc player and turn the volume down. My mother doesn't speak too much anymore. It takes too much effort. But if and when she does, I want to be sure to hear her. On her better days, it's not uncommon for my mother to whisper through haggard breaths that sound more like a broken cellular connection than a conversation, "Always remember, Cat. No matter what. Ignorance isn't bliss when you're dying."

It's also not uncommon for a story of the past to follow.

This morning when I left for school, my mother seemed to be having one of her "better days", which isn't exactly saying much since by definition "better" means she is awake. On these days, she is more aware of her suffering—as am I. But, sensing that she is now asleep, I immediately make myself busy, organizing the multitude of medicine vials littering the dresser and refolding the piles of clean bed linens, my back to the skeletal figure that has become my mother.

For all of my sixteen years of life, I have never been good at handling any sort of illness or bad news. In the face of death, words abandon me. And it's not often I cry unless I'm alone. I feel more like a fish out of water when faced with any type of tragedy, so it's no surprise, really, that in the face of my mother's death, I haven't quite figured out how to just *be* with her.

And I certainly don't *want* to see her as she is now, her face hollow, her skin so thin it seems almost transparent, a network of veins transporting poison at an alarming rate straight to her weakening heart.

She was beautiful once. Before the Virus. *Really* beautiful—her ebony hair tumbling in soft waves down to her slender waist, a stark contrast to her fair, porcelain-like skin. I would sit for hours brushing what seemed to a seven-year-old like an endless sea of night while she softly hummed a now long-forgotten Old World tune.

We couldn't have looked more different.

"Cat, who'd you get your lion's mane from?"

"Cat, were you adopted?"

"Cat, you're nowhere near as pretty as your mom."

Too often as a child, I was teased for looking nothing like my mother. I was awkward, clumsy, a little rough around the edges, my wavy blond hair and deep blue eyes wild. But if ever my kind-hearted, graceful mother was within earshot of the taunts and jeers, she would swoop in to save me and my fragile self-esteem.

"She's me and more," she'd tell them, a twinkle in her eyes, and I knew in my heart that she meant it. "Me and more."

"Me and more," I whisper now without realizing I've spoken the phrase aloud, and I find myself smiling for the second time today.

We were—my mother and I—happy once. Happy and healthy. Or so she's told me. It was too long ago, and I was too young to remember much about the time *before*. I mean, of course, we got sick occasionally. A stuffy nose or a rotten cough. Fevers that for me meant a few days off from everyday life and *maybe* a trip to the doctor's office. A listen of the lungs, a check of the glands, a tousle of the hair followed by a lollipop and a few days on the sofa. And the remedies? Popsicles, flat soda, over-the-counter medicines.

Antibiotics.

The truth is, illnesses were as common in my earlier years as they are now. The difference? When you get sick today, you die. Always, you die.

In today's world, you are never told, "Take two of these, sweetie; you'll feel better in the morning."

Instead and all too often, once you begin to show symptoms of the Virus, there is no promise of another morning.

Feel better never, is more like it.

And just like that, the harsh reality of the present returns along with a heavy weight against my heart. No music, no memory of what once was, could ever erase the fact that my mother and the world around us is, in fact, dying. It's a miracle she's held on as long as she has.

Most victims of the Virus don't last so long.

Without turning around, I brace myself against my mother's bed, my hand grabbing for a fistful of blanket, and I am suddenly startled as my mother's now-brittle hand grasps mine.

Caught off guard at first, alarmed, I cry out softly. Since her symptoms started, we have kept contact to a minimum. Oddly enough, she's not contagious. We both know this. In fact, the Virus isn't really—by textbook definition—a virus at all but an incurable infection stifled temporarily by the required vaccination given to each member of The Community upon admittance. The original disease was left to die outside the walls. What we brought in? A silent killer masked by the appearance of beautiful, thought-to-be healthy people.

Still, I pull my hand away quickly when my mother attempts to take mine because, lately, illness—whatever the form—seems to spread to anyone who gets too close.

A long, painful, suffocating moment passes. Awkward. I don't know if I should apologize. I want to hug my mother and at the same time, run screaming from the room. Instead, I inhale deeply, letting the breath linger in my lungs before releasing it, and press the palms of my hands onto the folded pile of linens before turning to face her.

Her dark muddy eyes are uncharacteristically clear. And for a fleeting moment, I catch a glimpse of the vibrant woman she once was.

"Mom, I—" I begin, but she cuts me off. She's not looking for an explanation from me.

Instead, her eyes shining, she says, "I still remember the night your father brought you to me," and pauses, inhaling two deep breaths of oxygen from the mask that has become her daily accessory. "You were so tiny. So perfect." Another break for oxygen. And a rare gentle smile that reaches the corners of her eyes. "I thought nothing in the world could be more beautiful. One of life's greatest miracles." She squeezes my hand ever so slightly, and I am at once overtaken with a mix of contradictory emotions. Often my mother, in the haze of her illness and morphine, reminisces dreamily about times before the Virus, but she has *never* spoken to me about my birth. She isn't supposed to talk about any of it.

Conversations of the Old World aren't exactly encouraged here in The Community.

It's difficult to forge ahead when your head is stuck in the past. Or so we're all told.

And you never know when someone might be listening. My eyes flash upward to the far corner of the room where a camera stares steely back at me, its red eye blinking.

Still, much of my mother's mumblings of her own younger years are forgiven—she's dying for crying out loud! But the story of my birth is one that's never retold. I have come to believe that it's just too painful for my mother—a time of immense joy she refuses to cloud with the horror of what our world has become.

Despite the anxiety that accompanies every rule I break—and, for this reason, I don't break many—my heart swells with intense longing—I want to *know* this story. What child wouldn't? And it's a few seconds before I recognize the sudden and uncharacteristic dampness on my cheeks as tears.

My mother, seeing that I've started to cry, turns back to the window, wheezing from the effort it has taken her to speak. She holds onto my hand and stares out into our small backyard. I am desperate to hear more. I wish more than anything I could wait for her to continue, that she were healthy and could talk freely about our past.

But I can't wait. Because she's sick. Probably days from death. There is no time for hesitation in these rare, cherished moments. I cannot spare even a fraction of a moment. Not to satisfy my own curiosity, my own longing.

I turn my head to check the time, not willing to let go of my mother's hand, and the red numbers on my mother's bedside clock seem to grow enormous, filling the entire space of the room.

8:23. *I've waited too long.*

And as if on cue, my mother winces, violent coughs seizing her, and panic sends my heart racing as I feverishly work to replace her intravenous bag of morphine before her pain becomes unbearable.

"Mom, I'm so sorry," I whisper, my hands as steady as they can be while frantically filling the syringe full of the liquid pleasure that in a few moments will pass through her ravaged veins. I squeeze the newly-filled bag to flush the medicine through her body more rapidly.

She settles after a brief shudder and closes her eyes, and I wait an eternity before lowering myself to her bed softly, not wanting to cause her any more pain and cursing my selfishness quietly.

I know better. I have been here before. Tempted by these brief, dream-like moments—when my mother's held captive by her memories and not her pain. I know these moments of clarity are rare, the only opportunities I have where I might just be allowed a glimpse into the past. Our past. My past. A story saved for our time alone as my father and the rest of The Community regard these tales as a waste of valuable time—time reserved for finding a cure.

But I know *better.*

I lie with her for a while, gently stroking her brittle hand, careful of her fragile skin, speckled with needle marks and bruises, and pray silently for her to wake up even though I know, I *know,* she suffers more when she's awake.

Outside the city's lights twinkle one final moment, and then everything is dark. Nine o'clock.

By habit and with automaticity that is well-rehearsed, I reach for the candles beneath my mother's bed and light them.

My mother sighs, and I imagine her letting go of the memory I most likely will never get the chance to know. But then she speaks again, "You can't keep him out, Cat," she wheezes frenziedly, and in a voice I hardly recognize, her eyes still closed. "No matter what. He'll come for us all. One day, you'll see. He will come for us all." She grabs the sheets, her knuckles white, as she is taken forcefully by an uncontrollable fit of coughs. I hold onto her, feeling her body wretch, afraid if I hold too tightly, she'll break.

"Who, Mom? Who is coming for us?" I ask, desperate for her answer, all the while knowing it will not come. Not tonight. Maybe not ever. So I cling to her softly until her coughs subside. I cling to her, knowing our time together is limited. That every minute that slowly passes could be her last.

Late into the night, when her breaths seem less labored, and my heart has calmed, I tiptoe quietly from the room.

The candles have long since burned out, so I don't notice until the following morning, when I'm finally changing out of yesterday's clothes, that my shoulder is stained dark red with her blood.

•   •   •   •   •

No one in The Community is supposed to speak of the past anymore, so there are no references to specific dates or times of the year. There is only *before* the Virus and *after*. Most people want to forget the times in between. The fear. The suffering. The decay of what was once a larger, happier, healthier society.

It's easier for most not to remember all they left behind, what they had to endure, and the laws of ethics they had to break in order to be *accepted* into The Community. You needn't harbor the guilt though; you aren't alone. A quick glance out the window or down the street brings immediate validation.

We all wear the same required identification cuffs.

I use mine now to enter The Academy: an old college medical building chosen to remind us young, impressionable, educable youth why we are here. To discover yet another miracle drug.

When the true disease initially emerged over a decade ago—first in the developing countries but then quickly spreading—and doctors failed to treat it even with last-resort antibiotics, plenty of so-called medical experts were quick to claim a cure, but only one doctor had been successful with seemingly stopping the rapidly spreading illness in its tracks. Still, the swiftly mounting demand for this new drug had far surpassed the supply. Thus, The Community was built to separate the sick from the healthy. A type of quarantine. And the new generation of its members, Generation Resistance, was charged with figuring out a way to stop the Virus for good.

Once upon a time, I was a wholehearted believer in this mission that I conceitedly believed was mine and mine alone. My father made sure of it.

But with my mother's currently declining health and my father's increasing neglect, I find my passion waning.

Today, I walk slowly and haphazardly down the hall of the school, bumping shoulders with a dozen or more of my classmates who ask the customary questions:

"What's wrong, Cat?"

"Is it your mother?"

"Cat, are you *feeling* ok?"

I ignore them all. I know how I must look; I can feel the bags under my eyes, heavy and dark as storm clouds, but it's nothing compared to the weight burrowing deep within my chest. And there are simply no words to describe it.

When I left my mother this morning, she was still sleeping, the latest morphine drip strong in her veins, and her breathing seemed steady. Rhema, arriving at sunrise, assured me she'd be fine. As fine as she could be. Still, I almost hadn't left. I had almost broken one of The Community's cardinal requirements: *Without education, there will be no cure. Attend classes daily.* But I needed to breathe air that wasn't tinged with sickness. I needed to be reminded of why I fight so hard for answers. Not just to save my mother. But for the sake of all The Community—me included. I needed some shred of hope left in a world that continues to unravel.

I'm still thinking about my mother and our late-evening conversation when I almost miss my classroom. But just as I stumble past, a hand, steady, strong and familiar, pulls me through the doorway.

"Cat!" Abel's voice is fierce but kind, bringing me back from the fog of my memories. He doesn't bother to ask if I'm all right. It's not a question we ask each other anymore. We've known each other far too long for small talk.

I force a half smile. "What? Do I look lost?" My voice is barely a whisper.

My friend tilts his head, offers me his arm, and I take it. His dark eyes are heavy with concern. "Your mom?" he asks though he doesn't need to. Abel knows me better than anyone in The Community. He's one of the few who does not hold a grudge because of my heredity.

I nod because I'm afraid if I speak my voice will shake and the tears will roll, an uncontrollable, raging river of grief. Already I feel the pools swelling in the corners of my eyes. The sides of my mouth are quivering. Abel, recognizing that the floodgates of my eyes threaten to burst open, gently but hurriedly guides me back out of the room and down the hallway I had only moments ago ventured.

Toward the front door.

"Abel?" I ask, trying half-heartedly to shake him off. But his hold tightens around my shoulders. *This is against the rules. We aren't allowed to skip class. This is wrong. We will be caught.* Still, I let him half drag, half guide me down the now empty hallway. "Abel?" I say again, but he's focused on the door leading out into The Community's commons.

"Come on," he says, conviction in his voice. "You and I need to take a walk."

•   •   •   •   •

Hurrying through the streets of The Community, it's hard to believe that the world around us is poisoned. People litter the market place, buzzing with the daily monotony of community life.

Forge ahead.

Mrs. Sheridan is busily working her produce stand, lining up melons and tomatoes and cucumbers, a colorful array of shapes and smells. Mr. Allen sweeps the sidewalks in front of his bakery. A small group of middle school children—our youngest and last remaining group of school-agers—runs boisterously across the street toward the canal, a young Ms. Flowers breathlessly trying to catch up. It looks picturesque. Almost postcard perfect. Almost. Except I know that on the third floor of Mrs. Sheridan's building, her son, only twenty-five is sick with late-stage symptoms of the Virus. And the shop next to Mr. Allen's? Closed. The owner having died just last week.

Abel tugs at my hand, and we hurry more swiftly through the busy street, my heart pounding. No one seems to notice us.

"Where are we going?" I whisper. But Abel ignores me and continues to half lead, half drag me through the city.

Above, the sky beyond the translucent ceiling of The Community is a beautiful robin's-egg blue. There are no clouds as far as the eye can see—as far as the walls of The Community allow you to see. And even though the temperature is set at a comfortable 75 degrees, I find myself sweating heavily.

I allow Abel to take me past the outskirts of the city. Past the old college grounds. Past fallen statues of once-great men who have long been forgotten. To a remote area of The Community where I am sure no one visits too often anymore. If at all. The roads are worn cobblestones. Weeds tower from the cracks, and I have to watch every step for fear of falling or twisting my ankle. Here in this area of The Community, homes have been abandoned or used for forgotten storage. Rooftops sag and windows gape like dark, sad eyes searching, longing for something. *A better time?*

Finally, after stumbling for what seems like miles down the hazardous cobblestone road, I pull at Abel's hand. I need to catch my breath, and there's a sharp ache growing near the lower right side of my abdomen. Clearly, I am out of shape. I had no idea The Community even stretched so far in this direction.

"It's ok," he tells me. "We're here." And his voice holds a subtle tone of wonder and awe.

With my hands on my knees, still panting, I look up and immediately understand Abel's reverence. Directly in front of us is a towering wall of emerald holly trees. And because they have been neglected for many years, it's almost impossible to see what lies beyond. *Almost* but not impossible. A paved path—maybe an old driveway—leads *through* the trees, winding its way to what appears to be a small, stone cottage shrouded in ivy like a forgotten secret. *Hansel and Gretel* I think instantly, recalling the Old-World story from my childhood, and walk as though in a trance to get closer.

To get a better look, I reach into the trees and move the branches aside, careful of the pointed leaves. It looks like something straight out of a fairytale. A long ago forgotten time. Before the Virus. Distinguishable among the sea of overgrown green is a red door with peeling paint that seems to beckon me. Something small, a hummingbird perhaps, hovers just beyond the leaves to my right. It seems remarkably still, suspended in air. Watching us. I wonder fleetingly how the tiny bird managed to get inside.

Without looking back at Abel, I whisper, "What is this place?"

Abel moves along the wall of trees and pulls back a few holly limbs to reveal a faded octagonal sign. Most of the words are illegible, weather-worn and tarnished. But one word has withstood the test of time.

Cemetery.

A shiver, starting with a tingle at the base of my neck, travels rapidly down my spine, and a heaviness, hot and suffocating fills my chest.

Why would he bring me here?

Abel, recognizing the horror in my face, says quickly, pointing through the rod-iron fence beyond the trees, "What I want to show you—what I *need* to show you—it's through *there*." He walks back toward me and attempts to take my hand. I refuse the gesture. My mother's blood on my shirt, her obvious pain, it's all too fresh in my mind. It's too close to this place. Again I wonder about Abel's intentions. What could be so important that in the wake of my mother's impending death, he'd bring me to the one place where death is inescapable? I feel myself harden, my trademark defense mechanism, and back away from the fence and Abel.

"This place hasn't been used in years, Cat." Abel's voice is a plea. *Forgive me*, it says. "It's just a forgotten piece of land." *I didn't mean to remind you of your mother. I didn't mean to hurt you.*

I turn away from Abel, as though to shield him from my utter disgust, and a silent moment passes between us. I'm trying to decide how to respond. On one hand, I know Abel is the one true friend I've got. He would never do anything to intentionally hurt me. On the other, I cannot ignore the fact that beyond the fence and eight feet under, lie the remains of our ancestors, and my mother is soon to join them.

I turn again and take a few steps closer to the whimsical, stone building that lies beyond the wall of ivy and am once again filled with an odd sense of longing. It is inexplicably beautiful. There's something about the path beyond that seems to call to me.

Walk this way, I imagine it saying. *Let me lead you away from the cruel reality of your life.*

Abel is suddenly beside me, but he doesn't dare touch me. He knows me better than that.

Without taking my eyes from the path beyond the fence, trying in vain not to see the endless sea of gravestones, I ask him quietly, "Why?" But there's much more to this one-worded question, and Abel knows it.

He sighs and thinks a moment before answering. "Have you ever felt like there's more to life than just this place?" I know instantly Abel is speaking of our lives within the walls of our small, often-suffocating community. I also know you aren't supposed to question these things. So I keep quiet, and he continues, "I saw something the other day, Cat. Something that makes me believe not everything we've been told *is* as we've been told."

Still, I say nothing. I am silenced by shock. Shock that my friend would bring me to a cemetery in the first place and shocked that it seems as though he's been spying on the very people who are here to protect us.

"Can I—," Abel starts, and then he turns to face me, his dark eyes pleading. "Cat, can I show you something? Will you come with me?"

Ever since we were young kids, I have trusted Abel. When my father left, when my mother got sick, his friendship never faltered. Even with all the recent rumors circulating through The Community, Abel has remained my rock. But what he's asking now is for me to betray everything I've ever been taught. We aren't supposed to question The Community and its requirements. Requirements put in place to protect us. Yet here Abel was, threatening everything I was raised to believe.

"Please, Cat. I think it's important." Abel's heightened voice lets me know he's beginning to panic. He looks at his wrist where his identification bracelet illuminates the time.

I nod because I can't bring myself to answer out loud and because I'm suddenly apprehensive of my childhood friend who in this moment feels more like a stranger. Abel returns my nod, as though reading my thoughts, and turns and inches along the fence until he comes to a break in the holly. Here, he pulls back the chain link to reveal a small opening just large enough for us to squeeze through, and without another word, he ducks through and disappears.

For a moment it seems as if I'm left standing in the road all alone, and in this moment's hesitation, I consider leaving my friend and running for home. What could they possibly be thinking back at The Academy? Four classmates gone in two days? There would be immense hopelessness. Panic even. The same emotions I felt just yesterday. Except Abel and I aren't sick. Neither of us are suffering from symptoms of the Virus.

"Cat, we need to hurry." From beyond the thick holly, Abel's usually smooth-as-velvet voice has grown slightly desperate. He's my only true friend, I remind myself. The damage back at The Academy is done. We can smooth it over later. The thought of abandoning the one true ally I've got who's not sick is one I cannot bear. So, with a trembling hand, I pull back the fence and step through to the other side.

I don't have time to get my bearings. Abel immediately takes my hand and leads me to the left, down a paved path lined with overgrown plants and grave markers, some tombs so large, they're actually built into the sides of the rolling hills of the cemetery. We climb steadily, and as we reach what appears to be the highest point of the cemetery, I hear what sounds like rushing water.

The river?

Graves are all around us now. One a tall metal cage, rusted and crumbling, stands prominently in the center of a circular path. I wonder who is buried here. Important people. *Once important*, I think. *Not anymore.* The names on the stones are all but impossible to read, but some of the dates are still legible. And astounding.

1825. 1845. 1892.

"Amazing, right?" Abel says but tugs on my hand to get me moving again. "We're almost there," he says. We continue on a few more yards, toward the towering wall that marks the end of The Community, the end of our manufactured protection, when Abel drops my hand and heads toward a part of the wall completely shrouded with ivy. He lifts the vines away, and I shudder, trying not to imagine what creatures are lurking within the leaves. Spiders, snakes, rodents of any kind? True, there aren't supposed to be any dangerous creatures in The Community, but then again I've seen strange droppings from time to time in our pantry back home, so I'm not entirely sure.

Abel works for another minute, grunting and swearing, and by the time he's done fiddling around in the thick brush, the back of his T-shirt is drenched in sweat.

I inch closer to my friend who is now intently looking at something, and once I'm standing directly over his shoulders, I freeze.

"Abel!" I can't contain my immediate fear. He's managed to dislodge *a piece of the wall*. The very wall put in place to protect us. I can't even begin to imagine the consequences we will endure if found out. But as I gaze out through the small opening, I am also filled with something other than fear: immense awe. The sounds of the rushing water. The faint scent of fish. We are staring into the face of a great tumultuous river.

Peering over Able's left shoulder, I can just make out large rocks scattered almost like a hopscotch game across the water to the far shoreline. A flock of long-billed birds glides downstream and disappear beneath a bridge. A bridge! It's all so shocking and...*beautiful*...and so very unbelievable.

"Here," Able backs up to let me take his spot in front of the gaping hole in the wall. From behind me, he says, "In a minute the boat will come back."

My eyes grow wide. "The boat?" All our lives, we have been told there is no leaving The Community. It's simply not safe. The Virus. The terribly evil men and women who have survived only to turn to crime and unspeakable violence. The very people we locked out.

"Listen to me, Cat," Abel says, his voice gravely serious. "I've been doing some thinking lately. When your mom got sick, when I saw how it affected you, I just couldn't stand by and do nothing. I couldn't just sit back and watch you suffer. So a few weeks ago, early one morning, I went for a walk. A long walk. I stumbled upon this place, and it got me wondering. What if? What if, you know, we don't *have* to stay here?" I'm still staring out onto the river, too shocked to reply, so Abel continues, "It leaves early. The boat. Around five-thirty. And returns each day right about now. A little over two hours. I don't know where they go or what they do."

"Who?" I manage to ask.

"I don't know exactly. It's too far to be sure. But—"

"But what, Abel?" I ask when he doesn't finish.

Abel sighs. "It's too far to see *who* is in the boat...but it's not too far to see how many."

"Ok?" My heart is racing because I think I know where he's going with this.

Abel sighs another heavy sigh, clearly worried about how I'll take his news. "Last time the boat left with two people. It came back with three."

"Survivors," I whisper, my eyes wide, but even I know this sounds absurd. The Community hasn't demonstrated concern for the well-being of outside survivors for years now.

"Then why not tell us? If there are people out there who have survived the Virus, why keep it a secret?"

Suddenly there's movement, a flash of color from the opposite shoreline, and I make out what unmistakably is a watercraft of some sort. I hear the muffled rumble of an engine and the boat races across the river, avoiding with great speed the rocks in its path. Almost as if this crew has navigated this exact course hundreds of times.

I stare in disbelief, my mouth agape. For the first time in my years within the wall, I feel extremely exposed.

The boat slows slightly as it approaches the wall to my left, and I swear, the boat is going to head straight into the concrete barrier. My hand instinctively goes to my mouth to stifle a scream, but the boat continues *through the wall*.

"There must be a door we can't see from here," Able explains the obvious. And I back up and out of the opening and collapse against the wall, knees to my chest, rocking back and forth. "There's something they're not telling us," Abel says after a minute.

"I don't know. I don't know," I reply, shaking my head. "Why?" I stare out into the cemetery, trying to make sense of it all. In the corner of my eye, something shimmers, and I think I see another hummingbird hovering just above a grave marker to my right.

"Why else would they make these runs? Bring *survivors* back? And not tell us?" Abel's voice interrupts my scattered thoughts. Nothing about any of this makes sense.

"How often do you come here?" I ask him not able to hide the shock in my voice.

"Enough times to know that no one will think to look for us here once they've realized we've gone AWOL." He offers me his hand, and I hesitate before I take it. My nerves are shot, and my legs unsteady. My mind is racing.

AWOL: an Old-World military term. *Absent without leave.* Without permission.

With Abel's words, I am once again abruptly brought back to planet Community. We've broken the rules, *many* rules, Abel and I. Panic surges. How long have we been gone? An hour? Maybe longer. Will they come looking for us? Of course, they'll come looking! They're probably searching for us now! Who will they send? Wall patrolmen? No. They are far too busy vigilantly guarding the outer walls of The Community to worry about two teenage kids who skipped classes.

Or are they? Abel had just shown me that members of The Community can, in fact, come and go from The Community. To where? For what purpose? We can only guess.

But I do know they *will* send someone to look for us. They *have to* send someone. Two Community members are missing, and with the preservation of life such a priority, The Community won't take the chances of something happening to even one of its members.

Not to mention Dr. Scott Grayson's little girl.

I shake my head. No.

"Cat?" Abel's voice, clearly concerned, seems a mile away and muffled.

Still, my mind continues to race, my heartbeat now a pounding, panicked drum in my chest and ears. Because I know there's only one person who would come looking for us. He would insist on it. And it's with this sickening realization that my hands begin to tremble. My face grows hot, my cheeks two scarlet flames. Moisture clouds my eyes, and it's an eternity before I recognize it as sweat. I am dizzy, and the world around me spins around and around and around like I'm three years old again, riding on that ridiculous, dizzying attraction where you sit in oversized teacups.

Except I'm not three. And I certainly am *not* having a good time.

My head swims, and it's not until the world has righted itself, and I see that Abel is kneeling over me that I realize I fainted.

2: WREN

The distant yet unmistakable sound of a revving motorbike abruptly interrupts what *had* been my perfectly peaceful morning gardening with Alice. The one chore I really don't seem to mind. Whether it's the quiet time I get to spend with my childhood friend or the fact that I have a hand—literally—in something so vital for our camp, I'm not sure.

Startled by the noise, a flock of birds previously resting on the surface of the reservoir to my right explodes into the air. My head instinctively jerks toward the roaring of the engine, and I knock into the basket of vegetables Alice and I only moments ago finished filling.

"Wren!" Alice's voice has a clear note of agitation to it. "Come *on!*" she complains.

"I'm sorry!" I say to her, giving her the look I know she understands, and Alice rolls her eyes. She's seen it before. She knows what's coming. I'm poised to run, but I remain locked in place, awaiting Alice's approval, pleading to her with my eyes.

"Seriously, Wren?" Alice's face falls, and her eyes roll again. "You're unbelievable," she says, but her softened tone lets me know that she's already given up the fight. I jump to my feet and brush the dirt from my hands, ready to hightail it out of there. My heart is already racing with anticipation. "Wren," Alice starts again, "your mother."

It's a pathetic attempt on Alice's part.

I shrug. "What she doesn't know—?" I wait for Alice to finish.

Alice holds up her hands in frustration. "I know, I know!" she says. "What she doesn't know, won't hurt her."

I smile a huge toothy grin of gratitude at Alice, who has, on more than one occasion picked up the slack where I've dropped it—literally—and without waiting for her to change her mind, take off running at top speed in the direction of the revving engine.

He's done it again, I fume. But my anger is surface deep and merely part of the chase that both Ryder and I have grown to enjoy these last few months.

"Ryder!" I scream his name into the wind even though I know he can't hear me, and there's no denying the feigned tone of irritation in my voice. I quickly find the path through our little neighborhood camp and pick up my pace even more. I am fast, there's no arguing that, but I know Ryder. And I know he'll make me work for this ride. He always does. It's Ryder's twisted way of flirting.

Tree limbs smack at my face, but I don't slow down, leaping over giant cracks in the old jogging trail, avoiding protruding roots that have long broken through the pavement like knobby fists angry at the condition of our current world.

And just like every other time I've run this route, I find myself imagining other young girls—girls not unlike Alice and me—but in their fashionable running gear jogging along this exact path. New mothers pushing strollers. Elderly couples hand-in-hand leisurely out for a walk. Everyone a picture-perfect image of health and ignorance, disastrously unaware of the rapidly approaching end of just about everything and everyone.

I exhale loudly, as though I can rid myself of such thoughts with this one breath, and push myself harder. I wind around a corner, burst through the tall gate that borders our camp, and I see him.

Ryder.

He is alone in the deserted and crumbling gas station parking lot. His gloved hands loosely grip the handles of the bike, and his body is positioned to leave, but his helmet is off, his sandy blond hair a straight-up mess.

"Damn, you, Ryder!" I yell, still a hundred yards away. He turns to face the direction of my voice and laughs a deep guttural laugh.

"I had just about lost my faith in you, girl!" he humorously shouts back, and there's no denying the over-exaggerated hint of his almost-southern drawl, nor his obvious up-and-down as he takes in the length of my body.

So like Ryder. I roll my eyes.

Now that I know he is, in fact, waiting for me, I slow to a jog. And as I approach him and the bike, he reaches down to reveal a second helmet, smiling coyly. I am walking now, and, against my better judgement decide to play into his charades, twirling around for him even though I know it's flirtatious and I shouldn't encourage him.

He whistles. "Damn, girl. You didn't think I'd go without you, did you?" His eyes twinkle, and I am reminded once again how hard it is to resist his charm. I know that's why he sometimes talks with that silly, exaggerated accent; he thinks it impresses me. If I'm being honest, it does. So does a man on a bike.

Still, I grab the helmet forcibly and strap it on, feigning frustration, no stranger to these games Ryder plays. He knows how much I cherish these supply runs, and he doesn't hesitate to use this knowledge against me. "You never know," I say, smiling smugly because of course, I do know. Ryder would never ever leave me. "Alice may just kill me," I continue as I mount the bike and wrap my arms tightly around his waist.

"Nah, you're with me, Wren. And you know how much she *loves* me." He slaps my thigh and revs the engine once more, and we're off before I can argue.

It takes just a few minutes to reach the highway. This was one of the reasons my mother and her small crew chose our camp's location. They weren't naive to think they could survive on their own. Sure my mother's an incredibly resourceful woman, and our small community *has* come a long way, living, as my mother refers to it, like our revolutionary ancestors. But our motorbikes and generators don't run on solar power; thus, we need supplies.

And it just so happens that for the past few months, Ryder, my closest male ally in the camp, has been elected as the weekly pick-up man.

We soar down the interstate, weaving in and out of abandoned, rusty cars, now just metal shells where the few surviving drifters sometimes find a night or two of refuge. In the weeks following the outbreak of the Virus, they were all gutted; engines, electronics, steering wheels, seats, even windshield wipers and floor mats were taken for various uses. And the drivers? I don't like to think about what happened to them. It makes me sick.

We fly through the unmanned toll booths—the EZ Pass lanes ironically no longer easy to navigate, too crowded with pieces of cars and debris—and I reach my left arm out and pretend to throw loose change. There's something about pretending life is as it once was that makes me feel freer. It's crazy, I know. But I still do it nevertheless.

The perpetual dreamer, my mother calls me.

Ryder, sensing I loosened my grip, turns to look over his shoulder. I can see his green eyes through the visor. *Ok?* they ask. I'm used to his protectiveness that at times smothers me; however, I also know how much my safety means to him, so I grab back onto his waist and squeeze hard. I swear even through his heavy biker jacket, I feel him relax.

Another half mile, and we'll be at the bridge. This is where we will stop. This is where we will wait.

•　•　•　•　•

And wait.

We wait for what I believe is a few hours, the sun creeping its way left over the river that seems smooth as glass beneath the bridge. Large rocks line the shoreline closest to us, and I again imagine life before the Virus. Sunbathers. Young families. Kayakers and fishermen. A time when people weren't afraid of what lay hidden beneath the water or in the woods. A time when illnesses were easily treatable. A time when survival simply meant getting out of bed each day.

But even now as I turn my eyes to Ryder, the unmistakable bulge near the small of his back reminds me just how unsafe these supply runs can be. And not just because of the unpredictability of who and what lives beyond the great wall that separates the privileged from the not-so-privileged, but because of the other survivors who coexist outside its doors with us.

A shiver interrupts the nervous tapping of my feet, and I realize I have moved far past the point of feeling antsy. It's not unusual for the drop-off to be a little later than expected, but this is the longest I remember ever having to wait.

"Something's wrong," I say out loud before I realize it.

Ryder's brow furrows. I can tell he feels the same way. Still, he replies, "Maybe. Maybe not."

I jump off the hood of the abandoned jeep that I swear by now has the imprint of my ass on it. "Come on, Ry, we've had to wait before, but this is ridiculous. Something's happened."

Ryder inhales deeply and stretches his long arms up over his head in an over-exaggerated, lazy stretch. "Listen, we'll wait for another hour. If no one shows, we'll head back," he says matter-of-factly, but by the hitch in his tone I can tell he's worried. He also hasn't been able to sit still for the past thirty minutes.

We are both acutely aware of how much we need these supplies. Without them, we'll run out of gas, clean water, and medical supplies just to name a few of the inventories that are "volunteered" by our one contact person within what our camp has come to refer to as The Dome. Without gas, it would take days to hike down the highway. And that's *if* you made it.

Without clean water, we'd be forced to drink from the reservoir beside our camp. Boiling water over a fire. Without the aid of matches.

"If no one shows?" I question, incredulous. "Ryder, if no one shows—"

He walks over to me and rests his large hands on my shoulders. "Babe, Don always shows, ok?" When I don't seem relieved, he continues, "Look, Don's late. He'll be here. He would have gotten word to us otherwise, Wren. Trust me."

I nod but am still not convinced.

"You know, you don't *have* to come with me," Ryder says after a few minutes of silence as he takes a seat back on the hood of the jeep, offering me his hand. I shove it away and, placing my boot onto the fender, gracefully leap onto the car. "I'm a big boy," he continues. "I can handle the supplies all by myself." And now there seems to be a hint of hurt behind his words. He's never been fond of my stubborn independence.

"We both know you like the company," I say, playfully elbowing him in the ribs.

There's another moment of silence between us as I stare out into the river flowing freely beneath the bridge, and I can feel his eyes on me. He's no longer in his typical playful mood.

"Wren," he says, "why *do* you like to come?"

Without looking away from the river, I respond, "Maybe *I* like the company."

I feel Ryder grow tense beside me, but he doesn't speak. So I am forced to answer more seriously. "Safety in numbers, remember?" I say. But he snorts loudly, not believing a word of it. It's true, I do worry about Ryder's safety on these supply runs, but that's not why I come.

The truth is, there's more to my curiosity of The Dome than even I understand.

And before I can stop myself, I admit aloud, "I don't know, Ry. There's something about that wall, you know?" I lift my head to face the immense concrete barrier that divides our world in two. On the opposite shoreline, the wall climbs steadily up, no windows, no doors that we can tell, a translucent domed ceiling too high to offer us any kind of view inside. Only once a week are we even offered evidence of life beyond the large wall. And even though we are all told that what lies beyond the wall is corrupt and unjust, every time a supply run is on the horizon, The Dome seems to beckon me like a beacon. I can't explain it. I also can't deny it.

"No, Wren, I don't know." Ryder's voice has grown ever-so-slightly frigid.

I shrug. "It's almost like I'm supposed to be there." And as soon as these words pass through my lips, I wish more than anything I could take them back.

•　　•　　•　　•

Agonizing hours slip past us, too quickly, like the water flowing rapidly beneath the bridge.

With every passing minute, my worries intensify. I worry about my mom, whether she's noticed I'm not in camp. It's true, I keep these supply runs with Ryder a secret from my mother, but it's the one truth I keep from her. And it's a big one. I worry, too, about the resources that might not come today and what impact that will have on our camp. I worry that I've pissed off Alice.

I just worry.

To pass the time and calm my nerves, I take to watching the angles of the shadows change, growing longer and more severe as the daylight hours diminish, and I allow my imagination to transform them into graceful dancers with slender, reaching arms. I am studying one tree's particularly beguiling shadows when from somewhere in the distance finally comes the faint hum of an automobile's engine. Immediately I am set on high alert.

I leap from the hood of the jeep, cursing loudly as my body rejects the sudden impact after sitting sedentary for so long.

"Shhh!" Ryder hisses. He turns to stare across the great eight-lane bridge, eyes shielded by his large hands. Through the haze of exhaust, a white van gradually materializes from far down the bridge. Without warning, Ryder turns and crashes into my body, sending me flying into the overgrown brush.

"Ryder, what the h—?" I start, but he cuts me off with a violent gesture then demandingly whispers, "*Put your helmet back on and stay out of sight!*" and runs full sprint to the start of the bridge, leaving me in his dust before I can protest.

It takes less than a minute to decide not to heed Ryder's advice. Because something about this drop-off just doesn't feel right.

Slowly, I crawl to the edge of the road to see the supply van come to a halt where Ryder stands arms outstretched as though asking, *What the hell has taken you so long?* But then his arms drop heavily to his side as not one but *two* men wearing black suits exit the vehicle. His right arm reaches behind to feel for his gun but then changes its mind. My chest pulses rapidly.

Something's wrong, something's wrong; my heart beats seem to shout within my ears. But still, I stay hidden. Still, I watch helplessly as Ryder confronts these two strangers on the bridge alone.

Two strangers. At first, I think it is a trick of the light, more shadows toying with my imagination. But it doesn't take me long to recognize that our Don is not either of the two men who have exited the vehicle.

Then who are they? And what's happened to Don?

The trio of men are too far away for me to discern any audible conversation—not with the roaring of the river below—but I can tell from their gestures and body language that the conversation isn't exactly conversational. I remain poised in a crouching position, ready to pounce if Ryder appears to be in more danger than I know he can handle.

"We can't risk being seen, Wren. Promise me you'll always be careful." My mother's pleading voice penetrates my thoughts. *"Promise me, Wren. This is important. Please."*

I shake my head, attempting to rid my mother's voice from my thoughts, having already broken, as I had so many times before, our camp's number one rule: All girls are to remain in camp. Unseen. For their safety. Period. The end.

For years, I had heeded the warning, too young to realize I *could* disobey my mother if I chose to, her steely tone enough to make the point. But as the years in camp passed, and I grew older, home began to feel more like a personal prison, my restlessness also growing until it became too large to ignore. And while I knew I probably shouldn't risk it, I soon found myself a defiant teenager with a thirst for the forbidden.

After a while, my mother's rule became just that: a rule. One that brought me a rush of adrenaline to break.

So break it I did. And often.

Before this moment, I believed Ryder would protect me should anything happen on these rebellious adventures, my mother's cautionary rule one of an overprotective parent.

Now, lying on my stomach in the tall grass on the side of the highway, watching helplessly as Ryder and the two other men disappear behind the van and out of sight, my mother's warnings seem justifiable. As the minutes pass at a painfully slow rate, I find myself making a decision. I inch cautiously over to the motorbike that sits precariously close to the road, and, trying not to make a sound, pry open the storage compartment at the back. I am not entirely sure what I plan to do, but feeling the cool metal of the second gun pressed into my palm brings me a brief rush of courage.

It doesn't last.

Who am I kidding? I've never fired a gun before. I'm not even sure how to *load* a gun. How am I going to pull the trigger, then?

I try thinking back to the day, three years ago, when I stumbled upon the men in camp—Ryder included—going over gun safety and our camp's ridiculously simple protocol for security. Before that day, I hadn't even thought the camp *had* any type of weaponry, let alone firearms. We were a peaceful "gated" community. In the beginning, we had even built our own version of a wall after the Virus, and that seemed to offer all the protection we needed.

Even raiders left us alone. I was told we aren't their type. Too many of us, too few of them. We aren't vulnerable. Nor are we valuable.

But I'm no longer a naive child, I remind myself. Since then, I have seen things, heard things. I know we aren't as safe and protected as I would like to believe.

And Ryder brings the guns on every supply run. Why? For protection. It was by mistake that I had discovered the second pistol, searching for a blanket while Ryder made the trade with Don a few months ago.

Hold the gun steady. Feet shoulder width apart, knees slightly bent. Extend your arms. Aim. Shoot.

Could I do it if I needed to?

With the gun held tightly in my left hand, I head as quietly as I can over to the van. The three men are still hidden from view, the back door of the van wide open, but now that I am closer, voices rise above the roaring river below.

"Shifted? What does that even mean? *Shifted?*" It's Ryder's voice, impatient and angry, followed by a muffled reply. Laughter? "Again, I'm not sure that *you're* hearing *me*. I don't do business with anyone except Don!"

I can tell by Ryder's tone that he is trying to convince the other men that he is in control of the situation; however, I can also tell that Ryder himself doesn't believe it. With Ryder's mention of Don's name, I am suddenly hyper-aware, too, that no one—I mean no one—except Don has ever dropped off supplies. Never once did I think to question why.

Something tells me now, though, that perhaps not everyone living beyond the great wall approves of these deliveries.

So what do these men want then?

At this point, sensing the rising tension, I begin to slink along the side of the van, carefully stepping over what's left of the rusting, jagged guardrail, my heart racing almost painfully in my chest.

Because the back door of the van is open, I can't see the men exactly, but I can see three pairs of feet. Ryder, obvious by his faded and worn riding boots, stands with his back to the open van while the other two men work in unison it seems pinning him, leaving Ryder no choice but to get past both if he needs to escape.

"Kid, just tell us what we want to know, and we'll hand you over your precious supplies," one of the men says with a gruff voice. The other grunts.

"I've got no reason to tell you *anything*," Ryder responds defiantly.

"Did you hear that, Leo? Kid, here, wants a reason."

I see one pair of shoes move so close to Ryder that they appear to smother him. Then I hear the unmistakable *click* of a gun set to fire. I don't think. I leap around the van's rear doors and take turns pointing my own weapon at the shoulders of each stranger like an indecisive child.

"Stop!" I scream because, frankly, I'm not exactly sure what else to say. My hands are sweating and shaking, the gun much heavier than I anticipated. It wavers up and down as I continue to alternate pointing the gun at the backs of the two men. At first, adrenaline empowers me, making me feel like a quasi-superhero. But then the reality of the scene materializes in front of me.

Ryder's face says it all. I've messed up.

He's standing at the one open mouth of the van where I can see supplies lining the walls of the *left* side of the storage area. The right side, however, is slightly ajar, one of the stranger's large hands still on the handle, frozen in the process of pulling open the door. It was the lock, I realize, that made the clicking sound I mistook as the gun's safety. *Shit. What now?*

"Wren," Ryder's voice is surprisingly calm. "Wren," he says again, "put the gun down, and go back to the bike." He's holding out his arm to me, signalling *stop*. "It's ok. Go. Now."

I take two steps to my left, back toward the guardrail, keeping the gun level with the strangers' backs.

"Little lady," the stranger closer to me, growls, "I suggest you listen to your boyfriend." His hands indicate surrender, but he begins to turn around.

"Don't!" I scream, sweat beading on my forehead.

"Promise me, Wren. Promise me you will remain unseen."

But the stranger has turned just enough to look me in the face. His brow furrows, a look of sheer perplexity shrouds his eyes. Then his mouth stretches into a crooked smile. "Well, well, well," he purrs and snaps his fingers toward his partner who is still facing the van door, through which I can now see Don bound and gagged in the corner.

"Hey, Leo, check this out," the man says.

"Man, I'm not about to be shot," Leo responds.

"Wren," Ryder says again. "Go back to the bike. I've got the situation under control." He indicates the gun tucked into the back of his jeans.

My eyes plead with him, but I continue to take small steps toward the bike.

"Leo, I'm telling you, man. Turn around. Boss man's not going to believe this."

At this, Ryder draws his weapon. "Enough!" he orders. "Wren. *Go. Back. To. The. Bike. Now.* Leo, untie Don. And, *you*," he turns to face the unnamed stranger. "Shut your flippin' mouth about my *girlfriend.*"

"Ok, ok, mate. Leo, we're good. We've got what we need. Dump the supplies, and let's go." There's a tone of accomplishment, haughty confidence, to his voice, and I can't for the life of me figure it out. There are, after all, two guns pointed in his direction.

And I am *just* a girl.

A girl.

In an instant, horrible images of greedy men desperate for affection...for...*sex*...fill my mind. *That's why!* I think appallingly, realizing I may have just put our entire camp at great risk.

Ryder cuts one more angry scowl in my direction, clearing my head in an instant, and I leave him to finish the exchange, my tail tucked between my legs.

Still, there are bits and pieces to this exchange I can't quite figure out. We've never traded Don for *anything.* He has, for whatever reason and for as long as I can remember, simply delivered to us the supplies our camp needed—no strings attached. Yet, here were these two men vying for a trade.

Of what? Information? Something more tangible? What had they asked Ryder?

I am sitting back on the jeep when I hear the van doors shut and the engine roar to life. I'm not sure how to explain my actions to Ryder. How I let my imagination and then my assumptions get the best of me. How I put us both in what could have been very real danger. So when he approaches with the filled duffel bags in hand, I keep my head bowed and follow him like a sulking, humiliated child back to the bike.

•   •   •   •   •

Our entire ride back down the interstate is done in silence. But now as we pull into camp, a million questions race through my mind. Who were the strangers on the bridge? What had they wanted? Why had they tied up Don? And why had they seemed so intrigued by me? Still, I keep my mouth shut. I don't dare ask Ryder. In truth, there is only one person I know I need to talk to. And I just don't know how I'm going to muster up the strength for what I know is a necessary conversation with my mother.

Ryder parks the bike just outside the garage where the supplies are housed and takes off his helmet. We sit for a moment before he helps himself off the bike and heads towards the trailer to unload it.

He doesn't bother offering me a hand. He's angry; I know it. But not at me. I know him well enough to know he's struggling with what *he* could have done differently. It's just like him. He blames himself.

Taking the hint, I leave him unloading the supplies by himself and walk toward the cabin I share with my mother. It's a modest three-bedroom house with a large garage my mother has managed to transform into a makeshift clinic. Her own little doc-in-a-box she likes to call it.

Our entire neighborhood is made up of what we all call cabins instead of houses. Why? I'm not sure. Maybe it gives us all the sense of a true camp, of camaraderie. Maybe it's because these cabins will never truly be our homes. They don't exactly belong to us. It's not like we pay mortgages on them.

I kick off my boots by the door and head toward the kitchen at the back of the cabin where I smell tonight's main course cooking. Silverware is click-clacking against pots and pans, and my mother is humming. There's someone else in the kitchen, too, I realize as I approach the doorway and hear a male's voice laughing at something my mother has either said or done.

I stand there in the opening to the kitchen and watch the scene unfolding in front of me. Bill, my mother's "friend" is helping with the vegetables—vegetables most likely cleaned up by Alice after my furious departure for supplies earlier.

Thinking of Alice right now intensifies my guilt, so I don't. After all, I've got bigger things to worry about.

Mom and Bill don't notice me at first, and I am glad. It's like watching a movie on the big screen, a picture-perfect, old romantic film.

Bill brings the bowl of tomatoes, peppers, and onions over to my mother, who is standing over the gas stove. Without speaking he wraps his burly arms around her, tipping the vegetables into the large bowl my mother is stirring as she sways back and forth—a dance that I feel I shouldn't be intruding.

I try backing out of the kitchen slowly, but as she turns to face Bill in what I imagine would have resulted in an intense make-out session, my mother sees me out of the corner of her eye.

"Wren!" she exclaims. "You're home!"

As if by magic, Bill is back behind the center island messing with what appears to be a lopsided loaf of bread.

I chuckle softly. "Hey, Mom," I say. "Hey, Bill." Despite the occurrence earlier on the bridge, I can't help smiling at the two of them acting like young teens caught in the act by a parent.

Bill doesn't look up, his cheeks scarlet. He's big and tough on the outside, but inside, I have learned, he is a teddy bear. And he's the closest thing I've had to a father figure since my dad died of the Virus when I was three.

"Listen, guys, I'm really sorry about earlier—"

My mother cuts me off with a wave of her hand. "Nonsense, honey. Alice wasn't happy, of course, but she explained to me what happened." She wipes her hands on her apron, turns, and winks at me, her eyes twinkling. "Come, give me a hug. I feel like I haven't seen you all day."

I am confused but let her wrap her arms around me anyway. She smells of spices and lavender, and I breathe her in heavily. Too often, I forget how much just the presence of her calms me. "Mom, I..." my voice trails off. She backs up, holding me at arm's length, and I know instantly that she recognizes the seriousness in my face.

She hugs me again and whispers in my ears, "We'll talk later, ok?"

And even though I sense she believes my worries are of no real significance, I nod, not wanting to have to admit my foolishness in front of Bill.

"Ok, now go wash up for dinner. It's our turn to host," she reminds me, and I groan knowing that as dinner hosts to the neighborhood camp, we will be up most of the night.

•　　•　　•　　•　　•

There are exactly thirty-two people living in our neighborhood camp. It makes the saying *small world* really ring true. Our youngest is ten, our oldest 67. Everyone knows everyone. Everyone knows everyone else's business. Everyone has opinions and flaws. And we all know what these limitations and weaknesses are. But we are a family. And we need each other, which is why our weekly neighborhood dinners are so important.

Our camp actually started with just seven survivors: five men, one woman—my mother—and a child—me. After the camp's inception, drifters trickled in, following rumors of an existing community of people. *Healthy* people. *Sane* people. And a doctor.

I was six when Alice arrived with her uncle. We became instant best friends—easy to do when there are so few to pick from. But from the moment we met, we were more like sisters than friends. We talked like sisters. Fought like sisters. Were jealous like sisters.

Still are, I think, imagining that Alice's resentment earlier in the day had less to do with the chores and more to do with Ryder's obvious feelings for me.

He certainly doesn't hide it.

Ryder.

I sigh, remembering the day Ryder stumbled in--nine years old, all alone, filthy and terrified. He'd traveled too many miles to count and had lost his family during the long, tortuous way. To this day, he doesn't talk about it. Not even to me. Alice was head over heels for Ryder almost instantly, following him around like a trained puppy. Ryder, however, was not interested in Alice, but instead spent his days playing outside in the dirt with me.

I watch the two of them now, sitting alone at one of our long, white folding tables—rescued no doubt from a restaurant that must have at one time served as a wedding reception venue. They seem deep in conversation. Well, Alice does anyway as she's doing most of the talking. Ryder's head is lowered, resting on his closed fists. I know what they're most likely talking about.

Me.

Because just as Ryder doesn't hide his feelings for me, Alice doesn't hide hers for him. It's a messy triangle. One that I don't feel like being a part of tonight.

I sigh again, heavily.

I know I should join the two of them, apologize to both, but it doesn't seem worth dealing with their combined disapproval. Instead, I scan the crowd for my mother.

I'm not sure what excuse Alice gave her earlier, but it's clear she doesn't know about what happened on the bridge today. Just thinking about it makes my heart race in anticipation.

When I can't find my mother, I begin absentmindedly clearing the tables that people have abandoned, walking amongst the crowded backyard smiling and responding politely to questions and statements from neighbors who tonight feel superficial.

Since dinner is usually followed by a neighborhood meeting where supplies are distributed among the campers, the backyard is arranged so that each table is facing the back deck. Bill, who usually does most of the talking at these weekly meetings as he is close to my mother and one of the original seven, takes the steps leading up to our large porch two at a time and stands smiling out at the crowd, seemingly unaware of the earlier occurrence on the bridge.

But tonight it's Ryder who takes the center stage of the porch, quickly following behind Bill, pausing to briefly shake his hand before whispering something in his ear. Bill's expression falters, but he nods, taking a seat.

"Today's supplies came," Ryder announces to the crowd after a few words of casual conversation. His accent is all but indecipherable, and his face is uncharacteristically solemn. A few people start to applaud but abruptly stop as they realize this isn't exactly great news. Ryder inhales deeply before continuing. "Our informant from The Dome let us know that the situation within the walls has *shifted*," Ryder twists the truth, deliberately leaving out the part about the other men, "and while we don't know exactly what this means, we need to prepare like today's run was our final pick up." He looks straight at me, and I lower my head, ashamed.

There are cries from the crowd. Bill looks completely befuddled, coming to a stand, and doesn't seem to know what to say or do in response to Ryder's announcement.

"What do you mean *shifted*?"

"Our final pick up?"

"What will we do?"

When I look back up, I see Ryder has pulled back his solid shoulders, and his face is stoic. He's no longer looking at me. He holds up his right hand to silence the crowd. "What this means is we are on our own. But we've always been on our own. We'll just have to work a bit harder now, that's all."

"That's all? That's *all*?" The camp is far from relieved by Ryder's speech. There is heated discussion rippling through the yard, and Ryder's steady features become panicked.

Men talk of storming The Dome. Women wrap arms around each other, fear rippling across their candle-lit faces.

Quickly, and as if on cue, my mother appears beside Ryder—as though conjured by his current need for her—and she places a hand on his back. She looks reassuringly out over the crowd, and I am filled with awe by her demeanor, which is both calming and powerful.

"My family," she says softly, tenderly, "I know that the news tonight is worrisome." She pauses to smile but cuts Ryder a look that says, *We'll talk later.* "What you must remember is that we started from very little and have grown. On our own." She looks again at Ryder, and he knows to give her the center stage. He takes a few steps back.

Bill to his left leans in to ask, "What happened?" But Ryder's gaze is locked on my mother who continues her speech.

"We will be fine without the aid from The Dome. We are strong. We are smart. We are family. We've already survived the unsurvivable. We. Will. Be. Ok."

And with her words, there is a hush over the crowd.

In the silence, I think I can hear my own heart beating.

"I know many of you must be afraid by this news, but fear is not foreign to us," my mother continues, the camp and I now hanging on her every word. "We have faced the Virus head on. We have persevered while our loved ones did not. We have experienced more tragedy in these last few years than many face in a lifetime. As long as we are together as a family, we will get through this. I promise you."

With her final word, the collective crowd sighs, and the sense of relief is almost tangible, handed to each member of the camp like a gift-wrapped box. Though a few men still whisper among themselves.

I, however, am not convinced by my mother's conviction. Because I've learned a thing or two about promises. They are all too often broken.

I'm living proof of that.

•　　•　　•　　•　　•

Later that night, after the final dish has been cleaned and put away, my mother brushes the mass of tangles from my unruly bob of hair while I sit staring at a reflection that doesn't quite seem to belong to me.

The hours following the camp dinner were spent in silence, me scrubbing dishes from boiled reservoir water while my mother and Bill whispered secretly in corners of the modest house, seemingly avoiding me at all costs.

And Ryder? He had quietly disappeared back to his own cabin to brood.

Now, nearly midnight, Bill is back at his own place and our cabin once again belongs to my mother and me alone.

For once I am speechless. I don't know what to say. What questions to ask. And I certainly don't know how to talk to my mom about what transpired earlier on the bridge. Of course, I know more than Ryder shared with the camp, and I am now afraid my mother will be even angrier with Ryder *and* me that we chose to keep it to ourselves. But how do I begin to share with her that I had—only hours before—broken the one promise she had begged me to keep?

"Something's troubling you," my mother says, her voice bringing me back to the present. "Are you worried about the supplies?"

I don't answer. I don't know how to, and she continues to brush my hair in silence for what seems like many tortuous minutes.

"Mom. Stop," I say, no longer able to endure the quiet. I take her hand and hold it, preventing her from taking another stroke of the brush. I know I've betrayed her, and each loving pass through my hair is a cruel reminder of the secret I keep. I turn to face her but can't seem to meet her eyes.

"Wren," she says softly. "Talk to me. What's the matter? Is this about the supplies? Did something happen between you and Ryder?" There is genuine concern in her voice.

I shake my head. My mother inhales deeply and puts down the brush. She turns to stare out the bedroom window, and I try to find the right words. Maybe I am wrong. Maybe my presence on the bridge today meant nothing significant. Maybe if I choose to keep the information locked away, then it will mean nothing. But I know I can't. I have to tell my mother everything. What will the consequences be once I do, though? Fear? Anger? Disappointment? I don't think I could bear my mother's anger, let alone disappointment.

There's a sharp, sudden pain in the palms of my hands and looking down I notice I've dug my fingernails into the flesh.

"I broke my promise to you, Mom," I finally say, and then the next few sentences come tumbling out. "I went with Ryder on the supply run today. I'm so sorry. I'm so sorry I didn't listen to you. There were other men with Don on the bridge, Mom." She continues to stare out the window, so I go on with my confession, thankful not to have to look her in the eyes. "They all *saw* me."

And I'm afraid I've put us all in jeopardy, Mom.

There's another minute of silence between us. The spoken information hovering in the air like a dense fog. I am sure my mother is trying to mask her concern.

But when she finally turns back around to face me, her eyes don't register the fear I think they should. Or the disappointment. Instead, she looks almost apologetic. Sad even. Like she hasn't heard a word I've just said.

"Mom," I say with more conviction this time around, "One of the men. On the bridge. He saw me, and the look in his eyes...." I'm not exactly sure how to describe it now. Hungry?

Still, my mother doesn't appear overly distressed by this information. Instead, she smiles sadly and seems lost in a memory the two of us clearly don't share.

"Maybe you didn't hear me correctly—" I begin, seriously worried that I somehow *still* haven't gotten the point across. Just another exaggerating teenager. But my mother stops me, raising her hand to touch me softly on the shoulder.

She lets yet another moment hover in the air, her hesitation causing me more distress. "Wren," she finally says, and while it sounds like she's trying to reassure me, the very edge of her voice is sharp. "It was only a matter of time." Her expression remains soft, and as she reaches out to touch my face, I lean into her palm, relishing the warmth of her gesture, and close my eyes. I feel her weight on the seat next to me and then her arms around my shoulders.

"Mom, I'm so sorry," I whisper, but she replies with a gentle, "Shhh. Shhh."

"I might have ruined everything," I continue.

"Nonsense, sweetie. It's my fault for ever thinking I could keep you hidden away forever." She pauses as though considering something. "You know, Wren," she starts to say, but her voice trails off as she changes her mind.

I give her a minute to finish, but when it's clear she's not planning to, I lean back to look her in the face. "What, Mom? What were you going to say?" Wrinkles of worry crease her forehead, and she suddenly seems years older. I am alarmed by her appearance. Alarmed and guilty. How had I not noticed this all before? Even with all my mother and I have been through, she's remained my rock. Now, however, she seems more like a wilting flower.

"Oh, darling," she cries, smiling and pulling me into a deep embrace. Her face is in my hair, and I feel her breathe me in. Her grip on my shoulders is tight.

"Mom," I say, my voice muffled by her neck. "Hey, mom, it's ok." I pull back and am relieved to see her still smiling. "We're going to be ok, remember? You said so yourself."

"Yes, sweetheart." She cups my face with her strong, calloused hands. "I believe what I told the camp tonight. As long as we stick together, we'll beat this hurdle." But there's a trace of uncertainty to her voice that fills me with doubt.

"Hurdle, huh?" I say, jabbing her in the side with my elbow, attempting to lighten the air in the room. "More like a mountain."

My mother laughs. A sound that warms the very depths of my core. "Like landing on the moon," she replies, hugging me again.

"Like surviving the Virus," I say, and she squeezes me tighter.

We rock back and forth together until my eyes grow heavy, my breathing steady and deep. And as I fall fast into the abyss of sleep, I completely forget about the conversation my mother tried to start but never finished.

•　•　•　•　•　•

When dawn's light awakens me the following morning, I am initially confused. There is a thundering noise in my head that I can't place, and I press my palms hard into my eye sockets, hoping to alleviate the throbbing ache beyond my temples. But the noise becomes louder and more panicked, and my eyes dart open as I fly to a sitting position.

At first, my vision is blurred as my sight adjusts to the sudden brightness of the room, and gradually, dizzyingly, my setting becomes clear. I must have fallen asleep in my mother's room.

I scan my sleeping arrangements quickly. I'm still in my clothes from last night, tucked into my mother's chaise. Her favorite afghan blanket is tangled at my feet. I kick it off now, and swivel my legs around, placing my feet, still in socks, onto the cool hardwood floor.

Bang! Bang! Bang!

There it is again! The incessant noise in my head! I can't seem to shake the feeling that this is all part of some bad dream I must have had during the night but can't quite recollect. My knees tremble as I rest my elbows on my thighs and drop my head, trying to find some clarity.

I breathe in, two, three, four…out, two, three, four.

"Claire!" *Bang! Bang!* "Wren!" *Bang! Bang! Bang!* "Open the damn door!"

And then it hits me. The sound. It's someone knocking at our cabin door.

No.

Not knocking. Pounding.

I stand quickly—too quickly—and I have to catch myself on the door frame of my mother's bedroom, swept up in a wave of dizziness.

My mother.

Where is she?

"Claire! Wren!" The bellows beyond our front door continue, muffled but unmistakably panicked. "I swear by any god left above! I'll break down this damn door!" Bill's voice. He sounds angry. Why would he be angry?

I shuffle down the hallway, each step growing steadier than the last.

"I'm coming!" I say as loudly as I can muster, grabbing onto the banister and making my way down the creaking stairs. *What time is it?* I wonder.

"Wren? Wren, is that you?" There's relief now in his voice. "Thank God. Open the door. I've been worried sick."

By this time I've reached the small foyer and am fumbling with the lock. After unlocking the handle, I reach almost instinctively for the chain at the top of the door, but my hand hits the metal dangling against the frame. Startled, I look up.

Something's not right, I think, shaking my head.

My mother never forgets to chain bolt the door. I turn and yank the handle, my chest tightening with a sudden dread of anticipation. *What the hell is going on?*

And like a force to be reckoned with, Bill storms into the cabin, pushing past me, his head on a swivel, searching up the stairs, back down the hallway to the kitchen, back again to the stairs, a wild desperation in his eyes.

"Bill," I say, and my voice is barely a whisper. I struggle to find my breath, frantic, anxiety a fist around my chest. "What's the matter?" I take hold of his strong arm and squeeze. It's the most contact he and I have ever had.

"Your mother. Where is she?" But he doesn't wait for me to answer. He is clambering up the stairs two at a time. "Claire!" he shouts. "Claire, tell me you're still here!"

"Bill, wait!" I scream, and I take off after him. "What's going on? Why are you here? Where is my mom?" My world seems to be crashing down around me. If Bill is here...if he's worried...then that can only mean one thing.

Something's very, very wrong. And that something has to do with my mother.

I hear a noise to my left and turn into my mother's room, crashing into Bill, who now cries freely on his knees.

"Oh, Claire," he cries. "I am so sorry. I never should have left you last night." The rest of his speech is muffled by his large hands that now cover his face, and I am left standing helpless above a man I never thought capable of breaking.

"Bill?" I question softly. I am trying hard not to break myself. "Where is my mom?"

But Bill shakes his head slowly.

I try again. "Where. Is. My. Mother?" And each word is its own sentence, hanging in the air like a dark cloud.

"Wren. I am so sorry." Bill's shoulders shake, but he doesn't look at me.

"I don't understand," I whisper, kneeling down beside the man who has become more like a father figure to me than just my mother's long-time boyfriend. Hesitantly, I rest my hand on his broad shoulder. "What could you possibly be sorry for? Where is she? Where is my mom?"

"Wren," Bill moans, tears now running freely down his face. "I couldn't stop them. Oh, God. I tried. I knew...I *knew* when I saw the van...I followed them as far as I could—"

"Knew what? Bill, knew *what*? What van? What is going on?" And this time I can't hide the panic, the fear in my voice. I run to the window and pull back the dusty blinds, but there's nothing to see. No van. No tracks. Only the lone motorcycle thrown haphazardly on its side where Bill left it.

Bill doesn't move from his spot on the floor. "Wren," he chokes, "she's gone. They took her. I'm so sorry."

At first, I don't acknowledge what he's said. I can't. My mother is our rock. She's the one thing that holds our camp together. And she was with me just hours ago. My knees buckle. I grab hold to the curtains framing the windows of my mother's bedroom. What will we do? What will I do?

"Who took her, Bill?" I manage to whisper.

At first, he doesn't answer me, still a sniveling mess on the floor.

"Bill," I say again, trying to hold myself together. "Answer me. Who took my mom?"

Looking up at me with red-rimmed eyes, Bill mumbles through his sobs, but I understand what he says nonetheless.

"The men from The Dome, Wren. They came in the middle of the night and took her. They took her, Wren. They took her." With this, Bill completely gives in to his despair, moaning so loudly I can't concentrate.

This is my fault, I think. It's too much of a coincidence not to be. The men on the bridge yesterday. They must have come back for me and left instead with my mother.

"What are we going to do?" Bill asks once he's gotten himself together enough to speak.

But I don't answer him. Because, although I know instinctively what *I'm* planning to do, I also know Bill simply won't stand for it.

3: CAT

"Cat, come on, wake up." There's a slight nudge of my shoulder, and I cringe, a shooting pain starting in my fingers snakes its way up my arm. "Cat, can you hear me?" Another nudge. Another shot of pain. "Wake up. Dr. Grayson's here to see you."

That does the trick. I force open my eyes to reveal a room I'm all too familiar with. There's a beeping just to the left of my bed, and I can hear the steady rhythm of my heartbeat from the machine to my right. At the sound of my father's name, though, it has grown faster.

I feel like a small child about to be scolded, and I am anything *but* looking forward to the conversation I know is coming.

"Catherine," my father says a little too smoothly. He's the only one in The Community to use my full given name. It's irksome. I turn to look at my father, who stands at the foot of my hospital bed. For whatever reason, he's masking the normal I'm-the-boss-of-you coolness to his voice. It's a facade, I know, and I don't play into his antics.

"Dr. Grayson," I offer back instead, staring him straight in the eyes despite the fogginess behind my own. I have learned from many years of practice that you can't show weakness in my father's presence. Weakness means failure. And when you fail in The Community, someone dies.

"Leave us," my father continues, not bothering to look toward the person he's speaking to, the chilled edge to his voice returning. I don't look either, but I know who roused me from sleep. I'd know his voice anywhere. The door to the hospital room closes as Abel leaves me alone to face my father, who immediately pulls a steel chair to the side of my bed and takes a seat. "How are you feeling?" he asks, but there's a genuine lack of concern to his tone.

"How am I feeling?" I narrow my gaze. "I'm fine."

"Fine," he repeats, pursing his lips.

I say nothing.

An icy moment of silence passes between us before he asks, "Did you enjoy your little stroll through the cemetery today, Catherine?"

Something else I've learned about my father: He doesn't like to waste any time beating around the bush.

"Abel took me on a walk. My mother—" But my father doesn't let me continue. He holds up his hand to silence me, and my mouth clamps shut obediently.

"What did you make of the boat?" Again, straight to the point.

"The what?" And I know as soon as the words leave my mouth I've made a mistake. Power is everything to my father, and I'm suddenly acutely aware of the fact that he would know everything about my whereabouts.

"Dear, Catherine," he jeers, and he's now completely dropped the concerned-father act. "Don't you know by now that you can't keep anything a secret from me?"

I decide it's best not to open my mouth this time.

"You skipped class."

Again I say nothing.

"When you skip class, you don't learn, Catherine." He grips my leg, and in any normal father-daughter interaction, this might be seen as an act of affection. But, truth be told, the only reason my father even cares about my well being is because I am one more workhorse to his team of makeshift scientists. This contact serves as a threat. "When you don't learn, my dear, you fail. And when you fail—"

"Someone dies," I finish before I can stop myself.

Instead of firing back at me, however, my father is silent, his face registering something resembling an understanding. Could it be there's a trace of sadness, too? I wonder. Is it possible that the one man in The Community with unfaltering confidence sees our community for what it's worth? A dying breed?

"Your mother," he says, interrupting my thoughts, "she's not doing well." And it doesn't feel like a question, but I nod my head anyway. "Do you wish to save her?"

"Of course I *wish* to save her," I almost scream. "You're the one who—" but here he holds up his hand again—not the hand on my leg, though; this one he tightens. I am trying hard not to tremble beneath his firm grip. It's not fear that makes me shake, though.

"If you wish to save her, Catherine, you will continue to attend your classes. You are smart. Driven. Not unlike me."

"I am nothing like you," I say a little too quickly through clenched teeth.

He laughs at this, but the laughter doesn't reach his eyes. "You don't see it, Catherine, because you don't want to see it. But you are more like me than you know."

I shake my head at his words, but I can't deny what he says is true. I've known since I was little that I was different from the other girls who grew up on our community block. I hadn't been interested in dolls or dress-up. Instead, I had begged and begged for telescopes and microscopes, building blocks, and coding puzzles. By seven, I was solving algebraic expressions and wowing my classmates with my ability to complete the Rubik's cube from behind my back. I was my father's pride, his little, shining protege. But the older I got, the more he pushed me to be just like him, and the more I quietly rebelled. I didn't want to save the world. I wanted to blend into it.

"I see the way Abel looks at you, Catherine," my father changes the subject, and I'm startled. When had he ever seen the two of us together? When had he even cared enough to notice?

"I don't know what you're talking about," I say. And this time I'm not lying.

My father laughs again, and his laughter reverberates around the hospital room, a lingering, echoing sound. "Of course you don't, dear. But I watched him watch you as you discovered the cemetery. He was concerned you'd react with fear and loathing. He was afraid he'd upset you. He cares about you deeply."

And as he talks, the hairs along the length of my arms stand errect. At first, I can't place what it is about his words that has my skin crawling, but when the cold, hard truth becomes clear to me, it's like a battering ram slamming against my ribcage. There's only one way he could have seen Abel and me in the cemetery. He must have been there with us. Had he followed us? And what on earth was he planning to do with this information? Because if there's one thing I know for certain about my father, it's the fact that everything he does serves a purpose. There's *always* a method to his madness. Always.

Still, to follow his own daughter? From school to the far ends of The Community? That would take too much of his precious research time.

Then it hits me. The hummingbird.

"Cameras?" I manage to squeak out the word, my throat and chest tightening, making it hard to breathe normally.

"They're quite remarkable, aren't they?" he asks. "So small. So delicate. Yet so clever and precise." He squeezes my leg again. "But of course you know they are; they're *your* creation." It is apparent by his expression that he has delighted in my struggle to uncover the truth.

Science fair project: seventh grade. A drone created to maneuver inconspicuously outside the walls of The Community to search for survivors. *My* tiny flying drone, however, had not been a hummingbird but disguised instead as a small speckled, brown bird. I never intended for it to be used as surveillance. The disguise was for anonymity and protection. Period. I won first place that year, and the replicated bird still sits on my nightstand in a glass case.

"You've been *spying on me?*" I accuse. And there are tears of rage in my eyes. I am so angry at this moment I don't know whether to run from the room or attack. I want to gouge my father's eyes out. I want to hurt him the way my heart has been hurting for the past few years. But my body is locked in place. I passively grab at the sheets of my hospital bed and silently will myself to calm down. He's used me, yet I can't ignore the fact that he's my father, my own flesh and blood. Still, he's *used* me.

My father laughs again, adding more fuel to my rage. "Spying, my dear? Oh, no. I have been keeping a close eye on the ones I hold dear. Trying to keep you safe."

And the argument of old comes back with a vengeance. "What makes you think it's your job to save us? To save *me?*" I ask. "Who says it's *you* who can keep us all safe?"

"Are you willing to leave it up to your friend, *Abel?*" He almost spits out his name.

I shrug, raising my brows, challenging him to continue. Whatever he has to say about Abel, I simply won't agree with it.

"Catherine," and his tone, still cold, carries an air of finality, "Abel hasn't exactly proven himself *able* in the academic classroom." It's not an opinion to debate. "He will not be the one to find the cure we need."

Again, my father speaks more truth than I care to admit. It's not that Abel isn't intelligent. It's just that he doesn't buy into the hype surrounding a possible cure.

"It's a waste of time, Cat," Abel's said too many times to count, and always I disagree. "Humans are innately greedy," he has argued in class. "Why do you think we are in the predicament we are in? There was one simple rule to antibiotic resistance: the fewer you use, the less likely resistance will develop. But we broke that rule. We humans did that. We caused this! What makes anyone think that even if we discover a new *cure*, we won't fall into the same cycle of resistance again?" Abel is willful, stubborn, and argumentative. He's always preferred playing the devil's advocate. Quite the opposite to my own passive disposition. It's probably why we get along so well.

It's also the cause of my father's disdain.

After many quiet minutes, I still haven't figured out where my father is going with this conversation, and I find myself growing impatient. Why the cameras? Why the secrets? Why the mention of Abel's obvious feelings for me? It's not my best interest he has in mind; I do know this.

"Abel's strong," he finally says after it is clear I won't respond to his insult of Abel's intelligence. At his mention of Abel's physique, I find myself subconsciously nodding as a sudden image of my friend standing resolute and tall in the cemetery flashes before my eyes. "But he makes you weak. I cannot afford your weaknesses."

I'm aghast. "This isn't just about *you*!" I shout.

My father nods. "It's about the safety of The Community," he agrees. "We need strength and protection in The Community almost as much as we need our little scientists." There is a deliberate pause to my father's speech. He wants me to figure it out. He wants me to realize the implications of his words. Dr. Grayson so enjoys his mind games, a way to slowly reveal the power and control he has over whomever he has chosen to play with. "We lost a vital member of our wall patrol team last week—"

"No!" I interrupt him with as much force as I can summon. But inside I whimper silently, *no, no, no, no.*

My father raises an eyebrow. "No?"

"Daddy, no." And while it disgusts me to call this man 'daddy', it's my one final hope that he'll change his mind, remember what it was like to love me as I once loved and adored him. "You can't send him to guard the wall." Tears tumble freely down my face. I no longer care about showing weakness. My world, my one steady friend, has been threatened. "I need him. You can't take him from me. You can't—"

"I can and will do whatever needs to be done."

The finality of his tone breaks me. I turn to my side and cry freely. Because I know what it means to protect The Community from atop the great wall. The men, they're more like mindless zombies, drones marching along the border, programmed to kill. And they never come home. Abel would rather die than patrol the wall. He's not a killer. I also know that once Dr. Grayson has made a decision, there is also no point of arguing.

I let my tears soak through my pillow and dampen my skin and hair. All my life, I have surrounded myself with the few people who make me feel safe, protected, happy. And now my mother is dying, and my father is going to take the one true friend I've got from my life.

After it becomes clear there will be no quick end to my tears, my father sighs heavily, but it's not a sign of remorse. It sounds much more like disgust. "You may think my methods of control are, for lack of a better term, ruthless," he begins, "however, I can assure you every measure I have put into place since the beginning of this community has kept you and the ones you love safe." With these words, I hear him turn toward the hospital window, and I roll over to steal a glance of his rigid form. Even from the back, my father, despite his age, looks young and powerful. I look past him out the window, and I imagine my mother listening to her music back at home.

It must be near evening because the lights seem to be dimming. In a short while, they will go dark until morning. That is how this community works. That is how Dr. Grayson and his band of un-merry men maintain power.

"Then why is Mom dying?" I ask, breaking the silence that has filled the small room.

My father's posture remains soldier-like.

"Mom's dying," I repeat. "Don't you even care?" But my father doesn't flinch, doesn't falter. And as the lights of The Community go out, I am left with the image of a man who no longer loves, who no longer feels anything.

•   •   •   •   •

I don't dare move a muscle until long after my father has gone. I don't want to see him again tonight. Or any time soon for that matter. I just want to go home and curl up on the couch in my mother's room and sleep. Or at least try to. Too many emotions crowd my head and heart, and I long for an escape.

When I finally do muster up the courage to leave, the corridors of the giant hospital are quiet save for the beeping of monitors and hushed televisions left on all night by their viewers. It's the one privilege the dying have in The Community: reruns of every ancient sitcom imaginable. The Community's rules no longer apply when you're knocking at death's door.

A heaviness weighs on my shoulders, and my left arm, now in a sling that I fitted for myself, throbs. I am angry that I allowed my fear of my father to get the best of me. I am angry that I fainted, that I ended up in a hospital bed basically shackled in place. I am angry that I had to endure the lecture of my father. I am angry about his threats toward Abel. I am just angry.

I am still fuming as I scan my identification bracelet and burst from the revolving doors into the cool, darkened streets of The Community. The ceiling above the hospital building is decorated with stars, tiny Community-made fireflies that appear to dance across the barrier designed to protect us all from what's beyond.

Protection. A recurring theme in The Community.

And isn't that what's important? I ask myself. My father, Dr. Grayson, often speaks of protection. In fact, every manufactured feature of The Community has its own unique place here in our small world, and all were specifically designed with one purpose in mind: it's people's safety.

I shake my head, still staring at the twinkling lights above. Then why do the people of The Community continue to die?

A noise to my left stops my thoughts in their tracks.

I turn. There's a shadowy figure hunched on top of the brick wall lining the entryway to the hospital, and my breath catches in my throat. I run to him without a moment's hesitation.

When I reach him, his head is at his knees, his strong hands tugging at his hair, and I cannot see his caramel-colored face, but I know who it is.

"Abel," I whisper.

He looks up, and my heart breaks. "Cat," he moans. "I've been worried sick. I thought--," he jumps down off the wall and takes me in his arms, inhaling the scent of my hair, which I'm pretty sure can't be pleasant. "I don't know what I thought," he finishes, relief in his voice.

We stand this way for a few minutes, just two people caught up in an emotional reunion, clinging to the existence of one another. I listen to Abel's heavy breathing, feel his chest rise and fall against my own. In a different time, a different world, we could have been happy. We could have enjoyed moments like these.

But not today. Not in this world. I gently push Abel away. "He's going to send you to patrol the wall, Abel," I whisper matter-of-factly because there's no other way to spin it. The decision has been made.

To my surprise, Abel's reaction is one of understanding instead of the horror I had anticipated. "I know," he says simply, almost gently. "I've known for some time that Dr. Grayson hasn't been too thrilled with my attempts to play devil's advocate in the classroom."

Despite the gravity of the situation, I laugh. "So that's what we're calling it now?" I jest half-heartedly, punching him lightly on the shoulder, remembering that merely an hour before I had conjured up the same term when thinking about Abel's consistent defiance in clinical. We've always been so in sync with one another, even as young children. "Maybe if you talk to him—" I start, but Abel's expression turns grave, and I stop mid-sentence.

"I was thinking we could just leave instead," he says, and there's something in his tone that frightens me.

"Leave?"

Abel grabs my arms, his grip firm, his eyes pleading. "Cat, I know what you're going to say, but we *need* to leave The Community. It's the only way. I won't survive as a patrolman. You know it. I know it. Dr. Grayson knows it. Why else would he send me? He's trying to punish you, Cat, by punishing me. He's trying to show you that he's still in control. He's using your fear of the Virus to keep you at bay. But we're prisoners here, Cat."

Two of the three things he says are true: Abel won't survive his post, and his sentence is my punishment.

One is nowhere near the truth.

"My fear of the Virus? Abel, I'm not *afraid*. Ghosts you can be afraid of. Monsters beneath your bed even! But you can't be afraid of something that's right in front of your face! The Virus is real, Abel. It's killing my mother!" There's a hint of venom to my words that I hadn't intended.

"What if it's not?"

I'm aghast at the suggestion. "That's not up for debate, Abel!" And there's no hiding my anger now. "The Virus is killing my mother. Right now. As we speak." I shake his arms off me. "How dare you even suggest that I leave her?"

Even in the dark, I can see Abel's face registering defeat. "I'm sorry, Cat. I didn't mean--" He moans in frustration and begins pacing the sidewalk, clearly at a loss for the right words to say. I assume he's trying to shield me from the pain he's obviously causing. But I'm not the only one who needs protecting right now, and he knows it. "Look," he begins carefully, "I understand how much you want to save your mother, but what happens when no one finds this *magic* cure we're all so desperately seeking? Someone else will get sick. Someone else will die." Abel stops pacing and turns to stare in the direction of the hidden cemetery. His supposed way out. "I'm going to die, Cat. I am. I can't stay here. If I stay, I die."

"Abel, that's not fair!" I cry incredulously. This is *not* the direction I thought our conversation would take tonight. "Are you saying that I have to choose? Abel? Are you seriously telling me it's you or *my mother*?"

Abel doesn't answer. He lowers his head, his deep brown eyes shrouded in anguish. "I want you to choose *us*, Cat," and his voice is barely a whisper.

"I want—no I *need*—to *do* something other than hide behind a lab coat and microscopes and results that just aren't coming. I just can't keep ignoring the simple fact that our friends and families are dying."

Forge ahead.

I roll my eyes. "I am NOT ignoring that fact, Abel!"

Abel's broad chest expands slowly. "No, I guess you're not. But I have been. Until now. I refuse to ignore it any longer. There are people here in this community—your father—who are keeping things from us. And I won't stand for it. Not when so many of us are dying. Cat, I want to know the truth beyond the walls of The Community. Don't you?"

"The truth is my mother's at home dying, Abel. The truth is I work too damn hard in clinical for you to tell me it's all just a waste of my time. You want to know what I think is a real waste of time? This conversation," I spit these words back at my friend who's never done anything to hurt me until now. My insides are churning with rage. "I've already spent far too much time and energy away from my mother today. I need to go."

I abruptly leave Abel standing alone by the hospital, his mouth agape. I haven't said it, but I don't have to. He knows. He asked me to choose, but there was never a choice to begin with. My mother needs me, and to hell if I'm not going to do everything in my power to save her.

I round the corner of the hospital and head toward the nearest and always largely stocked Off-Load rental building. It's a modest-sized kiosk manned tonight by The Community's head security guard and my parent's childhood friend, Don.

"Good evening, Cat," Don greets me gravely, and I am immediately taken aback. While it's true that Don is known around The Community as Dr. Grayson's right-hand man and thus can seem somewhat standoffish, he's always been kind to me. And especially kind to my mother. I know her current condition pains him, but when he visits—which isn't too often anymore—he always tries to make her smile. Now, however, beneath the eerie glow of the kiosk lights, he looks unsettled, a bruise, deep purple, surrounds his left eye.

For a second, I want to ask him if he's alright, if there's anything I can do for him, but the direness of my situation propels me in another direction. "I need wheels, Don," I say simply, and when it seems like he's planning to speak again, I add, "I'm in a hurry." Don closes his mouth abruptly and nods toward a small screen attached to the side of the kiosk, and I scan my bracelet, feeling little guilt at my curt responses.

"You can take one of the new ones, Cat. Number 107. It's fully charged."

I purse my lips and say a quiet, "Thank you," before heading to the rear of the small building.

"Oh, and, Cat?" I pause but don't turn around, my frustration rapidly mounting, which isn't exactly fair to Don. "This new edition, it's fast," he tells me. "And with your sling, you might find it harder to balance. So be careful." He seems to want to say something else (maybe ask about my mother) but stops, so I continue walking, grab the helmet with my good hand, scan my bracelet to unlock the small robotic disk, unfold the two footrests with a click of the remote, and take off toward home with one hand awkwardly controlling the handlebars.

I reach our row house in less than fifteen minutes, covering the uphill five miles more quickly than expected. Don wasn't kidding; the new and clearly improved Off-Load is lightning fast, and the sling, while difficult to get used to at first, did little to hinder my speed. It's amazing, the power of adrenaline. I tear up the front porch steps so quickly I don't even notice that it seems like every light in the house is on. Nor do I see the large white van parked just to the right of the house. Maybe if I had, I would have been more prepared for the horror awaiting me through the front door.

There's the soft click of the lock as I scan my bracelet, and then I open the door and charge into the foyer.

The first thing I do notice is the chill to the house. It reminds me of winter, a time when air temperature wasn't yet regulated. Instinctively, I hug my good arm around myself for warmth. My eyes dart to the living room to the right of the stairs where a lone figure sits slouched on the tattered couch. Rhema looks up slowly. She's surrounded by a mountain of tissues, and I don't have to look hard to see the pain in her swollen eyes. She doesn't say anything. She doesn't have to. I turn away from Rhema, and let my gaze travel down the narrow hallway, past the dining room table, past the tiny kitchen. That's when I see them.

Men in white suits. Putting a lifeless figure onto a gurney.

"Mom," I moan and head unsteadily to the rear of the house.

"Cat, don't," Rhema pleads, but I ignore her. I will myself forward, each step becoming more difficult, when a hand from seemingly out of nowhere grabs my elbow.

"Miss," and the voice is firm but kind. "There's nothing you can do for her."

For *her*.

"But she's my mother. Please," I beg, tears dripping from my chin. "I need to see her."

The man in white hesitates a few moments more but lets me pass, and for the moment I am grateful. Until I see my mother's face. Her dark hair is matted with blood, and the veins in her face are a ghastly purple, a sharp contrast against her ashen skin. I scan the gurney. There's blood everywhere. On her gown, on the linens, on the floor. As though it has seeped from every pore on her ravaged body.

I turn quickly toward the trash bin and am violently ill, my body racked with sobs between retching over and over and over again.

The pain of loss is unbearable. The feeling of guilt even worse.

"What have I done?" I repeatedly moan.

"Dear, Catherine," a voice comes quietly from the back door of the small room. I don't look up but instead hang uselessly over the trash bin, placing my head on my forearm, too weak to do anything more. Dr. Grayson cooly continues. "You were too late. You couldn't save her." There's a threatening tone to his voice that makes my body retch again. "Perhaps you'll put more effort into your classes now. *Tsk, tsk.*" He moves past me, past the lifeless form of my mother, his *wife*, and into the kitchen where he grabs a handful of nuts from the bowl on the island. From my place on the floor, I watch how he chews them deliberately, one by one, savoring each as though they represent a tiny, separate victory.

He did this, I think. *He killed her.* And my mother's warning from yesterday comes back with a sudden realization that leaves my eyes wide and my body retching once more.

"You can't keep him out, Cat. No matter what. He'll come for us all. One day."

4: WREN

The hours following my mother's kidnapping are a blur of packing, panicking, more frantic packing, and even more panicking.

So many questions race through my head, tumbling into one another, causing a nightmarish migraine. *Where had they taken her? What were they planning to do with her? Who* were *they?*

And Ryder? He hasn't left my side. He acts like a puppy fearful of abandonment, following me around whimpering nonsense about me not having to go, the trip is too dangerous, I'll get myself killed. All I hear is blah, blah, *blah.*

Bill, on the other hand, is as helpful as he can be. You know, between moments of intense grief and guilt. He blames himself. I blame myself, too. I had sensed in my mother a sort of quiet resignation the night before. My mother, normally steady and resolute, had seemed *off.* And I hadn't questioned it then, and now it is too late. I shouldn't have fallen asleep. I should have stayed by her side. Questioned her more about what was left unspoken. If I had, maybe the outcome would be different.

I head to the storage garage to finish loading my bags. Ryder, no surprise, is fast on my heels.

"Wren, you know you don't have to do this," he says for the umpteenth time. Blah, blah, *blah.* "You know how strong your mother is. She'll know what to do. She'll come back to us. You'll see." Blah, blah, *blah.* "I don't think she'd want you to follow her. It's too dangerous."

I continue the back-and-forth trips to the garage, saying nothing.

"At least let me come with you. Wren," and with this last attempt to speak to me, he places a strong hand on my shoulder. "Please."

I sigh, but continue my way over to the shelves at the rear of the garage to add some final necessary survival supplies to my pack. "You know as well as I do that you're needed here, Ryder. Bill needs you. Our family needs you."

I pick up a compass, check to make sure it works, and throw it into the zipper pouch at my waist.

"Bill can take care of the camp," Ryder replies, and I can't help but laugh in response.

"Bill's a mess, if you haven't noticed." I rummage through a drawer for a bit until I come across an old, rusting Swiss army knife. I open the blade, hold it to my index finger until a minuscule drop of blood appears. Good enough, I think, and after folding the blade, go to drop it into my pack before reconsidering. Swallowing the dread that I might actually have to use this knife as a weapon, I unzip my boots and tuck it to the side of my ankle instead. I gently shove past Ryder to weave my way through the cramped space to the one cabinet I had deliberately chosen for last.

Ryder lets me pass but continues to follow me. I find myself starting to get annoyed, but then I remind myself that it's because he cares about me that he's begging me to stay. I reach for the cool metal handle of the cabinet, lift it, and twist. Nothing. I try again. It still won't open.

Frustrated, I turn to face Ryder who is so close to me that our faces almost touch, and I shock myself by wondering what it would be like to kiss his mouth, just inches from my own. I shake away the thought.

"Can you help me?" I ask Ryder, turning my face any direction but his and placing my hands on my hips in hopes of displaying my annoyance. I refuse to leave Ryder with any reason to hang onto me. Onto the chance of *us.*

He sighs but does as I ask, digging out a ring of keys from his pocket and reaching around my waist to make contact with the lock. Once again, I find myself sharing very intimate space with Ryder, and my cheeks grow hot with embarrassment. I wait impatiently as he messes with the lock and wonder if his struggle with the key is intentional, if he's simply attempting to delay the inevitable. Holding onto me until he can no longer.

This little game goes on for a few more drawn-out, uncomfortable seconds until my frustration threatens to ooze from my pores. "Oh, for crying out loud, Ryder, let me try it!" I grab for the keys, but the cabinet opens finally, and Ryder backs away.

At first, I am shocked into silence, staring at the abundance of weaponry beyond the cabinet door. I knew the guns existed, I've had some up-close-and-personal interaction with them recently, in fact; however, before this moment, I never needed a reason to see the entire arsenal. Our existence in the camp, up until this moment, has been relatively quiet. Calm. Almost peaceful. As though the relationship between the people beyond the wall and our camp was mutualistic.

Not anymore.

The reality of the current situation is that the people on the other side of that wall have kidnapped my mother, my world. And I will need to cross into some seriously sketchy and dangerous parts of our world to get to her. The weapons are nonnegotiable.

My hands tremble as I reach in to take the least intimidating gun from a shelf littered with a half dozen look-alikes. "You'll need to load it for me," I tell Ryder, handing him the gun.

Ryder rolls his eyes, grabbing a box from a lower shelf. "I can't believe I'm allowing you to do this," he mumbles as he carefully loads the bullets and sets the safety.

"It's not up to you to let me go anywhere. This isn't your decision; it's mine."

Ryder rolls his eyes again but then nods as though making a decision about something important. Still, he hesitates before offering me the gun, and I immediately motion for him to lay it on the table, cursing myself that Ryder might see this as a moment of weakness on my part.

This is it, I think. *I'm really doing this.*

"Do you remember our first ride together?" Ryder asks, interrupting my thoughts and taking a seat on top of the motorbike that less than forty-eight hours ago had taken us for supplies. How quickly things can change. Yesterday we rode for clean water and gas; today I ride to save my mother.

"Of course I do," I say, and because I know that he's not going to let me leave without a proper goodbye, I take a seat opposite him on a pile of supply boxes.

Alone in the quiet, cramped space of the garage, I begin to fidget.

After a few awkward, drawn-out minutes, Ryder says, "You were so fiery. So full of life, riding with one arm out, challenging the wind." I smile because I can still remember how this felt, to be truly free of worries. It felt like *happiness.* Before Ryder showed up in camp, I was a mopey, brooding child. But after? He changed me. "You're still just as reckless," he finishes. My smile fades.

"Reckless?" I almost shout. "Reckless?" I jump down from the boxes, knocking the top one loudly to the floor, supplies spilling. "You're unbelievable! Reckless. Do you want to know what *I* think is reckless? Not doing a damn thing to save my mother. She's the one person who can keep us grounded, who keeps us safe. And every minute I spend saying goodbye to you is one less "reckless" minute I don't spend looking for her."

I make the move to leave. My own bike is fueled and waiting for me by the road. But Ryder isn't done with me yet.

"Wren, please don't go." He grabs my elbow, but I yank it free. "I'm not sure you realize how dangerous this little adventure of yours will be." There's a foreign but blatant disapproval and cruelty to Ryder's voice, and that's the final straw.

"My little *adventure?*" I explode. "Is that what you think I'm doing? Exploring the world? Traveling the unknown? A leisurely *vacay?* You've got to be kidding me!" I forcibly grab the gun that only a moment ago I was afraid to touch. I'm trying to prove a point even I don't believe in. Because I know what he's doing. His tactic is deliberate. But in trying to save me, he's pushing me farther out the door. This was never about him and me.

The moment of silence between us is deafening, and as the last of my supplies are thrown haphazardly into my army-style backpack, I push my anger aside. "I don't have a choice, Ry," I say, resisting the urge to turn and take his hand. My back is facing him, but I don't need to see his eyes to know what he's feeling.

"There is always a choice," he spats matter-of-factly.

"Ryder!" I plead, turning to face him. My tone is incredulous, anger threatening again like hot bile in my throat. "*They took my mother.*"

He nods, pursing his lips, starts to say something else but stops.

"What?" I ask. "Do you know something I don't?" The look in his eyes tells me he does. After all, he was present on the bridge yesterday. He heard every word that the strange men had said. But if he knows more than I do, he doesn't admit it now.

There is one final pause between us. An ever-so-brief and heart-breaking moment of silence before it's clear he finally registers *this is it.* It's done. I am leaving. His shoulders slacken, a signal that he's finally given up the fight. There's nothing more for him to say or do.

Yet still, he tries one more approach. It's Ryder after all. The same Ryder who once saw me fall from my bike but pretended not to notice because he knew my pride was precious. The same Ryder who brought me bandaids and nodded reassuringly as I spun the story that I was chased by a pack of wild dogs but fought them off all by myself. Ryder. My best friend in the whole wide messed-up world.

"Wren." And the desperation in his voice threatens to break down the walls of my defense. He steps towards me and clutches my face with his strong, calloused hands. His breathing is heavy as he looks at me, his emerald eyes darting back and forth, back and forth, as though he'll find some part of me, buried deep inside, that still longs to stay. "You can't leave." Pause. "I love you, damn it."

My eyes close. The world around us dissolves, almost comes to a stop it seems, and in my mind, lines begin to blur. Confusion threatens. I knew this was coming. It was inevitable. From the moment we met, I knew. I *knew* he would fall in love with me. But this world we live in, this disillusioned, corrupt world we call home isn't a place for his type of love. My heart flutters; I am sure he can feel it beneath his fingers that recklessly caress my face, my jaw, my neck as they desperately try to take in every inch of me to remember once I'm gone.

I take a deep breath and turn my head just as a lone tear escapes and makes its hurried descent down my cheek. My resolve to leave him without a shred of hope crumbles. I simply cannot do that to the one true friend I've got. The truth is, I know there's more than a slight chance I won't be coming back. Once I'm gone, I might never see Ryder again. And I know what that will do to him.

But I'm already gone. My heart left with my mother when *they* came and took her.

Ryder's hands fall heavy as stone to his sides.

"I've got to try, Ry," I whisper, wanting to leave it at that, but Ryder won't let me.

"I love you," he says again.

We stand there for what feels like many minutes, time suspended by Ryder's words, until finally I find enough nerve to get my next few words out. "You know I love you, too." And then more playfully, "I'll be back before you can miss me."

I place two fingers to my lips, gently touch them to his own, and turn and walk quickly out the door of the garage before he can say anything else. But not before I see his face register defeat. Not before I know I have failed; he doesn't believe me.

The truth is, I lied.

The heavy door closes behind me with a finality that echoes in my ears long after I've gone.

•　　•　　•　　•　　•

I climb onto the bike, determined to make one more stop before my final departure. Determined also not to cry.

There's a funny thing about the truth. It isn't always absolute. Part of me does love Ryder. It's just that most of me realizes that this love is pointless. I rev the engine, and without a second glance, speed off to Bill's place.

When I pull into his drive five minutes later, there's only one light on in his cabin. I lean the bike onto its kickstand, shut off the engine, and approach the house cautiously, knuckles white against my helmet. The dark has never felt like a friend to me, and tonight is no exception. Plus, I am not exactly looking forward to the conversation I'm about to have, but I know that it's immensely important.

I'm playing over the words I want to say to Bill, hand ready to knock, when the front door opens.

"Wren, hey," Bill manages to get out. His hair is disheveled, and his eyes are bloodshot. I lean in on my tiptoes and look over his shoulder to see a mostly empty bottle of what I imagine is moonshine on his living room table.

"Is it ok if I come in?" I ask. The sooner I get this conversation started, the sooner it will end, I tell myself.

"What? In? Of course! Come in!" His words are slurred and seem to carry a false joviality, but I nod in understanding, and he indicates I move toward the couch where he had obviously been sitting before my arrival. "Don't mind the mess," he says as I place my helmet on the table by the door and redirect myself to the reclining chair next to it instead. I don't need him to take the seat beside me.

He looks initially hurt, but he glances at the bottle on the table, and his face turns red with embarrassment.

"I don't usually do this," he says, grabbing the bottle with a shaking hand as though he aims to put it away. But then he thinks better of it, shrugs, and pours another healthy glass, emptying the bottle's contents.

"Bill—" I start, but he abruptly cuts me off.

"Wren, I'm so sorry about your mother. I—I never should have left her the other night. I just *knew* something would happen. She was in one of her moods, you know?"

And I do know. But I'm not here to talk about what could have been.

"Bill," I begin carefully, "I don't blame you, ok? I need you to know that. Blaming someone other than the men who took my mother isn't going to help." Bill shakes his head in protest, and my frustration mounts. What *is it* with these men? "Also, I need you to get yourself together because now that my mother's gone, the camp needs someone to stand in for her until I can bring her back." I pause, letting my words sink in. "Ryder is going to need your help."

There's a flash of horror in Bill's eyes. I knew this wasn't going to be easy. "What do you mean *until you bring her back?*" Bill cries. "You're not thinking of going after her, are you?"

I don't falter. "Of course, I'm *thinking* of going after her. She's my mother, Bill."

He stands a little too quickly, swaying from the alcohol. I sit back hard in my chair, resolute to make this conversation end as soon as I can and be on my way. I know that traveling at night will be risky; however, traveling during the day makes me a sitting duck.

"I refuse to lose you, too, Wren." He starts to move toward me, but I hold up my hand, standing, trying to appear braver than I actually feel. The sour smell of the alcohol on his breath has made me suddenly queasy.

"I'm not yours to lose, Bill," I say matter-of-factly, my voice hard. He flinches.

"Then you're just as reckless as your mother," he says sadly.

This is the second time today I've been called reckless, and it stings. It's even more infuriating to hear him reference my mother in the same way.

"My mother is anything but reckless."

Shaking his head again, Bill replies, "No. She was reckless last night, Wren. You might not want to believe it, but your mother *let* them take her. I don't know how she reached out to *him*, but she did. And he came and took her, Wren. And I wasn't there to stop it." At this, he falls heavily back onto the couch and is racked with sobs.

I am immediately confused. Alarmed even. "Bill," and I speak his name slowly. "What are you saying?"

"It's too late, Wren," he says through sobs. "It doesn't matter." He pulls a piece of folded paper from his shirt pocket and throws it forcefully— almost ridiculously because of the booze—onto the table. It slides across the wooden surface, then flutters to the floor at my feet.

Anger courses through my veins. "Doesn't matter? *Doesn't matter?*" I cross the space between us. "Bill, who is *he?* Why would my mother leave with anyone?" As I say the words, I still don't believe them. My mother would never go willingly to the very place she has taught us all to despise.

Would she?

"Bill," I say again when he doesn't immediately answer me. "Tell me what you're talking about!" But Bill still doesn't answer, and as he slumps back against the couch, I see that he has passed out. "Damn it, Bill! Wake up!" I roughly shake his shoulders, but this causes him to fall over, unresponsive. I inhale deeply, scan the room for anything that might seem out of place, that might tell me what he's talking about, and, seeing the piece of discarded paper lying on the carpet, lean down to pick it up. My hands tremble as I unfold what I immediately recognize as stationery belonging to my mother.

There's one sentence written in perfect long-abandoned cursive. I'd recognize the handwriting anywhere. I read and then reread the sentence over and over, more than a dozen times willing the words to change. Because I can't believe what I'm seeing.

Bill, whatever happens, don't let Wren follow me.

She knew. She knew they were coming for her, and she didn't stop them. She didn't tell me.

I frantically look to Bill who is now snoring loudly from his awkward position on the couch. I walk over to him and shake him roughly again and again, but he is out cold.

It's no use. I can't rely on Bill to help me any more than I can rely on Ryder. Of course, I understand why my mother would insist I not follow her. What isn't clear to me is *why* she would allow—maybe even initiate—her own kidnapping.

Well, it's no longer up to her, is it? I think. She's gone, and there's only one thing I can think of to do in this situation. Find her and bring her back. I grab my helmet, glance once more at Bill, open the door and head out into the night.

5: CAT

I can't seem to peel myself from the small couch in my mother's bedroom. It's been twelve hours since her death, but time has stopped for me. I don't eat. I don't sleep. A cool, hard numbness has taken refuge in my heart, and it seems perfectly content to stay put. When absolutely necessary, I crawl to the cluttered bathroom just beyond the room, making sure to avoid the mirror and my reflection. I know what I'll see, and I choose not to punish myself further.

After the men in white suits took my mother's lifeless body, they cleaned and gutted the room. No need for all the IVs and medicines any longer. They even took her hospital bed and extra linens, leaving the room looking more like the sitting room it was intended to be. Truth be told, my mother was one of the very few allowed to stay at home once she began showing symptoms of the Virus. Most people are taken to the hospital to die alone. Family rarely visited; they weren't really supposed to. And despite all the animosity I feel towards my father, I do know there are perks to being Dr. Scott Grayson's daughter. It's just that most of the time, the pain far outweighs these benefits.

Like now.

From the couch, I slowly scan the now near-empty room, searching for any remaining sign of my mother's existence. Her sweaters, normally draped over the furniture for when she was all-too-often cold, are already boxed up thanks to Rhema, and the rest of her clothes are still hanging upstairs in her old bedroom, abandoned when they became too big for my mother's emaciated form. There is only one object that remains, and my eyes stop to rest on the disc player sitting atop her once-bedside table. This relic, the one thing that seemed to bring my mother so much pleasure, brings for me the threat of fresh tears.

"Cat?" I pull my eyes away from the sad reminder. Rhema makes her way tentatively into the room, a steaming bowl on a tray in her hands. "Are you hungry?" Now that my mother's gone, Rhema has taken on the role of *my* nurse. I guess caring for people is in her blood.

At the thought of blood, my stomach churns, images of my mother's matted hair and red-soaked sheets fill my mind. I moan and shake my head.

"Cat, sweetie, you need to eat something," Rhema whispers but retreats from the room to place the tray on a table in the hallway before returning to talk to me. She's always had such good bedside manners. "Your mother would want you to carry on with your life, Cat. You know this as well as I do," she continues, gently taking a seat next to me on the floor. She scrunches up her face in disgust as she gets close to me and adds, "A shower might make you feel better, too."

I know as she says the words that she's right. My mother would hate to see me like this. But grief and guilt flood my veins much as the Virus flooded hers, and the physical pain that accompanies these emotions is debilitating. More tears threaten as I think of my mother, so helpless, dying by my father's hands. And where was I? Having a lover's quarrel with Abel.

And as if she reads my thoughts, Rhema says, "Abel came by to see you this morning, Cat. He's a mess. He's worried sick about you."

I still don't reply. My throat feels like it's coated in cotton.

Rhema strokes my hair before standing. "Ok, then. I'll check back with you around dinner time."

Once she has left the room, I tell myself to cry, to let it all out, that maybe once I get in one really good cry, the pain will finally wash away. But even my tears seem to abandon me in my darkest hours, and I lie staring at the ceiling, wishing I died alongside my mother.

•   •   •   •   •

Day two begins in the same slow, tortuous way as the previous one ended. But Rhema is pleased that I somehow manage to stomach a few sips of water and a handful of crackers. By mid-afternoon, however, I've made a decision. I cannot go on like a victim any longer. It was a dream, I think, that finally rekindled the fire within me, a dream of before the Virus. Or a dream of *after.* I can't be sure. Either way, upon waking, something simply felt different.

I make my way from the couch, careful not to move too fast—my head dizzy from lack of food, water, and restful sleep. And, as though without thinking, I find myself shuffling across the small room over to my mother's small bedside table where her beloved disc player sits gathering a fine layer of dust.

I rub my fingers along the buttons gently, once, twice, then linger over the word PLAY. I will myself to apply the pressure needed to start the mechanical relic, but it still takes several minutes and my eyes firmly shut to muster up the courage needed. There is a sudden whirring of the disc, and then the music starts. I lurch back slightly, the quiet of my two-day solitude now broken, but because I feel a sudden intense draw to the music, I sink deeply into the chair beside the table and close my eyes.

The melody of the album is haunting. But not sad. It's beautiful. Soulful. And so like my mother. The lyrics—in a language I don't recognize or understand—embrace my heart and carry it up and away. Past the ceiling of The Community. Past the pain and suffering. In the moments that follow, I feel a freedom that I haven't felt in years, since I was a child and my mother was healthy. I smile, imagining my mother as she once was before the Virus, and then I imagine her now as an angel, free of pain and suffering, her dark hair lustrous once more, her smile radiant.

I'm not certain how long I sit there, the disc continuing to play, but when I finally open my eyes, the light seeping through the blinds in the windows indicates it's closing in on sundown. Quickly, I gather the disc player, the albums, and a small framed picture of my mother and me from the early days of The Community that earlier I discovered beneath a couple of discarded books. I place each item gently in a canvas bag, throw it over my shoulder, and head toward the front door, a sudden and fierce determination driving each step.

I know what I need to do.

My father—Dr. Grayson—took my mother from me. Sure, the Virus would have killed her eventually, but he sped up the process. I know this to be true just as I know my mother is watching me from above. But he cannot steal our memories. If there's one thing my mother has taught me, it's the fact that the past is important, sacred. We should never forget what and where we came from. Otherwise, where we're headed won't make a lick of difference.

Forge ahead my ass.

Rhema catches me before I head out the front door. Her warm face is one of understanding, and as I take from her the brown paper bag I know she's packed with food, I whisper, "Thank you," and hug her tightly. "Please, don't leave yet, ok?" I say, still holding tightly onto her. *I'm not ready to be alone in this house. I can't take any more loss right now. I need you.* I don't say these final thoughts aloud, but I feel her nod against my neck. She is as familiar with loss as I am—many of us in The Community are—and as far as I know, I'm all she has left in this world.

The tragedy of my mother's illness—and now her death—has made us family.

After a few more tender moments, I push Rhema gently aside and head swiftly out the door.

•   •   •   •   •

When I reach the cemetery, the sun is just a half orb cut in the middle by the thick line of trees beyond the great wall. Once again, the rented Off-Load has done its job, getting me across The Community's limits in under twenty minutes. With my good arm, I carry the lightweight Off-Load, my helmet, and the bundle of my mother's belongings along the wall of holly trees. The last time I was here, the only thing on my mind was my mother's impending death. Now, today, I am here to honor it.

As I approach the broken area of chain link fence, I place the Off-Load and helmet at the base of an adjacent holly tree, so thick with leaves that they'll be hidden from view—hidden also from any invasively small lenses of flying cameras—carefully pull back a few branches, and climb through.

It's dark by the time I make my way up and around the paved path of the cemetery. But I planned for this. I don't want anyone to discover I am here, and, while I know Dr. Grayson is extremely intuitive, he's naive when it comes to the behaviors of the opposite sex, one of the many reasons my mother chose to stay behind in our modest row house when he left to join the rest of his medical team in their majestic hotel. I assume he believes I'll grieve for a few days and show up to class when my last tear is shed. He thinks he's won, and in a way he has. For now. At least that is what I want him to believe.

I do plan to go back to class. But not tomorrow. I don't want to look too strong, like I'm on a mission. Dr Grayson needs to think I'm suffering and that this suffering makes me weak. An obedient pawn to control. No, I decide. I'll let him believe I'm grieving for a few days before I return. And then I'll hit the ground running.

My breath is labored by the time I finally make it to the giant cage rusted by weather and time, and I sit heavily upon the collapsing stone barrier surrounding it. I know this is a place of importance, that the men and women buried here stood for something. That they fought hard to make a difference during their time here on earth. My mother was no different. Her battle may not have been the same, but still she fought—for a forgotten past, for an abandoned history. And I know in my heart of hearts this is the reason she is dead. There's something about the past that Dr. Grayson is desperate to keep hidden. This realization is clear to me now.

I unwrap the ancient disc player and the albums. I pull out the tiny framed photo of my mother and me. I lay them all on the ground, and for a moment, I am so overcome with grief that only my anger can drive me to continue. I stare up at the ceiling of The Community, at the stars and the brightness of the moon projected there.

"You think you can control me," I say a little too loudly into the night. And then more quietly, "But you're wrong. Father, you are so very wrong." I tear at the ground, hardened by neglect, and by the time I've finished digging a hole deep enough to hold all that my mother held dear, my fingernails are broken, bloody, and caked with soil.

Carefully, I place each item into the hole that will be their final resting place and cover them, each new level of dirt hardening my heart. I refuse to let my mother's death be in vain, and I vow to honor her memory with each day I live on. I owe her this much.

And as for my father? Dr. Scott Grayson? I'm not worried about what he'll do to me anymore. If he wanted me dead, he would have done it by now. No. He needs me. He all but said this as he stood there in the hospital room with me days ago. He needs me in clinical running labs, testing results. But for what? I'm no longer sure. What I am sure of, though, is that if anyone here in The Community can uncover what Dr. Grayson's so desperately seeking, it's his own flesh and blood.

I *will* find out what he's up to. And I will do what I can to stop him.

But first I owe someone an apology.

•　　•　　•　　•　　•

Abel's not home when I first reach the apartment he shares with a classmate. During the outbreak, Abel's parents, having been too old and too poor to make The Community's strict cuts, emptied their bank accounts and paid his way in. Part of me knows this is the real reason he wants to leave. So that he might find them again one day, still alive and thriving somewhere beyond the great walls of what we have been conditioned to call our home. Wondering about him as he wonders about them.

It isn't until the very early morning hours that Abel finally stumbles home. I see him before he sees me as I am masked in the shadows of his towering building. I remain sitting, unsure of what I'll say, how I'll even begin.

By the time he's at the foot of the steps, it's become clear to me that he's caught up in his own thoughts, so much so that he almost passes me, and I reach out to grab his hand as he takes yet another step.

"Cat!" he says, not able to mask his surprise. "What are you doing here? Is everything—? I mean, are you—?" He's at a loss for words, and I understand this completely. There are no words left here in our world that seem to fit casual conversations.

Attempting a smile, I reply, "It's ok, Abel. I'm...better." I motion for him to take a seat beside me. "In fact, I've just come from the cemetery," I tell him carefully, watching his face closely for his reaction.

His dark eyes come alive with hopeful disbelief. "The cemetery? Cat, why? What's going on? You're not thinking of leaving now, are you?" His voice is almost pleading. "Are you?" he asks again when I don't immediately answer.

I want to look away but can't and instead take his hands in mine. "No. I'm not," I whisper, tilting my head to remind him of the camera near his door, and my voice is serious. "I can't leave, Abel. But I do owe you an apology."

"I don't understand," he says, lowering his voice and pulling his hands from mine. "Why were in the cemetery then?"

"To say goodbye," I tell him. "To let my mother know I'm not done fighting for her." By the look on Abel's face, I can see he's still very confused. No one who dies in The Community is laid to rest anywhere. An incinerator keeps us all free of rotting, Virus-ridden corpses.

I rest my head in the palms of my hands suddenly very aware of how late it is and how tired I am. "Listen, Abel, I know you feel you need to leave, and I don't blame you for that. If there is something out there beyond these walls that Dr. Grayson doesn't want us to know about, then you're the one who's going to find it. I truly believe that. And I believe you, too. Something very wrong is going on here in The Community."

Earlier, before leaving the cemetery, I made sure to check the stone Abel pried loose in front of my very wide, very surprised eyes just days before. To be honest, I wholeheartedly expected it to be cemented firmly back into place. After all, Dr. Grayson watched Abel pull the stone from its position in the wall. He watched us while we watched the mysterious boat cross the river, a river, we were told too many times to count, that is never *ever* crossed. For safety reasons, of course. *Could this be the chance Abel needs to escape?* I wondered, and then, because any other alternative would have been too frightening to imagine, I decided that it was.

After taking a moment to digest my words, Abel continues, "And you think you're the one to stop it." It's more of a statement than a question.

"He's my father, Abel," I say, sighing. Each time I say this out loud, I hate the way it sounds. But it's the truth, and I can't keep running from it. "If there's anyone who knows Dr. Grayson, it's me. I'm his only living relative left." I turn to look at him, but Abel refuses to meet my eyes. "Look, I don't think I'm the one to stop anything. I'm not naive, Abel. I know what I'm up against, but I've made a promise to myself and to my mother. I will do what it takes to figure out what's going on here. I want the truth just as much as you do, but running from here won't change anything."

"It will keep us alive," Abel says, dejection heavy in his voice. "Cat, if Dr. Grayson," he pauses, grimaces, "if your father wants you dead, you're as good as dead. You know that, right?"

"I know," I say.

Abel nods, the corners of his mouth quivering. I've never seen him cry, and I don't expect to tonight, but my friend wears his pain clearly now. "I've got to leave," he says after a few moments heavy with silence. "It's the only way I'll survive."

"I know," I say again.

"I might never see you again, Cat," his voice breaks.

"I know, Abel. And I'm so sorry, but I can't go with you."

He surprises me by wrapping his strong arms around me, enveloping my small frame in his massive one. He doesn't shed a single tear, but his body shakes, and I hold onto him like tonight's the last night we'll see each other. Because it very well may be.

"I've loved you since we were children," he whispers. "I just thought you should know that. In case—" He doesn't finish this thought. He doesn't need to.

"And I've loved you, too," I say. I don't try to hold back my tears because this is the second goodbye I have been forced to make over the course of hours. Both Abel and my mother are the only two people I have ever loved more than myself, and I have to let them both go. It hurts like hell. It hurts more than I thought one person could hurt. But I know it's the right thing to do. I feel it in the deepest corner of my heart.

And maybe just maybe, the outcome won't be as terrible as I fear.

6: WREN

By the time I am finally ready to leave the camp, the night has grown increasingly cold, and I zip my heavy leather jacket all the way to my throat. For added protection from the wind, I wrap a tattered, itchy scarf around my face, leaving enough exposed so I can see. It's drawing closer and closer to the crisp autumn nights I used to look forward to, but tonight the bitter winds remind me of how little time I have to reach The Dome, rescue my mother, and return before the weather and roads turn even more treacherous than they already are, raiders and all.

As ready as I'll ever be, I shove my mother's hand-written note into the back pocket of my jeans, start the engine of my motorbike, take one final look at the cabin my mother and I have shared since I was a toddler, knowing very well I may never see it again, and take off heading north.

It is in my best interest, I know, to travel along the major roads in order to avoid any raiders or bands of refugees who tend to take cover in the woods at night, but as I merge onto the old, open highway, panic starts to set in, though I try in vain to ignore it. Being out in the open, paired with the thundering roar of my bike's engine, I feel utterly vulnerable. Still, despite my mounting fear, I race along the four-lane highway toward the lights of the giant wall that glow like a beacon in the dark night sky.

As I weave in and out of debris and large cracks in the pavement, my thoughts go again to the many questions that have presented themselves since last night. Why did my mother choose not to tell me her plan? What *was* her plan even? And what on earth did she think she'd accomplish once she found herself a prisoner on the other side of the wall? Nothing adds up. Not the reaction of the strangers on the bridge. Not my mother's all-too-calm mood the previous night. And certainly not the note my mom left for Bill.

My current situation feels like a puzzle with missing pieces, pieces that, without a doubt, I believe I will find once I'm inside The Dome. This brings me to my next larger-than-life challenge. It is, of course, foolish to assume that there is an easy way inside those giant walls. Even though I personally hadn't witnessed the many men, armed heavily with artillery of every size, style, and power, standing guard atop the wall, my mother never hesitated to recount the horror of the earlier days of The Divide, of gunshots that came so steadily they could almost be mistaken for celebratory fireworks. *Almost*—except for the screams of anguish that accompanied them.

A cold shiver starting in my gut snakes its way up and around my shoulders like a noose waiting to tighten, and with this panic comes the first of many shattering waves of doubt. Of course, I knew the risks of this rescue mission and chose to come this far anyway. But now, as the lights of the wall grow brighter, I feel like a small child with stage fright, alone in the spotlight. Except the price of failure, I know, will be more than just my pride.

I pull my bike over into a large gravel area where the highway meets the bridge. It has been less than forty-eight hours since Ryder and I encountered the strange men on the bridge in this very location. But it feels like years. I walk the bike as far off the road as possible, careful of any traps hidden in the towering weeds, my paranoia just as thick.

Once I'm far enough back, I slide to the ground with my head to my knees, my back resting against my propped bike.

Think, think, think, I will myself. Don and the strangers from yesterday are obviously able to cross the bridge with no problems. Come and go as they please. Then again, they are members of the privileged society beyond the wall. They drive a marked van. They carry their own weapons.

I, on the other hand, am an armed stranger with transportation that leaves me open and exposed. Not to mention my mission tonight is one aimed at destroying anyone who stands in the way of me rescuing my mother.

No, I won't be waltzing easily across the bridge to knock on any doors tonight. I need to find another way. Coincidentally happening upon an abandoned boat is too much to hope for, and even *if* I did secure one, what would keep the armed men of The Dome from shooting at me? A vessel of any size would be fair game.

So then what?

Time passes slowly as I sit there with my head bent, my heart drumming in my ears. A wave of hopelessness threatens to bury me, and I'm considering heading back to camp with my tail tucked between my legs when the roaring of the river gives me an idea.

Before heading down the sloping bank, I push my bike farther into the brush and try my best to cover it with broken branches and leaves. While it's unusual to encounter refugees and raiders this close to the main highway this time of night, my mother and I will need the bike to get us home once we make it back across the river.

If we make it back. I can't stop the thought. Still, I stand back to admire my handy work, and once I'm satisfied, I head cautiously down the slope, the sound of the rushing river camouflaging the steady pounding of my heart.

When I reach the bank, a slow smile spreads across my face, and I imagine that in another life, I would have enjoyed this moment immensely. The view of the river from the bridge doesn't do it justice. Now, at an equal level to the rapids, gleaming and sparkling beneath the moonlight, I am breathless, taken aback by the powerful beauty. But it's not just the sheer magnitude of the river that causes me to smile. It's what I see scattered like stepping stones above the surface.

Rocks.

It has been a typical dry end to the hot summer months. A sporadic storm here and there, but otherwise very little accumulating rain. And because of this, the water level of the river is down. Way down. Low enough that I am almost certain the rocks stretch all the way across to the opposite shore. Even better than that, the path of rocks is close enough to the cement supports of the bridge, that I am certain I will be shrouded in shadows as I cross.

I can do this, I think, the doubts from earlier drowning with this new revelation. I tell myself not to worry about what happens once I'm firmly planted on the other side of the river. I just have to take it one rock at a time.

With a deep breath, I secure my supplies, including the gun held in place at my waist, take my mother's note from my pocket for added motivation, and step out carefully onto the rock nearest to the embankment. I apply forward pressure, and, finding that it's secure, make to move out onto the rushing water.

I'm not exactly sure what happens next, but something slams into me from my left, and I'm falling head first into the raging river before I can regain my balance. The cold of the water slaps my face, and immediately I am ripped downstream with such force, I panic, try to scream. Water fills my lungs, and I choke. I try to scream again but only manage to swallow more water. This continues time and time again as the river tosses me downstream like an old rag doll. I resurface for a few seconds, attempt to inhale a deep breath, and am pulled back down again with the powerful surge of the current. My body crashes into a large rock, and I feel my left leg split in two. The pain is unbearable.

For the next few tortuous minutes, the current tosses me angrily down the river, my body repeatedly thrown against the rocks that earlier I thought would save me. Just as I decide the river will be the death of me and I'm fading into darkness, my strength and will waning, I become tangled up in what feels like a net, and two hands yank me from the water and drag me to the shore.

Then everything goes black.

•　•　•　•　•

"Mamma, mamma, she's awake!"

I moan and attempt to bring my left hand to my aching, throbbing head but can't. I'm sprawled out on a splintered wooden floor, and I hurt. Everywhere.

The little voice starts again, "Momma! Come up here! She's awake! The girl's awake!" And after another moment of no response, "*Momma!*"

There's the sound of pounding feet and a door opening, and as my eyes adjust to the dim, muted light, a figure emerges from the shadows.

"Well, well, well," it says. Momma? "Look who's decided to join the party. Darla, go fetch me some water." The little girl mutters a weak complaint but shuffles from the room.

I moan again and try once more to lift my arms with no luck.

The figure beside me chuckles. "Sorry about that, love," it says. "But you can't never be too careful today. Am I right?" The figure nudges my leg that I notice is wrapped crudely in filthy bandages.

"Where am I?" I manage to whisper.

"Well, it ain't the Holiday Inn!"

There are hurried footsteps from beyond the door; the little girl is back, panting. "Here, Momma. Here's the water," she says breathlessly.

A chipped glass is shoved in my face, two dirty little hands encircling it. Suddenly acutely aware of my parched throat, I tilt my head back, allowing the little girl to pour the water into my mouth, and greedily begin to swallow. As soon as the water hits my throat, however, I wretch, spewing the cup's contents all down my front and into the child's face.

The little girl cries out, and Momma roars with laughter. "Didn't you hear me say this isn't the Holiday Inn? Darla, go fill this cup back up. Fool girl needs to drink."

"But, Momma," the little girl whines, wiping her hands across her face, which only manages to smear the dirt even worse.

"No buts, little lady. Get!"

Darla leaves again, her head bent.

Momma turns her attention back to me. "Name's Jenny," she says, closing the distance between us and sitting down beside me on the floor. "I know the water tastes awful, but you get used to it. You need to drink." Jenny laughs again. "Though your gut's gonna hate you after."

A moment of silence passes between us as Jenny considers my bandages. "You must of pissed someone off somethin' terrible for them to shove you in those waters," she says. "You were in pretty bad shape when we found you yesterday. Wasn't sure you'd pull through." Jenny smiles, revealing a mouth full of rotten teeth.

I cringe, and she notices, putting her face so close to mine, I can smell her putrid breath. "Where did you come from, honey?" she asks, wrinkling her nose as she scrutinizes my face. "You seem cleaner than most." She fiddles with my matted hair still damp from my trip down the river, and a look almost like envy shrouds her eyes.

I pull my head away.

Jenny shrugs. "Well," she says. "When Sam gets back, we'll figure out what to do with you. I reckon we can get a pretty penny for your pretty face." Jenny stands and heads toward the door.

Panic motivates me to find my voice. "Wait!" I cry earnestly. Jenny turns around, her eyebrows raised in question. "Did you say you...you found me yesterday?"

"Last night, actually," Jenny responds. "Sam was fishing when you smacked right into him. Made him drop his net. He wasn't too happy with you." Jenny laughs. It seems this woman finds everything funny. It's vexatious. "Sam was gonna skin you and cook you up right then and there for ruining supper."

I'm not sure I hear her correctly. "Wait, what?" I ask.

Jenny howls again. "Lord, child, you're not too bright, are you? Darla might have more sense than you! Sam sure can be meaner than a snake, but he'd never *kill* nobody. Though I do believe a part of him was hoping you wouldn't make it." With this, she cackles her way out the door.

As soon as she's gone, I immediately begin to assess my situation. My hands are bound behind my back with a fraying rope, the loose strings scratching my wrists. I vainly try to wriggle them free, but the uncomfortable strain to my shoulders makes me stop. I'm awkwardly propped up against a wall in a room with boarded up windows, and hints of the sun filter through the cracks in the boards, mocking me. My gun is gone, and there's no way I can check for my knife.

What now? I think. What now? I've already wasted at least twelve hours, and I'm not any closer to my mom than when I left. And Jenny? Clearly, all her marbles aren't intact. And this Sam character wants to serve me up for dinner. I shake my head, trying to rid my thoughts of all the possible horrible scenarios.

I hear a small voice crying about something to someone from somewhere else in the drafty house, and turn my head to listen, but the words are all muffled by the walls that separate us.

Darla.

Jenny and Sam might be hanging onto the cliff of humanity, one foot tap dancing on the opposing side, but Darla's still young. Young enough to hope. Yes, I decide, if there's any way I'm getting out of here it's through the kid. But I can't do anything in the meantime but wait.

So I do.

Outside I hear the distant sound of thunder and the pitter-patter of raindrops falling on the roof above. To my right a puddle forms, the ceiling riddled with leaks from years of neglect. I think about the last time it rained. How Ryder and I, barefoot through the tall grass just beyond our camp, had gone running, laughing and chasing each other until we reached the far end of the reservoir surrounding our camp.

How simple life had seemed then.

How happy.

How stupid I had been.

•　　•　　•　　•　　•

There is no more light filtering in through the cracks in the boarded-up windows when the door to my new prison opens again.

The footsteps are heavy, clearly not Darla's, and it's with a sinking dread, I realize I am about to formally meet Sam.

"Girl, wake up!" he demands in a voice that propels me to stretch taller against the wall.

"I'm awake," I tell him meekly.

Sam walks over to me and kicks my bandaged leg. I cry out in pain. Sam laughs. *What's with these people?* "Where you from?" he asks once his clear enjoyment of watching me suffer subsides.

"From down the highway," I tell him, as another idea seizes me, recalling the filthy water Jenny served me earlier. "Please, please," I beg. "My camp. We have supplies. Clean water and food. I know if you help me get back to them, they'll reward you—"

Sam cuts me off, laughing loudly again. "You're an idiot fool if you think I'm gonna believe some girl who just so happened to wash up on my territory." His tone becomes serious. "Someone *pushed* you in, girl. I'm not so sure your so-called camp even *wants* you back."

My mouth falls open to protest, but something that he says makes me stop. Someone pushed me in. *Pushed* me in. It couldn't possibly be true, I think, but when I try to recall the exact moment I fell into the river, something in my memory tells me that Sam might just be right. Someone or something forced me into the river. But who? And, more importantly, why?

"So you see," Sam continues gravely, "we have quite the predicament on our hands, now don't we?"

I say nothing, my mind still struggling to unravel the thread of confusion in my head, throbbing from dehydration.

"We'll figure it all out in the morning, I suppose," Sam says almost to himself. "Yesss," he hisses, "we'll find a use for you, girl." And my eyes go wide as I swear he licks his lips with pleasure. Then he laughs once more as he heads out the door, slamming it in his wake.

I squeeze my eyes tight and begin to cry. How stupid was I to believe that I could survive on my own? How ignorant was I to think I could save my mother all by myself? And all at once, my longing for my mother fills me with such despair, I bring my knees to my chest and wail. I don't care who hears me.

I'm still crying hours later when the door creaks open hesitantly, and someone tiptoes into the room.

"Hey," Darla's tiny voice whispers. "Hey, please don't cry," she says and comes over to sit beside me on the cold floor. I sniffle, and she takes her filthy hand to gently wipe away my tears. The gesture is so sincere, it causes me to cry harder.

"Please," I say to her. "Please, let me go. Untie my hands, Darla. I have a mother just like you. Please."

Darla doesn't say anything at first but continues to stroke my cheek. She can't be more than six or seven years old, and if my despair wasn't so immeasurable, I might find it comical that my life now depends on such a young child.

"Momma won't be happy," Darla whispers.

"No, she won't," I agree. "But, Darla, *my* momma—" I can't finish the thought.

Darla takes my face into her hands and looks into my eyes. "Sam will beat me senseless," she says seriously. I lean my cheek into her hand.

"He'll kill me," I tell her. Darla purses her lips and nods.

"I don't want him to hurt you," she whispers so faintly I'm not at all sure she even spoke the words.

"So let me go, Darla. Please," I beg. She wraps her arms around me tightly for just a moment and then scuttles from the room, quietly shutting the door again.

Alone again with the pounding of my heart, I start to really panic. *Am I wrong about Darla?* I wonder. *Am I foolish to hope she'll let me go?* The house seems to breathe heavily with me, the creaking of the boards and shutters the only other sounds. I wait for what seems like an eternity before the door inches open again, and Darla hurries over to my side.

"I got scissors," she whispers, pushing me forward to get to my bound wrists.

My relief is palpable. "Oh, Darla! Thank you! Thank you!" When the blade accidentally nicks my skin, I wince. "Careful," I tell her, thinking about the more-than-likely possibility of rust. Of infection. "Just cut the ropes, Darla, ok?"

Darla doesn't speak, her tongue hanging out of the side of her mouth to indicate her deep concentration. When I feel the ropes finally slacken, I yank my arms free and embrace the courageous young girl who has risked more than she even knows to save a perfect stranger.

"Darla," I start, but she pulls at my hands.

"Come on," she whispers, her eyes full of fright. "Momma and Sam are sleeping, but they'll wake easily if we make too much noise."

I nod, check quickly for the knife I know will not be there, and climb gingerly to my feet, testing out my injured leg. It hurts, but adrenaline makes the pain bearable. I want to run from the house, thunder down the stairs and out the door, but I have Darla to think about. For her sake, I need to get as far away from this house before Jenny and Sam wake. Maybe then she can spin the story that I escaped on my own. I bend down and pick up the scissors Darla discarded after cutting through my ropes and pocket them. I don't know what happened to the rest of my supplies, and though I'm not sure how much they'll protect me, scissors, for now, will have to do.

I follow Darla down the stairs as she attempts to point to where I should walk to avoid creaking boards, but every other step I make a mistake, and the entire house seems to shudder.

I'm limping out the front door when Darla stops. I drop her tiny hand and turn to look her in the eyes, which seem far too solemn for such a young child. She backs up slowly, nods once, and shuts the door before I can even tell her, "Goodbye."

I turn and look out into the darkness. *So this is it,* I think. I'm back to where I started. But at least I'm nobody's dinner. I listen intently for the sound of the river, and when I think I hear it off to my left, I hobble down the rickety front steps of the house in that direction as quickly and quietly as I can.

It's at least half of a mile from the house to the river, I estimate, and once I'm standing on the shore, I search upriver for the great bridge that's supposed to take me to The Dome to find my mother. It's no use. I must have traveled a considerable distance downriver. The bridge is nowhere in sight.

I take a moment to examine my leg. The bandages have managed to stop the bleeding, but the swelling is pretty bad, and I worry about possible infection, what might happen if I don't get it cleaned and treated soon. *There's nothing I can do about it now,* I remind myself, and, taking a deep breath and repositioning the bandages, I take off upriver.

By the time the outline of the great bridge is, once again, illuminated by the glow of The Dome, I am relieved but exhausted, the initial adrenaline having worn off, and my battered leg throbs in protest. It's been almost two days since my last bite of food and sip of clean water, and after a short-lived internal debate, I collapse against a large oak tree. *One minute,* I tell myself. *You've got one minute to rest.*

But it takes half that time to fall asleep.

I am not exactly sure how long I'm out, but when I awaken, it's to the sound of a twig snapping from somewhere close by and to my right. I'm groggy from sleep, so my reaction time is hindered. I rub my eyelids, and try to stand, but it's too late.

A bright beam of light temporarily blinds me, and, falling back against the tree, I try to shield my eyes with my hands.

A voice cuts through the night. "See? I told you it was her," the voice says and laughs maniacally. "Didn't I tell you it was her?"

Sam.

A large cloaked figure emerges from the shadows and lifts me off the ground. I try to fight, but it's no use. I scream and am shaken so hard my brain rattles. The cloaked figure hurriedly carries me in the direction opposite of Sam and toward the bridge.

"Hey!" Sam yells. "Hey, you told me if I helped you find her, I'd be rewarded!" The man carrying me grunts. "Hey!" Sam screams again, his voice growing fainter as the distance between us rapidly expands. "A deal's a deal!"

My captor shifts me onto his other arm and turns to look in Sam's direction. "I'll let you and your slut wife live," he says gruffly. "I'll even throw in the child for free. That should be reward enough." He continues to walk through the thick woods, scaling rocks and fallen trees with surprising ease, until we reach what appears to be a road. I continue to struggle, but the man carrying me is so strong it's no use.

"Let me go!" I scream, and I'm shocked when he tosses me to the ground like a sack of flour. Ignoring my leg that screams in protest, I start to get up, to run for my life, but the man's heel comes down on my chest, and the breath is momentarily knocked out of me.

"Little lady, you're gonna be my ticket to the inside," he says. Then he kicks me so incredibly hard in the side of the head, I'm out like a light.

• • • • •

The first thing I notice upon waking is the utter darkness of my new surroundings, and at first, I fear I can't see at all. When I attempt to bring my hands to my eyes to check for the hindrance of fabric, however, I find that I am bound both by the wrists and ankles. A moan escapes my lips.

Not again, I think, and pull frantically at the chains.

"It's no use," comes a quiet voice from behind me, and I jolt on instinct toward the opposite direction, fear like fire in my heart. I try to break free again but am stopped short by the pain in my head. "Oh," I moan.

"Don't struggle," the voice continues. "It's no use." I squeeze my eyelids tightly together, trying to clear my head, to make sense of my current desperate situation. "You're in a basement." The voice is male. "It'll do no good to scream." Fellow captive? Raider? I'm not sure.

I try again to speak, but only panicked whispers make it past my lips.

I hear a heavy sigh. It is clear from the direction of his voice, the figure behind me hasn't moved, and there's something about his tone that sounds comforting. I decide, for the time being, he's just as much a prisoner as I am and tentatively relax, exhausted, against my restraints.

"Listen, I know you're frightened," the voice continues, "but it will do you no good to fight right now. You've been drugged. He calls himself a raider. The effects will wear off soon, but for now, you should try to conserve as much energy as you can." The soothing quality of the voice remains, but it does little to calm me, and I slump heavily against the barrier at my back as images of the river and its path of rocks, of Sam, Jenny, and Darla, come hurtling into my mind's eye. Ryder was right. I was a fool to think I could rescue my mother on my own.

In less than seventy-two hours, I realize, I have found myself a prisoner not once, but twice, first captured by Jenny and Sam and now a raider. Hot tears roll down my cheeks and drip onto the cold cement I have been chained to. My chest heaves, and I gasp for breath. I hadn't even made it *to* The Dome.

"Hey," the voice comes again in the dark, "please. Please, don't cry." I hear the movement of chains, and a large warm hand emerges from around the corner to touch me on the leg. On impulse, I jerk away, and I hear a loud intake of breath. "I-I'm sorry. I didn't mean to—." He withdraws his hand. I can't speak, so I don't even try to tell him that it's not his touch that frightens me but what the raider has in store for me that has my entire body trembling like a leaf. I know what raiders do to girls like me, and suddenly I wish I had died at the mercy of the raging river. At least then death would have been quick.

The soothing voice on the opposite side of the divide continues to speak to me, but I'm no longer listening. And as the drugs and shock take hold of me once again, I am tossed into a fitful sleep.

•　　•　　•　　•　　•

When I wake, my neck is stiff and my body sore, but the searing pain in my head from earlier has lessened. The darkness of my new prison has also lifted a bit; there's now a dim light radiating from somewhere above that creates a room full of shadows.

I glance down at my shackled, still-bandaged leg, recalling the earlier touch of the stranger apparently just inches away from where I lie chained. Is he still there? Could he possibly be of help to me? My gut tells me he *wants* to help me—even if he can't. At this point, what do I have to lose? I swallow hard, inhale deeply, clear my throat, and try my voice. "Hello?" I whisper. My voice still sounds like it's riddled with shards of glass, but at least I can speak. I clear my throat again. "Hey, are you awake?" I ask.

There's movement from behind me, and relief rushes over me as I imagine whoever is on the other side of the wall sitting up and turning his head toward the direction of my reclaimed voice. At first, he doesn't speak, and I worry that something's happened to him.

"You got your voice back," he eventually says.

I let out the breath I am holding. "I got my voice back," I reply, "Sort of."

"How are you feeling?" he asks, and with this question, I try shaking free of the chains again, but with far less force than earlier. The pain in both my head and leg is still there, but it isn't nearly as unbearable as before.

"Surprisingly, not as bad as I think I should."

My fellow prisoner grunts. "Yeah, well, you've probably been given another hefty cocktail, but this time I imagine you were dosed with a pretty awesome pain medication instead of a sedative. It's actually quite amazing— our captor's resources."

Immediately baffled, I ask, "Why on earth would a raider want to make me feel better?"

This time there's no mistaking the irritation as my cellmate grunts again. "I guess we're not dealing with an ordinary raider," he replies.

While it's true I don't have much, if any, personal experience with raiders, I do know that they're known for making a profit off wandering survivors. Children traveling alone make easy prey and tasty treats for the starving refugees, no longer holding onto their humanity. As for the young women? I shudder, willing away the unforgiving images.

"It doesn't make sense," I say.

"What's even more unusual than the drugs," he continues, "is how this guy *takes care* of us." There's something venomous about the way he says this. "Wait until breakfast is served. You'll see."

"Breakfast?" the word almost catches in my throat. My stomach growls, reminding me that I haven't eaten since the night of my mother's disappearance. My dry mouth waters involuntarily.

"When Jeb first told me about the food, I didn't believe him either," he says. "But then dinner was served. And, get this, we were even offered seconds." He laughs when he hears my sharp intake of air. "Don't get too excited, though. There's no silverware."

My head is reeling. Drugs? Food? Jeb? "Wait. I still don't understand. Who is Jeb?"

"Jeb was here when I was brought in. So was Mackenzie." There's a sincere tone of sadness to his voice now. "I imagine you arrived down here not long after Jeb was taken up there." I look up toward the ceiling of the basement where I imagine the face belonging to the voice looks as well.

"What happened to him?" I whisper, not certain I really want to know.

I hear chains jingle and envision the figure behind me shrugging. "If I had to guess? He was sold into The Community. Jeb had all kinds of theories."

Again, I am confused by his words. "The what?"

"You know, the giant wall? The place of healthy, happy, dying citizens?" The venom to his voice is back, and I take it there's something extremely personal between him and this so-called community.

"You're talking about The Dome?" I ask.

"Yeah, but I'm learning only outsiders call it that," he replies.

"Outsiders?" I ask incredulously. "Are you saying that you *lived* on the other side?"

He laughs, but his laughter carries no good humor. "If you can call it that," he says. "But I am no more a prisoner here than I was living there."

I sit against the wall in shock. Here I was trying to get *into* The Dome to save my mother, and this guy recently escaped from it. Something about our meeting feels like fate, and my heart lifts ever so slightly. Hope. Could it be that maybe, just maybe this stranger is my ticket in? I look to my shackled feet. Sure, there *is* the "small" matter of the raider to deal with before I can consider anything else. But still, a pocket-sized confidence burrows its way back into my soul, and I marvel at how little it takes to make me realize there's still fight in me left.

I turn slightly to my right and gingerly offer my hand. My one chance of escaping this raider and making it into The Dome, I realize, is with the help of this stranger who clearly knows how. And I don't believe he'll help me if he doesn't trust me. If the two of us are going to form any sort of valuable relationship, it needs to start with an offering. An offering and a name.

My fellow captive hesitates to take my hand at first, and for a moment, I think he won't accept my gesture, remembering my own rejection of his touch just hours before. But then I hear his chains moving, and a moment later his large, warm hand envelopes mine and he softly pumps it up and down.

"My name's Wren," I tell him.

"It's nice to meet you, Wren. My name's Abel."

• • • • •

Abel wasn't kidding about the food.

It isn't but a few minutes after our official introductions that our captor rears his face, shrouded in silvery hair, storming down the basement stairs with a tray of delicious-smelling food.

Growing up in camp, an edible delicacy consisted of a bountiful salad with more than two colors of vegetables. Every now and again, our hunters would bring enough deer or turkey around to share, but, without the proper marinades and spices, the meat was always rather bland and all too often overcooked. Not to mention, no one was ever really what I'd classify as full after a meal.

My first morning in captivity, however, Abel and I eat like kings—well, kings without forks. There are scrambled eggs and sausages smothered with a thick, deliciously salty gravy, piles of pancakes sticky with syrup, and potatoes so tender, they seem to dissolve on my tongue. By the time I am finally finished eating, I lean heavily against the wall that separates me from my new ally, and then later sink awkwardly onto the cement before falling into a deep sleep, the gravy and syrup still a greasy mess on my face.

That evening, Abel informs me that our dinners are likely laced with sedatives as each night he follows the same routine: eat, eat even more, and then crash. At first, I am relieved. I am growing stronger and stronger with each meal and subsequent rest, and this, I am certain, will increase my odds.

But my relief isn't quite as profuse as my full bladder.

"Abel," I say with hesitation after awakening from my breakfast comma. I'm not entirely sure how to tell this boy I've just met that I seriously have to pee, but the ache in my abdomen is almost unbearable.

"I-uh, I need to-uh—"

"Use the toilet?" he interjects. "I know. It's a funny thing about food and water. They go in. They have to come back out."

When Abel doesn't offer a solution, I whisper, "So what do I do?" And I can't hide the alarm in my voice. The idea of soiling myself isn't exactly appealing. Neither is the idea of individually confronting the raider.

"You hold it."

"*Hold it?*" I hiss. "What if I can't hold it?"

"He'll come to get us soon. He always does."

My head reels. He'll come to get us? I think appallingly. But what does that mean? Where will he take us? And just when I think I'll be flooding the cement floor of our prison, the door to the basement opens. I wince as the light from above temporarily blinds me, a million tiny stars dancing across my closed eyelids.

"All right, Newbie, you first. Time to take a walk," a voice grunts from the top of the stairs.

Abel immediately gropes for my hand.

"Listen," he whispers. "Everything will be ok." But hearing the fear in his voice, I am anything but assured.

Footsteps thunder down the stairs, and I'm not sure which is louder, my pounding heart or this burly raider clamoring down the stairs.

"What do I do?" I barely whisper, inching as close to Abel's direction as I can.

"He's taking you up, Wren. It'll be ok. Just do what he says."

"Abel, I can't," I cry, still yanking at my chains in vain.

"Just do what he says, Wren," Abel repeats. "You'll be safe as long as you just do what he says."

The problem is I'm not exactly good at following *anyone*'s orders. And I'm not too sure I believe that even if I do, everything will end up okay. This is a raider we're dealing with after all. I pull at the chains one last time, desperate to go anywhere but with this disgusting man upstairs. Alone.

Thud. The raider has made his heavy descent to the bottom of the steps. He pauses and laughs. "Poor thing," he chides. "You seem afraid." Here he laughs again as he approaches my trembling form. "Hands!" he commands.

I don't think. I lift my chained hands up to where I imagine he can reach them, sickened by my lack of motivation to fight. My eyes are shut tight, and I am reminded of the time Ryder and I played hide-n-seek late into the night when we were ten. The attic I chose to hide in wasn't unoccupied as I had thought. Only when I finally noticed the moving ceiling did I realize I was now sharing the space with a roomful of bats. *Rats with wings.* I don't know how long I sat there, wound up tightly into a ball on the floor, but when Ryder finally found me there trembling, I didn't hesitate. Fear propelled me to take his hand and slowly make our way out into the dark of night.

It's a different kind of fear that propels me now.

I feel the chain holding my arms in place slacken. Then I hear the cock of the gun. Cool metal is pressed to my temple. "Try anything, and you're dead," he says, and I know he means it. The smell of his breath lingers in the stale air as he bends and unlocks my ankles as well. "Get up!"

I stand on legs that don't feel strong enough to support an ant but resolve not to show any more weakness in the face of the raider. He spins me around, and in one clumsy but swift movement, unlocks my wrist cuffs, wrenches my arms behind my back, and immediately locks them again. He grabs my right arm with one of his meaty hands and presses the gun into the small of my back with the other.

"Move," he growls and pushes me toward the stairs. I have to shuffle because my ankles are still cuffed.

Abel says nothing as I disappear up the basement stairs.

When we reach the ground-floor landing, the raider knocks me into the door, and the force of my body sends it swinging from its hinges. Before it reels back, the raider throws me into the room, and the door slams behind me, causing me to startle.

"You seem jumpy, Newbie," the raider jests. "What's a-matter? Never seen a raider before, eh?" When he smiles, his teeth, surprisingly white and intact, mock me and my mounting panic.

I don't answer. The truth is he's right. In all my years living in camp, I never once encountered a raider. But I don't want him to know this.

"Don't worry, Sweet Cheeks," he says, his hot breath in my ear. I turn my face away, but he takes the gun and pushes it into my flesh, forcing my eyes to his. "I'm under strict orders to bring you in unharmed," he hisses, and at my immediate and obviously surprised expression, he laughs loudly. "I said unharmed. Not untouched." At this, he grabs my breast forcibly, making a noise sounding half like laughter and half like a groan. Immediately, tears sting the corner of my eyes, and again, I try to turn my head away, but the raider has another idea. Keeping the gun pressed firmly into my cheek, he plants his fish lips on mine, his wiry beard scratching my skin. I gag on impulse, and when his tongue makes its way past my lips, I bite down as hard as I can, the coppery taste of blood filling my mouth, causing me to retch again.

"Bitch!" the raider cries out, but it sounds more like *bith* as he grabs his tongue, blood dripping through his fingers. I stumble backward as he regains a bit of his composure and lunges toward me. His shoulder slams against the door frame just to my left, and I move as fast as I can down the hallway, cuffs cutting into my ankles with each encumbered step.

When a blast suddenly comes from behind and pieces of drywall pelt me from somewhere above, I fall to my knees and curl up against the wall at the end of the hall, remembering with horror the raider's gun.

This is it, I think. *I'm going to die.*

I don't move, but instead try to fold deeper into myself, as I did that night in the attic many years ago, bracing for the pain of the impending bullet tearing through my body. But there's only the laughter of the raider, towering over me.

"I told you, Sweet Cheeks," he says menacingly before spitting out a mouthful of blood on the floor next to me. "I'm not to harm you." He picks me up by my hair, and I cry out. He shoves me into a room with a soiled mattress and heaps of filthy clothing. "And if I'm anything," he continues, "I'm a man of my word." The heel of his boot meets the base of my spine with immense force, and I fly forward onto the dirty makeshift bed, crying out in pain and shock.

I try not to let my face touch the dirty mattress, covered in stains of God knows what, and for a second I want to laugh because how funny is it that I'm worried about smothering my face in filth when this raider is about to rape and possibly kill me? When I hear the unmistakable jingle of his belt buckle, however, I bury my face into the fabric unable to face the grim reality of the situation.

"Don't worry, Sweet Cheeks," the raider spits. "You're gonna love it."

PART II

7: ABEL

The escape. That's the easy part. Wait until lights out. Move a rock. Climb through. Walk away. Leaving Cat behind is another story. I replay our conversation from earlier this morning over in my mind.

"I want the truth just as much as you do," Cat had said, *"but running from here won't change anything."*

A small part of me agrees with her. Running never solves anything. And yet here I am running anyway. Slowly. But nevertheless running.

Once I finally do reach the outskirts of The Community, it takes me longer than I would like to admit to conjure up the motivation to climb through the towering wall of holly trees that disguise my way out.

Since childhood, Cat has been my one constant. The one person who seems to give a damn about me, the poor boy whose parents had to buy his way into the safety of The Community. How can I just leave her behind?

Then again, I've known since I was a young child that things aren't quite as they seem in our so-called safe community. But in recent months, I finally reached my breaking point. Leave it to the kid who was made an orphan for "his own protection" to make a stink.

It is ironic, I think now, as I head silently through the dark cemetery, that after thirteen years of "safe" living in The Community, the security of my life now depends on my escape.

Thirteen years, I lament, passing by the long-forgotten graves of our ancestors. Thirteen years without parents. Thirteen years without a sense of belonging. Thirteen years without really *living*.

And why? Because humans are innately reckless and self-absorbed. And our ancestors were no exception, using up all the wonder drugs and leaving the future generations with nothing.

It takes me only a few minutes to reach the top of the cemetery where the once-important, tall metal cage towers above me like the grim reaper himself, ready to swallow me whole. I kick the cage hard, a sudden anger welling up in my gut. And it hurts. All of it. The fact that, despite all attempts, the people in The Community are still dying. The fact that I might never see Cat again. The fact that *I* might not even see the dawn of the next day. And the fact that all of this could have been prevented in the first place.

"Damn you!" I scream at the cage. "Damn all of you!" I storm around the circle of graves, kicking and screaming like a small child with a tantrum and letting go of all the suppressed anguish I've had to keep hidden from The Community and its leaders my entire life. "This is all your fault," I shout up at the ceiling of The Community. And then I start to laugh. A high-pitched maniacal sound. The cage in the cemetery. The giant wall. *We're trapped*, I think. *All of us. Lured in by the promise of a better life. We're no different from caged animals.*

And yet I'm leaving my one true friend behind the bars of The Community. Held captive by the grief caused by her mother's death. A puppet on strings controlled by her delusional father.

My chest heaves as I collapse against the tall barrier that separates me from the unknown. What waits for me out there? I wonder. Is it better than what I face here in The Community? Is it worth the possibility of losing it all?

I don't know, I don't know. But I think it *has* to be. I can no longer consider the alternative. Dr. Grayson, Cat's father, has sealed my fate.

Forge ahead, I think cynically one last time and then turn and dislodge the large stone from the original foundation of the cemetery wall, burying any doubts and lingering thoughts of Cat deep into my subconscious.

Immediately, the smell of the river hits me, and I don't hesitate. I squeeze my large frame through the gap in the wall. Once I'm through, dirty, my clothes torn, I fashion the stone back into place and head out into the darkness of what lies beyond.

•　　•　　•　　•　　•

I walk all night. The chill in the air is not at all what I anticipated, having lived in a climate-controlled environment most of my life; however, it's nothing I can't handle. What unnerves me the most about the world beyond the wall is the darkness. Always in The Community, there is a constant glow, even in the dead of night, but here, out in the wilderness, the darkness is so thick I often fear my next step. Because of this, I decide to follow the path of the long-abandoned railroad tracks that seem to snake along the banks of the river to the south. I also hope that the tracks will lead me to a bridge across the river.

In the shadow of the great wall, I feel as though I am under constant surveillance, and my immediate goal is to get as far away from The Community as possible. Crossing the river would make me feel a whole lot better.

When dawn finally veils the earth in a blanket of gold, I am rewarded by what I believe is, in fact, a bridge a few miles off in the distant haze, and although I am exhausted, I hasten my steps. Now that the darkness is lifting, the sense that I am being watched returns. I don't dare to turn around, however. I'm afraid of what I'll see. What I'll feel. What I'll regret.

By the time I reach the bridge, the sun is now high in the sky, and I've sweated through my two layers of clothing. I smell of sweat and earth, and I realize that besides my immediate goal of putting as much distance between The Community and me as possible, I haven't given much thought about how I plan to survive out here if there are, indeed, no survivors.

I need to find shelter. I need to find food and clean water. I wrinkle my nose: I'm going to need to bathe.

I survey the old bridge. Surprisingly, it seems to be in pretty good shape. Because it was built to support the weight of train cars, it has withstood the many years of neglect. I shield my eyes to look down the tracks to the opposite side of the river bank. I scan the edge, east then west, but see nothing out of the ordinary. The only movements are the current of the river and some type of bird that flies low, looking, I assume, for food.

"You and me both," I say to him quietly before taking a seat at the base of the bridge to open the sack I packed hastily the day before with a loaf of bread, some dried fruit, and a canteen of water. While I rest, I make a more thorough plan. I'll cross the bridge and continue to travel along the river. The water source, I imagine, would make setting up camp nearby ideal. Maybe others thought so too.

I'm packing up my meager supplies when I first hear the noise. It's the unmistakable rumble of an engine. A boat? A car? I turn in every direction, trying to decipher the direction of the sound. With the raging river so close by, it's difficult to tell. But then I see it: a white blur of a vehicle traveling just beyond the trees on the south side of the river.

My heart races. At first, I am alarmed. The driver could very well be a member of Dr. Grayson's guard sent to find me. Then again, I knew the risks when I escaped. And I need to be optimistic that maybe—just maybe—the occupants of the vehicle are proof of survivors. Optimistic but cautious, I decide and climb out onto the bridge.

The white vehicle has disappeared into the woods beyond the river's edge, but the bridge doesn't provide much cover, so I crawl tediously across the steel grooves, ignoring the growing discomfort in my knees.

It takes me much longer than anticipated to cross the river. A half-hour, maybe longer. But by the time I reach the end of the bridge, I am filled with an immense sense of accomplishment, the adrenaline coursing through my veins like the flowing river now at my back. I leap off the bridge and head quickly into the trees, my confidence mounting with the increased camouflage of the forest.

Now, to follow that vehicle, I think, and head in the direction I believe it has gone. I don't travel long—maybe ten minutes—before I reach a paved road, and even through the overgrown woods, as I travel, traces of human life begin to emerge. Rusty mailboxes, open and empty, like hungry mouths waiting to be fed. Long, winding driveways, leading, I am sure, to once-desired real estate properties. Private! Riverfront! And the views!

I can't help but smile sadly.

This is proof of a once-happy society. Of a generation where illness and infection were so-easily treated. Maybe it's possible a new society has risen from its ashes.

I choose the third driveway on my left for no other reason than I've always believed that good things happen in threes—or is it bad things always happen in threes? I shrug. Either way, I'm eager to explore the house I know I'll find at its end.

When I finally do reach the top, however, I am overcome with such an overpowering sense of sadness, I am all but forced to my knees and stare. I can tell that once upon a time, the house was a beautiful, magnificent structure, its architecture modern and constructed of so many windows I can't imagine its occupants ever being able to sleep. But its facade has been cruelly graffitied. Windows shattered, the torn draperies billowing out of the splintering frames, like arms reaching, reaching.

Let us go. Let us go.

I shiver despite the afternoon heat. And even though the shell of the house seems to beckon me, it takes me a long time to muster up the courage to inch closer. Once I do, I see that its foundation is made up of three great stories with a basement sloping off the back of the house, and I decide to walk around to investigate. Walking up to the front door just doesn't feel right.

I stay close to the house, my hand on the exterior wall, and when I get to the back yard, I gasp. How had I not smelled it? A fire recently extinguished sits abandoned and smoldering in its pit. Two rickety chairs are sitting nearby. Trash litters the landscape.

Could it be?

I stand motionless, my heart racing, listening for anything that might indicate who these people are. Innocuous survivors? Pillaging savages? Members of The Community? But I hear nothing but the distant roar of the river blending with the sounds of nature.

I'm inching closer to the fire pit, hoping that whoever was here earlier might have left behind possible remnants of food, when a drop of water lands on my cheek. Then another. I stop and hold my hands out as more droplets fall from the sky. I know what this is of course: rain. But because it's been thirteen years since I've felt it on my skin, it startles me at first. After a few moments, I tilt my head to the sky and let the water roll down my face, and find myself smiling again. It feels clean. Fresh.

After a few minutes of gentle drizzle, however, the raindrops come faster and faster, and when I hear the faint rumble of what I remember to be thunder, I know I need to find shelter. And fast.

I could easily head back to the front of the house and climb through a broken window, but the rain is steady now, and since I'll be temporarily protected by the decking that extends from the first floor above, I quickly begin to examine the back of the house for any obvious clues that might tell me who these people are and whether or not I should risk breaking in.

The windows of the basement have been crudely boarded up. The French doors also boarded, chained, and padlocked. I wonder briefly if this happened pre-Virus or after. I pull on the chains, fiddle with the lock. Finally, because I don't know what else to do in the interim, I knock hard on the splintering boards.

A flock of birds taking refuge in a nearby tree takes flight, startled by the sudden disruption.

I'm not sure what I expect to happen. The doors are locked from the outside, after all. I'm ready to flee in an instant if I need to, but when voices from within the house break through the steady sound of the rain hitting the trees and ground around me, I am frozen in place.

I know that I am a large, strong, very capable young man. It takes a lot to rattle me. But these voices from the basement weaken my resolve, and I am suddenly very, very frightened.

Because the people shouting from beyond the locked doors don't sound like innocuous survivors.

They sound panicked. Afraid. Desperate.

I'm still standing there, frozen in place, voices screaming at me from the other side of the door, when something blunt and heavy hits me from behind.

I stumble backward, making contact with a solid figure who grabs me by the arms.

I try to turn around, my head swimming, but the figure behind me brings what I guess is his own head down to hit me again.

Then everything goes dark.

●　　　●　　　●

When I come to, my face is covered by a sack made from some sort of very uncomfortable, scratchy material, and I am in a sitting position. My arms are bound tightly and awkwardly around a chair, and when I try to move them, my muscles scream in protest. The soft light filtering through the fabric indicates it's still daytime, but I can't be sure how long I've been unconscious.

My head throbs fiercely, and I moan, squeezing my eyes tightly shut, trying to think.

"Nice of you to join us."

The cool voice cuts through the air like a cruel joke. At first, I can't believe it. I think my mind must be playing tricks on me. A consequence of the blunt-force trauma to my skull. It can't be right. Because even though his muffled voice has more pleasantry to it than usual, I would know it anywhere.

Dr. Grayson.

So. I escaped only to find myself back in the clutches of The Community.

"I'm curious," Dr. Grayson continues. "What did you possibly imagine you'd accomplish by leaving, Abel?"

I don't answer.

There's movement to my right. Someone else is in the room.

"Did you really think I would let you just walk out of The Community and abandon your given post?" There's the sound of a chair scraping across the floor, and I feel Dr. Grayson's presence at my side. He grabs me by the wrists and twirls my identification bracelet once around, and almost immediately, I recognize the very stupid and very consequential mistake I have made.

Of course. My required bracelet. He's tracked me. He's tracking us all. And I was so accustomed to wearing it that I never once considered its true purpose.

Dr. Grayson laughs, relishing my ignorance. From my many conversations with Cat, I have come to learn that exposing the weaknesses in others bolsters Dr. Grayson's own feelings of importance. It's fuel to his fire of greed.

A moment passes between us before he speaks again. "I have to admit, Abel. I am surprised you were so eager to leave Catherine behind. How must she have felt knowing that you *chose* to abandon her in a time of such great despair?"

Cat's given name in his mouth infuriates me. How dare he speak about her as though he cares? I want to scream at him, "I had no choice!" but still I say nothing. He wants me to be angry. He wants me to react. So I bury my fury deep inside.

"*Tsk, tsk,*" he continues. "What to do with you now?" He pauses again for effect then gets his mouth so close to my ear, I can feel his hot breath through the coarse fabric covering my face. "You're *nothing*, Son, if not a pawn," he whispers. "You will do whatever it is *I* need you to do. Or you die. It's that simple." He stands and puts his hand heavily on my shoulder. I don't move a muscle.

"Put him in the basement for now," he orders. He's no longer talking to me. "And bring me one of the other prisoners."

There's a grunt of confirmation, and my arms are yanked back abruptly, the chair I'm sitting on sent flying foward. It happens so fast, I don't have time to react. My face hits hard on the cold floor, and a coppery taste fills my mouth.

Someone laughs. The chair is roughly removed from my arms, the wood burning my skin, and I'm lifted to my feet.

"Walk, Pretty Boy," says a gruff male voice, and I'm shoved hard in the back. "You're mine now," the man growls as he leads me to the basement door and down thirteen steps. It's difficult to breathe with the cloth over my face, but when we reach the floor of the basement, the unmistakable stench of urine penetrates the fabric, and I have to fight the urge to gag.

"Make room, boys," the man says. "Fresh meat coming in." We shuffle awkwardly across the space, and then I'm thrown heavily against a wall.

There is the sound of shackles moving as I'm chained to the floor. "You, up!" he orders someone else. More chains move.

"Wait!" comes a panicked cry. "Please, wait!"

The sack is ripped from my head. I blink rapidly, trying to adjust my eyes to the scene unfolding in front of me. There are three other boys in the room with us. One is hunched over by the far wall of the basement, not moving. The other two are near the base of the steps and are scrambling to move as far away from our captor as they can, but because they are both also chained to their surroundings, they have nowhere to go.

"Hmm," says the man in charge of the current situation, jeering through his thick silver beard. He's holding a gun in one hand, pointing it back and forth between the two boys as if playing eeny-meeny-miny-moe, the childhood counting rhyme.

It's sick to watch, both boys trembling in anticipation.

He pauses on the boy who I imagine is the one who cried out earlier. Tears zigzag down his dirty face. He can't be older than ten years old. The man moves in on him quickly, and the burlap sack is thrown over his face, the gun now pressed to his temple.

"Make this difficult for me, and I'll blow your brains out." The boy is lifted like a rag doll to his feet, unshackled, and dragged to the steps. Before the two ascend, the man turns back to address the remaining prisoners.

He smiles a wicked, too-bright smile. "Don't worry, boys. I'll be back." And he leads the whimpering boy up the stairs and slams the door with his heel.

The noise of the slamming door reverberates around the basement. Above, I hear the sound of feet shuffling overhead. A door closing. Then nothing. I wait for someone to speak. But there seems to be a blanket of temporary relief covering the boy who wasn't chosen; he's staring out into nothing, his chest rising and falling. The hunched figure against the far wall still doesn't move.

I take in my surroundings. The basement itself is quite large with a door leading to another room to my left. A bathroom perhaps. I swivel my head as best as I can and decide that the wall I've been chained to is some type of half-wall of cabinets. An old bar maybe? There's a lip of countertop directly over my head. The boarded-up doors and windows of the basement are to my right.

The thunder outside has ceased, and I curse myself and my haste to find shelter. I realize, of course, I don't have much experience surviving in the wilderness. Still, I could have avoided this. I could have been more cautious.

"Quite the view, huh?" comes a voice from across the room. It's the hunched figure. He's awake and apparently eager for conversation. The other boy watches to see how I'll respond.

I shake my chains. "Sure, if you're into sadism and human torture." My answer is sarcastic, but cautious.

The boy snorts. "Maybe I am," he replies.

A moment of silence passes between us before the boy speaks again. "It could be worse, you know?" I don't. "Although by the looks of your clothes, I'd say you've fared better than the rest of us," he says eyeing me up and down suspiciously.

I remind him grimly, "Right now, I figure we're all in the same boat, so what does it matter how we're dressed?" I lift my shackled arms for emphasis.

"Fair enough," the boy says, nodding. And then after a pause of consideration, adds, "Name's Jeb. Him over there, that's MacKenzie."

"Mac," the kid mumbles quietly. "I go by Mac."

"Yeah, yeah, yeah," Jeb says. "Like it matters down here. Our raider friend loves his nicknames."

"Raider?" I ask.

Jeb's eyes narrow. "Where you from, boy?"

I consider whether or not I should answer truthfully. My guess, though? I've got a better chance of getting out of here alive if I know exactly what it is that's going on. And Jeb seems to be willing to offer information.

"Not from around here," I decide to answer.

Jeb snorts again. "I'd say so," he responds, leaning back against the wall and awkwardly crossing his arms. "Raiders, my friend," he continues with a jeer, "are scum of the earth left to pick off what's left of humanity." He doesn't elaborate, but he doesn't have to. I can easily fill in any blanks. It is part of Community doctrine to educate its youth on the sufferings of those left *outside* its walls. More propaganda put into place to remind its members why life within the walls is far superior than the alternative of life outside.

"And Dr. Gray—"I start but then change my mind. "I mean the other man? Upstairs. What's his deal?"

Jeb narrows his eyes again, and I fear I've said too much. "You must be talking about the man in charge," Jeb says, and I am more than excited he knows who I'm talking about. "I imagine he's in it for the same reasons."

"And that is?" I ask.

"What's your name, boy?" Jeb asks, sitting up and leaning forward to get a better look at me.

I settle for the truth. "Abel."

"Well, Abel," Jeb says, "Rumor has it, we're bound for some great big experiment."

"Don't say that," Mac whines.

"Don't what? Don't admit the truth? Stop trying to deny it, Mac. You know, and I know that they're fattening us up for the slaughter." Jeb turns to me. "Remember when I said it could be worse?" I nod. "Well, wait until you get a load of the food."

My head is reeling. "What do you mean by 'some great experiment'?" I ask, ignoring the mention of food.

Jeb rolls his eyes. "Man, haven't you heard? They're *dying* on the other side of that great wall. Their miracle vaccine? It didn't work." He laughs. "Who would have thought life would be better out here after all?" He laughs again, raising his arms as high as he can.

"What are you saying?" I ask, but I already know what he is insinuating. Still, I need to hear it.

"Specimens, man," Jeb says, relaxing back against the wall. "That's all we are."

Mac starts to whimper.

Jeb continues, picking at something on the wall next to him, seemingly talking to himself now, his voice lowered, "Some mad scientist is gonna inject us with who-knows-what and then cut us all into tiny, little pieces. And for what? To save all the rich and powerful people inside that wall." With this, he spits on the floor. "At least the food's good, right, Mac?"

Mac doesn't respond, and the basement fills with a silence so thick I struggle to breathe.

8: RYDER

As soon as Wren shuts the door, my mind goes berserk with conflict. Should I follow her? Should I not? Should I band together a group of willing men to storm The Dome?

What does Wren *really* want me to do?

The thing is, if I know Wren as well as I believe I do, following her after she explicitly asked me not to would infuriate her. Still, not following her could prove to be the gravest mistake of my life.

And then there's the matter of the proposed trade on the bridge yesterday, which I chose not to tell Wren about. I thought the information would cause her to react irrationally, which she did all on her own anyway.

I shake my head in frustration, recalling the events from the previous day, and how Claire reacted (or didn't react) when I disclosed the fact that the men on the bridge had asked for *her*. By name. "The people from The Dome *know* you, Claire," I told her, but she only patted my shoulder and agreed that telling Wren would cause more harm than good.

Right.

I head back to my cabin to clear my thoughts and make a plan, but all I end up doing is pacing a trench in my hardwood floors.

"*You're needed here, Ryder,*" Wren said. "*Bill needs you. Our family needs you.*"

Truth be told, the one person I want more than anything to need me doesn't. Wren was right. She's strong and fierce and resourceful. If anyone stands a chance of breaking into that great wall, it's her.

Still, while I know this to be true deep within my gut, my heart says otherwise: *Follow her,* it tells me with each beat. *Follow her, you fool!*

Hours later, I've made up my mind and am throwing clothing and other travel essentials into a duffle bag when there's a loud knock at my door. My brow furrows as I slowly and quietly move toward the door, breathing deeply. It's late. Or early. Well after midnight. There are only two people I can guess who would show up right now, and one of them is more than likely drowning in his "secret" stash of moonshine.

I open the door with caution, and as soon as I take one look at Alice standing on the opposite side of my front door, I know something's wrong. Her fiery hair is disheveled with debris caught up in its curls like she's stood in front of an industrial-sized fan deep in the woods. Her olive eyes are wild.

"Alice," I say. "What—?" but she cuts me off, attempting to brush past me. I don't budge, and she stands on tiptoes to look over my shoulder. I try to block her view because I know what she's looking for. Too late. She recoils as though from a repugnant smell when she sees my half-packed bags. As she turns to go, I grab her arm, and she tries to yank it from my grasp.

"Let me go!" she screams, her voice almost manic.

"Alice, what's going on?" I demand.

She continues to fight my grasp for a moment more. "I *said* let me go!" she says again, but her voice holds less conviction, and she collapses on the front porch of my cabin, sobbing. "She left you," she mumbles into her arms when her crying subsides just enough to get the words out. "She left you, and you still love her enough to go after her."

I take a deep breath, trying not to get angry. This isn't anything new. Alice fabricated this love triangle between Wren, her, and me a long time ago. There have been too many times to count when she's shown up sobbing on my cabin steps.

"Alice," I say, "please get up. We can talk about this, ok?" I offer her my hand, but she swats it away.

"She left you!" she screams, the almost-manic conviction back. "Why? Why do you still love her?"

My frustration with Alice's all-to-familiar charade mounts swiftly. She's looking at me with those pleading eyes that make me want to roll mine. "She didn't leave me, Alice," I remind her. "She left *us*. And if you haven't heard," I take a calming breath in and out, "her mother was kidnapped."

"To hell with her mother!" Alice shouts. And then, as though thinking twice about her choice of words, adds, "Oh, I forgot just how *precious* Wren's mother is to everyone. Oh, Claire! Can I do anything for you, Claire? You're so amazing, *Claire.* Thank you for saving us all, *Claire.* It's ridiculous just how much everyone worships her! Claire says jump, and everyone in camp yells, "How high?'" Her voice is now one of a high-pitched, whining child, and suddenly it all becomes crystal clear to me: Alice's resentment for Wren and her mother, her desperate need for affection.

"Alice," I say calmly, "it's not Wren's fault your mother's dead." I brace myself for the major meltdown I know is coming. It's what she wants, I guess, my shoulder to cry on. So I gently scoot her over and take a seat next to her. As much as Alice's antics drive me crazy, I can't ignore how closely I relate to her story. I, too, lost both my parents to the Virus. I know first hand what it feels like to be an outcast and an orphan. To have no real sense of belonging.

That is until I found Claire. And Wren. Instant family.

Alice still sniffles beside me, her face buried in her freckled hands.

"Alice," I remind her, "Wren and Claire are your family, too."

"Ha!" she responds, but she starts crying again. "Family doesn't abandon you when you need them the most. They don't just *leave* you."

I glance toward the door. "Look, if this is about me leaving—"

"Of course it's about you, Ryder! It's always been about you! I was just a little girl, and you and Wren, you both were *so* enamored by each other. She forgot about me and dolls and dress up to play with *you*! I wanted that, too! But you never gave me the time of day!" Alice is back to whining.

"Alice," and I can hear my southern drawl coming out as it tends to do when I'm trying to impress Wren or, in this case, when I'm extremely irritated, "you're actin' like a small child." I stand up, clearly recognizing that this conversation isn't going anywhere fast. I need to finish packing. I've wasted enough time.

I head into the living room where my duffle bag is turned on its side, spilling out the haphazardly packed contents: clothes, canned foods, matches. I grab the canteen I found earlier and toss that in too, scooping up the rest of the overturned supplies as I do.

I'm lacing up my riding boots when I look up to see Alice standing in the doorway with an odd look on her face. It's a mixture of pity and satisfaction, her lips curled up at the edges. I ignore her, something I'm apparently quite used to doing, and continue to lace up my boots. When I'm finished, I stand, fully anticipating that Alice has gone; however, to my surprise, she's still standing there in the doorway with the same bizarre look on her face.

Something in my gut tenses.

It must show in my face because her smile falters a bit. She casually smoothes back her tangled mess of red hair, and something falls to the floor. It seems to happen in slow motion. We both follow the small piece of branch with our eyes, and when I catch her looking at me, I can tell she knows I know.

"You've been on my bike," I say matter-of-factly.

Alice stands a bit taller, holding her shoulders back as though to prove a point. "It's not *your* bike," she says coldly.

True. "So you've been riding one of the camp's bikes, then?"

She shrugs, and the tight feeling in my gut worsens. "Are you surprised I know how, Ryder?" she asks.

I shake my head in disbelief. This is a new side of Alice, and I find myself liking her even less.

"You know," she continues, "I'm just as resourceful as your precious Wren. Sometimes," and as she continues to talk she stares out into the space behind me, a dreamy quality to her voice, "when you two are off doing God knows what, I just drive. To nowhere, really. But I like to think I can drive to the edge of the earth where the Virus never existed."

"Where?" I ask, halting her memories in their tracks. "Alice, where did you go *tonight*?"

She shrugs again, and I feel something deep within me snap. I close the space between us so fast Alice has no time to react. I grab her wrists forcibly and squeeze.

"Where have you been tonight, Alice?" I demand.

Alice tries to shake free. "Ryder, you're hurting me!" she cries, and her voice has returned to normal. But I don't care. Something tells me that Alice didn't take the bike tonight for some joyride. "Ryder, please! Let me go!"

"I'm gonna ask you one more time, Alice," I say as calmly as I can manage. "Where did you take the bike?"

"Ryder!" An alarmed male's voice cuts through my rage. Bill. I drop Alice's wrists, and she stares at them blankly, the deep red marks already a perfect circumference around each one. "Ryder," Bill says again, "what on earth is going on here?" His face is haggard, and his eyes bloodshot. He's stumbling.

Alice starts to laugh a strange maniacal laugh. Bill backs up a few steps, holding up his arms.

"Woah," he says, clearly not sure what to make of the scene before him. "I get that we're all upset about Claire—"

Alice cuts him short with another laugh. "I don't give a damn about Claire!" she shouts at Bill. "You," she says, pointing at Bill, "and *you*," this time pointing at me, "and everyone else in camp care what happens to Claire." Her voice is icy. "I, on the other hand, I couldn't care less."

"Alice, what's gotten into you?" Bill's question is directed at Alice, but he's looking for some sort of answer from me.

"I think something's happened to Wren," I tell Bill through gritted teeth. Alice laughs again.

"Why would you think something's happened to Wren? Where is she? I thought she…wait." Bill doesn't finish, a look of confusion coming over his face.

I am overcome with panic. I turn back to Alice, trying a new approach—anything to get answers from a girl who's clearly gone mad with jealousy. "Darlin'," I say to her as sweetly as I can summon, "can you tell me, please? What have you done to Wren?"

Her anger returns like a boomerang, fast and furious. "It's too late for that, Ryder! It's too damn little and too damn late."

"Ryder, where did Wren go?" Bill sounds as frantic as I feel now. I wave him off. Bill may have been too drunk to remember, but I certainly wasn't going to let his befuddlement stand in my way of figuring out the truth.

"You followed her," I say to Alice.

She nods. "It was easy," she says. "I've been following you both for years. I know where you go and what you do. How the two of you talk and laugh about me."

Again, I feel like I've been punched hard in the gut. "Alice I never—we never—"

She cuts me off. "Don't. I don't want to hear it. Don't pretend I don't know how you both made a mockery of my feelings. Every time your precious Wren left me behind to pick up her mess, she never once was thinking about *me*. And it was all because of you, Ryder." Her voice trails off. "You want to know the saddest part, though?"

I nod my head because I don't want Alice to stop talking yet. Not until I know the truth.

"She never loved you like I did."

I inhale deeply and try once more. "Alice, please," I say. "What have you done to Wren?"

In the early light of dawn, her eyes look mad. "I followed her to the river, Ryder," she says, picking at her fingernails absentmindedly and shrugging. Her voice is so nonchalant, I almost can't believe what comes out of her mouth next. "I followed her to the river, and then I pushed her in."

•　　•　　•　　•　　•

The shock of the situation cloaks me like a heavy shroud as Bill and I escort Alice, who hasn't spoken since her admittance, back to the cabin she shares with her uncle. I also say nothing and let Bill take the lead.

Thoughts—awful thoughts—try to invade my mind. Images of Wren's body torn to shreds by the unsuspecting rocks beneath the rapids. Wren's body washed upon the shore, only to be discovered by raiders. Wren. My body convulses, and Bill, noticing, puts one of his big hands on my shoulder.

"Look," Bill whispers so Alice can't hear, "I'm not about to tell you that Wren's all right. But if I know Wren, she's anything but a quitter." He pats my back a little too hard for comfort. "You hear me, Ryder? Your Wren's a survivor. Just like her mom." His voice breaks, and he lets his hand fall.

We continue to the cabin in silence. Neither Bill nor I know what we're going to say to Alice's uncle. There hasn't been any real human conflict in the camp since its inception. It's not like we're going to put her on trial for involuntary manslaughter. This is new territory. Territory I'm not ready to figure out right now when all I want to do is find Wren. I'm also not ready to concede that Wren is dead.

I need to believe that she's still alive.

Turns out, we don't have to tell Alice's uncle anything. As soon as he answers the door, Alice falls into his arms sobbing, her story spilling out for the second time tonight.

And when the cabin door shuts them in, Bill looks at me as if to say, "You ready?"

When I don't speak, he nods his head as though deciding on something of significance. "Come on," he says, heading down the gravel driveway. I look at him, and I realize I must look lost. He motions me with his hand. "Come on, kid. You and I need to figure some things out before we head out of camp tonight. And I need a drink."

I follow Bill reluctantly. What I really want to do is get on my bike and fly away from the horror of Alice's story. Find Wren alive and live happily and healthily ever after. But my heavy legs won't let me. They seem to know something I do not. *How is this not my fault?* I think. *I should have demanded I go with her.*

At Bill's, he pours a stiff drink, considers the glass, hands it to me, and gets another from his dusty cupboard. He doesn't bother to wipe or even blow it clean but pours the strong, clear liquid almost to the top.

I stare at the glass before tipping back its contents in one swift swallow. It burns like hell all the way down, the fire settling in the pit of my stomach. I cough. Bill reaches for my glass to refill it, but I hold up my hand.

"No, really. I'm awake now," I tell him, still wincing from the sting of the alcohol.

He takes a generous gulp of his own drink. "Good," he says, "because we're going to need to have all our wits about us if we're going to save Wren and her mom." I notice how he doesn't say her name and wonder if it's deliberate, if he can't bring himself to say it.

"So what's your plan?" I ask him. "Because I'm already packed."

Bill laughs. "As it turns out, so am I."

"Well, then. I guess it's settled. We leave. Right now." I make the move to stand.

Bill holds up a hand to stop me, and I see the tremors in his fingers. "Now, hold on just a second, Ryder." He takes another hearty sip. "We're going to want to travel by night. And we have a duty to prepare the camp for our absence." He inhales heavily. "Plus," he says, "There are a few things we need to settle here. Between you and me."

"Such as?" I ask, but I have a feeling I know where this is going.

Bill sighs. "I'm not an idiot," he starts. "There are two things I know for a fact: One, Claire left willingly. And two, she wouldn't have done that if she didn't have a darn good reason to." He finishes his drink, sets the empty glass on the table, and looks me square in the eyes. "The way I figure it, something more must have happened on that bridge the other day. Something you didn't tell the rest of us. Something to scare the shit out of Claire."

I nod but need some clarification, too. "You said Claire left willingly? How do you know that?"

"She left a note," Bill says, and something about this must seem funny to him because he laughs. "She left me a goddamn note," he repeats, shaking his head.

"What did it say?" I press.

"She told me not to let Wren follow her," Bill says, his laughter subsiding and his features growing serious. "So, what did I do? I got drunk and let Wren go."

"Bill," I say, "this is *not* your fault. Nothing was going to stand in Wren's way. Believe me when I say I tried."

Bill nods, reaches for the bottle on the floor, but then changes his mind. "So what are you not telling me?" he asks.

There's no need to sugar coat anything at this point, so I just come out with it. "Two men had Don bound and gagged in the trunk of the supply van. They asked about Claire. They *knew* her name," I tell Bill, who surprises me by nodding. *Why the hell does this information not seem to bother anyone but me?* I wonder but continue the story, "Wren was just trying to help but—" I immediately hear myself defending her and stop and start again. "These strangers on the bridge, Bill, they—they saw Wren."

Bill's eyes go wide at this, his face suddenly very pale. After a moment, I see sweat beading on his forehead. He stands but has to steady himself. He pours another large drink and gulps it down.

"Bill?"

"You—you say they saw her?" he asks, looking at me intently with his red-rimmed eyes.

"Yeah, but—"

"Did they say anything?"

"Yeah, sure—"

"Tell me exactly what they said, Ryder."

Panic mixes with frustration. "I don't know, Bill! I don't remember! It's not like I was taking notes! They *looked* at her. They—they—" And then it's like I'm back on the bridge, watching Wren, so damn reckless, so damn beautiful, pointing the gun she doesn't know how to fire at these two men like she's so damn brave. "They said their boss was gonna be happy or something like that."

Bill nods as if this makes all the sense in the world. He seems to consider something for a moment, then nods again.

"No wonder she left," he says to himself.

"Who, Claire? Bill, what the hell does it all mean?"

He considers me a moment, nods again. "It means, Ryder, it's time to get moving." Bill walks over and holds out a hand. "Come on. Let's go inform the camp and then let's go get our girls."

•　　•　　•　　•　　•

The following morning, after informing the members of our camp, who were a little too enthusiastic that they join us but even more frightened to actually *do* anything, Bill and I wait until dark to make our departure.

As there are only two bikes in the camp—and Wren took one of them—Bill is forced to ride with me tandem style. And it's not the intimacy I need tonight. It's awkward, unbalanced, and uncomfortable. But it's the only option we have. There is no way I am letting Bill drive; even with my helmet, I can smell the booze on his breath.

98

It takes less than twenty minutes to reach the bridge, but it feels like an eternity. The uncertainty of what Bill and I will find weighs heavily on my shoulders. *If we find anything at all,* I remind myself.

I pull the bike off the highway onto the shoulder, and as I lean the bike abruptly to one side, Bill all but falls off, muttering, "Oof," when he lands.

I immediately pull the loaded gun from my sack and slip it into the back of my belted cargo pants and am already searching the surroundings for evidence of Wren when I hear Bill mutter behind me, "I'm getting old." Personally, I don't have time for it. If Bill slows me down, he gets left behind. Period. I hesitantly offer Bill the second gun I packed for him earlier, not meeting his eyes as I do. He hesitantly takes it.

For just a moment, I feel an inkling of guilt tugging at my heart. He doesn't know it's not loaded. I figure I'll wait until he's sober enough to hold it steady to fill him in.

After the awkward exchange of the weapon, I continue with my search, and it doesn't take me long to find the second bike. Wren has covered it in a thick blanket of branches and leaves; however, it's not hard to spot an out-of-place motorcycle. Seeing it abandoned, however, brings such a powerful wave of grief I almost double over, my hands on the bike's cold seat. After a moment, I swallow it down the best I can and start my descent to the river's edge, Bill right behind me now.

"I followed her to the river, Ryder. I followed her to the river, and then I pushed her in."

The shock of Alice's admittance clearly hasn't worn off because, even now, as I search for signs of a struggle, I wonder how on earth she could have done it. Did she confront Wren? Was there an argument? Did Wren have the chance to fight back? Was Wren even aware it was her childhood friend who pushed her in?

I reach the edge of the vast river and drop to my knees. What must Wren have been thinking as she went tumbling into the cold water? Had she been terrified? Angry? In pain? I want to scream her name loudly to the heavens. I want to hear her voice in response. I want to turn back the hands of time and hold her in my arms. *I wouldn't let her go this time,* I think. *I wouldn't let her leave.*

Bill's hand finds my shoulder.

"Hey, kid. You all right?" he asks, and I nod, quickly wiping away my tears of anger. "Good, 'cause I think you should come take a look at this," he says seriously, and I jump to my feet. My eyes meet Bill's for a moment, and it seems he recognizes the unspoken question I want to ask him but can't: *Do I want to see?*

Bill nods and heads toward the base of the looming bridge and points out to the center of the river.

"See those there?"

I squint. "The rocks?"

Bill nods. "My guess? Wren was down here scouting out a way to get across this river. What better way than those rocks? See? They stretch all the way across, and they're close enough to the base of the bridge that Wren would have been better protected from view." Bill kneels down, grunting as he does, and starts to search the ground around the water's edge. I do the same.

After a few minutes of sifting through sticks, mud, and various debris, with no success, I take a seat, suddenly feeling very foolish. I'm not even sure what we're looking for.

Bill, taking notice, shuffles over and plops down beside me, saying nothing.

"This is a waste of time," I say, looking out into the churning waters of the river. "We already know Wren went *into* the water, Bill." I pause, shaking my head. "We should head downstream to see if she *came out.*"

"Where she came out," Bill corrects me.

I shake my head again. Denial isn't going to save me now. "Bill, I think we should face the fact that Wren—"

But Bill cuts me off. "I can't accept that, Ryder. I just can't." He gets to his feet again and starts off down the river's edge. I stay right where I am but turn back to the river as though the waters can give me the answer I so desperately need. An emotion, foreign and strong, begins to stir deep within me, heating up my very core. And it binds me to my place by the water's edge because I know what it is. Murderous rage. I clench my fists, my jaw taut. My breathing becomes heavy and more rapid. The shock of Alice's crime is no longer alive within me. I realize, with certainty, I want to kill her. If Wren's gone? I *will* kill her.

I don't know how long I sit there simmering before Bill begins to yell from somewhere far down the river. "Ryder!" His muffled voice cuts through my rage like a hot knife. "Ryder!" he screams again. "Get your ass over here! It's Wren," and I swear I hear him laugh. "It's Wren!"

I jump to my feet, powered by a sudden, immense hope, and sprint the half-mile between Bill and me in an instant.

Except it's not Wren that Bill has found. It's her near-empty pack of supplies. I pick it up and hold it, turning it over and over in my hands as though the truth of the situation will spill out at my feet. The look of disappointment on my face when I meet Bill's eyes forces him to speak.

"Don't look at me that way," he says. "Look." He's pointing now to the smooth narrow path that I hadn't noticed before. It leads from the river straight to where Wren's bag was found. "Someone was dragged from the water, Ryder."

He's right. The depression of the ground, the narrow snaking trenches, the width of the path—they all indicate *something* the size of a human body was, without a doubt, dragged from the depths of the river, but I don't ask the questions I know we both are considering. *Was it Wren? And if so, was she alive?*

"And look here," Bill says, kneeling in the damp earth. "These look like footprints."

Again, Bill is right.

"Why would someone pull her out if she wasn't alive, Ryder?"

I can't answer him. In a normal world, there would be no other explanation. But in ours? There are hungry, desperate degenerates. Savages who, after surviving the Virus, would do anything to survive anything else. And in order to survive, one must eat.

A chill runs through my spine. Overhead a bird launches into the air, rustling the branches, and my senses are sent into overdrive. To my right, a small rodent scurries up a tree. Suddenly, everything seems much, much too *clear,* and I'm feeling extremely exposed, standing here even in the thick of the forest. The dawn is slowing breaking, and the reflection on the water casts a soft golden veil over the river's surface.

Without saying another word, I begin to follow the faint imprints of soles that lead away from the river. Bill catches up, and we continue on together for another half mile, not speaking, the woods growing less and less dense until we come across a paved road. There are deep tire tracks on the far side a little farther up. It looks as though the vehicle must have recently spun out.

Had Wren been inside that vehicle? I wonder.

Bill is panting next to me, his hands on his knees, as I debate our next move. His shirt is drenched in sweat, and his eyes are bloodshot. Clearly, the booze has worn off.

"I think we should follow this road," I say to him.

He looks up at me with a pained expression. "Maybe we could find some sort of wheels?" he suggests.

I almost laugh, but hold back. "Bill, even if we do manage to find a car with gasoline, it's been over a decade since the outbreak. The gasoline won't be any good."

"We could go back to the bike," he says, but even I can hear the doubt in his voice.

"And what? Drag it all the way down here?" I ask. After a moment I continue, "Look, the bike is loud. Too loud. We have no idea what type of person drove this vehicle. Do you really want to get caught when we're just setting out? If Wren's alive—"

"She is," Bill says quickly.

"Ok. So she's alive. And in the hands of God knows what type of person." I look down the road. "If I'm a betting man, I'd say the car—or truck—drove that way," I say pointing back in the direction of the bridge where a trail of dried mud disappears down the length of the road. "I really think our best bet is to follow it by foot and see what we find."

"I was afraid you were going to say that."

I shrug. "Go back, if you want." I really don't need Bill slowing me down, but the idea of going on alone makes me nervous as hell. I don't admit this to Bill, though.

"Hell no," Bill replies firmly. "What kind of man would that make me?"

I'm serious as a heart attack when I answer. "A rational one," I tell him and wonder, just briefly, if maybe, just maybe, we should just head back to camp. Except there's one not-so-small problem with that.

Wren's out there, alive or not, and I don't plan to rest until I find out what's happened to her.

9: ABEL

It's been twenty-four hours since my capture. I keep track of time by the light that filters through the minute gaps in the boarded-up doors, casting shadows that I use like a sundial to count the hours.

Mac is no longer with us. He was taken up late last night, a whimpering, heaping mess of a boy "dragged to the lab" according to Jeb. I wonder if Dr. Grayson was here to escort him across the river, or if Dr. Grayson can only be bothered when the hostages are of his inner circle.

Even in the face of the inevitability that I, too, will eventually be taken back to The Community, I feel my optimism gradually blossoming as my strength grows with each of the meals we are, in fact, fed sans silverware.

If I'm being honest, I'm shocked that I'm allowed to eat at all and wonder if this is an oversight on Dr. Grayson's part. Then again, it would be uncharacteristic of Dr. Grayson to overlook *any* detail. No matter how small. Perhaps he's just *that* sure I'm not going anywhere.

Following our after-meal slumbers, Jeb and I attempt to pass the time with redundant rounds of twenty questions.

Me: How did you survive the outbreak? And after? How did you survive after? What's it like living on the outside? Are there any more signs of the Virus? What happened to your family?

Jeb: How'd you get selected for the Great Divide? What's it like inside? Why'd you want to leave? Are the chicks hot?

It's all small talk, really. Half-hearted conversations to get through the slow torment of time passing by at a snail's pace.

That is until Jeb mentions his encounter with Dr. Grayson. He doesn't actually say his name, but because I am acutely aware of his direct involvement with this particular raider, it is clearer than crystal from Jeb's initial description that's who he means. I stop Jeb mid-sentence and make him start again, my interests more than piqued. I sit up straighter.

"So like I was saying," Jeb begins again, a note of irritation to his voice from being cut off, "I met the guy in charge not long after I got here."

"Wait a minute, Jeb. You actually *met* him?" I ask.

"Ok, so I didn't, like, shake his hand or anything." I hear Jeb's chains jingle and watch him relax against the far wall, ready to tell his story. "As it happened, I was on the shitter when he showed up, and our friendly raider dropped everything, I mean everything, for this guy—even his guard," Jeb pauses dramatically for what feels like five minutes. My jaw clenches. *Why am I just now hearing this?*

"So this guy shows up," Jeb continues, "and I hear the raider all but run to let him in, leaving me alone to do my business. Needless to say, as I was no longer a priority, of course, I eased my pants back on and tried to high-tail it outta there." Jeb pauses. Again. It's not one of his more endearing qualities. He's so damn dramatic.

Still, I play into Jeb's drama asking, "So what happened?"

"Well, sorry to spoil the ending for you, but I didn't make it," he jests, shaking his chains. I, however, am far from amused.

"Clearly," I say dryly because there's no point in trying to rush him.

"Right. So here I am, shuffling down the hallway like an idiot in my shackles, trying not to make too much noise, when I realize that unless I find a master key or plan to hack my limbs off, I'm not *really* going anywhere." At this point in his story, a trace of dejection creeps into his voice, and my frustration wanes slightly. I can almost feel the wind in his sail of hope die.

"Jeb, I'm sorry, man. That sucks," I say, and I mean it, my recent experience with the taste of freedom still as fresh as the debilitating hopelessness that comes after losing it.

"It wasn't all for nothing, though," Jeb says after a heavy moment of silence, the dream-like, light-hearted quality to his voice returning.

"How so?" I ask, genuinely surprised that his story has a potentially satisfying ending. I mean, he's still shackled to a wall, after all.

Jeb tilts his head to the ceiling, clearly envisioning something that's not there. "'Cause, man, when I returned to the bathroom, the raider and his boss were arguing so loud I could hear every word they said."

The hairs on my arms stand tall, and, sensing something of significant importance is about to be revealed, I am on the edge of my chains—literally. I'm not entirely sure what I expect him to say, but Jeb doesn't know Dr. Grayson. I do. And if Dr. Scott Grayson is angry about something, it involves The Community. And if it involves The Community, that means it involves me. Cat, too.

"What were they arguing about?" I pry. I am no longer able to hide the anxiety Jeb's dramatic pauses have caused, and I can sense that Jeb realizes this, but still he torments me with his lazy retelling of the story. It's almost as though he is savoring the final taste of his last meal on earth.

"A girl," he says simply.

My stomach does a somersault. "A girl?" I manage to ask. I can barely get the words out because there's only one girl I know who can cause Dr. Grayson such angst.

"Man. A beautiful girl," Jeb responds, bending his knees to rest his elbows on top. He looks right at me, and even though the room is dim, I see him smile wistfully. "The raider, he showed me her picture after his boss had gone. He said—and I promise you, man, it's the honest truth—he said, "Maybe if you're lucky, I'll catch this one and send her down with you awhile.'"

"Wait, Jeb, back up," I tell him. "What was the argument about?"

But it is clear Jeb couldn't care less about the content of the argument. He's hyper-focused on the image of Cat dancing through his head. My stomach churns.

"Man, I don't know," Jeb says. "I guess it wasn't *actually* an argument. A loud discussion, really. Something about a missing girl worth a lot—and I mean a lot of loot." Jeb is back to staring longingly at the ceiling of the basement. "Man, you know what else the raider told me he'd do if he caught her? He said he might even let me go. Said this girl might just be his ticket to the inside, you know? Beyond the wall and shit. Like I'd want to go in there!"

My head is swimming with questions. There's a fear rising in my gut that has me frozen in place. If Dr. Grayson is, in fact, looking for a missing girl, and that girl is, as I suspect, Cat, then that means she, for whatever reason, had a change of heart and left The Community. And if she left, then that must mean that she's out here looking for me.

It also means she's in very real danger.

What could have changed her mind? I wonder. And then, before I get too caught up in the assumption that the girl in the photo is, in fact, Cat, I ask Jeb, "What did she look like? The girl in the photo, Jeb. Can you describe her for me?" And when I don't immediately get a response, beg, "Jeb, *please.*"

"Easy, man. Easy. You want to see for yourself? I bet you anything that sicko has the picture tacked up someplace he can wack off to it. Heck, he'll probably show it to you if you ask!"

My nauseousness escalates. "Jeb, please. Tell me what she looks like."

"Man, ok, ok!" I can tell by Jeb's tone he thinks I'm just some lonely guy desperate for a fix. "Fair skin. Freckled. Lips you could bite, ya know? And thick, *clean* blond hair. The kind you want to bury yourself in," he replies dreamily, inhaling loudly as though he can smell it through his imagination. He lets out his breath slowly, continuing, "She has the most beautiful blue eyes, too. Deep blue. Like the deepest part of the ocean."

And I know it. I know it with every fiber of my being. Cat is the girl in the photo. Which means she's somewhere out here in Raiderville. And Dr. Grayson knows it.

My breathing is rapid, my pulse quickening. "Jeb, did this boss—the guy in charge—did he say anything specific about this girl? Did he mention why he's looking for her?"

"Man, I tell you. You ask the funniest questions. Who cares *why* he's looking for her? I just hope he finds her! Didn't you hear me? She could be our way out!"

"Jeb, I'm serious. Can you remember anything this guy might have said? Anything at all?"

"All I know is this, man. He's desperate to find her," and he pauses one final time as he stretches out on the concrete floor. This is Jeb's not-so-subtle way of telling me he's done with story time. But before he drifts off into one of his lengthy silences that usually indicates naptime, he rises to his elbow as though startled.

"Hey, wait!" he exclaims, a note of pride to his voice. "I do remember something now that I think about it!"

"What?" I ask, not able to hide my impatience. "What did he say?"

But Jeb doesn't get the chance to tell me because the door to the basement suddenly opens and the raider thunders down the stairs.

Jeb doesn't even put up a fight.

"Guess you didn't find the girl, huh?" he says disappointingly. His comment gets him a hard punch to the gut.

I watch helplessly as Jeb, head down, lumbers up the stairs, his shackles clinking like discordant windchimes, with the raider in tow. Before the two of them disappear from view, Jeb turns around once more to say, "Hey, Abel. I sure hope he finds her for your sake." And then the door to the basement closes, leaving me in silence so palpable, I can hear the beating of my own heart.

I sure as hell hope he doesn't, I think.

•　　•　　•　　•　　•

When I wake early the next morning, it's to the pounding of the raider's feet tramping down the basement steps. It's too dark outside for me to clearly see, but the raider's labored breathing indicates he's carrying something heavy--his latest hostage. Instead of using Jeb's recently vacated spot, however, the raider carries his new victim around to the far side of the bar as though he doesn't want me to see what he's doing. *Or who he's brought down,* I think.

At first, this frustrates me. There was something honest about Jeb's and my conversations because we could see each other's eyes. But the sudden nearness of this new person gradually dissolves the consummate loneliness that seems to emanate from every nook and cranny of the basement, replacing it with an unfamiliar and welcomed warmth. Misery loves company after all.

Hours pass before there's any indication of life from the opposite side of the wall, but I'm not surprised, recalling how the raider used his large skull to knock me unconscious days before. It starts with a moan and then the familiar jingle of chains. I stay silent at first, unsure how to start the you're-probably-going-to-die-but-at-least-the-food's-great conversation. After a few minutes, though, the clanging of metal becomes more frantic, and I decide it's time to make my presence known.

"It's no use," I say as quietly and calmly as I can, not wanting to elicit fear, but I hear the sudden and violent yank of metal anyway and know that I failed.

"Don't struggle," I urge, but then realize that maybe this isn't the right thing to say. "It's no use," I continue, recognizing the need to reassure this hostage that I, too, am a prisoner. "You're in a basement. It'll do no good to scream."

Still, there is no response, but the frantic movement of metal has stopped, so I keep talking. "Listen, I know you're frightened," I say, "but it will do you no good to fight right now. You've been drugged. He calls himself a raider. The effects will wear off soon, but for now, you should try to conserve as much energy as you can."

The person on the other side remains silent for a few moments more before the crying starts. Something about the sound of it breaks my heart. The quick intake of sobs, the shallow breathing, it feels familiar somehow and fills me with such immense sadness I can't help myself. "Please," I implore, "please, don't cry," and without thinking it through, I reach around the wall and come in contact with the stranger, who jerks away on impulse. "I-I'm sorry," I say quickly. "I didn't mean to—."

But the figure on the opposite side of the divide continues to cry until he or she falls into a fitful sleep that keeps me awake despite how tired I am.

•　　•　　•　　•　　•

When I finally drift off to sleep, I dream I am back at the top of the cemetery, with the river to my south and Cat lying next to me. She's talking quietly, staring up at the ceiling of The Community except it looks different. Like it's not the man-made sky of our world but the *real* sky with real constellations and real shooting stars.

She gasps as one streaks across its ebony backdrop. Her genuine surprise makes me smile.

"Make a wish," I say to her dreamily and then give her a moment to do so. I love watching her, her eyes closed, a solemn look on her face. The corner of her mouth twitches, and I resist the urge to kiss it. "Well?" I ask her.

"Well what?"

"What did you wish for?"

"What I always wish for," she whispers. I don't ask her to elaborate because I know what she wishes for with every breath that she takes. She wishes for her mother. She yearns for her mother to still be alive and well as much as I wish this dream, this imagined moment, were real, and I could reach out my hand to touch her. "What about you, Abel?"

"I wish you would come with me," I tell her without pause. She considers this a moment and nods, lips pursed. This isn't news to Cat; she's heard it before. This time, however, she doesn't immediately turn me down.

"What if I did leave with you?" she asks instead, still gazing out into the night. "Do you think we'd make it? To the end of it all?"

"What do you mean by *the end of it* all? I answer her question with a question.

"You know," she whispers romantically, "to the end of all life's pain and suffering."

I find myself shaking my head, though she's not looking at me but at the twinkling stars overhead. "Cat, life's not supposed to work like that," I tell her matter-a-factly.

"What if it did?"

I don't answer her right away. I feel certain that I'm so close to getting what I want like it's just out of reach of my grasp as long as I just say the right thing, but something about what she says makes me falter.

"Abel, what if it did?" she asks again, but right when I think I might have my answer, the cemetery landscape dissolves into darkness.

"Hello?"

I turn to look for the source of the voice, but Cat seems to have disappeared, too, swallowed by the suffocating darkness.

"Hello?" she whispers again, farther away now. My heart races with panic. I don't want to lose Cat, not again, but no matter what direction I turn, she's gone. "Hey, are you awake?" I turn over, my chains clink-clanking as I do. The voice and the sounds of my imprisonment are enough to make me realize that it's not Cat who speaks to me now. The voice belongs to the person chained to the opposite side of the bar. The bar I've been chained to. The bar in the basement of the raider who holds me prisoner. And this voice—it belongs to a girl. Because of this all-too-sudden transition from fiction to reality, it takes more than a moment to shake off my dream and recollect my thoughts. At first, I fear that it's Cat chained to the wall behind me, but she would have recognized my voice immediately—drugs or no drugs. I relax a little against the wall.

"You got your voice back," I say, still trying to maneuver through the haze that was my dream.

"I got my voice back," she says. "Sort of."

When the girl speaks this time, with a note of lightness to her tone, my heart does a somersault. Even though I know—*I know*—without a doubt that it's not Cat who speaks these words to me, something about her voice makes me think about her. Maybe it's the dream. Maybe it's the fact that my longing for Cat at this moment is so great, it's almost paralyzing. This is when it all materializes for me. All my life, I tried to protect Cat, but now, in my darkest hour, shackled to this girl, I feel this objective shift.

The word *fate* hovers just out of reach of my subconscious, and my sudden desire to *know* this girl like I know Cat grows immense. As though my life and maybe Cat's depends on it.

So we talk. About Jeb's theories and about my own. About the strangeness of this situation. Why she's trying to break into the wall. Why I fled. I learn her name is Wren and she's looking for her mother who is a prisoner now of The Community. Of Dr. Grayson's. The similarity of Cat's own plight with her mother and Dr. Grayson doesn't evade me. In fact, the more Wren and I speak, the more I feel like I *could* be talking to Cat. The hitch in her tone when she's upset, the soft sigh when she's considering something. It is all *so* Cat. They would be friends, I decide. Yes, if they could meet, Wren and Cat would really like one another. The thought makes me markedly sad.

Later that evening, when the raider storms down the stairs to take Wren up, the helplessness that has been building for the better part of my life reaches its limit and spills over. I reach for her hand, and she takes it, trembling. I tell her with as much certainty to my voice as I can summon, that everything will be ok, but I know it in my soul that it won't be. This raider will show her no mercy. When she speaks my name, I feel my heart split in two for the second time in four days.

"Abel, I can't," she cries. "Please."

But I can do nothing.

The raider takes her up the stairs and slams the door.

Seconds later, a gun goes off. I can only pray its target isn't Wren.

When the raider returns her hours later to her chains, at first, I'm relieved. She's alive. But she's not the same. She doesn't speak. She doesn't eat. And each moment that passes between us feels like an abyss growing so deep, soon there will be no way out.

I'll lose her, too, I think. I'll lose Wren just as I've lost Cat.

I reach for her hand, desperate to comfort her. She doesn't take it.

10: RYDER

We walk for about two miles before Bill needs a break. And by break I mean he hurries into the woods to violently wretch for a solid ten minutes behind a tree. The sound of the rushing river to our right fails to mask Bill's obvious distress. The alcohol has finally made its toxic way from his body.

While I wait, I fidget. I'm not at all happy about this detox detour, but it gives me some time to collect my thoughts. Bill and I haven't yet encountered anyone on our thirty-minute trek down the crumbling paved road; however, there have been a few signs of recent life: dying embers from an earlier fire, discarded remnants of food, a sad, forgotten child's doll, filthy and missing one eye.

Despite my mounting frustration, a voice from deep within my gut tells me we're heading in the right direction. Still, it would make me feel better to find someone—*any*one—with helpful information that could lead us to Wren's current whereabouts.

I look past the line of trees that separates me from the tumultuous river, where The Dome rises as though from the waters to tower over the rest of the world like a watchman at his post.

In my peripheral line of sight, Bill comes to a stand, unsteadily, his hand still pressed hard into the bark of the tree, his knuckles white. "Ready?" I call to him.

Bill stays in the bent-over, rigid stance for a minute more before he nods and turns to face me. I sigh. He looks like serious shit.

"Bill—" I start, but he cuts me off with a wave of a hand.

"Ryder, I'm good," he says, though his voice lacks conviction. He continues to walk past me down the road, and I quickly follow suit. After walking a few minutes, Bill panting like an over-run dog, I reach into my pack and hand him my canteen. He has, I know, finished off his water supply already, and I'm sure he's dying of thirst after his vomit fest. When he sees the peace offering, however, his face grows hard. "Look, Ryder. I get it. I'm sort of a mess right now."

"Sort of?" I say before I can stop myself.

Bill nods, closing his eyes briefly. "Sure," he says, "I deserve that." He gently pushes my canteen away. "Still, I'm not a charity case. I know I brought this on myself. I couldn't deal when Claire left. I just couldn't face the reality of the situation." He looks at me with a pained expression on his face. "But what choice do I have now, huh?"

"You could go back to camp," I remind him simply.

"And leave you to save the women? To get all the glory?" He shoves me lightly on the shoulder, but I don't smile. He starts to walk ahead of me again.

"This isn't about glory, Bill."

Bill stops and turns to face me again. "Of course I know it's not about glory, Ryder. It's about Claire and Wren. They're out there somewhere. Probably in serious danger. And, as much as I want this to just be about that, about saving them, I won't be able to live if Claire's not with me."

I don't respond. How can I? As selfish as it is to admit it, I need Wren, too, and I'm not sure that *I* can go on without her by my side.

Bill seems to understand my silence. He reaches for the canteen I offered moments ago. "Truce?" he asks.

I hand him over the water. "Truce," I tell him, and I mean it. Harboring my resentment for even this long has slowed me down. I watch Bill carefully take a sip and then hand the canteen back over. "I hope you didn't backwash," I say, only half joking.

"Protein," Bill jests, and I fake gag. It feels good to not be serious even though I know the moment is short lived. I take a sip of water, gulping it quickly down before I notice any residual food particles from Bill, and look to the tree line ahead of us.

"So, what do you think?" Bill asks as I absentmindedly screw the lid back on the canteen. "We still heading in the right direction?" But I almost don't hear him, my face still tilted toward the sky ahead of us, squinting. Without answering Bill, I continue slowly down the road, not taking my eyes off the thin black line rising like a piece of thread pulled to the heavens. "Is that what I think it is?" Bill asks, following my gaze and hurrying to catch up beside me.

"Smoke," I say simply.

Bill laughs. "Smoke!" he says a little too loudly, a note of optimism to his tone. "But that means—" I cut Bill off again.

"People." And my tone does not hold the same lightness to it as Bill's. I stop and let my eyes travel along the tree line to where the smoke appears to begin. "I reckon it's still a few miles ahead," I tell Bill, the sudden reality of the situation sending the hairs on my arms on end. Before, when there was only the *possibility* of other survivors, our situation hadn't exactly felt *real*. As though we could simply travel this road, find the girls safe, and return to camp. Now, though, this evidence of life mere miles ahead of us reminds me just how dire our situation is.

I reach for my gun, cock it. Bill does the same. The noise from Bill's empty gun brings me back to my senses. I sigh and kneel to the ground, setting my weapon carefully on the ground beside me. From my pack, I pull out our meager supply of ammunition. I take a handful of bullets and offer them to Bill. He looks confused for a moment before snorting and taking the ammunition from me.

"You never cease to amaze me, kid." And then as he begins loading his empty weapon, says, "I can't say I blame you. I'm not even sure I trust myself with this." I know from the tone of his voice he's serious.

"Bill, we have no idea what we're up against," I remind him, taking my gun from the ground and standing. "You don't have to use it. Just let me take the lead, ok?"

"Deal," he says simply. "Look, Ryder—" I stop him before he can get all sentimental on me.

"There will be time for that later," I say to Bill who nods. I look down the seemingly empty road and then back to Bill. "You ready?"

"As ready as I'll ever be," he says, and, our guns at the ready, we head in the direction of the smoke.

• • • • •

It takes us a few hours to reach the part of the road parallel to the line of smoke that has remained steady and strong as we travel. I am only slightly surprised to discover a narrow path leading from the road up the hill through the forest of towering trees that appears to lead straight to the origin of the smoke. I imagine whoever is manning the fire at its end would need easy access to the river. Still, it feels a tad too convenient.

Bill has already started up the path. "Hey," I hiss, "you want to discuss our plan first?"

To my surprise, Bill chuckles. "Plan, huh?" he says, but he doesn't turn around, nor does he stop. Instead, he holds his gun in the air and waves it carelessly. "Way I figure it, the element of surprise is plan enough."

I shake my head but realize that Bill is probably right. I duck through the trees to follow behind Bill, and we climb through the thick branches that scratch at my arms and face, my calves screaming in protest. The pain doesn't bother me, though. Whatever Wren is facing, I fear her suffering is much worse.

When we are near enough to smell the smoldering embers of the fire, I reach out to grab Bill's arm. We're close. In fact, just ahead of us, through the trees, I can see a rather large opening. And there in the middle of the clearing is a fire.

Bill takes another step and a twig snaps. He stumbles forward into a dozen or so metal cans that are strung up like wind chimes around the clearing. The noise is deafening in the silence.

"Shhh," I whisper, but it's too late.

"Who's there?" a voice cries out from somewhere in the clearing. Frantically, I look all around but see no one.

"Ryder?" Bill says so quietly I almost don't hear him.

Without thinking it through, I burst through the remaining trees, my hands raised in surrender. "We mean you no harm," I say loudly, spinning around and around the clearing looking for any trace of the voice.

Laughter. It seems to reverberate off the trees that now surround me on all sides. I don't know what to make of it. On the surface, the laughter seems friendly; however, I know better than to rely on my initial instincts in a world where nothing is certain.

"We mean you no harm," I repeat more sternly, and the laughter stops.

"Well, why *would* you want to harm an old man like me?" Into the clearing on my right steps a tall, bearded man, beady eyes twinkling in the sun. I stand a bit taller and look him over. His hair is matted but clean and cut; his over-large clothes hang off his form like a heavy, wet blanket. Still, there's something about this man that seems strong, confident. Misleading.

I feel Bill close to me on my left, his breathing heavy. I let my hands fall to my sides, my gun gripped tightly, a trembling finger still on the trigger. The old man looks to my weapon, and he smiles. The smile doesn't reach his eyes.

"You mean me no harm, eh?" he says chuckling. I see now that he's carrying a pile of kindling, and after considering me a moment, he walks confidently over to the center of the clearing and starts to place the small logs on the dying fire. There is a steaming pot of liquid hanging from a rusting metal hook that's staked into the ground, and I catch a whiff of something earthy cooking.

He takes a seat by the fire and starts to stir the pot. "You hungry?" he asks us without looking away from the steaming liquid.

Bill and I trade looks. Bill nods, and I turn back to the stranger.

"Yeah," I say. "Actually, we're starving." Still, we remain rooted to our spots, and after a few more awkward minutes, the old man chuckles again.

"Well, then, what are you waiting for?"

Bill and I walk hesitantly over to where the man has rolled up a couple of logs and sit down cautiously. Bill is uncomfortably close to me at first, and I am forced to scoot closer to the man, where I think I can faintly smell his body odor, a mix of earth and sweat. Not necessarily unpleasant.

The man works to rinse out a few of the tin bowls scattered haphazardly around his camp and then proceeds to fill them to the brim with the liquid from the pot. He hands them both to me, and I pass one to Bill. We both wait until the man has taken the first sip. He looks at us, the broth from the bowl dripping down his beard. He smiles again, wiping his mouth with the back of his hand, and I am shocked to see he has all his teeth.

"Sorry there are no spoons," he says to us, and I carefully lift the bowl to my mouth and take a sip. Immediately, the warmth spreads throughout my empty stomach, and I sigh, closing my eyes briefly to savor the moment. The broth tastes of the earth—mushrooms maybe—but it's far from disagreeable, and I help myself to a larger gulp.

We sit like this for a while, Bill, the old man, and I, until all the bowls have been drained and our hunger alleviated.

"So," the man says to break the silence, "what are you fellas doing in these parts of the woods?"

I look at Bill, who remains silent.

"We're looking for someone," I tell the man. And then I extend my hand. "My name's Ryder. And he's Bill," I say, tilting my head in Bill's direction.

The old man continues to smile. "Well, Ryder and Bill, I have to say I'm surprised to have visitors. Not too many people around these parts anymore. At least not the kind who come out willingly in the daylight," he says, his eyes still shining. "Name's Wes," he tells us, sizing us up. "I've been out here on my own since my wife passed not too long ago." He indicates a pile of stones set against one edge of the clearing that I assume mark her grave. "Lost the kids with the final wave of the Virus, but the wife and I managed to avoid it. Somehow." I expect to see his eyes turn sad, remembering, but still, they carry the same twinkling humor from earlier.

"What about you boys?" he continues. "You both look a little too refined to be refugees."

"We have a camp," Bill tells him before I can interject. "It's not too far down the highway, but it's pretty substantial. And we have a doctor—" Bill stops short. "Had a doctor, I mean."

"Oh, yeah?" Wes says, surprised. I try to make eye contact with Bill, to tell him with a look that he's probably said too much, but Bill is caught up in the moment.

"That's who we're looking for actually," Bill says softly. "She and her daughter…" His voice trails off.

"*She*, eh?" Wes looks a little too intrigued by this information than I would like. "Well, I dare say I won't be of much help to you, but you're both welcome to stick around a while till you get your bearings about you."

"Well, we appreciate that, Wes," I say as earnestly as I can muster. "And thanks for the soup."

Wes nods. "Like I said before, it's been a while since I've had any sort of mutual company." He gives me another toothy grin that unnerves me. Something about the way he says this makes me think he's stretching the truth a bit.

"You mean to tell us that there aren't any other survivors around?" Bill asks, incredulous.

"Now, I didn't say that," Wes responds, and again there's something in his tone that returns the hair on my arms to standing.

"What did you say, then?" I ask him.

"Your camp," Wes says, ignoring my question, "I'm guessing you've been left alone then?"

"We're pretty protected," I tell him. "There are quite a few of us, and we're armed." I wave my gun for emphasis. "So raiders tend to leave us be." There's no need to share with Wes exactly how many members we have in camp.

"So, you're familiar with the raiders then, eh?" Wes asks.

"Of course we are," Bill responds. "We're not idiots." I shoot Bill another sharp look. He turns his hands over and shrugs as though to ask, *What?*

Wes laughs, slapping his knee. "Of course not! Never said you were. Forgive me," he says. "Like I said, I'm not used to having casual conversation with strangers these days."

Bill squints his eyes, looking at Wes suspiciously. "Why do the raiders leave *you* alone?" he asks.

Wes shrugs. "I guess they don't consider me to be much of a threat," he says, but I think there's more to this reason than he lets on. He stands, and again, I sense his unusual strength. His movements are fluid and deliberate. I get to my feet, too, and this makes Wes chuckle some more. "Jumpy, aren't ya, Cowboy?" he comments, and I lock eyes with Bill who also stands.

"Do you think you could point us in the direction of these raiders?" I ask.

Wes walks about the clearing, hanging up garments on branches. Through the trees beyond and amidst the hanging metal cans that must serve as some sort of alarm system, I think I recognize some sort of makeshift shelter. "Well, boys, I think I can do you better than that."

Another look passes between Bill and me. Bill arches his eyebrows.

"And by that, you mean?" I ask Wes.

"Stick around, boys," he says seriously, looking back over his shoulder and sneering. "You want raiders? You'll get 'em." At this, he chuckles one final time, then disappears into the forest.

•　•　•　•　•

Bill and I decide to stick close to Wes' camp after he's gone. It's too close to lights out, and as strange as he seems, we need answers to Wren's possible whereabouts. Wes could be our ticket. To pass the time while we wait for Wes' return, Bill and I devise an open-ended shell of a plan. If looney-tune Wes turns out to be a dead end, we'll stay until daybreak and continue down the road in search of other, less bizarre, signs of life.

"He's off his flippin' rocker," Bill says as the sun starts to dip below the tree lines. It's clear my traveling partner hasn't been able to shake the nagging feeling that Wes doesn't exactly have our best interests in mind. A cool breeze has started, and I find myself inching closer and closer to the fire that Bill and I have managed to keep going in Wes' absence. The chill in the air is like a ticking clock, reminding me of just how little time we have left until the autumn nights turn brutal. The sudden, intense longing for the warmth of camp and for Wren takes me by surprise, and I fight back tears.

"You ok?" Bill asks softly from across the fire. I nod, not wanting to speak. All around me, it feels as though every tree, every woodland creature is watching us, listening.

When I hear the crunch of branches underfoot and the rattling of the cans, I startle, coming to a quick stand, my gun pointed at the shadows to my right.

"Easy, Cowboy," Wes says, emerging from the darkness. "It's only me." From the open sack in his arms, I see an array of goods: a variety of plants, sticks, and what looks like fish.

"You've been busy," I say, still pointing the gun in Wes' direction.

Wes nods at the fire. "So have you." He doesn't offer thanks. "You boys still hungry?" he asks instead. Of course we are, but neither Bill nor I answer him. "'Cause I've just been fishing," he says, flashing the strange smile I've come to expect from this bearded stranger.

Wes sets down the kindling and starts to arrange a crude grill over the fire. When he's satisfied with it, he pulls out a knife, and I immediately bristle. This is the first indication that Wes is armed, and this, along with the ambiguousness of his answers from earlier, sets me further on edge. I watch as, with care and skill, Wes begins to skin the fish and place it among his gathered herbs on the fire. He begins to whistle. The eerie sound is carried off into the forest with the wind.

In just minutes, the fish is thoroughly cooked, and we eat with our fingers in silence, the darkness around us thick as a blanket. Surprisingly, the fish is good—better than good, actually—and I have to admire Wes and his ability to have survived so long on his own. More than once, I find myself staring at him, attempting to figure him out, but Wes just eats and watches the fire.

After the plates have been scraped clean and collected, I expect the three of us to continue our conversations around the fire, but Wes has something else in mind. He walks to the edge of the clearing, grabs a bucket I hadn't noticed before now, and abruptly throws a pile of what looks like dirt onto the already dying fire. It happens so quickly, I cry out.

"What did you do that for?" I ask, already feeling the chill of the night returning.

Wes chuckles. My jaw clenches; I am beginning to find his laughter quite irritating.

"Seriously!" I respond a little more vehemently than I intended.

This makes him laugh harder. "Oh, *seriously*, eh?" he mocks. "Well, in that case—" But he doesn't finish the statement, still chuckling at the joke only he seems to understand. "Seriously, he says, eh?" Wes continues to mumble as he walks along the outskirts of the clearing, adjusting the hanging cans that surround his camp. After a few minutes, without so much as a nod of the head as good night, he heads into his small tent and pulls the flaps shut.

"Well," Bill says, "I guess that's that."

I look at him, my eyes wide. "What a freak," I whisper.

"You're telling me," Bill says, rolling his log away from what used to be the fire and stretching out on the dirt. He pulls his jacket off to use as a pillow. "Listen, you want to take first watch, or you want me to? Because I sure could use a few winks." Bill yawns and closes his eyes, not waiting for me to answer. In minutes, he is snoring. I snort, flabbergasted.

Personally, I no longer think traveling at night is such a terrible option if it gets us the hell away from Wes and his camp. But I realize that unless I choose to leave Bill behind in sleep, I'm stuck standing guard for now. Plus, there's something in my gut telling me Wes can, in fact, get us closer to Wren.

Late into the evening while Bill sleeps soundly to my left, I take in the surroundings of our small camp that seem to grow smaller still with each minute the evening closes on us. I can no longer see beyond the tree line, the glow of the moon unable to penetrate the thick forest, and sitting in the middle of the open clearing, I feel like an animal on display at the zoo. Except I can't see who's watching. It makes me nervous in a suffocating, claustrophobic kind of way. And even though exhaustion seeps from every pore in my rigid body, my legs sore and cramping, I get to my feet to pace the outer circle of the clearing. There's no way I'm sleeping through the night, I realize. Not after what Wes said earlier about raiders. I've never liked the dark much, but the uncertainty of what lurks beyond the clearing now multiplies my terror.

I'm not sure how long I walk the circle of the clearing before the noises start. They are off in the distance at first, and I can't decide where they're coming from. Then quickly I realize the sounds are everywhere. Feet crashing through underbrush? Whispered conversations? Faraway screams of agony? I think I can even hear what sounds like distant dogs barking. I hold my gun tightly and consider waking Bill but am frozen to my place on the outer ring of the clearing, turning first one way and then another, waiting for the ambush I feel for certain will come.

The noises become increasingly louder. And louder. Until they sound as though they are right on top of me.

When Wes' handmade alarms go off somewhere to my right, I don't hesitate. On impulse, I turn, squeeze my trembling finger on the gun's trigger, and fire my weapon out into the trees. There's a loud grunt, and then the woods explode with chaos, the sound of scattering, frantic feet spreading in all directions. Bill bolts upright to see me still standing with my gun in my shaking hand, pointing out into the darkness.

"Ryder, what the hell?" he cries.

"Shhh!" I hiss. "There's someone out there." But the woods have become silent again.

"What do you mean someone's out there? How do you know? What did you hear?"

I ignore Bill's rapid-fire questions and instead march over to where Wes's tent stands eerily still. With the gun still in my hand, I push open the flap of the crude shelter and squint through the darkness, but the tent is empty save for a pile of clothes in the corner.

"What the—" I whisper.

"What is it? Is he gone?"

I back out into the clearing, my eyes still on Wes' tent as though I expect him to materialize out of the discarded pile of fabric lying on the ground.

"Ryder?" Bill asks, and his voice is frantic. "What the hell were you shooting at?"

"I don't know!" I yell, and then a little more quietly, "I don't know."

I can barely see Bill in the darkness, but by the whites of his eyes, I know he's terrified. "Ryder, let's get out of here," he whispers, but his voice is uncertain.

"And go where?" I ask. "We have no idea where we are, where Wes is." I walk back out into the clearing to pick up Bill's jacket. I toss it to him. "Here, put this back on." The jacket hits him square in the chest, and he has to bend to pick it up.

"What do you want to do?" Bill asks me.

I consider all our options. None are great. Ultimately, though, what the situation boils down to is the fact that Bill and I have no idea where we are or where we are going. As far as staying safe is concerned, being surrounded by hanging metal cans might be the best choice.

"We stay here until morning," I say to Bill. "Then we get as far away from here as quickly as possible."

For the rest of the evening and early morning, Bill and I sit back to back, our guns sitting atop our bended knees, ready to fire.

Wes doesn't return, and part of me, remembering the loud grunt from the woods earlier, wonders if he hadn't played a part in the madness of the night.

"You want raiders? You'll get 'em."

Wes' voice echoes in my mind. Had he been right? Had we just encountered raiders and not known it? What had they wanted? Where had they gone? Where was Wes?

As dawn shed's it's hazy glow on the clearing, I nudge Bill who has once again fallen prey to his exhaustion.

"Come on," I say, getting to my feet. "Time to get moving."

Bill obliges but says nothing.

Before we leave the camp of nightmares, however, my intuition and curiosity propels me over to the stones Wes indicated earlier mark the graves of his family. When I'm close enough to touch my foot to the pile, I gasp. Because the stones aren't actually stones at all.

They're human skulls.

PART III

11: CAT

A few years after the initial outbreak, when I was three, my mother took me to a nearby amusement park.

By this time, developing countries had already been ravaged by the seemingly incurable and quickly spreading disease that antibiotics clearly stood no chance against. Millions were already dead or suffering with symptoms too grim to describe on the evening news. The states, however, were just beginning to feel the effects of the Virus.

Many people, typical doomsday preppers prepared to survive any and all end-of-civilization circumstances began sequestering themselves in underground bunkers and hoarding cans and cans of food. Large grocery chains even started mass-producing and selling so-called survival kits containing foods like freeze-dried broccoli, green beans, corn, dehydrated apples, and other grains and proteins believed to have a shelf life of up to thirty years.

Other not-so-prepared people began protesting. Riots broke out in major cities. Fires were set. Buildings bombed. People murdered.

Being three years old at the time, I was mostly sheltered from the horrors of the world. My mother worked hard to make sure of that. Which is why, so many years ago, we ended up at the amusement park.

My mother had not been like the doomsday preppers or the naysayers—not even close. She was instead among the very few optimists left in our dying, cynical world, and I believe it was this fact that made my childhood one that I remember as fondly as I do.

When we arrived at the amusement park, the parking lot was empty, save for a handful of vehicles. There were no lines for rides. There were actually very few employees there to run the place, but my mother's beauty and kind-hearted nature was magnetic, and within minutes of walking through the park she easily convinced one worker to join us on our adventure. So for one very magical day, my mother and I had, again and again and again, ridden our favorite rides: the spinning teacups, the carousel, the roller coaster I wasn't exactly tall enough to ride. Who cared about park regulations when the Virus would kill us all eventually?

Everything was going great, a picture-perfect day in a not-so-picture-perfect world. Until the power in the park went out, temporarily leaving my mother and me stranded on a roller coaster high above the ground. I vividly remember my terror, how I sobbed and screamed to be let down, clinging onto my mother's shoulder. For hours we remained trapped at the top of that coaster, my mother's arms wrapped around me while I cried.

When the ride finally got going again, and we were docked safely on solid ground, I set out running, trying to get as far away from the ride as I could, yanking at my mother's hand.

But my mother wouldn't let me run. Instead, she knelt beside me and took my wet cheeks gently in her hands and said, "Darling, Cat. It's ok. It's ok to be afraid. But we cannot run from our fears, sweetheart. We must face them. Do you understand?"

I remember shaking my head earnestly in protest, but my mother's hands on my face remained firm.

"We need to get back up on that coaster, Cat. Come on. Trust me."

Frightened and trembling though I was, I obliged, and together the two of us got back onto the ride. The first time around, I clung to my mother, afraid to open my eyes. But by the third time, my terror from earlier was forgotten, and I reached my tiny arms into the air, squealing with delight.

My mother, like many times before, had been right.

Running from your fears never solves anything. It hadn't when I was three, and it certainly wasn't going to now.

Just days ago, Abel suggested that Dr. Grayson was using my fear of the Virus to control me. But he was wrong about that. I'm not afraid of the Virus. What I fear most is my inability to stop it.

The thought of Abel now, after our tearful goodbyes days ago, fills me with a mix of sadness and apprehension. Part of me fears that he's left The Community. The other part of me fears he hasn't. There's no way for me to know if Abel's been captured and ordered to patrol the wall or not. Not unless Dr. Grayson wants me to know.

It's this added fear, though, that propels me to devise the plan I am determined to stick to. And that plan starts with clinical.

As I head down the streets of The Community, toward the educational buildings, I am surprised by the lightness of my steps.

I hadn't slept a wink the previous night, but instead filled up pages and pages of an old journal of my mother's I found hidden deep within one of her dresser drawers. I didn't dare read a single page, though I was, at times, tempted. It just felt too private. Too personal. Instead, I paperclipped the used pages together and started fresh with just one question.

What is Dr. Grayson hiding?

From there, I wrote down everything of significance I could think of. From the miniature flying cameras to my mother's nightmarish death. Anything that I believed Dr. Grayson had manipulated—even orchestrated—since the inception of The Community went down in the pages of the journal. By the time I finished, almost ten pages were filled, my right hand cramped from writing for hours.

Now, as I walk confidently through The Community, I contemplate the revelations from last night. There are at least two details I am sure of: Dr. Grayson is desperate for a cure, and this desperation led directly to the murder of my mother. Of course, I realize that my mother's fate was sealed the moment she started showing symptoms of the Virus. But Dr. Grayson was the one who ultimately pulled the plug on her life.

But why? To prove a point to his faltering daughter? Or to remind me that I am, in fact, under his complete control? We all are.

All my life, I have been conditioned to believe that what Dr. Grayson stands for is, for lack of a better word, good. He was, after all, the one to discover the vaccine's potential to keep the majority of The Community's members alive longer.

At the heart of everything, Dr. Grayson has, since the dawn of The Community, consistently claimed his only motive to be our protection. Then why kill my mother? Why threaten Abel? If he truly has everyone's best interest in mind, why allow *any* member of The Community to suffer?

It doesn't make any sense.

At the medical building's heavy doors, I scan my bracelet, and something in the distant corner of my mind awakens with a jolt. It's as if the faint click of the lock triggers a once-burnt-out light bulb in my brain to ignite.

Oh my god. Oh my *god*, I realize all at once with horror. The bracelets! Of course! I twist the slender band around and around my wrist. Dr. Grayson's tracking us. Has been since the beginning. The realization makes me nauseous. First the flying cameras and now this. How had I not realized?

I start to feverishly remove the identification cuff but stop, shaking my head. No. I want Dr. Grayson to know where I am today. I *need* him to know. For once, I think, I can use his clever devices against him. The thought makes me laugh out loud, and before I realize it, students traveling the hallway alongside me are staring.

I purse my lips, feigning seriousness, and continue to my first lab.

As usual, our instructor has set up all our necessary daily materials. Piles and piles of equations. Notes to analyze. Blood samples. *From where?* I find myself questioning for the first time in my life. It's not like we have a weekly blood drive here in The Community. In fact, we've never been asked to donate *anything*. And yet, not once have I wondered where the samples come from. I just assumed....

I open the journal and jot down a single phrase:

Need to get inside Dr. Grayson's lab.

Then I close the journal, slip it back into my bag, and begin to flip through the pages of procedures, all written in the same familiar, neat script of Dr. Grayson's. His typical daily orders. Drills, they are called by all our instructors, but I now see them for what they really are. Every day in clinical it is the same. Follow the photocopied directions. Record the outcomes. Report anything of significance to the teacher who in return, sends the information to the lab—to Dr. Grayson and his scientific colleagues.

Like an obedient daughter and student, I do what I am told this morning. I need to keep as low a profile as possible right now, and so I record my results diligently and report them to Dr. Lawson, who flips through my calculations with a scowl on her long horse-like face, the red-rimmed spectacles sitting low on her pointy nose.

"Good work," she says, robotically without looking at me.

"Thank you," I say, and turn to go back to my seat. Now to figure out how to get into Dr. Grayson's lab.

My next class is Microbiology, my favorite, even though most of my peers consider the subject to be quite uninteresting. What had Abel called it once? Unsexy? A quiet laugh escapes my lips despite the wave of sadness that washes over me at the memory of Abel.

Specifically, there are two details that make Microbiology even more appealing today. First, the class requires zero interactions with other classmates. Instead, I can spend my ninety minutes hovered over microscopes, studying—or pretending to study—various microbes. Second, the classroom is located on the first floor of the massive building we also use as our hospital. Dr. Grayson's lab is on the sixth.

When I arrive, five minutes early, I hesitate outside the lobby doors for a moment, trying to still my pounding heart. In order for my plan to work, I need to elicit help, and I'm increasingly worried that no one here in The Community will come willingly to my aid.

Not now that Abel's gone.

I scan my bracelet and push my way through the revolving doors, but instead of heading to the left to Microbiology, I make my way across the slowly-emptying first-floor lobby.

"Hey, Cat!" a cheerful voice calls from behind an unnecessarily tall reception desk near the rear of the lobby, the phrase *Forge Ahead* etched into its dark wood. Behind it, a continuous wall of water cascades peacefully into a seemingly bottomless pool only to return again to the top and start again. I resist the urge to roll my eyes. It's all about perception in The Community.

I put on my happy face, smiling perhaps a little too brightly at Mikaela Woody, a former classmate turned receptionist. "Hey, Mikaela!" I say cheerfully, and at first, she seems a bit taken aback by my over-the-top excitement. I guess in recent years, I *have* become quite the introvert, with Abel as the only friend to sit with me at lunch and partner with me during labs. But as Mikaela is one of those girls who is *always* so sweet, she shrugs off my unusual geniality and tucks her long wavy blond hair behind her ears.

"How are you, Cat?" she asks earnestly, watching me as I watch her closely. An awkward second passes between us before I get myself together.

"I'm ok," I tell her honestly. "Except I haven't seen Abel around today." Obviously, I *have* to say something about Abel. It would seem uncharacteristic of me not to be with him now as we both are in Microbiology this block of time.

"Hmmm," Mikaela says softly, and the sympathy in her eyes lets me know she believes there's been a row between Abel and me. Another girl, perhaps, has gotten between us. I'm all right with her believing this. Her compassionate nature will work in my favor here.

I shrug, standing on tiptoes to cross my arms on top of the reception desk. I lean in as closely as I can. "To be honest, I'm quite upset by the whole ordeal." Mikaela's eyes grow wide with curiosity. She's not one to gossip, but if she can be of any help at all to anyone, she will. It's what she thrives on: helping others in emotional crisis. This is the trait that landed her the job as one of Dr. Grayson's receptionists, a menial position, but one that I aim to benefit from today. So I continue. "It's nothing, really," I say quietly, looking around to make sure no one else is listening, "but sometimes I think Abel doesn't actually have what it takes if you know what I mean."

Mikaela nods in agreement, reaching out to put a warm hand on top of mine. "But you guys are so sweet together," she says, and she gives my arm a light squeeze, flashing me a genuine smile. "I'm *sure* you guys will work things out, Cat. He's probably just going through a phase, you know?"

"I don't know," I whisper, feigning disparagement. "My father doesn't approve..." I allow my voice to fade out, turning away. I'm trying to stick as close to the truth as I can in order to seem more sincere.

Mikaela squeezes my arm gently again. "Listen, Cat. I get it. I do. My dad *hates* Cole," she reminds me. And I force a laugh. "It's hard when we're all so close to one another, you know?" *Oh, how I do*, I think, nodding. "Well," she says, checking her bracelet for the time. "You'd better hurry to class. You don't want to be late."

This is it, I think, my heart pounding again. Acting has never been my forte, so I plow ahead without hesitating, afraid I might change my mind. I look to my own wrist, shake it twice, and abruptly cry out. "Oh, no! My identification bracelet! It doesn't seem to be working!" I frantically look around the first-floor lobby, my eyes wide. There are a few final stragglers making their way to Microbiology, but no one is paying attention to Mikaela and me, determined themselves to get to class on time. "Dr. Jensen—"

Mikaela doesn't let me finish. She's already unclasping her bracelet like I hoped she would. "Here," she says. "Use mine. I don't get off until four, so you can use it until then. That'll give you a few extra hours to get yours fixed, too. Repairs are done on the second floor. Room 236. They'll have your bracelet up and running again in no time at all."

I smile a big toothy grin and squeal. Were there not a large, hulking desk separating us, I might give Mikaela a genuine hug. "Thank you!" I say, putting her bracelet on my opposite wrist. "I owe you big time!"

Mikaela waves me off (After all, what's the big deal, right? It's *just* a bracelet!), and I fly down the corridor to Microbiology where class with Dr. Jensen has already begun. I can hear his monotonous voice coming from inside the classroom as I scan my own identification bracelet and let myself in quietly. I need to let Dr. Grayson know I've made it to class. I also need to let him know once I've left.

Dr. Jensen looks at me disapprovingly but continues to lecture about today's microbes. I slide into my seat at the back and concentrate on my breathing; I need to calm down if I'm going to make any rational decisions. Except there's nothing rational about anything I'm planning to do.

Somehow I make it through the tortuous ninety minutes of class, and when the bell chimes, the time on my wrist reads 11:30. Perfect, I think, as I pack up my books. Most of the building will be out for their lunch break. This gives me at least an hour to break into Dr. Grayson's lab and see what I can dig up. If any alarms should go off using Mikaela's bracelet, I can claim I dropped it somewhere looking for maintenance. Act now, I decide. Apologize later.

Lights flicker on and off, sensitized by my presence, as I maneuver down the now-empty hallway toward the elevators. Behind me, the drone of voices grows fainter as people exit the building for lunch. Once alone at the elevator, I scan my bracelet, press the button for the lift and wait, staring at the reflective metal of the doors. It could be anyone, I decide, looking back at me. Anyone with blond wavy hair, that is. In fact, as long as you can't see my face clearly, I could very well be Mikaela Woody. Still, I lower my chin to my chest, hoping to evade any security cameras in the corridor. *You can never be too careful*, I think.

It feels like an eternity before the elevator reaches the ground floor, a soft *ding* signaling its arrival. I don't wait until the door fully opens, but duck inside and hit the button indicating the second floor three or four times as though this might make the doors close more quickly. The floor of the elevator lurches noticeably, forcing me to brace myself on the handrail for support, and then begins to climb toward my destination.

Once on the second floor, I head swiftly toward room 236, smiling nervously at the handful of community members that loiter in the halls. But instead of turning into the Maintenance and Repairs department, I duck through the door to the adjacent women's restroom. I'm counting on proximity to solidify my alibi, and, finding no other alternative, hide my bracelet at the bottom of an artificial potted fern.

Back on the elevator, my left foot fidgets as I stare at the closed door, not sure what to expect once it opens. Two, three, four, five. Each floor I pass, I say a silent prayer that no other member of The Community will be waiting to get on the elevator.

Six.

Only one time before had I ventured to this floor, to Dr. Grayson's lab. Only once in my lifetime had I allowed the cloak of reverence to drop just enough to give me the courage to break through the barriers my father began putting into place the moment the mere idea of The Community was conceived. And it had been on the morning my mother first showed signs of the Virus. I remember running at full speed down the streets of The Community, tears streaming freely down my face, desperately needing to be told by the one man I admired above all that my mother, my rock, would be ok.

But when the door to my father's office opened that day, there had been no remorse, no inkling of sympathy in the creases of his face. Instead, he had stood there cold, like a statue, eyes unblinking and shut the door in my face without so much as an, "I'm sorry."

That's the moment I stopped referring to Dr. Grayson as my father.

And now my mother is dead, and I am back again in hopes of uncovering *why*.

The doors of the elevator open, and I am relieved to see the corridors dark. When I step onto the sixth-floor landing, lights flicker on, and I look first left toward Dr. Grayson's office and then right down the hall toward the labs, listening for any indication of Dr. Grayson or his team of scientists. When it seems as though the coast is clear, I turn left and head silently down the hallway, hugging the wall for comfort.

I figure my best bet is to head directly to Dr. Grayson's office. Make sure he's not there.

If I'm caught, I rationalize, then I can just say I came looking for him. To let him know I'm ready to fight the good fight. His fight. Whatever that may be.

His door looms tall and menacing at the end of the hallway. I knock once. Twice. Then I try the knob that I know won't open without an identification bracelet. I hesitate, my heart pounding. Will there be flashing red lights? A siren? A community-wide alarm that will send Dr. Grayson and patrolmen heading in this direction? There's no way of knowing unless I try.

With a trembling arm, I lift my wrist to the scanner and close my eyes. I press Mikaela's bracelet to the small screen and wait for the click.

Nothing happens. I open my eyes and try again, hoping that maybe, just *maybe*, I hadn't gotten the bracelet close enough. Still, nothing.

I sigh. Of course. *Of course*, members of The Community would require special clearance to get into Dr. Grayson's office—even trusted employees. Even immediate family. I wouldn't be surprised if Dr. Grayson himself is the only one with permission to enter. This fuels my belief that he does, in fact, have something to hide. I do an about-face and head back down the hallway to Dr. Grayson's lab. Would security clearance be the same? There is one way to find out.

At the large double doors with the sign *Authorized Personnel Only* I scan Mikaela's bracelet. Nothing.

"Damn it!" I whisper because at first, I think the bracelet doesn't work, but then the indicator light on the handle turns green, and I let out the breath I didn't realize I was holding. At first, I'm so stunned I don't move, but my shock quickly turns to quiet jubilation as I realize this is my chance. My plan had worked!

Gently, I push down the door handle and the metal doors open. I push my way inside. Like the hallway, the lab is dark. I can hear the scurrying sounds of animals and the low and steady beeping of monitors, but no one seems to be around.

I set the timer on Mikaela's identification bracelet to ten minutes. Wherever Dr. Grayson and his minions have gone for lunch, I figure there is a very small window of time to investigate.

There are monitors everywhere, and I have to swallow the fear that someone somewhere is watching me now in order to will myself forward.

I head toward the back of the large lab first, lights flickering on as I do. I figure I'll work myself back to the door in case I am forced to make a quick exit. Along the back wall, there is a row of three large metal doors, each with a red indicator light blinking ominously above. As I approach, I see what appear to be rectangular digital monitors beside each door. Heart rates. Blood pressures. Temperatures. But of what? Of whom? I attempt to scan Mikaela's bracelet but am not surprised when the doors remain locked. There are, of course, limits to where even employees of Dr. Grayson are allowed.

I lean in to listen for any sounds beyond the doors that might tell me what lies beyond when from somewhere behind the middle door I think I hear moaning. I recoil back a few feet, my heart pounding so violently I think I can hear it.

I scan the area around the doors, but there's nothing except the monitors to indicate what is locked inside.

Backing up slowly, I move now to the rows and rows of cages that line the right side of the lab. On the table tops, there are less-advanced methods of monitoring the status of the animals: clipboards with all but illegible scripts detailing current conditions, ages, stages, and symptoms.

One monkey, wheezing on a filthy cage floor, blood pooled around its mouth is documented to be in Stage 5—whatever that means—and, according to the notes, all attempts to prolong life have failed. I put the clipboard back down beside the cage and move on in horror. These sad dying animals are everywhere, and my heart breaks again and again as I read their assigned clipboards, all indicating inevitable and grave outcomes.

It's all quite difficult to stomach, but, other than the strange three doors that I have no way of breaking through, nothing seems to jump out at me as terribly *off*. Everyone in The Community expects there to be a level of experimentation. Lives are at stake here. And this is, after all, a *laboratory*.

As I'm turning to leave empty-handed, however, I bump into a table I hadn't noticed before. The protruding corner digs into my thigh, and I'm rubbing out the Charley horse when the name of the small caged mammal jumps out at me from the silver tag near the bottom of its cage.

Mr. Jingles.

Isn't that odd? I marvel, watching the little white mouse spin his wheel with such speed and endurance I think it might come loose and spin its way out of the cage and across the floor of the lab. *Like he's trying to escape,* I think, and I am reminded of the birthday when I received my first and only pet. In The Community, there is no allowing for pets, of course. *All life is sacred and must be used accordingly.* The Community's way of saying animals are for experimenting. Period. No ifs-ands-or-buts about it.

Unless you are Dr. Scott Grayson's little girl. Then, and only then, exceptions can be made.

So for my tenth year of life, I wasn't shocked to unwrap the tiniest of boxes to find a small white creature with a pink nose and tail, its tiny, twitching silver whiskers and beady eyes staring back at me. Immediately, I fell in love with the mouse my father called Mr. Jingles.

Coincidence? I wonder, then shake my head foolishly. There are no coincidences with Dr. Grayson.

I search for the mouse's clipboard but quickly realize that, unlike the other lab animals, Mr. Jingles doesn't have one. Also, unlike all the other animals, this little mouse seems *healthy*. I run my hands gingerly over the top of the cool metal table and then down each side until my fingers close on what feels like some sort of button. I push it and jump back startled as a small screen materializes out of thin air above the cage.

At first, I just stare at the mouse's vitals, a mix of reds, greens, and yellows dancing across the monitor hovering in space. The mouse's heart rate is strong, temperature normal. What makes this little guy so unique? I wonder, reaching my hand out to touch the virtual clipboard. When my fingers swipe across the screen, the image changes. The screen is dated at the top—yesterday's date. I continue to swipe through the history of vitals and notes.

There are months and months of data, and as I continue to scan the remarks, it becomes very apparent that this creature is special. Important even. Despite what appears to be countless attempts to infect the mouse with the Virus, he has, for whatever reason, remained immune to it.

I stop reading the notes and scan hurriedly all the way back to the beginning of the log, but it takes much longer than anticipated. My identification bracelet vibrates, reminding me that I don't have much time—if any—left.

"Come on. Come on," I plead with the machine, and when I think that I'll never reach the beginning of this little mouse's existence, the screen stops reacting to my feverish swipes.

My eyes freeze on the date at the top, disbelief causing me to falter.

It can't be, I think. It's not possible.

October 12, 2069.

Three years after the onset of the Virus. And—perhaps more unsettling—seven years *before* my father presented me with my very own Mr. Jingles.

I rack my brain, trying to recall my little pet's fate. But I don't have to try too hard. Because I *do* remember what happened to my Mr. Jingles. Dr. Grayson had taken my beloved pet with him when he left my mother and me two years later, when I was twelve. I just assumed the mouse died.

It should have died, I think. It should *be* dead.

Because the average lifespan of the common laboratory mouse is a mere two years—maybe three in the perfectly engineered environment.

I can't believe what I'm seeing. My head starts to spin. If the records on this mouse are accurate, this Mr. Jingles is around thirteen years old.

"It's not possible," I whisper, taking a step closer to the table and peering into the cage at the tiny marvel.

Mr. Jingles stops running for just a second, staring back up at me, its tiny pink nose and silver whiskers twitching like they had all those years ago.

The implications are so far-fetched, I find it suddenly difficult to breathe, goosebumps errupting down my arms. It *is* my Mr. Jingles, I realize, looking into the little mouse's eyes. I just know it is. But how?

The mouse's little whiskers twitch again, and the realization that *this is my pet* makes me giddy, and I laugh, the noise bringing me back to my current reality. Panicked by the sudden break in silence, I look around the lab filled with so much suffering, then turn my attention back to the tiny marvel.

How had Dr. Grayson done it? I wonder. Found a way to halt time? To prolong life? To stop the Virus in its tracks? And why—*why*—is he keeping this seemingly fantastic medical breakthrough from us all? Isn't this *good* news?

My wrist buzzes again, and I start to back up slowly from the cage at first, not wanting to leave just yet, but then I break into a slow run, fleeing the laboratory and the little mouse thinking only one thing.

Dr. Grayson knows—has known for some time now—how to halt the symptoms of the Virus. And possibly even extend life! Yet he has chosen to do nothing. *Nothing!*

I sprint down the hallway toward the elevators, my anger mounting with each step that propels me, lights flickering on and off in my wake like lightning.

12: WREN

Day two, I think. I measure time by the meals I don't touch and my all-too-often trips up the basement stairs. I don't speak. Not to Abel. Not to the raider. Not to myself. I turn myself off. To everything.

•　•　•　•

By mid-day, I'm operating on autopilot. I continue to refuse the food that's brought, much to the raiders chagrin. I don't drink the water. I think dying of dehydration or starvation will be better than by the hands of my merciless captor.

Every now and then, Abel's voice breaks through my despair. "Don't let him win, Wren. Please. Don't give up." And there's something in his voice that makes me think he's said these same words to someone else. Someone else who didn't take his advice. Still, it doesn't make me any more inclined to listen.

"Why?" I whisper after he's begged too many times to count. "What's the point anymore?" My voice is as faint as the trace of hope that lingers in the far corner of my heart, but Abel hears and grabs hold of it.

Chains clink and shuffle on the opposite side of the barrier. "I'm still here," he reminds me softly.

"I don't want to be," I whisper back so quietly I'm not sure Abel hears me.

"Think about your mom," he pleads.

But I can't.

Because the cold, hard truth is that if what Bill told me is true, my mother's recklessness is just as much to blame for what's happened to me as my own.

•   •   •   •   •

Later that afternoon, when it becomes evident I don't wish to talk, Abel fills the void with stories. He talks to me about a girl named Cat from inside the wall. About growing up in The Community. About the resurgence of the Virus. I half-heartedly listen. What does it matter, after all? But then he talks to me at length about the man named Dr. Grayson and his connection to the vile raider who has taken us prisoner.

"He claims to be searching for a cure," Abel tells me. His methods, though, are cold, calculating, manipulative.

They would have to be to become involved with a raider.

"Jeb thinks he's using the hostages—us—as human guinea pigs," Abel continues. "Test subjects for his experimental drugs."

And as Abel talks, something Bill said to me before I left camp comes back into focus with the introduction of this Dr. Grayson. Bill revealed that on the night of her kidnapping, my mother "reached out" to someone. No, not someone, I recall. Specifically, a *him*. Initially, I assumed he was referring to Don. Whom else would my mother know inside The Dome? But then it dawns on me. Like Dr. Grayson, my mother is a doctor. Could my mother possibly *know* this man, I wonder? And if so, why would my mother, a kind-hearted, loving person wish to associate herself with someone with so little regard for human life?

I am still pondering this new information later when the basement door opens above, and the sound of boots clamber heavily down the stairs. The light from upstairs penetrates the thick darkness of the basement.

What time is it? I wonder. At first, I think I must have fallen asleep and am dreaming because there's no denying that there's something significantly different about the sound of the raider's steps this time. They seem lighter, more civilized even. Still, on instinct, I will myself numb, my adopted defense mechanism to ward off the pain the raider will inevitably inflict upon me, and close my eyes.

I hear Abel gasp, which makes me shut my eyes tighter, red stars reflected on the backs of each eyelid. I vaguely hear him whisper the word, "You!" which reinforces my fear, and I keep myself in a tight little ball on the floor, my knees to my chest. I know the drill. The raider will beat me into submission until I stand or he has to carry me. There's little fight left in me and I have almost nothing left to prove.

When my shackles are undone, however, it's not by the raider's rough, unforgiving hands. To my utter disbelief, strong, careful arms wrap around me instead, lifting me gently, my legs draping over one side. I release my breath, and without opening my eyes, bury my face into the stranger's chest, the relief that it's not the raider so tangible it overpowers me. My savior smells of clean linen.

Abel protests, crying out, "Why can't you just leave her alone?" Does he not realize that it's not the raider who has come for me?

The man who carries me up and out of the basement says nothing at first. With ease and a kind of tenderness, he brings me to a dimly lit room filled with a cool breeze that does its best to clear the putrid scent of the basement from my nose. He lays me down on a couch and kneels near my head, placing a hand gently, hesitantly, on my filthy face, brushing aside my matted hair.

"Stay here," he orders softly. "I'm going to take care of something. I'll be right back." His words are deliberate but kind, and I listen, nodding my head slightly.

The man stands and heads out of the room, his footsteps echoing toward the rear of the house. Still, my relief locks me to my place on the couch.

When the shouting starts, still I remain where I am, not sure I even have the strength to walk—let alone run—away. Then, amidst the angered voices, comes the unmistakable *pop!* of a gun being fired followed by footsteps that walk assuredly back to where I lie trembling on the couch.

"It's ok," the same voice from moments earlier says, kneeling again beside my head. "Do you think you can walk?"

I shake my head.

The man sighs heavily. He places a strong hand on my cheek, one finger brushing a tear from my eye. Tenderly. He sighs again. "Corrine," he says softly. "I really need you to walk."

At the sound of my given name, my eyes flutter open, and I look my savior square in the face, drawing in a breath. His green eyes stare back at me with such concern and affection, it makes my heart do a somersault.

"What did you call me?" I whisper.

Lines form at the corner of his eyes. He's smiling without actually smiling. "Of course. Forgive me," he says. "I believe your mother has renounced that name." He brushes another strand of hair from my face, and I prop myself up on my trembling elbow. "Wren, is it now?"

"Who *are* you?" I ask. "And how do you know my name? My mother?"

The man sighs again. "Do you think you can walk?" he asks once more, ignoring my questions.

Again, I shake my head, still staring at this stranger's handsome, clean-shaven face. Something about him makes me yearn to trust him. Something else urges me to be extremely wary.

The man turns his gaze to the front door. I do the same. Outside, the orange orb of the sun glows so low and bright through the wall of windows, I have to squint, my eyes not yet adjusted to the light after spending the last few days and nights in darkness.

Still staring out the door, the man says, "If you want to see your mother, Corrine, we need to move. Now." When I don't answer or make any attempt to move, he continues, "I can carry you most of the way, but the hillside leading down to the river will prove most difficult unless you can manage on your own." He turns back to me, and his eyes are once again soft, questioning.

I swing my legs over the side of the couch, testing their strength, and place my hands on my knees, preparing to stand.

The man nods approvingly. "Good." He turns to leave. I stand up carefully, but I don't follow him. Not yet. When he realizes this, he stops, hanging his head slightly. In frustration? I wonder. Well, he's not the only one who's frustrated, I think.

"You said you know where my mother is?"

"I do," he replies, not turning around.

"Is she—is she all right, then?"

"She is."

I consider this a moment longer.

"You're Dr. Grayson, aren't you?"

The man turns abruptly at the sound of his name, but his look is not one of surprise. He is smiling, his bright white teeth gleaming. "I am," he says simply.

I turn back to the basement door. "What about Abel?" I ask.

Dr. Grayson's smile falters slightly. "Ah, you've made a friend down there, have you?"

"Will you save him, too?" I'm still staring at the door, torn between what I want to do and what I feel I *need* to do.

"Corrine," Dr. Grayson says, serious this time, "the only way you're going to see your mother is if we leave now. Without Abel."

My heart sinks. "But you will come back for him," I say.

It's not exactly a question, and even though Dr. Grayson nods, there's something in his face that causes me to believe he's not exactly being honest. Still, I bury this suspicion deep within my heart. Regardless of what I feel for

Abel, I have been presented with a clear path leading straight to my mother. I cannot let this opportunity pass me by. I have suffered too much and lost too much time already.

"Ok," I finally say.

"Ok." Dr. Grayson smiles again, offering me his arm. I take two careful steps closer to the man who has just saved my life, not entirely sure that my rescue is his ultimate motive nor my safety his primary concern, and together we head out into the setting sun.

13: RYDER

After the discovery of the skulls, Bill and I climb back down the hill in silence to find the road and continue in the direction we were traveling before we saw the rising smoke. Our canteens are both empty, and it won't be long before the side effects of dehydration take hold of us.

Still, we don't stop, trying to put as much distance between us and Wes' camp as possible.

After many long, arduous hours of traveling with no real destination in mind and no food or water, Bill and I stumble upon an abandoned train. We search the length of it, finding it utterly silent. Bill looks at me with pleading eyes, and I know what he wants: to rest. I do, too. So, we set about finding a suitable car in which to spend the remaining afternoon hours and possibly the night. Near the end of the train, we successfully find an empty car with a sliding door. We climb up and together wrench the heavy door shut. With the protection of the four walls of the train car, I am finally able to give into much-needed sleep, knowing full well that Bill will be right behind me. Neither of us offers to keep watch.

What does it matter? I think sadly, before drifting off into oblivion. We have no idea what we're doing or where we're going. We're like cats chasing our tails. Hopeless.

My afternoon slumber is fitful. I don't dream. Instead, I toss and turn violently on the floor of the train car, sweating despite the cool metal bed. When I wake next, it's to the dull aching in my neck and the sound of Bill snoring contentedly beside me. Without waking him, I crawl to the door of the train car and, as quietly as I can, pry it open. Light immediately blinds me through the narrow opening.

At first, I'm confused. I fully anticipated to be greeted by the night sky; however, when I realize what has happened, my confusion turns to horror. "Shit!" I say, jumping from the train car and shielding my eyes to locate the position of the sun. It's directly overhead. "Shit!" I say again. We've somehow managed to sleep not just the night away but most of the new day. "Bill!" I hiss, placing my head inside the train car. "Bill, come on! Get up!"

"Hey, ok," Bill mumbles but makes no attempt to move.

I let out a groan of frustration. "BILL!" I shout this time. "It's the middle of the day! We've got to get going!" But even as these words leave my lips, I know they lack conviction. Suddenly, I'm not sure why I'm so frantic. Still, what's the alternative? I ask myself. Turn back to camp? Go home like two sad dogs with our tails between our legs?

On the far side of the train car, Bill sits up. "Middle of the day?" he mumbles, rubbing his eyes. "That means—"

"I know what it means, Bill. Come on."

Bill drags himself to the edge of the car and sits, rubbing his temples and attempting to wet his lips. "Damn, I'm thirsty," he says and then adds, "and hungry."

My own stomach is so empty, I feel nauseous. Other than the meager meals of fish and soup at Wes' camp, we've had nothing to eat since leaving in search of Wren. We won't make it much longer without food and a water source.

"Listen, Bill. We need to find water. A stream off the river, maybe. I have a few matches. We can start a fire and boil the water as best we can, but we need to find something to put it in."

"Yeah, ok," Bill says, still rubbing his head. "There's bound to be *something* in these train cars."

"There's bound to be," I say, but I don't necessarily believe it. Every survivor of the Virus has been where Bill and I are now: starving and dehydrated. The likelihood of finding anything left unpillaged, I know, is slim to none.

Nevertheless, we search every car. Mostly, we find scraps: of metal, plastic, and wood. One car is half-filled with gravel. I scoop a few handfuls into my sack for the fire. The best we can find for water is an aluminum can that appears to have minimal rust. I'm not at all sure about the FDA's take on boiling water in an old can; however, they're not around at the moment to fill me in, so I use my knife to cut the can lengthwise and bend the sharp edges inward. It will have to do.

Bill and I stumble upon a stream shortly after leaving the main road to head closer to the river that roars in the distance. I kneel to carefully fill up the small, pitiful can with water while Bill collects wood for the fire. After digging a shallow hole and filling it with the confiscated gravel, Bill places the kindling in a teepee-like fashion. Because the wood is still damp from the rain showers earlier in the week, it takes almost all of our matches to get the fire going, but once it does, we celebrate soberly with rust and earth-flavored water, making several trips to the stream for more.

Once our thirst is temporarily quenched, I cover the fire with the remaining gravel and toss the aluminum can in my bag.

"Back to the road?" Bill asks dejectedly.

"Back to the road," I reply. What other choice do we have?

The two of us head silently through the forest back to the paved road and walk along in silence for many minutes. There's nothing left to say. I cannot offer Bill any words of encouragement. It would just be a lie. But I also don't need to rub the hopelessness I feel in his face.

When the muffled but unmistakable sound of a gunshot reverberates through the trees, breaking the silence, a flock of birds to my right takes flight, and Bill and I stop dead in our tracks.

I reach for my own gun and look to Bill. "We should check that out," I say quietly, still listening for signs of life—or struggle—in the distance.

"I had a feeling you were going to say that," Bill says, but he takes his gun out, too.

"Come on," I say, "It didn't sound far."

"I know." Bill sounds disappointed.

"It could be Wren," I remind him. "Or Claire."

Bill holds up his hands in surrender. "Ok, ok."

We continue to walk until we come across a string of driveways leading up into the woods. The mailboxes are sad reminders of the people who once lived here, and the surrounding trees and vines have crept their way across the paths that were once large enough for cars but now barely allow for human travel. All except one. The third one on the left.

I stop to examine it, bending down to investigate the shoulder of the road where it meets the driveway. The dirt has been disturbed. Probably recently as there are tracks of mud climbing away from the road as far as I can see.

"Tire tracks?" Bill asks.

I nod. "Looks like it to me. The recent rain would have washed this away," I say, indicating the dried mud. "They have to be pretty fresh."

"So let's go check it out," Bill says, but he sounds far from enthusiastic.

I've already started up the drive, my heart pounding, and Bill struggles to keep up with my newly energized steps, his breathing labored.

"Hey, what's with the hurry?" Bill asks. "Don't you want to wait until nightfall?"

But I don't answer Bill. There's something about this path that awakens my determination. *Wren has been here*, I think. I can feel her.

When we reach the top of the driveway, I don't stop. I head toward the house, which is seemingly constructed of windows, and am quick to find shelter at its base. The graffitied words *Keep Out* and *Danger* stare menacingly at me like large black eyes. I do not heed their warnings. Slinking beneath the gaping windows, I keep my eyes on the front porch steps. I wait. I listen. Nothing. It's now or never I think, and, taking the steps two at a time, avoiding the rotten planks, I burst through the front door of the house, the old wood giving way against the full weight of my body.

Inside, I inhale deeply, realizing suddenly that I have been all the while holding my breath. I hear Bill come in behind me.

"Ryder," he whispers. "What the hell, man?"

I hold out my hand to silence him. "Just listen," I order.

We stand in the once-swanky, large foyer, listening for any sound that might indicate what we're up against. Faintly, I think I hear noises coming from below the floor.

"Do you hear that?" I ask Bill.

He nods. "Yeah," he says, his voice trembling a little. "What do you think it is?"

I shake my head. "I don't know, but it sounds like it's coming from a basement. My pounding heart races even faster. *Could it be Wren?* I wonder. *Could she really be here?*

"Come on," I say, signaling the direction with my gun. "There's a door over there past the kitchen."

As we walk past, I can see the kitchen sink is filled to the brim with dirty dishes, some sort of small flies hovering around them. I nod to Bill who nods back.

Someone has been here recently.

At the basement door, I press my ear up against the splintering wood, and sure enough, I hear the sound again.

Clinking chains.

"Someone's down there," I whisper to Bill who looks white as a sheet. He keeps glancing back over his shoulder as though expecting someone to jump out of the shadows at any moment.

Using my foot, I nudge the door to the basement open. The smell hits me like a wave: urine, filth, and fear. My heart falls to my feet. Moments before I was hoping we'd find Wren here in this house, but now I'm silently praying we won't.

I gingerly step out onto the first board leading down into the dark basement. It buckles slightly beneath my weight and groans in protest. I keep my forward momentum going at a snail's pace, terrified of what I'll find once I reach the bottom.

Just enough light filters through the boarded up door and windows that I can make out an empty room with empty shackles along one wall. When I reach the last step, however, a voice cries out to my right. I turn abruptly.

"Hey!" a figure chained beneath the bar along the fall wall cries. "Help me!"

I brace myself and lift my gun. "Who are you?" I ask.

"Look," the prisoner says frantically, attempting to break free from his chains, "there's not much time. Dr. Grayson could return at any moment. Quick! Find the keys. The raider...I think he's been shot. Look there!"

I don't understand half of what this stranger says; however, the sheer panic in his voice is clear.

Still, I need to know one thing before I can help this man.

"A girl," I say breathlessly. "A girl named Wren. Have you...have you seen her?" *Please, please,* please, I silently beg.

"Wait, what? Wren? Yes!" And the prisoner laughs, but there's little humor in the sound. "Yes, I know her! Quick," he says frantically again, yanking at his chains, "Dr. Grayson took her! We can still catch them! You're armed. We have a chance! Go! Find the keys and let me out of here!"

Again, I don't follow all of what this stranger says; however, I'm filled with such emotion at the revelation that Wren's alive, that I don't think. I run up the stairs, past Bill, and through the first floor rooms.

The dead raider is in the kitchen, sitting slumped in a chair, blood pooled all around his head that rests against the Formica table top. The lazy *drip, drip, drip* of the blood hitting the floor lets me know that he hasn't been dead long.

I approach the slouched man cautiously, even though it's clear he won't be attacking anyone anytime soon—or *ever.* But when I get close enough, I gasp loudly. The clothing. The beard. I know this man. Wes.

I don't have time to contemplate the *how* or *why* of the situation. Instead, I survey Wes' body quickly but don't see any keys.

"Great," I murmur, getting closer to the corpse. I'll have to reach into his pockets. Holding my breath—again, I'm not sure what fuels my fear here;

Wes is clearly dead, after all—I reach into first one pocket and then the other.

Jackpot! My fingers close around what feels like a ring of tiny metal keys. I grab them and sprint back to the basement. Bill is still standing at the top looking at me like I'm crazy.

"Ryder—"

I don't listen. I push past him and fly back down the basement steps.

Once I am kneeling before the chained stranger who holds his hands out to me like an offering, shaking his cuffs frantically, however, I hesitate.

"Come on!" he says. "Hurry!"

I consider the situation a moment longer. He claims to know Wren. That he can lead us to her. But what if he's lying to save himself? I decide I need a little more proof that I can trust this guy before setting him free.

"How do I know you're telling the truth? About Wren, I mean," I say to him, trying to find confirmation in his eyes.

He looks at me earnestly. "Why would I lie?" he asks, and then realizing that there actually are a million reasons to be dishonest right now, he shakes his head and lowers his arms. "Look, she was here, ok? She told me she was looking for her mother. And Dr. Grayson..." He shakes his head again. "Nevermind. Please," he pleads desperately, "uncuff me, and I'll take you to her."

There's something about this stranger that makes me want to believe what he says. Nevertheless, I ask, "Why should I trust you?"

"Because if you don't, Wren could die," he says.

With trembling hands, I start to unlock his shackles. "I'm Ryder," I say as I work quickly, trying first one key and then another until I hear the click of the shackles unlocking.

"Abel," he tells me, shimmying his legs over to make it easier for me to unlock the remaining chains that bind him to the wall. "And Wren? She's in a bad way."

"Is she hurt?" I ask, not certain I want the answer.

"She's alive," he says. "But the sooner we can get to her, the better."

The shackles are off, and both Abel and I get to our feet a tad too quickly, Abel stumbling a bit as he does. Once he steadies himself, he reaches out to shake my hand. I oblige, pumping his hand up and down firmly once.

"Ok," I say, swinging my arm in the direction of the steps. "Lead the way."

Abel considers me for a second, then nods and brushes past me to climb the stairs.

He startles when he first encounters Bill on the first floor but sensing his harmlessness, relaxes. "He with you?" Abel asks.

"Most of the time," I respond.

Abel's lip curls up, offering me a lopsided grin. "Well, boys. I hope you're not afraid of heights," he says.

Bill and I exchange one final look before the three of us head out the front door after Wren.

14: ABEL

At first, I'm not entirely sure what to make of Bill and Ryder. Bill, obviously the older of the pair, seems to be the one taking orders from this Ryder kid, who behaves more like a sullen cowboy than anything. Once leaving the house of horrors, Ryder says nothing. Asks zero questions. Tearing through the trees with melodramatic force. Bill, on the other hand, stumbling to keep the pace, doesn't shut up.

Both Ryder's silence and Bill's incessant questions quickly give me a headache.

Just get them to the bridge, I think. *Get them to the bridge, point them in the right direction and—*

The problem is I haven't decided what comes after that.

By the time we finally break through the thick veil of trees that opens to the river, Bill's interrogation has stopped, and Ryder's pace has quickened. He shouts orders at Bill who continues to lag behind. Heck, it is a struggle for *me* to keep up. But Ryder's fury is understandable.

I sense another emotion welling up inside me now. Guilt. Ryder's girl, my comrade from the basement—Wren—is somewhere inside The Community, and a not-so-small part of me feels responsible for her capture by the hands of Dr. Grayson. Not once, but twice now, I have been unable to stop the good doctor: first, from controlling Cat and now from kidnapping Wren.

And for what purpose?

I recall the story Jeb spun for me on his final day in captivity. Of his attempted escape and the overheard and heated conversation between Dr. Grayson and the raider. Of the picture that had to be—just *had* to be—of Cat.

"Fair skin. Freckled. And wavy blond hair. The kind you want to bury yourself in. Almost wild," Jeb had described. And eyes like the ocean.

Just like Cat.

Except...

There's no logical reason for me to believe that Cat followed after me. Left The Community she so desperately wants to protect. She said it herself. She was planning to stay to uncover the truths surrounding Dr. Grayson and his involvement in her mother's death.

An incessant little voice inside my head screams for another explanation.

And then it hits me.

Wren. Not once while in the basement had I seen her face. But I had heard her voice. And so much of what she said and how she said it was so like Cat. Thoughtful. Kind. But with a fire, a rugged eagerness that was different. Could it be that the girl in the photograph was actually Wren, not Cat? And what would that mean if it was? Why would Dr. Grayson be seeking someone *outside* The Community? Perhaps even more importantly, what does he plan to do with her?

My headache grows worse, a symptom I know of impending dehydration, and I wonder what I should do. Should I entrust this information—really just presumptions—to two total strangers? Or do I keep it to myself and leave Ryder and Bill in the dark?

I glance ahead to Ryder who, having been pointed in the general direction of the bridge, has taken the lead of our accidental traveling posse, leaving Bill to huff and puff and complain behind me, and decide to wait a bit longer to determine whether or not I can fully trust these two with my suspicions.

We travel in silence for an additional ten minutes or so, and by the time we reach the railway bridge, I find myself questioning my plans once again. Now that we have come this far, I could very easily explain to Bill and Ryder how to get to the cemetery and dislodge the piece of the wall, leading them into The Community. After that, the two of them could go after Wren all on their own.

Or I could go with them.

Neither choice seems great, having recently experienced the lack of humanity outside the great wall I once called home and Dr. Grayson's clear and twisted connection to it; however, I now feel an obligation to Wren, the girl I know so little about but suddenly seem profoundly connected to. For reasons I don't quite understand, some undeniable part of me wants to make sure she's ok. Also, I miss Cat. Terribly.

"Don't tell me we have to cross that thing," Bill mutters, coming up behind me panting like a dog. My thoughts of Cat interrupted momentarily, I laugh softly but don't answer him.

Ryder is already climbing up and onto the platform of the bridge, and I imagine if he has to, he'll leave his struggling travel companion behind. He's a man on a mission, I think, and hurry to climb onto the scaffolding after him.

"Your friend," I say to Ryder's back, as it makes me a little uneasy to travel side-by-side down a narrow bridge next to a guy I just met, "I don't think he's going to make it much farther."

Ryder snorts and says dismissively, "He'll be fine," not bothering to stop and check.

So the three of us continue across the bridge without speaking, the only sounds the rushing waters below and Bill's haggard breathing.

It takes only half the time as it had taken me just days before to reach the end of the bridge as we do so on foot and not our knees, but once we do, enough time has passed that I have finally made up my mind. As much as I don't want to be back inside the walls of The Community, a prisoner once again of Dr. Grayson's, I realize I really have no better choice, so I will continue with them to the cemetery. From there, I will find Cat, the only person I truly trust in the world and tell her what I've learned. Together, I hope the two of us will figure out the rest.

As for Ryder and Bill? I'll point them in the direction of Dr. Grayson's lab and wish them good luck. The bulge on Ryder's back reminds me that the pair is armed. If and how they plan to use these weapons, I'm not sure, but they are better equipped to handle conflict right now than I am. And part of me honestly believes that they will find Wren there.

Part of me doesn't.

"Now what?" Ryder asks me.

I look off into the distance toward the towering wall.

"Now, we break into what you boys call The Dome," I say in response.

Ryder nods but surprisingly takes a seat. Bill, finally catching up, all but falls from the bridge, and collapses to the ground beside his friend.

"We have a few hours until daybreak," Ryder says, leaning back against a tree. "We need a plan." He glances at Bill, who is panting, laid out on the ground like he's been shot. "And water. Soon."

Of course, I know this to be true. And although I have been fed and watered each day of my recent captivity, my mounting headache lets me know I'll be suffering from lack of nutrients soon, too, sweating as profusely as I have tonight. Ryder and Bill are, I imagine, much worse off. Again, I am faced with a conundrum. What would it say about my character if I simply left these two on their own in a world they know nothing about? Not to mention a corrupt and fearful world?

They would be sitting ducks. Strangers. Threats even. Simply put, I would be setting Ryder and Bill up to fail even before giving them a shred of a chance.

And I still have my identification bracelet. I shake my wrist, weighing the benefits against the consequences. This bracelet...it could serve us well or get us caught, I recognize with frustration. But what other choice do I have? Do *we* have?

I sigh heavily. "We need a plan," I agree with Ryder, but Bill is the one to answer.

"A plan, huh?" he says with his eyes still closed, back pressed against the ground. "What fun would that be?"

I ignore him. "If we go now, we will reach the cemetery with plenty of dark left to keep us covered. The lack of daylight should help us go unnoticed for a little while, but I have to warn you, there are cameras everywhere."

Bill is suddenly alert, eyes open. "Cameras?" he asks incredulously, a reminder of Ryder and Bill's less-than-privileged living.

"Cameras," I reply. "And these cameras won't necessarily *look* like cameras either." I don't elaborate.

"Ok, Abel," Ryder says seriously, "what do you suggest we do once we're on the inside?"

I consider his question a moment. Really, there's only one real option that will buy us more time. "We'll need to cross the main commons and head to Cat's."

I don't realize I've said this out loud until Ryder asks suspiciously, "Cat? As in a person? Do you really think it's a good idea to involve more people?"

I lean against a nearby tree and consider how to answer. Ryder's concern is, of course, valid. I, too, am unsure who to trust at this point. But I do trust Cat. "She's a friend," I tell Ryder simply and then add, "I have a roommate who won't necessarily be receptive to two strangers from the outside in his house. You have to remember, we were taught from an early age to *fear* people like you. Cat, on the other hand," I pause here, careful with my words, "she lives alone." I deliberately leave out the part that Cat just so happens to be Dr. Grayson's estranged daughter. I don't need another reason for Bill and Ryder to be suspicious. Instead, I insist, "She'll be more than willing to help us. Trust me."

Ryder opens his mouth to say something, his eyebrows arched, but then changes his mind. Instead, he turns to Bill and offers him a hand. "Time to go, Bill," he says matter of factly. "If this Dr. Grayson guy has Wren, you'd better believe he's got Claire, too."

Bill, not worrying about his pride, gladly takes Ryder's hand. Ryder overemphasizes a loud grunt as he all but pulls the entire weight of Bill to a standing position, and we once again continue our journey to The Community.

"When we get back to camp, I am going to get myself in better shape," Bill says, but because of his light tone, I don't believe a word of it.

"Tell you what," Ryder tells him, "let's just get *back* to camp—with our girls—and then you can join me anytime for a workout."

Bill snorts. "Yeah, yeah, sure, Hercules."

"So how do you know this Dr. Grayson?" Ryder asks, directing his attention now to me. "And what do you think he wants with Wren and her mom? Why go through such lengths to kidnap them after all this time?"

"Claire wasn't kidnapped, Ryder," Bill pipes up, disparagingly.

Ryder waves him silent. But not before Bill's comment awakens the little voice inside my head from earlier. If Claire wasn't kidnapped, it means she went with Dr. Grayson willingly, and if she went with Dr. Grayson willingly, then it must mean she knows him, too. *The plot keeps thickening*, I think. And Dr. Grayson has, as usual, found himself at the center. I decide to ignore Bill's outburst for the time being and address Ryder's questions. "How do I know Dr. Grayson? For starters, he controls everything in The Community where I was raised," I tell them.

"The Community?" Ryder and Bill say in unison.

"The society beyond the wall. That's what we call it. The Community. More like The Dead End." I chuckle at this, but there is no humor in my laughter.

Neither Ryder nor Bill responds, so I continue. "When I was little, I thought—no, I was taught to believe—that the wall was built for our protection. That the people living on the outside were sick. Incurably sick. And the vaccine I was forced to receive? It was going to keep me alive. It was going to keep all of us in The Community alive. But that's not what happened. About a decade after The Community closed its doors to the outside, people began to get sick again. Really sick. Not all at once, of course, but year after year, more and more people began to show signs of the Virus.

And while most people at first denied that the vaccine had anything to do with it, eventually we all came to believe that it did."

"And Wren and Claire?"

I shake my head, but I'm sure in the dark Ryder and Bill can't see it. "No idea," I tell them both honestly.

"But if you had to guess?"

I stop walking to face Ryder, who has apparently adopted Bill's role of inquisitor. We face each other in a sort of casual standoff, and I realize as if seeing Ryder in the flesh for the first time that we are actually around the same age. "Look, Ryder, I don't have a clue. Ok? Dr. Grayson, for as long as I have lived in The Community, has taught us all to disregard the people living outside the wall. There was no hope and no use for them." Just saying the words out loud makes me cringe. Them. Us. As a kid, it hadn't seemed so preposterous, but now? "In there," I say, pointing in the direction of The Community still veiled by darkness, "we're brainwashed to believe. And as much as I hate to admit it, until just recently, I bought into Dr. Grayson's hype."

Ryder contemplates this for a moment, the glow of the moon reflecting off his eyes that never once leave mine. "What made you change your mind?"

To break Ryder's glare, I start walking again, and by the crunch of brush behind me, I know that Ryder follows closely behind. "A few weeks ago, I saw him leaving The Community. On a boat. For hours at a time."

"This was odd, then? Him leaving?" Ryder keeps the questions coming. I completely understand his need for answers, but I'm beginning to feel as though I'm a specimen beneath Dr. Grayson's many microscopes. It makes me uncomfortable.

I sigh and reply with a simple, "Yes," but I can't help but wonder to myself, *Hasn't he heard a word I've said?* "Like I said before, we were taught to fear the outside. No one was supposed to leave. It was forbidden. It wasn't safe. Yet here was the man in charge breaking the very rule he insisted not be broken. Ever. It got me thinking."

Ryder's barrage of questions finally stops, and once again we continue at a slow crawl toward the cemetery.

When we're nearly there, the distant glow of The Community casting an eerie yellowish-green color over the outside world, Ryder speaks again, but it's not to me. I'm not entirely sure he's addressing Bill either. "Claire knew this man once," he says with a tone that makes me think he's come to a conclusion about something that's been bothering him for quite a while.

And although it doesn't sound to me like a question, Bill answers, "Yes. Once."

"Wren, too," Ryder whispers in the dark. Again it doesn't sound like a question but instead as if he's just now figuring out the final few pieces of a rather large and difficult puzzle. As I listen to this exchange between Ryder and Bill, my own wheels start to turn again. Who is Ryder referring to? Dr. Grayson?

"Yes," Bill says, "but she wouldn't remember. She was too young."

Woah. What? My pulse quickens. It's actually obnoxious, this conversation between Ryder and Bill. Ambiguous. Claire, Wren, *him.*

"She knew him as a child?" Ryder asks.

"Yes, as a very young child."

"Claire and Dr. Grayson...were they...?" He can't seem to finish his thought.

So Bill does it for him. "Were they *involved?*" He seems sickened by these words in his mouth. "Yes." Bill says this final word so softly I'm not sure he even speaks this aloud or if it is the wind that carries the impossible truth.

And at once, this revelation makes me falter, causing me to trip over my feet. It's clear by the hitch in Bill's voice that it's difficult for him to get these words out. But it's just as difficult for me to hear them. Dr. Grayson and Claire? Wren's mother? Cat's father? Still my wheels turn. Faster and faster. Because I know where Ryder is going with this, and, frankly, I'm too stunned to interrupt.

The three of us, strangers, united by the uncertainty and corruption of today's world stand as if suspended by time, yards away from the entrance to the cemetery. We might as well be miles from our destination, though, because all at once a heavy and thick fog of deceit descends upon us, smothering us, and preventing us from moving any farther.

"He really is her father, then?" and there's a palpable sadness to Ryder's voice.

I brace myself against a nearby tree.

Bill doesn't reply.

"Is he, Bill?" Ryder's voice is now heightened. "Is this man—Dr. Grayson—is he Wren's father?"

Bill lifts his arms in the air as if surrendering and backs up a few paces. "Ryder, I'm sorry. Honestly. I shouldn't have kept this from you, but Claire, she—"

"Just answer the damn question, Bill!" Ryder screams, but it might as well be me demanding the answer.

"Yes. I'm sorry, Ryder, but Dr. Grayson is Wren's father."

And with these words, it's like the entire universe shifts. Dr. Grayson, Wren's father? Could this really be possible? Something about this truth makes sense but doesn't make sense. The memory of Wren's voice from the basement, the many conversations between Cat and me...the two girls' voices jumbling together, indistinguishable from one another. But that would mean—

"Wren and Cat are sisters," I whisper.

15: WREN

By the time Dr. Grayson and I reach the shore of the river, I am exhausted, both mentally and physically. However, my motivation to be once again reunited with my mother keeps my muscles moving. All my life I have wondered what the inside of The Dome is like. I felt drawn to it in some bizarre way, and now that I am one boat ride away, this longing intensifies with the knowledge that my mother is just through its walls.

No additional conversation passes between Dr. Grayson and me as we navigate across the rough waters that days before I thought would lead to my death. That night seems like a lifetime ago.

Every now and again, though, Dr. Grayson turns back to look at me like I'm some sort of ghost he expects to disappear at any minute.

I'm not sure what to make of this doctor. Listening to Abel, I should despise him and all he stands for; however, there's no denying the fact that he saved my life. And his gentleness and concern for me earlier...that can't possibly be an act. Can it? Something tells me that it can.

Approaching the wall of The Dome, it seems to grow even taller and more menacing, and just when I fear we will crash into its concrete sides, a door lifts allowing us to pass right through. Within seconds, we are drifting down a narrow stretch of water in some sort of dimly-lit, underground passageway.

How easy it is, I think, for Dr. Grayson to come and go as he pleases. All of a sudden, life feels entirely unfair. So many of us are struggling to survive on the outside when the privileged members inside can come and go as they need. It's just not right.

Are they so privileged, though? I wonder, remembering the stories Abel told me. About being trapped. About the resurgence of the Virus. About Cat's plight. Maybe life, I think, isn't that much better on the inside after all, and my motivation turns to apprehension. What—other than my mother—will I find on the other side?

Dr. Grayson docks the boat a hundred yards in, where two men wait for him, guns at the ready, backs against the wall of the tunnel. Quickly, Dr. Grayson tosses them the lines, and they tie the boat securely to the awaiting posts. They don't make eye contact but instead behave like soldier drones following unspoken orders, their faces strange blank canvases.

"It's all right," Dr. Grayson tells me, breaking the silence of our travels. He motions for me to stand and exit the boat. I obey because I'm not sure what other choice I have at this point.

Once steady on the dock, I turn to face Dr. Grayson. "What now?" I ask him.

He climbs onto the steel planks beside me and places his hand on the small of my back.

"How about I take you somewhere you can clean up and get some rest?" he asks, urging me forward.

"I'm not tired," I lie.

Dr. Grayson stares at me a moment, pursing his lips as though coming to the conclusion of some hidden internal struggle, and nods. "So you say, Corrine. But I can't take you to see your mother in the state you're in."

I look down at my torn and bloodied clothes, and I understand immediately what Dr. Grayson means. My mother would never forgive herself if she saw me like this.

So we walk, Dr. Grayson and I, through the tunnel that leads us, I assume, into The Dome, light from the walls reflecting off the waters in an eerie iridescent dance.

When we reach the end of the underground passageway, the canal waters seem to disappear beneath the wall, and we turn right into an alcove where we are greeted with a large metal door. Here, Dr. Grayson scans his wrist, and for the first time, I notice the bracelet he wears. It seems to allow him to enter otherwise restricted locations, and I vow to find a way to get one myself.

We travel up one, two, three, four floors before stopping, and the elevator doors open to reveal the most beautiful foyer I have ever seen. Even with only the lights from the elevator illuminating the space, I can see the rich plushness of the oriental carpet, the vaulted ceilings, the crystal chandelier, mirrors everywhere. I gasp. Dr. Grayson chuckles.

"Lovely, isn't it?"

I don't know how to respond. Again, I feel Dr. Grayson's hand on the small of my back, and I step off the elevator. As I do, lights all around us flicker on, and I cry out, "Oh!"

This makes Dr. Grayson chuckle again. "So much you've missed out on," he says sincerely. "The lights, they are activated by your presence, by your movement. Go on," he urges. "Walk. You'll see."

As I head down the luxurious hallway of mirrors, lights turn on and off like lightning in a faraway storm—silent yet illuminating.

"Where is everyone?" I whisper.

"Asleep," Dr. Grayson answers simply.

We take another elevator up even higher, stopping on floor nine. Near the end of yet another hallway, Dr. Grayson stops at a pair of doors. He hesitates a moment, then scans his bracelet. I hear the click of the lock disengaging. Dr. Grayson pushes open the door on the left and holds it for me.

I walk past him so slowly, I think I can hear him breathing. I look once more into his eyes, and the reverence is back. Who is this man? I find myself wondering again. And what is his connection to me? To my mother? He tilts his head toward the room, and I continue past Dr. Grayson into the large space.

Once again, the injustice of the world strikes me like a slap to the face. The four-poster bed covered in thick blankets of silk, the draperies covering the windows, so tall they appear to reach all the way to the ceiling, the carpet my shoes sink immediately into...*my shoes*! Without hesitating, I bend to take off my boots covered in mud and grime.

Dr. Grayson places a warm hand on my shoulder, and I stand back up, my eyes blurring.

"It's fine," he whispers. "Leave them there. I'll get them later."

"I've never seen anything so...so *rich*," I admit.

Dr. Grayson opens his mouth to say something but then changes his mind.

We stand there in silence for a moment, Dr. Grayson looking at me as though afraid I am just a figment of his imagination, that if he were to close his eyes and open them again, I'd be gone.

"The washroom is through there," Dr. Grayson says, pointing to another large door in the far right corner of the room. "There are toiletries, a robe.

Please make yourself comfortable, Corrine." He seems to hang on my name for a bit too long like it doesn't quite fit in his mouth.

When I don't make to move toward the bathroom, Dr. Grayson turns to leave. With his hand on the door, his back to me, he says, "I'll be back with some clean clothes later. Do see that you get some rest." Then he's gone, the door closing in his wake.

There's a faint click as the door closes, and I hurry back to the heavy door and reach for the doorknob, knowing what I'll find when I attempt to turn it. Still, I try anyway, and for the third time in less than a week, I find myself a prisoner yet again.

16: CAT

After leaving the lab, retrieving my identification bracelet from its hiding spot, and all but throwing Mikaela's on the reception desk with a rushed, "Thanks!" I make my way to the cemetery. My feet have a mind of their own, leading me to the very place where I buried my mother's treasures.

The three locked doors. Mr. Jingles. A possible cure. Everything is jumbled up inside my head.

"What do I do?" I ask the sky, my mother, anyone who is listening. Then, when I don't get an answer, I blanket my face with my hands and begin to sob.

I have no one, I think miserably.

No one.

I am utterly and sadly alone. Alone with the knowledge that the one person in charge of The Community's safety, Dr. Grayson, my father, is lying—has been lying—about, well, everything.

So how, then, do I stop him?

I break into his office, that's how I tell myself. But bypassing his security, as I found out today, is going to prove no small feat.

Then it dawns on me.

There is one person—*was* one person, I think—who I am sure at some point had access to Dr. Grayson's office. The one person he was supposed to have cherished until death.

Sienne Grayson. My mother. Dr. Grayson's once-beloved wife.

But she's dead, I remind myself. Who knows what has become of her identification bracelet? It's not as though we're accepting applicants to join The Community, so the bracelets wouldn't be recycled in that way. Then what happened to them when their owners died? Were they tossed out with the bodies? Incinerated? Melted into nothing?

I inhale deeply, sitting back against the great wall that marks the end of The Community. I know what I have to do, but there is no part of me that wants to do it. I'm not sure how long I sit there, my back pressed up against the cool concrete. But after a while, when I finally feel I am able, I pull myself to a standing position, and, facing the closing darkness of the evening, vow that first thing tomorrow morning, I will make my way to the incinerator. Once there, I will see for myself whether anything at all remains of my mother. Or if everything, every trace of her, has been turned to ash as I fear.

Forge ahead, I think. Then I spit on the ground, set my shoulders, and make my way from the cemetery.

•   •   •   •   •

Early the next morning, while waiting for the incinerator doors to open, my plans take a dramatic turn, and I have to admit, part of me is just fine with this.

The incinerator, which happens to be directly next door to Dr. Grayson's office, his lab, and my Microbiology class, is dark as pitch when I arrive, the sad and lonely workers who run the place having not yet arrived. I try my identification bracelet, but I know before I do that it won't work. Nevertheless, I attempt to turn the handle. Just as I expect: locked up tight.

I still haven't quite worked out what I plan to say as my excuse for visiting the incinerator; however, the employees, whose job is disposing of the deceased, aren't exactly what I would describe as conversational. My guess is they won't put up much of a fuss if any about my presence. I am Catherine Grayson, after all.

While I wait, sitting impatiently on the sidewalk curb, my feet fidgeting, a whirring noise from off to my right startles me. I look up, half expecting to see overzealous students passing through the academic building's door, heading to class early to get a jump start on labs. Hopeful overachievers as I once was. What I see, however, makes me do a double take. Because even though it's early and the lights of The Community are muted, it's not too dim to mask the lone figure who exits the building now and makes his way purposefully across the commons of The Community.

I can tell immediately by his gait that it's Dr. Grayson. I had, after all, spent the better part of my early adolescent years idolizing the man.

He doesn't see me as I abruptly jump to my feet and duck behind the building, keeping my eyes glued to him as he moves hurriedly down the street. His head is bent in thought, a large duffle bag slung over his right shoulder.

160

It's clear to me where he's heading: the expansive and swanky hotel he and the other important members of The Community call home, and even though I realize this means I am free to explore the dark, broiling depths of the incinerator without fear of being found out, I choose to follow Dr. Grayson instead. There's something about the way he moves—with obvious intent—that makes me think his destination is more important than breaking into his office.

I stick close to the buildings, letting Dr. Grayson have the street. There are very few people out at this hour—most shops haven't opened their doors yet—but there are just enough members of The Community meandering through the commons to blow my cover if I'm seen.

I glance at my wrist. It's a quarter past six o'clock. The sun is just beginning to climb above the dome of our world, but still, its warm glow sheds hues of gold over everything it touches. Odd. Dr. Grayson, once at work, usually stays until the early hours of the following day, breaking only for "emergencies" like chasing down his defiant daughter in a cemetery. In fact, wracking my brain, I can't for the life of me remember a time that I have *ever* seen my father out in the commons during the daylight hours.

I used to joke with my mother that my father was a vampire. This was, of course, when I still considered Dr. Grayson a member of our family.

Something clearly is on his mind this morning, though.

It takes only minutes to reach the grand hotel that stands tall against The Community's wall like a sovereign soldier, and from around the side of a smaller nearby building, I watch Dr. Grayson scan his bracelet and push his way through the large revolving doors that lead into the lobby. I glance fleetingly at my own identification cuff, but I'm not worried about restricted access. Dr. Grayson lives in a public building, which, if I'm being honest, is a hell of a great way to maintain civilian trust. Whatever Dr. Grayson's been hiding, hasn't been here at the hotel.

Until now, I think.

I watch from the outside as he makes his way to the elevators and punches a button. I'm too far away to tell which floor he will be landing on. As soon as the metal doors close on him, however, I make my way into the lobby and jog over to the elevators, watching the numbers climb from floor to floor.

It stops at nine. The top floor. The penthouse. This is where Dr. Grayson lives. I know because I've been there a few times. When in my mind, he was still my father and not some mad, neglectful scientist.

I'm just about to push the button indicating *Up* when a hand lands heavily on my shoulder. I'm so surprised, I gasp.

"Cat, I'm so sorry to frighten you!"

Ugh. Don.

I turn and offer him a smile that I can feel looks fake. He returns it all the same, but the smile doesn't reach his eyes that instead reflect concern.

"You never returned the rented Off-Load," he tells me simply. "I'm assuming it no longer has a charge—"

"Don, I'm sorry," and my sigh of relief is a bit too loud. *I can handle* this, I think. "My mother's illness, her death—I just forgot. Really." I place my hand on his, hoping that he'll remove it from my shoulder.

He doesn't.

"I'm sorry," I say again, lifting his hand this time. "I'll be sure to return it as soon as I can. I can't imagine anyone has missed it."

Don lets his hand fall to his side, but he doesn't say anything. I shake my head, crossing my arms over my chest. I don't have time for this.

"Listen—"

"No, Cat. *You* listen," Don says, cutting me off, and there's a sudden cold and commanding tone to his voice that is so unlike anything I've ever heard from Don, it locks me in my place. He looks over his shoulder to make sure no one else is in earshot before he whispers next, "If your father catches you here, there's going to be trouble."

Please, I think. Tell me something I don't already know.

"Go home," Don continues. "Take care of yourself. Don't worry about what your father's doing. It's all for your—"

I can't help laughing aloud haughtily. "Protection?" I almost shout then lower my voice. "You think he cares about me? About you? About any of us?" With this, I lean over and all but punch the *Up* button for the elevator. "Don, do yourself a favor," I chide, "and mind your own business."

It's uncharacteristic of me to be so cruel with words, but I am beyond frustrated now.

Don, not heeding my advice, continues, his voice a frantic whisper. "Cat, there are things going on here that you simply *don't* understand."

At first, I am shocked that Don, my mother's dear childhood friend, could be involved with Dr. Grayson's dark side. But quickly, my shock and frustration morph into rage. I turn on him just as the elevator reaches the ground floor.

"Oh, I understand, all right," I manage to say through gritted teeth. "I understand that people in The Community continue to die, and people like

Dr. Grayson—people like *you* apparently—aren't exactly doing all you can to stop it."

Ding. The elevator doors open behind me, and I back onto the lift with two large strides, my eyes still locked on Don's as the doors slide shut with a soft *whoosh*.

Alone in the elevator, I lean heavily against the back wall. First Dr. Grayson and now Don. My mother trusted Don. But obviously Don and possibly many others are as much involved in Dr. Grayson's plot as Dr. Grayson is himself.

What is going on here?

After a minute, I realize that I haven't yet indicated my desired destinition, and before the door of the elevator can open again, I quickly press the circle indicating floor eight. I figure once on this floor, I can take the stairs, so I'll not be seen if Dr. Grayson happens to be in the hallways when the doors open.

I have seen only two floors of this grand hotel, the ground floor and Dr. Grayson's, so when the door opens up into the hallway, and I step out onto the cool marble floor, I am a bit taken aback. All I have seen of this hotel has been soft, warm, cozy. This floor, however, feels terribly cold.

I scan the corridor. There are rows and rows of doors, of course. It's a hotel, after all. But these doors seem more substantial, nameplates beside each one. When I'm close enough to read them, it begins to make sense.

Patrolman 10567. I move to the next. Patrolman 10568.

So this is where the members of the wall patrol live. *This is where Abel would have lived*, I think. And then, because I am not sure, I wonder, *Is he here now?* My heart races with apprehensive uneasiness. Of course, there's no way to know if Abel is, in fact, one of Dr. Grayson's patrolmen relocated here as the names on the door aren't names, but the thought excites me for many opposing reasons nevertheless.

I let it go for now and turn toward the stairs. I'll have to figure out Abel's whereabouts later. For now, I need to focus my attention on Dr. Grayson and what he's up to.

Once in the stairwell, I climb slowly, my hands sliding up the railing. And when I'm standing on the landing for the ninth floor, it takes me many minutes to muster up the courage to push open the door, my heart hammering in my chest.

Carefully, with the door cracked, I peek my head through and scan the hallway. There's no one as far as my eyes can tell. I listen, but other than the sound of my breathing, so loud I worry someone will hear me, there is only silence, so I step out onto the plush carpet of the penthouse floor.

Every two rooms, there is a shallow alcove with a beautiful arrangement of artificial plants, a mirror, and a light fixture, so I cross the wide hallway and begin to slide down the far side of the wall, where I can quickly duck out of sight if a door opens.

I know Dr. Grayson's room number. 916. It's at the end of the hall in the opposite direction of the stairs, so I have quite a bit of ground to cover without being seen. I have no idea which of Dr. Grayson's team resides on this same floor, but if I had to guess, none of them would be alarmed to see me. They also wouldn't be thrilled as Dr. Grayson's disdain for his one daughter isn't exactly a secret. The thought of getting caught now revs up my anxiety tenfold, and this anxiety is almost enough to make me turn around. To head back to the incinerator like I originally planned.

But then I hear the voices. Two voices. One clearly Dr. Grayson's. The other one is female.

Now, two things immediately shock me about this. The first being that my mother is only days dead. I find it difficult to believe that even Dr. Grayson, as frigid and heartless as he has become, would be so callous as to have a new girlfriend. Secondly, my father hasn't cared about *anyone*—let alone a woman—other than himself in too many years to count.

So then who is she?

Slowly, I inch closer to room 916, but when I'm one room away, I stop abruptly, nearly falling over. The voices are not, I realize, coming from Dr. Grayson's room but the one *next door.*

But it isn't this revelation that halts my feet dead in their tracks. It isn't the fact that I'm actually terrified to be so near to what I believe are the answers to so many of my recently developed questions. It's the fact that this voice, the voice of the mystery girl within the room, sounds oddly familiar, like listening to your own recorded voice played back but not believing that it's *you,* all the while knowing that it is.

Because the voice belonging to the girl talking to Dr. Grayson just through the hotel door...it's mine.

Shock momentarily cements me to the floor, my eyes wide and breathing halted, but when I do regain a sliver of composure, my thoughts drive me to flee. Back down the hallway and down the stairs, not wanting to wait for the elevator. Not wanting to know what—or *who*—lies beyond the doors of room 914.

I feel as though I've gone temporarily insane, and it hits me: Don was right. There are too many things I don't understand. My mother's death. Mr. Jingles. Dr. Grayson's secrets.

What the hell has he done?

17: WREN

Rap, rap, rap!

When the persistent knock comes at my door early the next morning, at first, I don't hear it. Finally clean and presented with an over-sized, luxurious bed, I had fallen fast and hard into a deep sleep. No dreams. Thankfully, no nightmares either.

Upon waking and hearing the frantic sound, however, I am immediately transported back in time to the morning my mother went missing.

I bolt upright, panicked, the thin shoulder strap of the nightgown I found hung behind the bathroom door slipping from my shoulder. Ignoring this, I rub my eyes, attempting to clear away the sleep that still clouds them. *Where the hell am I?*

When the knock comes again more fervently this time, my gaze turns toward the enormous door that is difficult to make out because the room is so dark, the blinds pulled tight. I shimmy from the bed, the sheets a tangled mess at my feet, and sink my bare feet into the plush carpet. To collect my thoughts and my bearings, I bend my forehead to my knees and breathe heavily. In and out. In and out. With each exhale, the fog obscuring my thoughts slowly lifts, and my memories of last night return.

Dr. Grayson brought me here, I remember. Told me he had my mother. Then locked me in. He *locked* me in. *So why is he knocking when he knows I can't open the damn door?*

Fear seizes me, my heart pounding. *What if it's not Dr. Grayson? What if it's someone else? What if it's one of the men from the bridge?* After all I've recently been through, I'm not sure my will can survive another attack. I feel extremely fragile like I might literally split in two. If it's not Dr. Grayson, I don't know what I'll do. *Well, there's only one way to find out.*

Heart still racing, I stand, make my way over to the door, and, standing on tiptoe, trying not to make a sound, I look through the peephole. Sure enough, it's Dr. Grayson standing alone in the hotel corridor, looking serious and a bit harassed, a medium-size duffle bag thrown over his shoulder. My relief is tangible, and, without taking my eyes from the lone figure in the hallway, I try the door handle. Jiggle it. It's still locked from the outside. Hearing my futile attempt to open the door, Dr. Grayson's head jerks upward.

His eyes! Startled, I leap backward away from his powerful stare, and immediately, the door is opened, quickly closed, and Dr. Grayson and I are standing face to face in the now not-quite-big-enough hotel room.

We remain locked in our positions for an uncomfortable moment, he and I, watching each other intensely. The only sound the heavy breaths we both take.

Dr. Grayson is the first to break the silence.

"Corrine, you look—"

I stop him there, reminding him, "My name is Wren." I hadn't gone by my full given name since the Great Divide when the doors to The Dome were closed, and my mother and I forced to flee. We were just getting settled in our new camp when my mother jokingly called me Wren for the first time, chiding that I was like a baby bird anxious to leave the nest but not yet ready to fly. Apparently, I had been a difficult child to keep an eye on. The nickname stuck. I wasn't about to let it go.

"Of course, of course," he says, not taking his eyes off mine. "Well, Wren, sleep has done you some good." With a jolt, I remember how scantily I am dressed and wrap my arms tightly across my body, attempting to conceal as much bare skin as possible. Dr. Grayson, recognizing my discomfort, turns away from me as he slides the duffle bag off his shoulder and tosses it onto the bed. "I believe the clothes are all your size and will be to your liking. Take as much time as you need, but do remember, your mother is anxiously waiting to see you." With these words, he lifts his arms, indicating I go change in the bathroom.

"You'll take me to her then? Today?"

"As soon as you're ready. I thought it would be nice if we could all have breakfast together." The intonation of his voice when he says the word *nice* arouses my suspicions. And when he speaks, it's almost as though Dr. Grayson is studying me, the way his eyes are so serious. Like he's gauging my reactions, trying to read me like a textbook. It makes me feel exposed.

I open my mouth to respond but change my mind, wanting desperately to get out of the skimpy nightgown and go see my mother. I turn, grab the duffle bag, and close myself into the bathroom. Instinctively, I go to lock the door but see there is no lock on the inside—*figures*—, so I push the piece of substantial furniture, housing the ridiculously unnecessary supply of extra towels, in front of the door. I can't be sure, but I think I hear Dr. Grayson chuckle.

I place the duffle bag onto the counter and start to unzip it but stop, raising my eyes to the large mirror that hangs above the sink. What I see makes me gasp. Of course, it's me in the reflection, but it's not me at the same time. I'm different somehow. Less rugged. Sleep *has* done me a world of good, though my eyes are still haunted. I reach my left hand up to stroke my characteristically unruly blond hair and almost can't believe it. The shampoo has worked a miracle. I actually almost smile because instead of encountering an obstacle of stubborn tangles, when I run my fingers through my hair now, the short soft waves are actually smooth as silk. As I had gone to sleep with it still damp, I hadn't noticed.

For a moment I wonder what Ryder would think if he could see me now.

I sigh heavily, repressing the depressing thought, and begin to sift through the bag. All of the clothing is made of incredibly light and soft material, dainty. *Girly,* I think. It's nothing like what I would wear back at camp. *Then again, I'm not in camp anymore, am I?* I have absolutely no idea what the weather temperature is like now that I'm *inside.*

I opt for a pair of light-weight jeans that I slip carefully over my still-bandaged leg and a simple blue T-shirt. When I look once more at my reflection, my already deep blue eyes seem even bluer.

You clean up good, girl, I imagine Ryder saying with his silly accent, but the thought doesn't make me smile. I sit down on the lip of the large tub and rock gently back and forth, not ready to face Dr. Grayson just yet. There's something about him...something almost phony. I want to trust him. I want to believe he's going to take me to my mother. He did, after all, save my life. Plus, my mother must have some logical reason to come back to him. She must.

Then again, I can't just forget about the strange men on the bridge, how evil they had felt. And the way they looked at me....

Was Dr. Grayson their boss? If so, why would he be happy to see *me?* And why would this occurrence on the bridge make my mother run?

I know the answer is right in front of my face, but I can't quite figure it out. It's incredibly frustrating. With one final, heavy sigh, I set my shoulders, stand, and clear the barricade. *It's now or never,* I tell myself and let myself out of the bathroom.

Dr. Grayson has made the bed and is sitting at the desk in the corner, where he closely monitors a type of holographic screen of images that hover in the air in front of his face. When he hears me, he quickly presses a button on the desk and the scenes disappear.

Again, Dr. Grayson gives me an intense once over that makes me uncomfortable. He walks back into the bathroom and comes back with a hooded sweatshirt. "Put this on," he says, and I wonder briefly if this is his attempt to keep me hidden or protect me. My gut tells me to dismiss the latter. Once I have the lightweight jacket on, he fits the hood over my head and then nods as though pleased, stands, and moves toward the door. When I don't immediately follow, he says, "Aren't you coming?"

Something stirs inside me. It takes only a second for me to recognize it as fear. A voice inside my head pleads with me not to go with this man. *Run! There's just too much you still don't know,* it screams. So standing my ground, I ask, "How do you know my mother?"

Dr. Grayson, facing the door, his hand on the knob, doesn't turn around. "This conversation can wait until the three of us are reunited." The authority to his voice should be enough for me to acquiesce, but there's something about the word he uses: *reunited.* It doesn't quite make sense. Unless—

"How do you know my mother?" I ask him again, shifting from one foot to the other in a kind of nervous dance.

"Corrine—"

"Wren," I say through clenched teeth. Dr. Grayson laughs. It infuriates me. "My mother," I say, "she knew you once. Before the Virus. Before The Great Divide. Am I right?" Still, Dr. Grayson keeps his back to me, which all but gives me my answer. I marinate on this for a moment, the wheels in my head spinning. Dr. Grayson remains locked in his place. *Reunited.* "Does this mean...does this mean that you knew me too?"

Dr. Grayson's reaction to my last question is so abrupt, I don't have time to move out of his way. Within seconds, he's in my face, his strong hands gripping my shoulders, and I cry out in shock and pain. My gentle savior from the previous day is gone, replaced by a mad man, his green eyes wild with fury.

"Your mother is waiting," Dr. Grayson growls. "Shall we go?"

It's not exactly a question, but I nod vigorously.

Keeping his strong hold on my shoulder, he urges me awkwardly to the door then pushes me out. As we head down the hallway of the hotel, I silently beg someone to open a door...any door. If only someone could see me with this man, I think, then I'll be ok. But the corridor is deserted, eerily quiet. So quiet, in fact, that when Dr. Grayson punches the button summoning the elevator, I jump. Dr. Grayson's grip on my shoulder tightens.

Once the elevator doors have closed, he releases me, and I fall back against the wall. "You didn't have to do that," I say meekly, rubbing my aching shoulder.

Dr. Grayson doesn't look at me, but I see his chest rise and fall heavily. "Corrine, you need to understand that I don't *want* to hurt you. You are important to me. As is your mother." He pauses, rubbing his temple as though this conversation is giving him a headache. "But I need you to listen. Follow directions. Time is not on our side. Do you understand?"

I don't, but whisper, "Yes," anyway.

"Good. Now, when the doors to the elevator open," his words roll off his tongue slowly, almost lazily, like he is talking to a small child, "we are going to be underground. Beneath The Community. We will travel to our next location this way. You are not to be seen. Do you understand, Corrine?"

I don't bother to correct him this time but instead answer again with, "Yes."

Once we're walking through the dimly lit tunnel beneath what Dr. Grayson calls The Community, I find myself coming back to my conscious senses. Like my mother, Dr. Grayson has ordered me to remain unseen. But why? To protect me or to hide what it is that he is involved in? *Am I in real danger here?* I wonder. *Is my mother?*

When it seems as though we've been walking forever, Dr. Grayson and I come to a pair of giant steel doors with a rather large and ominous sign bolted to the center of the left side: *Do Not Enter. Authorized Personnel ONLY.* The combination of red and black on white seems sinister, and I'm not sure I want to know what's through these doors.

My mother is, I tell myself, and I feel a fragment of my resolve return.

Dr. Grayson, lifting his wrist to the scanner, easily disarms the lock, pulls open the heavy door, and holds it open for me to pass through. Despite my persistent feelings of alarm, this time I don't hesitate to do as Dr. Grayson says but instead make my way slowly across the threshold and into yet another empty corridor, lights flickering on ahead with each of my forward steps.

When I'm just about twenty paces in, Dr. Grayson grabs my arm, and I'm yanked backwards, caught off guard. "We're taking the steps this time," he says, pulling me toward another metal door I hadn't noticed. When we're through, and it closes behind us, the sound echoes around the stairwell like a hammer hitting its target, growing fainter with each passing blow. When the sound finally stops, it's so quiet, I'm almost afraid to breathe. I certainly don't plan to speak, but Dr. Grayson has other intentions.

"Your hair," he says, breaking the agonizing silence, "you keep it short."

I don't know what to say but find myself bringing my hand up to touch the hoodie that covers my shoulder-length locks.

Dr. Grayson continues speaking when it's clear I'm not going to respond. "I suppose it's easier that way on the outside, no?"

We move up another two flights.

"Has life been difficult for you? Have you been educated?"

The suggested insult propels me to answer this time. "Of course I have been *educated*," I say a little louder than I had anticipated. "My mother—"

Dr. Grayson, who is a few steps above me, raises his arm laughing. "I know, I know! Of course, your mother would have seen to it that you were. I just had to ask. You know, Corrine, I have to admit, I do love your fire. It is quite unexpected."

I want to ask, *What* did *you expect of me?* But I keep my mouth shut. We seem to have reached our destination anyway as Dr. Grayson has paused on the sixth-floor platform, and, being so close to what I believed to be impossible just days before, my thoughts are now only of my mother.

I am so anxious, I nearly plow past Dr. Grayson who, once again unlocks the door to the next—and hopefully final—hallway of our journey using the device encircling his wrist. I feel like a caged animal about to taste my long-awaited freedom when Dr. Grayson again grabs my shoulder forcibly and hisses in my ear. "You talk to no one, Corrine. Understand? If someone talks to you, nod in response. Do not answer any questions. In fact, try to keep your head down." He lets my shoulder go, but I feel his palm press into the small of my back to guide me. Or to keep me under control.

I'm so afraid that something will go wrong right now that I have every intention to follow Dr. Grayson's orders. The thought of *anything* preventing me from being reunited with my mother at this point sinks my heart to my stomach.

Reunited.

Dr. Grayson said earlier that he would wait to answer my questions once we were all—my mother, Dr. Grayson, and me—reunited. Which clearly implies he knew me once. That I knew him. *Were they old colleagues?* I wonder.

Traveling slowly and awkwardly down the hallway, Dr. Grayson and I run into a handful of men, some traveling in pairs, all dressed in similar dark suits and white lab coats. They nod courteously at us but don't seem at all concerned that there's a stranger in their presence. Odd. All of it. Dr. Grayson's abruptly shifting demeanor, the demands to go unnoticed, and now the men who don't balk at my company.

When we reach the end of the hallway, Dr. Grayson scans his bracelet and opens the door to an impressive office. He coaxes me in with the palm of his hand and guides me over to a really-comfortable-looking leather couch.

"Sit here," he tells me and waits for me to listen before walking across the expansive office that I see through the windows overlooks the almost-surreal world within The Dome. He stops at the door to the adjoining room, hesitates, and then quickly disappears beyond, the lock clicking with a sound of finality as the door closes behind him.

Once he's gone, I remove my jacket, dropping it onto the back of the couch, and make my way over to the wall of windows as though in a trance. What I see beyond takes my breath away, and for a moment, my apprehension dissolves into utter awe. It's beautiful. Foliage of every color surrounds what appears to be a type of courtyard. And the sky! A perfect robin's-egg blue. A handful of people scurry across the streets, exiting and entering buildings, like little marching ants with purpose. It reminds me of the time before the Virus, and I am overcome with immense longing.

Voices from the adjoining room suddenly shatter my reverie, and I'm brought back to my current, disconcerting reality.

Leaving the enchanting view behind, I creep across the office space and lean my ear against the cool wood of the door, listening. I can just make out what the voices are saying.

"It was for her own good, Claire. She would have died out there. Searching for you. And I couldn't let that happen." Dr. Grayson. And his voice is gravely serious.

A sound of a chair scraping across the floor is followed by a voice I would know anywhere. My mother. "Let me see her, Scott," she says angrily. "Let me see her *now*."

Without thinking, I begin jiggling the handle frantically, and then, when it registers that the door is locked and I won't be getting in on my own, I start to pound on the wood with such force I think it might splinter. "Mom!" I scream. "Mom! Open the door! It's me, Wren! Mom please—"

There is more shuffling of furniture, mixed with my mother's enraged reply to my shouting, "Scott, she's here? You brought her *here?*"

"Claire—"

But Dr. Grayson doesn't finish his sentence because the door separating me from my mother opens, and with a force that is undeniably driven by the inherent bond between a mother and her child, we fall into each other's embrace sobbing.

18: RYDER

I have to admit, when we finally make it to the cemetery after The Great Sister Revelation, I more than half expect our plan to hit a major snag. After all, this shady Dr. Grayson character continues to be ten steps ahead of us all and perfectly capable of manipulating the situation for his benefit.

He's also apparently quite the cheating dirtbag.

Why shouldn't I, then, assume the worst? That this miracle rock Abel managed to dislodge just days ago in order to escape has since been cemented back into place?

Imagine my surprise when shortly after we arrive at the cemetery wall I watch as Abel easily pushes aside the stone to reveal a hole just large enough for us all to crawl through. I almost laugh out loud but throwing a quick glance in Bill's direction makes me stifle it. *Well, maybe not* all *of us*, I think.

Abel, now standing, attempts to dust his hands off on his filthy cargo pants and presents to Bill and me this gift as though anticipating applause. I don't flinch. "You first," I say, and when a look of disappointment crosses his face, I add, "This is your rodeo. How are we supposed to know you're not walking us straight into a trap?"

Abel sighs heavily. "Man, I thought we were past all that," he says, clearly frustrated. "You want to rescue Wren, don't you? Well, she's through that rabbit hole. So, Ry*der*, you're just going to have to swallow your tough-man facade and trust me on this."

I don't like the way he emphasizes the final syllable of my name. He sounds like a smartass. "You first," I repeat, and Abel, shrugging, gets to his knees and shimmies through the hole within seconds. Once he disappears through the wall, I get to my knees and scout out what I can see of the cemetery through the small opening. Abel waits over by a giant cage of sorts, looking around suspiciously. The sun is just starting to creep above the horizon, casting this new world in a soft golden haze. And while the morning air outside the wall is cool, the breeze escaping through the opening feels degrees warmer.

I back up and climb to my feet. "What do you think?" I ask Bill. "He seems legit, right?"

Beneath the glow of The Dome, Bill looks apologetic. "Listen, Ryder, I'm sorry I didn't tell you about Wren. Claire...she made me promise, and she *never* said anything about a sister."

I'm not really in the forgiving mood at the moment, so I simply say, "It doesn't matter. I know now. We're all on the same page."

"Are we?" Bill asks.

I glance toward the narrow hole in the wall. "I think we can trust Abel. Besides, what other choice do we have?"

Bill's face is stricken. "It's not Abel I'm worried about," he says seriously, and I know he's worried I've lost my faith in him. After a quiet, thoughtful moment, however, Bill's tone turns lighter. "I'm more concerned about the size of that hole."

Despite the situation, I can't help but laugh. After all, Bill is the only father figure I've had growing up in camp. He might be a pain in the ass at times, but he's still family. "Oh, you're greasy enough at this point, you'll just slide right through," I tell him, but I'm not sure I believe a word of it. "How 'bout you go first. If I have to, I'll push, and Abel can pull. We'll get you through one way or the other."

Bill doesn't look convinced, but, mumbling something unintelligible, gets level with the hole to investigate it for himself before taking in a large breath and blowing it all out loudly. Then, before he can change his mind, he sticks first both his arms and then his head through the hole in the wall.

After some grunting, cursing, and sweating, we manage to get Bill's large frame through to the other side, torn clothes and all, and when it's my turn, I find the close space of the hole a bit unnerving but easy enough to slide through on my own.

Once we're all standing in the cemetery, a moment of reverie passes, Bill and I taking in the vast cemetery covered—and I mean covered—with crumbling gravestones and markers of various sizes. It's unlike anything I have ever seen before, and I am awed to my core. I can tell Bill is too.

Abel, on the other hand, seems to be recounting a memory or dream of some sort, his face blanketed in what I think is sadness. Using his foot, he haphazardly kicks the stone back into place with some effort and heads down the winding, paved path that snakes its way down into the center of the cemetery. "Come on," he says, his back to us. "The sun is almost up. The

Community members will be waking soon, and we need to keep you two hidden from view as long as we can."

I glance down at my clothing. "You know, Abel, you don't look much better."

"You're right," he says. "But these people *know* me, remember? It's a small world here in The great Community," he says, holding out his arms, not hiding his note of contempt. "Everybody knows everybody. And that means they won't know you."

The three of us continue walking in silence until we reach a towering wall of ivy that does its best to shroud the imposing fence that rises from the ground.

When he notices Bill and me staring at the chain links in disbelief, Abel says, "Don't worry. There's a loose piece of fence just over there." He points a little farther up ahead. "We can walk right through. Easily. Bill, too."

"Well, that's good to know," Bill mumbles.

"Look, guys," Abel continues seriously, "Getting across the square isn't going to be a walk in the park. We need to keep close to buildings, which means it's going to take us nearly twice as long to get up the hill to Cat's. I'd say it's a good three or four miles, so by the time we get close, the sun will be up and people will be out and about."

I reach around to feel for the cool gun that rests against my hip, and it ignites my courage. "I'm not worried about being seen," I say.

Abel's face goes rigid. "The people here aren't violent, Ryder," he tells me seriously. "They're just as innocent and in the dark as I am. As the two of you claim to be. Dr. Grayson and his men are your targets. Not them. I won't take you to safety unless you can guarantee you'll leave the people of The Community alone. Just stay out of sight, ok? If you're seen, these people, they'll want to run *from you*. They won't want to attack. They will, however, make enough of a scene that we'll be caught. And if we're caught, then you, me, Bill, the girls...we're all as good as dead."

"Ok," I tell him simply, and I mean it. All I want is to find Wren and Claire and get the hell out of this mess of a world. If staying out of sight is what I need to do, then I'll do it. Heck, between avoiding raiders like Wes and drinking rust-flavored water, this should be a cake walk.

"Ok," Abel repeats.

"Ok," Bill adds for good measure, and with no more time wasted, Abel leads us through the fence and into his so-called community.

At first, I'm not impressed. There doesn't seem to be anything fancy or new about this place. In fact, the roads are worn cobblestones and the houses dark and empty. It feels sad...deserted...and not at all how I envisioned it.

Once we get closer to the square, however, the setting starts to transform entirely. The pathetic excuses for houses are replaced by taller, sleeker, and swankier buildings. The landscapes are colorful and well-manicured, meticulous even. Too perfect.

I've never seen anything like it, not even in the deepest and happiest corners of my memories.

"It's still early," Abel whispers, inching down the road that has become smooth pavement lined with equally spaced and identical shrubs, "just after six. The early birds will be out and about soon—"

Abel stops short, holding out his arms, indicating Bill and I do the same.

"What is it?" Bill, just about to bump into me, whispers a little too close to my ears.

I nudge him away. "I don't know," I say.

"Shhh!" Abel is now crouched near the base of the building nearest us on our left, looking around the corner at something. I move up behind him, but he frantically waves me back. I groan in protest. It's more than frustrating for me to be kept out of the loop, and I fidget from one foot to the other with anticipation.

"What's going on?" Bill asks again, which exacerbates my irritation. I don't answer him. "Does he see something?"

Abel mumbles something I don't quite catch and then turns to face Bill and me. The look on his face is one of pure perplexion. "I can't believe it," he says. "I don't know what I expected, but it's so uncharacteristic. I didn't think—" Here he pauses, his look of confusion morphing into fear.

"What *is* it?" I whisper.

"Dr. Grayson," Abel responds quietly, deep in thought. "He's on the move."

"So what do we do?" I ask.

"Head to Cat's. If Dr. Grayson is using precious time to abandon his lab, then there's definitely something shady going on."

"We should follow him!" I say.

Abel shakes his head. "Are you crazy?"

"He could lead us straight to Wren. And to Claire. You said so yourself, this behavior is uncharacteristic for Dr. Grayson. Have you considered that maybe he's traveling so early in the day because he doesn't want to be seen? And that he doesn't want to be seen because he's holding two people hostage?" My breaths come out ragged. I feel like a wrongly convicted prisinor who's cell has been left slightly ajar. This is our chance, I just know it, but Abel's on a different mission.

"Look," Abel says, and this time around he sounds truly sympathetic, "you're probably right. And I know how much you want to find Wren. To know she's safe."

"I feel a *but* coming on," Bill grumbles.

"You don't know Dr. Grayson like I do," Abel reminds us. "He's got a plan for everything. If you follow him now? My guess is you'd be walking right into the lion's den."

"I think I can handle a lion," I say, reaching once again for the gun tucked into the waist of my pants.

"So what? You plan to just shoot him dead, then?"

"Why not? He shot Wes in the back of the head. Execution style. Who's to say he won't do the same to us? To Claire and Wren?"

At the mention of the raider's name, Abel's brow furrows with confusion for a fleeting moment, but then he shrugs. "Look, if the two of you want to save Wren and Claire, then you need to listen to me. Not your impulses. You don't know Dr. Grayson like I do. You don't know this community. We should find Cat, get something to eat, and make a plan."

At the mention of food, my stomach rumbles, and as much as I hate to admit it, I know Abel is right. In our current condition, we wouldn't stand a chance against a cockroach, let alone a roach the size of a human. So I swallow every desire that I have to follow Dr. Grayson, stretch out my arm, and say, "Lead the way."

Abel nods and leads us in a roundabout way around the square. By the time we finally reach the hill Abel mentioned earlier, the sun is inching higher across the ceiling of The Dome, bathing the perfect row houses along the street in a bright, warm light, the temperature all the while remaining comfortable. As the three of us keep to the shadows, people of all ages begin to emerge from their front doors and head down the street toward the square, some walking, others riding on machines that resemble stand-up motorcycles.

"Crazy," I mumble to myself. Everyone here seems oddly content, as though they have nothing in the world to fear.

"They don't know," Abel whispers as though reading my thoughts. "They fight every day for a cure that more than likely isn't even possible."

"But they seem so *happy*," I say.

"Forge ahead," Abel says mockingly.

I shrug. "What other choice do they have?"

"Fight," Abel suggests.

"How can they fight something they don't know exists?"

Abel shakes his head and points, apparently done with the conversation. "Cat's house is at the top of this street on the left-side corner. Come on. We're almost there."

Bill, who hasn't uttered a word since leaving the square, grumbles a quiet, "Thank God."

The block of houses lining the street appears to grow taller as we walk up the steep hill, and it spans a little over a quarter of a mile with ten houses all piled on top of one another in a strangely precise way. Cat's house, which sits on the corner, is equally as quaint as all the others, the outside tidy and well manicured like the rest of the yards on her block. But the air around the structure seems colder somehow. I glance to the sky. The sun doesn't quite reach the house, which I notice is oddly tucked back a few feet farther from the road than its surrounding neighbors, basking it in shadows. A shiver travels the course of my spine.

The sound of a front door opening on the quiet street sends us all diving behind a nearby shrub, and I watch as a young girl, who looks to be around eleven or twelve years old, hops down the steps of her row house, bag slung over her shoulder, and heads down the hill by herself.

"That's Sarah. She's probably heading to clinical," Abel whispers. "She's late, but her father started showing symptoms of the Virus a few weeks ago, so she won't be reprimanded. Cat has been walking with her when she can. I'm guessing this means she's not home." I can tell he's trying to convince himself that there's nothing at all amiss with this fact, but there's a note of uneasiness to his tone.

"Come on," Abel says, pushing past me. A branch slaps me in the face, and I flinch.

"Easy!" I complain, but Abel ignores me.

"Let's go around back. Cat keeps the back gate unlocked, and the fence will keep us shielded from view while we wait for her."

Sure enough, when we round the corner and try the gate, it opens with ease, creaking slightly on its hinges. The discordant sound in such a seemingly perfect neighborhood takes me by surprise.

Abel doesn't even wait for the gate to close before he's rounding the back stoop and mounting the stairs. He knocks softly once. Then harder. And harder still until my nerves are shot, and I call out, "Um, I don't think she's home, Abel."

The disappointment on Abel's face when he turns around is palpable. "No," he says with concern, "I don't think she is." He stares off into the small backyard. "I can't believe she'd go to clinical," Abel mutters to himself. "But then again, why wouldn't she?" He descends the steps slowly, deep in thought.

Now that we've reached our destination, I am suddenly acutely aware of my parched throat. "Hey, Abel? There's no chance another one of Cat's doors is unlocked, is there?"

Abel doesn't bother to look at me when he answers. He looks instead to his wrist. "Not without one of these," he says.

I am momentarily confused. "But...you have one."

"It only works where it's been programmed to work," Abel tells me.

"Of course it does," comes Bill's feeble reply from the ground where he collapsed seconds after clearing the gate. I nudge him with the toe of my boot.

"So are we just planning to wait until Cat comes home then?" I ask. "Because we're not even sure she'll be coming home at all—"

The words have hardly left my mouth when the unlocked gate flies open.

"Abel!" a girl's voice cries, and a blur of color jolts past me and throws itself into Abel's arms, almost knocking him over with the force of the embrace. I'm not sure who's more shocked: Abel, Bill, or me.

Bill sits up at the same time that I do a double take. The voice, it's not just *some* girl's. It's Wren's.

"Wren?" Bill's shocked voice breaks apart the embrace. I'm stunned into silence. Even from the back, the hair, the build, the way she stands holding Abel at arm's length as though she's afraid he's not real. It's just like Wren.

The girl, after softly, lovingly brushing her hand through Abel's hair, slowly turns to face Bill and me.

Simultaneously, Bill and I shout, "Wren!" and I'm crossing the small distance of the yard so quickly I don't have time to recognize the of confusion that crosses over her face. Before she can stop me, I'm all over her, hugging her, kissing her.

The slap comes so abruptly, and with such power, for a moment I see stars. I back up three paces, staring at Wren in horror. "What the hell, Wren? What d'ya do that for?" My hand is on my cheek where I can already feel the swelling heat from the impact.

Wren's wiping her face, clearly disgusted. Bill and Abel stare at the scene in front of them, mouths agape. "I don't know who you think you are," she says fiercely, fire in her blue eyes. "And I don't know who you think *I* am.

But my name's not Wren." She looks to Abel for help, but he just shakes his head in disbelief. She turns back to me, and I swear—I *swear*—she must be brainwashed because it is Wren. I blink hard once. But nothing changes.

"Wren—"

"I told you. My name is not Wren. Abel? A little help here," she says.

Abel puts a hand on my arm. "Ryder, are you ok?"

I shrug off his gesture. "Of course I'm ok. *She's* the one who's not ok. What's wrong with her? What did Dr. Grayson do to her?"

"To *who*? To Cat?"

And then it hits me. They're sisters. *Oh, my god. They're sisters.* It finally sinks in that Cat and Wren really do share the same creep of a father. So naturally, they're going to look alike. But exactly alike?

Bill has joined the party and is standing next to me staring at Cat as I try to work this out. "Ryder," he says softly like he's telling me a secret, "she looks exactly like Wren." *Like I hadn't noticed.*

"Yeah, I know," I say, shaking my head slowly.

"But that means—"

"I know what it means," I say, but it's Abel's voice that puts it out in the open for all of us to hear.

"They're twins."

19: CAT

I'm nursing my second cup of tea, my hands loosely fingering the mug that has long grown cold, when the truth of the situation finally comes crashing down on me like a giant wave. Even though I'm sitting at the same counter in the same kitchen that has been a part of my home since I was very little, in this moment I feel like a stranger. Lost. *That about sums it up*, I think. I'm lost. Utterly lost.

In just a matter of days, in fact, I had lost so much of what I once held dear. My mother. My best friend. And not just once. I lost her twice. *Twice.* First, to the clutches of the Virus. Then to the web of lies my father began to spin the moment I was conceived.

"Cat, who'd you get your lion's mane from?"

"Cat, were you adopted?"

"Cat, you're nowhere near as pretty as your mom."

The taunting voices from my childhood come back like a swarm of incessant bees, the words stinging over and over and over again. *It all makes sense now*, I think. I don't look like my beautiful, charming, lovely mother...because she isn't biologically my mother after all. The realization, finally sinking in, carries me out to sea and rocks me, and as I plummet deeper into my ocean of despair, I lose the ability to breathe.

Abel, recognizing my struggle, hurries over to me, placing his strong arms around me tightly. "Cat, it's ok," he says, his voice comforting. "It's going to be ok. Just breathe for me. Please. Just breathe."

I gasp and, finding my voice, cry out, "Abel, my mother. She's not my mother. She—" My voice trails off.

Abel doesn't loosen his grip around my shoulders. "I know," he whispers, his mouth in my hair. "I know, Cat."

"Why?" I cry. "Why would he do this? Why would he lie about this? What was in it for him?" Because there's always *something* in it for Dr. Grayson.

My chest heaves again as I choke on the tears that now flow freely down my face, a river of suppressed grief that spills onto the counter where I rest my head. "Why would *she* lie to me, Abel?"

Abel strokes my face, attempting to wipe away the tears, but they are relentless. "Your mother loved you, Cat. Hold onto that, ok? So she wasn't your mother by blood. That doesn't mean she wasn't your *mother*. She loved you like a daughter. She raised you like her daughter. She protected you—"

I raise my head abruptly, my wet hair matted to my cheek, "And he killed her, Able! Dr. Grayson killed her, and I let him. I let him!" At the thought of my father, my grief morphs into something much stronger, heat bubbling up from my gut and filling my veins. Rage. "We've got to stop him, Abel," I say, my voice resolute. "We've got to stop him for good."

A chair scrapes across the floor to my right as a figure stands. My head instinctively jerks in the direction of the noise. Flooded by emotions, I have completely forgotten about the two strangers from the outside.

"We need to find Wren first," the one named Ryder says. "And Claire." His eyes meet mine briefly before turning his gaze to the floor, his cheeks scarlet.

Of course, I think. Wren and Claire. My sister and my true mother. The idea is so unbelievable that it doesn't seem real, but something about the two names *feels* familiar, like a part of me has always known that something in my life was missing. "I know where Wren is," I say suddenly, the memory of her voice—a voice so much like my own—resurfacing. "Dr. Grayson has her in the hotel near the heart of The Community."

"Are you sure?" Abel asks, incredulously.

I nod. "I heard her, Abel. Just hours ago. I was so close to her, and I had no idea...." My voice trails off.

"He must have been going to see her when we saw him earlier," Abel says.

From his seat, Ryder huffs angrily but says nothing.

"And Claire?" the other stranger, Bill, asks.

I shake my head. "I don't know where Dr. Grayson is keeping her. She could be at the hotel, too. I don't know. I'm sorry." The helplessness that envelops me brings on more tears.

"It's not your fault, Cat," Abel says softly. "None of this is your fault. It's Dr. Grayson's, ok?" Abel embraces me again, and I lean into his chest gratefully, clinging to his T-shirt. I hadn't realized just how badly I missed him.

Ryder clears his throat. "Not to break up this touching reunion, but can we talk about what we're going to do to rescue Wren and Claire?"

I ignore him, another startling revelation from earlier ricocheting through my mind. "Abel!" I cry. "Dr. Grayson's lab. Mr. Jingles. My little pet mouse. He's alive." My words come out broken but with force.

Abel's brow wrinkles with confusion. "Slow down, Cat. What do you mean Mr. Jingles is alive? And what does Dr. Grayson currently have to do with a pet you had when you were little?" I can tell by his over-the-top consoling tone he thinks I must be going crazy.

"I was in Dr. Grayson's lab yesterday—"

"You were *what?*" Abel cuts me off, horrified. "How?"

I wave off his question. "Dr. Grayson has been experimenting on animals," I tell Abel. Ryder mumbles something under his breath. "Most appear to be suffering with horrible symptoms. From the Virus, probably. But not Mr. Jingles. He's alive and seemingly healthy."

"Cat, that's not possible," Abel says.

"I know it's not *supposed* to be possible, Abel. But Mr. Jingles is alive. It's him. There's a detailed log of his existence. I *saw* it."

Abel seems to be doing the math in his head. "That would make him at least ten years old, Cat!"

"Thirteen, actually."

Ryder begins to fidget, tapping his foot impatiently. "This is fascinating and all, but I'm a bit more concerned about Wren and Claire—"

"It's more than fascinating," Abel says, astoundingly, cutting Ryder off. "What you're insinuating, Cat, is that Dr. Grayson has found a way to prolong life."

"And stop the Virus, Abel. The charts indicate that Mr. Jingles has been exposed to the Virus—many, many times—but continues to stay healthy."

"This doesn't make sense," Abel whispers.

"What doesn't make any *sense* is *why* we haven't left to find Wren and Claire yet," Ryder growls.

"Ok," Abel says, speaking now to Ryder. "Ok." Then he turns back to me, grabs my hand, and squeezes. "We'll figure out what's going on with Mr. Jingles after we rescue Wren and Claire."

I nod.

"Finally," Bill mutters from his chair, his head tilted back, eyes closed.

Abel glances at his bracelet. "It's almost lunchtime," he reports. "There will be far too many people out and about right now. I say we wait another hour or so and then head to the hotel. Also, as much as I hate the idea, I think we should separate. Ryder and I can take the lead and Cat and Bill can follow five to ten minutes behind. It'll be less likely that anyone will notice us if we travel in pairs."

Abel doesn't say it, but I know by his tone he doesn't exactly want me to be alone with Ryder. Recollecting Ryder's desperate kiss from earlier, I can't say I blame him.

"There's an old bike path down by the canal that hardly gets used anymore," I suggest. "It leads back behind the hotel."

"What about the armed guards at the top of the wall?" Bill asks. "Won't they see us?"

Abel and I both shake our heads, but I am the one who answers. "They are programmed to watch the exterior of The Community. I don't think Dr. Grayson ever once considered that any of his people would revolt from the inside."

"So he does have a weakness," Ryder mumbles.

"Everyone has flaws," I say. "Dr. Grayson's greatest one might just be his belief that he has none."

Abel nods. "He also doesn't know I've come back to The Community with armed reinforcements. At least I'm hoping he doesn't." Abel looks down at his wrist.

"Well, if he does and he's tracking us, then it's not going to matter if we're armed or not." I look to my own bracelet. "It's so frustrating," I say. "We're going to need these to access the hotel or any other building for that matter. Yet, Dr. Grayson has been using these to spy on us all."

"A Catch-22," Bill mutters.

Abel nods, and as though reading my thoughts, takes off his bracelet. "We'll be good with just yours, Cat. I, for one, am tired of playing by Dr. Grayson's rules." He smiles wryly at me. "You got a hammer?"

"My pleasure," I say, and open the cabinet where my mother and I keep our meager supply of DIY tools. *My mother and I.* I wonder if there will ever come a time when I won't think of her as my mother. I grab the hammer. "May I?" I ask Abel.

"Of course," Abel says, holding out his hand and taking a step back.

I inhale deeply, raise the hammer up and over my head, and with one steady and powerful blow, bring the head of the tool down so hard on the granite countertop that the force of the blow makes my arms vibrate with shock. Pieces of Abel's identification bracelet are sent flying, one jagged shard pelting me in the face. I don't even flinch. The moment feels too gratifying.

"Impressive," Ryder remarks, and I think he means it. He then turns his attention to Abel. "I guess this makes you a dead man walking."

"I've been a dead man walking since my parents handed me over to The Community."

"Well, you're quite the handsome zombie," I tell Abel, hearing the sadness in his voice at the mention of his parents, and plant a soft kiss on his cheek. Ryder blanches in disgust.

Obviously sensing the awkwardness of the situation, Bill clears his throat and says, "Ok, shall we pack up some supplies and hit the road?"

Abel and I pull apart, and I look at the two desperate and impatient strangers from the outside as though seeing them for the first time. I know what they're feeling, and I empathize. Just days before I wanted nothing more than to save my dying mother. The feeling of helplessness, of anguish, it's unbearable even in the better moments. "I have a couple of bags in my room upstairs," I say. "We can pack a few water bottles and some food." I rummage through a drawer and pull out a large serrated knife. "A couple more weapons won't hurt either."

Ryder whistles. "Now you're talking," he says.

A few minutes later after Ryder and Bill disappear upstairs to wash up, Abel pulls me into a tender embrace, and for a moment we don't speak. I know what he's thinking, though. Because I'm thinking it, too. His breath is in my hair, and I match my inhales and exhales to his steady rhythm.

"I'm sorry I left you, Cat," Abel whispers.

"I'm not," I respond into his chest, pulling him closer. Another moment passes, and I pull away slightly to peer into his warm face. "I needed to get myself together, Abel. You gave me the space to do that. You helped open my eyes to this mess we're in. I've been blind. We've all been blinded. Dr. Grayson...my father—"

Abel cuts me off. "Dr. Grayson might be your father, Cat, but he does *not* define who you are. *You* are not your father, Cat. Never forget that."

I nod, but I'm not sure I believe all that he says. "What if we can't stop him?"

"All we can do is try," Abel says.

"And if we fail?"

"Then we go down fighting, Cat."

"I won't be able to pull the trigger, Abel. No matter how much pain he's caused me, no matter how many lies he's told, if he won't reason with us, if it comes down to an ultimatum, I won't be able to kill my own father."

"It won't come to that," Abel says, but his voice lacks conviction.

"We can't just leave either," I say more to myself than to Abel. "As much as I want to, we can't just run from this. It wouldn't be right. The Community deserves to know the truth."

Abel's chest rises and falls with a heavy sigh. "I know, Cat. Besides, it's no better out there. Believe me. And even if we did decide to run, what's to stop Dr. Grayson from hunting us down? No," Abel says, "if we want our freedom, we have to go straight to the source that's controlling it."

My hold on Abel tightens. I know he's right. Dr. Grayson won't just *let* anyone saunter out of The Community if he can help it. He will come after us. But I'm struggling with just how much the two us—now the four of us—can do to stop the man with so much power.

The six of us really, I think, remembering with heavy certainty Claire and Wren's existence. My biological mother and sister. No, not just *sister*. Twin sister. Somewhere deep within myself, I always felt like something was missing from my life. Now that the missing pieces to the puzzle have finally been made clear, however, I can't quite seem to accept the truth.

As if reading my thoughts, Abel whispers, "I met her, Cat. Your sister. Wren."

At first, I am thrown off kilter by this new revelation, but it's not entirely clear to me what shocks me the most: the fact that Abel has spent more time with my twin than I probably have, or the fact that he is just now telling me about it. Was he reluctant to share this information? I lean back to examine Abel's facial expressions. His brown eyes are filled with concern. I raise my eyebrows, willing him to continue.

"She's so much like you," he tells me. "I never saw her face, but her voice...it was like a pleasant memory. We were both prisoners of Dr. Grayson's. On the outside. Though I don't believe Dr. Grayson realized the raider had Wren in shackles."

"In shackles? Abel, I don't understand. What's a raider? Why would Dr. Grayson let you leave The Community only to come after you once you had?"

"To ensure I wasn't going to cause him any more problems. He left me in that basement to die, Cat."

Before I can ask any more questions, footsteps thunder on the stairs and echo down the hall. As Abel and I pull apart once again, Ryder and Bill appear framed in the kitchen doorway. For just a moment, I do a double-take. Bill, whose face is no longer dirt-smudged and sweaty, still looks tired, the purple bags under his eyes heavy. Ryder, however, looks like a new man, his thick dirty-blond hair wetted down and brushed, and his sun-kissed skin is bright.

The word *handsome* hovers in the far corners of my thoughts, but I dismiss it quickly.

"We ready?" Ryder asks, looking directly at me.

I tear my eyes away from Ryder's tilted smile, my cheeks flushing scarlet this time around, and make myself busy, filling sacks full of dried fruits and crackers. I clear my throat. "There are a few fillable water bottles in the cabinet to the right of the sink," I tell no one in particular, trying to sound nonchalant. "Top shelf." I hear one of my house guests begin to rummage through the glassware.

While Abel, Bill and I finish packing all of the supplies in wearable canvas bags, Ryder empties his cartridge of bullets onto the kitchen table, to count them I guess. Or to bolster his confidence. I watch him from the corner of my eyes as he loads all but one back into the gun. This one he absentmindedly pushes to the top of the table and lets roll lazily back. I can't help but smile sadly as I remember my mother complaining about the one leg of the table that didn't quite match all the others, causing the table to wobble when I worked through my homework. I never seemed to notice, but because I knew how much it bothered her, I tried to fix it by putting a piece of chewing gum at the bottom of the uneven leg.

Looking now, I see only a trace of the gum that has become hardened by the years. *Like me*, I think, wearily.

Hands press softly on my shoulders, lifting me from the depths of my memory, and I lean back into Abel's firm chest. "I miss her," I say quietly.

"I know, Cat."

"She would want me to fight," I say.

"She would," comes Abel's soft reply.

I turn to face Abel once again. "So what are we waiting for?" I ask.

"You," he says simply.

I nod. "I'm ready," I tell him honestly. "I'm not sure what to expect when we find Wren and Claire," my voice trails off slightly, "but I'm ready to find out."

Abel goes to look at his wrist, forgetting his shattered identification bracelet for the moment, then looks to me.

"It's a quarter after one," I tell him. "Time to get this show on the road."

Abel nods. "It's now or never," he says before turning to address Ryder. "You ready?" he asks him.

Ryder gets to his feet so quickly, the chair goes flying back into the wall where it leaves a mark. For some reason, this infuriates me. I let him know.

"I get that you're anxious to get to Wren," I say curtly, "but you could at least show my house a little more respect."

Ryder's hurt expression surprises me, but he recovers easily. "Sorry," he tells me, but I don't believe he is.

Abel steps in between us. "If this is going to work, we have to learn to get along," he says to us all. "From here on out, we're a team. Us against Dr. Grayson and whoever else is involved. Can we handle that?" When Abel receives three reluctant nods, he continues. "Good. So Ryder, we need to get going. Cat," Abel says, turning to me, "wait five to ten minutes and then follow us, down to the bike path along the canal. Try to appear relaxed but with a purpose. There's no reason for anyone to question us unless they are mixed up with Dr. Grayson. If this is the case, and you're seen—"

"Run," I say, finishing Abel's sentence.

"Run," he agrees.

Ryder fingers the gun at his side, but before he can speak, Abel interjects. "We use our weapons as a last resort," he tells us all, but he directs the comment at Ryder.

If looks could kill, I think.

Ryder tucks the gun away, clearly disgruntled.

On their way out the door, Abel pulls me aside one last time and looks me earnestly in the face before planting a quick but gentle kiss on my cheek. He opens his mouth to say something, but I hold up my hand to his lips.

"Don't," I say quietly. "I'll see you at the hotel, ok?"

Abel smiles, but it doesn't reach his eyes. "Ok," he says, but he doesn't make moves to leave.

I give him a gentle shove. "Go," I whisper imploringly. This time he listens. And as the door closes behind him, leaving me alone in the house with Bill, an ominous feeling overcomes me, the voice inside my head relentless.

"Don't let him leave you again," it says. *"Don't let him leave."*

20: ABEL

Ryder and I don't utter a single word until we reach the bike path. On one hand, I realize we are in a similar precarious plight, but I just can't seem to bring myself to empathize with him. The way he looked at Cat, the way he tried to kiss her—there was too much intensity there. Simply put, Ryder makes me nervous.

He's like a loose cannon, I think, pushing a low hanging branch from out of my way and hurrying down the narrow path that winds its sheltered way to the canal.

When we reach the bike trail that runs along the slowly moving waters of our community's aqueduct, Ryder breaks the silence.

"Awfully quiet around here," he says, and at first it's unclear whether he's talking about the two of us or The Community as a whole.

I choose to believe he means the latter and answer honestly, "There *were* around seventy-five hundred of us to start, give or take," I say, "but these last few years have been rough. Reminiscent of the days of the initial outbreak. At first, only a few were sick, but then, more and more people started showing signs of the Virus. We don't exactly have a community census, so I can't be sure how many have died." I look out across the waters until my eyes stop to rest on the giant wall that rises to the sky. To the heavens. "If I had to guess, though, I'd say our numbers have been cut in half."

"Why haven't more of you tried to escape then? Aren't you and everyone else here afraid of getting sick?"

"It's not contagious," I tell Ryder simply.

Ryder scoffs. "A virus by definition is contagious!"

At Ryder's loud outburst, I glance up and down the bike path and toward the direction of the square. The hotel looms tall and prominent in the distance, and I imagine Dr. Grayson and Wren alone in one room. The thought makes me cringe. "Not this one," I mutter, continuing on down the path, not eager to explain the convoluted history of a virus that isn't exactly a virus but a mutated illness.

Ryder is fast on my heels. "What do you mean *not this one?*" he asks, clearly irritated. When I don't immediately answer him, he pulls at my arm. I yank it away.

"It's a side effect, ok?"

"A side effect," Ryder repeats.

"The only way *in* was with a vaccine," I say. "There were limited quantities. It was pricey. People were desperate, willing to believe anything."

A moment of silence passes between us as we continue walking. Every now and then I glance quickly over my shoulders looking for signs of Bill and Cat, but the path is winding, and I can't see too far down it.

"Did you?" Ryder asks after a while.

"Did I what?"

"Believe," he says.

"I was young," I tell him truthfully. "I wasn't given the chance to decide anything. My parents were trying to protect me. I guess they believed it was the safest decision."

"So then you could become sick. Cat, too?"

"Sure," I say simply. It's a fact that I've come to terms with.

Ryder seems to think on this a minute. "Back at Cat's house, she said something about a mouse."

"Mr. Jingles," I remind him.

"Sure, yeah, Mr. Jingles. Do you think she's right? Do you think Dr. Grayson has the cure for this so-called side effect?"

Honestly, I'm not sure what I believe other than the fact that Dr. Grayson is corrupt and power hungry. "I wouldn't put anything past him at this point," I say to Ryder.

"I'll kill him," Ryder says, and from the tone of his voice, I know he's telling the truth. "If he's harmed Wren in any way...I swear I'll kill the bastard."

We have nearly reached the part in the path that runs parallel to the hotel, and I stop to face Ryder. "Look, we need to remember who Dr. Grayson really is."

"Who he really is, is a cheating, murdering—"

"He's also Cat and Wren's father," I remind him.

"So what? Wren didn't even know of his existence before this whole ordeal started. She thought her father was dead. And your girl Cat doesn't seem too enthralled by him either."

Ryder's flippant reference to Cat infuriates me. How dare he pretend to *know* her? I step so close to Ryder that I can see the pores on his face. I am taller than he is by half a foot, and I use this difference now to challenge him. "That might be true," I say, "but you will not kill *anyone*—not even Dr. Grayson—unless it's absolutely necessary."

Ryder backs up a few paces, his hands up in a weak attempt at surrender. He doesn't say anything, but I know he's embarrassed, his pride wounded.

I turn back to the bike path and locate the trail that leads to the courtyard behind the hotel. There's a bench up near the break in the treeline to the right. I indicate to Ryder to follow me and head straight for it. "We can wait for Cat and Bill here," I say, taking a seat on the ground next to the bench. I reach into my bag for my water, take a swig, and recline against the cool bark of the tree behind me.

Ryder, still sulking, doesn't sit, but takes out his water too. He swallows with a loud gulp and says sourly, "This whole situation is so messed up."

"Tell me about it," I say.

There's a hint of venom to his voice when Ryder speaks next. "You know, we were fine before this Dr. Grayson character meddled with our camp. Wren, Claire, Bill, and me...we had a good thing going. We were happy. We were free. We didn't need—"

"Didn't need what?" I interject Ryder's verbal pity party. "Food, clean water? Gas? Where did your supplies come from, huh?"

Ryder is clearly surprised I know about the supply runs, but Wren disclosed everything when we were in captivity. About the supply runs and the creeps on the bridge—most likely, Dr. Grayson's personal armed guards. About her life in the camp.

"We would have been fine without any of it," Ryder grumbles.

"Maybe you're right," I tell him, "but would that have been fair to Wren and Claire?"

Ryder kicks at the rocks in the dirt near his feet like a sullen child. "What do you think happened?" he asks me after a while, and I know he's referring to the fact that Wren and Claire left The Community while Dr. Grayson and Cat stayed.

"I don't know," I say, "but if I had to guess, Dr. Grayson didn't just *let* them leave."

Before Ryder can reply, I hear Cat's voice from down the path. In a moment, she and Bill appear around a bend, and I stand, waving my arms. I hear Ryder's intake of air beside me as he too gets to his feet. Even from a distance, Cat's smile is breathtaking.

Once the pair of them nears the break in the treeline, I can tell by Bill's face that he's enjoyed his time alone with Cat, and I bet he spent the entire journey talking about Claire. Cat's step seems lighter as well. *Good,* I think. She's going to need a clear head in order to face what's ahead.

I ignore the powerful urge to embrace Cat once she's within arm's reach, and she winks at me, showing me she understands. "Bill tells me my mother's a doctor, too," she says simply, her hand on Bill's arm. He beams. It's as though being in Cat's presence has revived him. "That she all but single-handedly resurrected a community of healthy and happy people straight from the ashes of the Virus."

"It's true," Ryder offers, but his voice is cold. "But I still don't understand why she would leave one daughter behind. Especially if she knew what a monster Dr. Grayson was—"

I cut Ryder off with a shove.

"Hey!" he cries, rubbing his chest where my hand struck him.

"Watch it," I growl.

Cat steps between us in an instant. "Cut it out, you two," she scolds as though talking to two young toddlers. "If Claire left me behind, Ryder, she must have had a damn good reason, ok? But it's not your problem to figure out. It's mine." She turns her attention to me. "Abel, I'm thinking we enter through the door near the kitchen. There's a set of emergency stairs just through the door that will take us all the way up to the top floors. I don't believe too many people use them, so we should be ok."

"You're not worried about it being restricted?" Ryder asks.

"It's a public building. And a historical relic. Restaurants, shops, a theater even. A little slice of the Old-World in our new one, and it's open to anyone in The Community," Cat tells him simply.

"This place doesn't make any sense," Ryder mumbles.

"It's all about appearances," Cat says. "Dr. Grayson doesn't want anyone to become suspicious. If the people of The Community are entertained, then their attention isn't on him."

"Clearly, he's doing a great job."

Sensing the conversation is about to take a turn for the worst, I interject. "Shall we?" I ask to the group, and when no one answers add, "I say it's now or never."

With one final questioning look at Ryder, Cat takes the lead, and we cut through the treeline that backs right up to the empty parking lot. The door to the kitchen is marked with a sign explaining that only employees and guests of the hotel should enter, and for whatever reason this makes me laugh. Cat cuts me a look that asks, *Are you ok?* I flash her a reassuring smile. She stares at me for a moment longer before raising her identification bracelet to the screen to the side of the door. There's a small *click* and Cat pushes lightly on the handle, hesitates briefly, and then nudges the door open a crack. She peeks in while the rest of us wait anxiously. Backing her head out, she whispers, "Move quickly and quietly," then shimmies her way through the door and is gone.

I indicate to Bill to follow next. Then goes Ryder. I bring up the rear, glancing around the kitchen long enough to see there are a few people busily working near the sinks before darting across the landing to the stairs. There's another slightly noisier door that we all hurry our way through, and when it shuts behind me, the four of us all let out our breaths at once.

"Just out of curiosity, how many flights are we climbing?" Bill asks, his hands on his knees. He's looking up the spiraling stairway in dismay.

Cat follows his stare. "Nine," she says. "We'll take a break if you need it, Bill."

He shakes his head. "I'll be fine," he says simply, standing tall and making a move toward the first step. "For you, Cat. You and Wren and Claire." With these words, Bill starts to climb the stairs with purpose. Ryder looks at me, his brows raised, and shrugs before following quickly behind Bill.

Cat doesn't move, though. She's still gazing up the stairwell, an odd expression on her face. I take her hand. "You can do this," I whisper in her ear.

"Can I?" she asks quietly.

"Of course you can. They're your family, Cat."

"What if I'm wrong, Abel?" Her voice is trembling. "What if she left me behind because she *wanted* to?"

I pull Cat to me. "Have you met yourself, Cat?" I whisper into her hair. "There is no one on this earth who would ever *want* to leave you."

I feel Cat's chest pulse with a small chuckle. She backs up and lightly punches me on the shoulder. "You're a dork," she says lightly.

"Yeah, but I'm the dork who's never been wrong," I say.

"Never been wrong, huh? What about the time—"

I don't let her finish. I pull her back to me and kiss her. Cat's eyes are wide at first, but then she kisses me back, her hands in my hair, desperate. I feel her tears on my cheeks and kiss her harder. Our hearts pound against each other, and for a moment, I am swept away.

Ryder's voice from somewhere above us breaks the spell. "You guys coming, or what?"

Cat and I break apart, breathing heavily. I take her face in my hands and look her square in the eyes. "Let's do this," I say. "Together."

Cat nods twice and heads toward the steps with me close behind her. The four of us climb in silence. When we reach the eighth-floor landing, however, Cat pauses for a moment, looking at the large metal door that leads out into the hallway.

"That's where you would be," she whispers to me. "This floor is reserved for wall patrolmen."

"I'm not, though, Cat. I'm here. With you. Come on. One more flight to go." I place my hand on the small of her back and urge her on up the final flight of stairs.

Bill and Ryder are waiting for us when we reach the ninth floor landing. "We thought you'd want to have the honor," Bill says, holding his hand out to the door.

The rest seems to happen in slow motion: the door opens, and the four of us walk as if in a trance down the long corridor until we reach room 914. Here Cat stops and rests her palms against the door. Bill, Ryder, and I wait, none of us wanting to rush this moment for her. We watch as she places one hand to the door handle before lifting her bracelet to the small screen above it. My heart is hammering so hard in my chest, I think anyone could see it. *Was that the sound of the door unlocking?* I wonder. But when Cat tries the handle, it won't budge.

Clearly frustrated, she begins to pound on the door. No one comes to answer it. No one calls out from inside the room.

Gingerly, I approach Cat whose pounding has become more of a pathetic slap, her palms hitting the door more slowly each time, and place my hand on her shoulder.

"She was here, Abel," Cat says. "I know I heard her."

"Cat," I begin, but she stops me short.

"She was here!" she all but shouts. "She and Dr. Grayson...they were here together. And I left her. Like a coward, I ran! I didn't even try to help her!"

"You didn't know, Cat," Bill says coming up behind us. Ryder, his face ashen, remains locked in his place by the wall.

"They've gone to the lab," Cat says suddenly, her eyes wild. "He's taken her to the lab. I know it. I can't explain it, but I *feel* it. We have go. We need to—"

The sound of the elevator doors opening behind us stops Cat in the middle of her sentence. The four of us turn at once and in unison to face the figure stepping off the lift, all of us, no doubt, wanting it to be Dr. Grayson but at the same time fearing what will happen if it is.

When the figure turns to face us, Ryder and Bill, recognizing who it is, let out a collective sigh of relief. Cat, however, cries out and just about knocks me over as she runs past at a full sprint toward the man.

The figure at the far end of the hall doesn't move as Cat begins pounding on his chest and screaming. "Why? Why did you let this happen? You knew all along, didn't you? *Didn't you?* You were her friend, and you *knew!* Why didn't anyone tell me, Don? Why didn't she tell me?"

Don gently grabs Cat's wrists to stop her beating. "Cat, I'm sorry. I told you to leave it alone. I told you you'd be hurt."

Cat drops to a sobbing heap at Don's feet. All the while, Bill, Ryder, and I watch as Don takes a seat beside Cat's trembling body.

"Your mother didn't want to hurt you, Cat," Don says with sincerity in his voice, and at first it's unclear who he is referring to. The woman who raised Cat or Claire. "She made me promise never to let you find out. And Claire—"

At the mention of her name, Bill gasps.

"Claire didn't know." Something about the way he talks about Claire feels *off.* Dismissive. Like he's talking about someone he doesn't much care for.

Cat looks up into Don's face. "Didn't know? How could a mother *not* know?"

Don shakes his head, his tone softening again. "I know it's hard to understand, but circumstances back then were dire. There were riots. Fires were set everywhere. People panicked. And your sister, she was sick."

Cat sniffles. "Don, I don't understand. What does any of this have to do with why my mother left me behind? How could she not *know* she was leaving me behind?"

Don sighs heavily. "Cat, there was a terrible bombing at the lab where Claire and Sienne were working...where you were living—"

"What are you saying, Don?"

"Many people were killed that night. Many bodies unaccounted for." Don pauses and cups Cat's damp face in his hands. "Cat, your real mother, Claire, she left because she believed...." Once again, Don's voice trails off but not before the trace of disdain when referring to Claire returns.

"She believed what, Don? *What?*" Cat pleads.

Don blinks once and says what we all know is coming. "Cat, your mother left you behind because she thought you were dead."

21: WREN

Even though it's only been days since we last saw each other, watching my mother from across the table now, she looks years different. Not exactly older. Just not like her usual cool, collected self. In this moment, her eyes are intensely watching me, her cheeks set and scarlet. Every now and then she lightly squeezes my hands, her arms outstretched across the table. It's like she's trying to prove to herself that my presence is real.

Dr. Grayson stands in the corner, a poised and stoic statue. He, like my mother, hasn't taken his eyes off me. Not for a second.

A million questions race through my mind, but I'm not sure whether or not I should ask them in front of Dr. Grayson. So I keep my mouth shut and wait, my heart beating against my chest like a drum.

My mother squeezes my hands again, opens her mouth, and then closes it. She seems as unsure as I am.

From the corner of my eye, I see Dr. Grayson take a few steps in our direction. His cool voice breaks the silence that has filled the room like a heavy fog. "Claire," he says a little too slowly, too calmly, "don't you think it's time to—"

My mother releases my hands and lifts an arm up to quiet Dr. Grayson. Her deliberate defiance of him surprises me. "Please don't begin to lecture me about time, Scott," she says, her eyes still locked on mine.

Dr. Grayson takes a step back.

My mother's hands once again envelope mine. This time, she speaks directly to me, "Wren, honey," she begins, smiling sadly. Her eyes shine with tears that threaten to fall. "You look...are you...?"

I'm torn. On one hand, I want to tell her I'm fine. However, despite how much I want to forget my time in captivity with the raider, I simply can't. And I can't lie to my mother, so I don't. "Mom, please just tell me what's going on," I whisper, leaning across the table as though this will keep the conversation between the two of us. Dr. Grayson excluded.

My mother's legs, crossed beneath the table begin to bounce nervously, the water in the cup sitting to her left rippling slightly. This time it's my turn to grip her hands tightly. "Mom, what's going on? Why did you leave?"

A tear that seconds ago threatened to spill makes its lonely way down my mother's cheek and drops onto the tabletop where it pools on the glossy surface. This side of my mother is completely foreign to me; I can't ever remember a time when I saw her cry. Not once. I don't know how to respond. So again I ask, "What's going on, Mom? Tell me, please. Why are we here?"

"Wren, there's so much I need to tell you, but first you must promise me something." Her voice is firm, but quiet.

I nod my head, my eyebrows raised. "Of course," I tell her earnestly.

"Promise me you'll forgive me."

I can't help it. I almost laugh out loud. It's so preposterous. "Forgive *you*? Mom, I'm the one who didn't listen! I'm the one who broke my promise to *you*. I'm the one who caused this mess!"

She lowers her eyes to the floor, and her reply is so quiet, I'm not sure I hear her correctly. "If only that were true."

"I've had enough of these charades!" booms Dr. Grayson from the corner. "If you don't tell her, Claire, I will!"

At this, my mother gets to her feet and is in Dr. Grayson's face so fast I think she might actually hit him. "You will keep your mouth shut, or I will leave. Do you hear that? I. Will. Leave."

"Again," Dr. Grayson says without hesitation and with a sneer. "You will leave *again*." He looks over my mother's shoulder to meet my eyes, and like a punch to the gut, it hits me. This is the moment—as Dr. Grayson's eyes meet mine from across the room—it all finally makes sense to me. The intensity in his stare. The gentle way he carried me from the basement. The way he and my mother argue. *Reunited.*

"Wait," I say, standing slowly on unstable feet, knocking my chair back a few inches. "Wait. Mom, you said...you told me my father was dead," my voice trails off. "Tell me you weren't lying about that," I whisper, my hand on my forehead. "No, no, no, no. Mom, is he...is Dr. Grayson?" I can't finish the question I already know the answer to. My throat tightens. I turn on my heels to face him. "You are, aren't you?" I ask. "You're *him*. You're my father."

Dr. Grayson surprises me by clapping, and the unexpected sound sends me tumbling back a couple of paces, and I almost topple over my chair. "See, Claire? Even after all these years, she's figured it out."

Helplessly, I look to my mother for reassurance. For clarity. For *anything* that will soften the blow of this betrayal. But she's looking with wide eyes at Dr. Grayson whose large plastered grin makes my stomach churn. "Mom?" I ask, the panic obvious in my voice. My mother doesn't take her eyes from Dr. Grayson's, so I say again, louder this time, "Mom?"

But it is not my mom who answers me. It's Dr. Grayson. "Corrine—"

The mention, once again, of my birth name sends me over the edge. I snap. I don't let him finish, fresh fury fueling my sudden tenacity. "My name is Wren!" I shout at him, my entire body shaking. "Don't you dare do that! Don't you dare act like you *know* me! You don't know anything about me!" I look again to my mother, whose wide eyes stare now at me. My mother, who has always protected me, who has always done right by me. There's no way, I realize with such certainty, she would have left my father if it weren't the *only* option she had left. *No way.* I close the space that separates us in seconds, grabbing her hand and tugging. "Mom, it's ok. I'm not mad at you, all right? Let's go. Let's just go back to camp."

As I turn to head toward the door, however, my mother pulls my hand from hers. Shocked, I turn to face her. "Wren," she says, "I'm so sorry, but I can't leave with you."

"Of course you can leave with me," I say, reaching again for her hand, more than ready to abandon the past few days behind in a cloud of dust. "Ryder and Bill...they'll be waiting—"

My mother gives me the look that I know means she's serious and places her hands firmly on my shoulders. "Listen to me, Wren," she says. "Dr. Grayson will escort you back across the river." She seems to be talking to me, but her tone is directed at Dr. Grayson. "He'll see to it you make it back safely to camp."

"I will do no such thing," Dr. Grayson interjects.

My mother nods at me in a futile attempt to reassure me and turns to face Dr. Grayson. "Scott, you don't need her. You have me. Let her go, and I will help you and your community in any way I can. You have my word."

Dr. Grayson laughs, but there is no humor in it. Goosebumps snake their way up my arms. "You underestimate me, darling," he says to my mother, and I watch the color drain from her cheeks as she clearly registers what he means.

Still, she whispers, "I'm not sure I know what you—"

Dr. Grayson laughs again louder this time, cutting her off mid-sentence. "Oh, I think you do, love."

My head pivots first to my mother, then to Dr. Grayson, and back again to my mother as the two of them argue over a point I don't understand.

"Scott." My mother's voice is now a plea, and her obvious panic quickly becomes my own.

"You didn't honestly think I'd forget, did you?" Dr. Grayson asks. "She's my daughter. *Our* daughter, Claire. All these years, I thought, no, you made me believe—" For just a second, Dr. Grayson seems at a loss for the right words, but then he regains his composure, setting his shoulders. "By every account, Claire, you and I both know Corrine should be dead." He pauses for dramatic effect. It works; my mom sucks in her breath. "Which, of course, can only mean one thing."

Wait, did he say dead?

"Scott, please," my mother begs.

Ignoring her, Dr. Grayson shifts his attention back to me. He watches me carefully for a moment, as though I were a painting he must analyze before his lips curl up in what looks like amusement. "You don't know, do you?" he asks me.

I can't seem to find my voice, so I shake my head weakly.

Dr. Grayson looks at Claire in disbelief, his eyebrows raised. "You haven't told her." It's not a question.

My mother's hand is over her mouth, her face ashen. She doesn't respond.

"Shall I tell her, then?" Dr. Grayson asks. "Or would you like the pleasure?"

My mother's eyes are pleading, but still, she says nothing.

The secret hovering in the air between the three of us becomes suffocating. *As if the revelation of my father isn't enough*, I think, my heart drumming in my ears, my head dizzy. The fear in my mother's eyes tells me whatever truth I'm about to discover isn't the stuff dreams are made of.

"Scott, don't. *Please*," my mother continues to beg, but I can tell she's given up the fight. It's too late, and she knows it.

"Both of you stop!" I scream, at last finding my voice. "Mom, what is it? Tell me what's going on. What does he mean *I should be dead?*"

Still shaking her head, my mother whispers, "You were sick, Wren. Really, really sick."

"I was sick," I repeat. "So what?"

"You don't understand," she says, her eyes sad. "Sweetie, you were *sick*."

When she says this again, with emphasis on her final word, what she says—what she means—still takes a moment to sink in. Growing up in camp,

I witnessed plenty of illnesses—most of them minor. My mother, she made us all better. We were a careful, meticulous group of people, utilizing all kinds of natural, herbal remedies alongside basic first-aid tools. To date, we haven't lost a single member of our small community to sickness. Not since the Virus was contained.

The Virus.

"Sweetie, you were sick. "My mother's voice plays back through my mind like a recording. *Sick, sick, sick.*

Before I realize it, I'm shaking my head back and forth, but my mother doesn't say anything else. In this moment she looks utterly helpless. Almost afraid. "I was sick," I say to her. She nods. "With—with *the* Virus?" She nods again. "But how?" I ask.

She grabs for my hands, her eyes shining with tears. "Wren, I didn't have a choice."

"Mom, what did you do?" At this point, I'm thoroughly confused. Because there is no cure for the Virus. She would have told me if there were. She would have told the world.

"It's incredible, really," Dr. Grayson says, but I ignore him.

"Mom," I say again but slowly this time as though I am talking to a young child. "How did you do it? How did you do to make me better?"

"I—" she starts, but changes course. "It's difficult to explain."

"Actually, it's quite simple to *explain*," Dr. Grayson interrupts.

My mother cuts him a sharp look. "It would be for you," she says coldly before once again softening her voice to address me. "Wren, listen, honey. You were *dying.* Ok? I panicked. I didn't want to lose you." Here she pauses yet again as if she can delay the inevitable.

"Mom, just tell me what you did. Please."

"Your father and I...Sienne...we were all working so hard to find a way to stop the Virus. But so many people were dying, Wren. It was all happening so fast. We didn't have time to—to be as thorough as we should have been." She inhales deeply before continuing, "Then you got sick. I panicked. Your father was working on a way to *prevent* the Virus, but you were already dying. You needed me, and I couldn't do anything to save you."

"But you *did*, Mom. You did save me. I'm still here. I'm still alive."

"Yes, you're still alive," she says softly.

"How?"

With nothing left to say but the truth of how she successfully halted the so-called unstoppable Virus, my mother lowers her eyes to the floor. Dr. Grayson takes a deliberate step closer to her. Then another. When he's standing right beside her, he does something that seems completely out of character. He takes her hand in his, a slow, sympathetic smile forming.

My mother looks at him for a moment and blinks as two tears, one from each eye, drop heavily onto her blouse. "I'm a hypocrite, Scott," she says sadly. "The very thing I hated you for only *dreaming* of doing, I actually did. *To our daughter*, Scott."

Dr. Grayson takes her face in his hands and looks steadfastly into her eyes. "You did what you had to do to save her life, Claire."

"It wasn't my place to make that choice for her!"

Dr. Grayson sighs with disagreement. "It's like I've said all along, Claire. Sometimes drastic times call for drastic measures. You said it yourself: Everyone was dying. Everyone was going to die, Claire. Corrine was going to die."

My mother backs away slowly, Dr. Grayson's arms dropping to his side. "Maybe I should have let her," she says quietly.

Her words cut like a knife. "What are you saying, Mom? That I'd be better off dead?"

She turns on her heels suddenly as though she's forgotten my presence, her face pained. "Wren, of course not! But I'd already lost your sister—"

Both Dr. Grayson and I speak at once: "You *what?*" Dr. Grayson says just as the words, "My *sister?*" escape my lips. *There's no way I heard her correctly*, I think. But the look of dismay on my mother's face, her mouth agape, tells me otherwise.

"Claire," Dr. Grayson says firmly, "Catherine's *not* dead."

Catherine?

My mother shakes her head, her forehead wrinkled in pity. "Scott, she is. I saw it happen! I watched as the lab—our home—was bombed. Cat was still there. She wasn't with me. She was with Sienne. And Sienne—" My mother can't finish the sentence, riddled with grief.

I grip the chair to my right tightly, afraid I might fall over. Nothing, *nothing* is happening the way it should. The way I imagined it would. When I left camp days ago, my only plan was to find my mother and bring her home.

What happened with Sam, the raider, Abel, Dr. Grayson...naively, I anticipated none of it. I blame this on learned ignorance brought on by the fact that I was raised in such a sheltered environment. A camp where the only violence was the slaughter of animals caught by our hunters and traps. But this? A father who hadn't left me after all...a sister I never knew existed...an incurable illness cured? This I blame on the lies I was raised to believe. Lies told to me by the one person I never thought could lie to *anyone,* let alone her own flesh and blood daughter.

"Sienne didn't die in the bombing either," Dr. Grayson tells my mother matter-of-factly.

Her eyes grow large. "Are you saying they're alive? Scott, are they here? Is Cat here?" I can see my mother's chest rising and falling rapidly as she desperately tries to come to terms with this information. Suddenly, I'm no longer the only one who feels betrayed. "Why would you not tell me? Why would you—?"

"What? Let you believe your daughter was dead?" Dr. Grayson challenges my mother.

"That's not fair!" my mother shouts back.

"What's not fair, is the fact that you—"

I can't listen to the two of them arguing any longer. My head is pounding, and my vision blurred. Carefully and without making a sound, I let go of the chair I've been holding on to for support and tiptoe over to the door. I push down on the handle and, finding the door already slightly ajar, slip out into the cool hallway. I stand for a moment, my back against the door, breathing heavily. Dr. Grayson and my mother continue to argue, but I no longer hear what they say. At this moment, I realize I've never felt more alone.

I stay this way for a moment, trying to make sense of it all. When I can't, I head unsteadily back to the stairwell Dr. Grayson escorted me up hours earlier and try the handle, but it is locked tight. Having no other option, I turn and slowly walk in the opposite direction down the empty corridor to the elevator doors. When I press the button indicating down, however, it doesn't light up, and although some part of my subconscious mind anticipated this, the utter helplessness I feel almost destroys me.

"Come on," I beg quietly pushing the small circular button again and again. Still, nothing happens. *It's no use*, I think. *I don't have one of those fancy bracelets.* I sink to my knees and bury my face in my hands. *It's no use*, I think again. I'm trapped.

All my life, I realize, I have been trapped by some force: first the Virus, then the fences of my camp, and now this—this crazy, upside-down world where you need special clearance to go anywhere.

I moan. *My entire life has been one big lie*, I think, tears slipping through my trembling fingers. Images of the tumultuous river where I almost lost my fight to live, invade my mind, and I recall the earlier words of my mother. *Maybe she's right*, I think. I would be better off dead.

Lost in my ocean of despair, I don't hear the gears of the rising elevator. Nor do I notice when the metal door begins to slide open, and Ryder steps off.

It isn't until he speaks that the spell I'm under breaks ever-so-slightly, and I'm lifted abruptly to my feet. At first, I'm too stunned to believe it's really him, but then I fall heavily into Ryder's chest and hold on as though my life depends on it, flooded with relief.

"Wren! Oh, my god, Wren! It's you! It's really you!"

Ryder tries to lift my face, but I don't let him. I want to fade into darkness with him holding me. I want to forget it all: the pain, the deceit, the betrayal.

All of it.

"Wren, it's me," he whispers in my ear. "It's ok. It's just me."

But it's not ok, I think. *It's never going to be ok again.* And it's with this thought that my body is racked with grief so immense I know no other way to cope with it but to just let go.

So I do. I let go.

PART IV

22: RYDER

"What's wrong with her?" Abel and Cat both ask, stepping off the elevator just as Wren goes limp in my arms.

Her head, cradled at first by my shoulder, falls backward slightly as I shift my weight, strands of her wavy blond hair cascading over my arm. Carefully, with my free hand, I tuck a golden lock behind her ear. If it weren't for our current situation, I'd swear she was sleeping. I have to resist the urge to kiss her mouth. "I don't know," I tell them, examining Wren's face, which has grown eerily pale, emphasizing the freckles that pepper her cheeks and nose. "Shock maybe?"

"Well, wake her up!" Bill says frantically. "She might be able to tell us where Dr. Grayson's keeping Claire!"

Before I can object, the door at the end of the hallway flies open with a resounding *whoosh* and a man of grand stature, who I immediately assume to be the infamous Dr. Grayson, and Claire appear suddenly framed like a frozen scene in a horror film. When the door slams against the wall, the hinges protest angrily, and behind me, Cat cries out. I jump back, sending Wren's head rolling to the side.

Then all hell breaks loose.

Before I'm able to process exactly what's happening, I'm knocked sideways with such force that I drop Wren to the floor as Bill plows past me like a charging bull—a mere blur of color. I immediately drop to my knees beside Wren's small fallen form to make sure she's still in one piece.

"Claire!" Bill cries out, but he doesn't even cover half the space between them before he drops like a two-hundred-pound sack of flour to the floor, a loud *oof!* escaping his lips. Every head in the suddenly very-tight-feeling corridor turns toward Dr. Grayson, who stands with his right arm outstretched with what appears to be some sort of gun in his hand.

Claire makes a move toward Bill's folded mass, a look of horror on her face, but Dr. Grayson forcibly grabs her arm and pulls her back. With his other arm, he lifts his wrist and speaks quietly into the bracelet he wears. He's too far away for me to decipher what he says or who he says it to.

No one else moves. In all the confusion, I forget for the moment I, like Dr. Grayson, am armed. Time seems to halt in its tracks. I study Bill's body looking for any indication that he's still alive, but I can't tell if he's breathing or not. The only consolation is the fact that there doesn't seem to be any trace of blood anywhere on or around him. I want to sigh with relief, but I'm too scared I'll be soon to join him if I do.

It's Cat who makes the next move, leaping over me and her sister's unmoving form to put herself directly in the middle of the fray. Dr. Grayson points his weapon at her, but he doesn't pull the trigger. Seeing that he doesn't appear to want to shoot her, Cat, with a slow purpose walks over to where Dr. Grayson and her mother stand.

The mother she found out about just hours before.

Claire's sharp intake of breath while watching her daughter close the gap between them is followed by the whispered word, "Catherine?" The echo of her name makes its way almost lazily down the hall. Behind me, I hear Abel shift nervously, protectively, on his feet. I squeeze Wren's shoulders. I know exactly how he's feeling.

When she's close enough, Cat lifts a hand tentatively to her mother's hair, nearly the same color and texture as her own. Claire mirrors her daughter's movement but takes Cat's hand in hers. "You're really my mother, then," Cat says softly, the corner of her lips turning into a slight smile.

Claire nods, her face wet with fresh tears. "I'm really your mother," she replies, smiling.

Everyone watches the moment in silence, not willing to interrupt. Even Dr. Grayson seems to be caught up in the tender reunion, but his weapon remains poised and ready, pointed now at Abel, Wren, and me.

From the far end of the hallway, doors begin to open, and the small space is immediately filled with chaos once again as a dozen men wearing white suits and tinted masks storm the corridor. They surround us all, guns pointed in every direction. A handful of them continue down the corridor until they reach Dr. Grayson, Claire, and Cat where they yank the mother and daughter pair apart roughly.

"Hey!" Cat shouts, fighting to get away. "Get your minions off me," she demands of her father.

"Take them to the boardroom," Dr. Grayson calmly orders.

"Just the two of them?" one man asks gruffly, his voice muffled by his mask.

"And her," Dr. Grayson says nodding in Wren's direction. "Be especially careful with her."

I go to stand, but the butt of one of the men's guns hits me square in the center of my back, and I drop back down to my knees. In one swift, fluid motion, another one of Dr. Grayson's men lifts Wren up into his burly arms.

Again I try to stand, finally remembering my own weapon tucked into the waist of my pants, but before I can reach for it, my hands are wrenched backward and painfully cuffed. Over my shoulder, I see that Abel is in the same predicament, his hands chained, too, behind his back.

Bill, who remains a lifeless fallen heap on the floor, is also handcuffed and hoisted up into a standing position by two men who all-too-easily drag him past a stunned Abel and me.

"Where are you taking them?" Cat asks with panic and anger in her voice. But her father doesn't answer her, and I watch helplessly as a swarm of men herd Claire and Cat unwillingly through the door that moments before Dr. Grayson and Claire had exited. Wren, still unconscious, brings up the rear, her motionless body flung haphazardly over the shoulders of the man who carries her.

The sound of the door shutting behind them drops my heart to the floor.

"Up you go," a man says as he simultaneously grabs onto my arms. He pats me down, searching for any concealed weapons. When his hand closes on my gun, he lifts it up and out, bragging to his cronies, "Well, looky what we have here."

"Search them all," Dr. Grayson orders from down the hall. "Even the unconscious one. He'll be waking up in an hour or two, and we don't want him giving us any more trouble."

"Affirmative, Boss. Where are we taking them?"

A leer forms on Dr. Grayson's face. "To the labs," he says menacingly. "I do believe Abel will recognize his cellmate."

Abel, who hasn't said a word through this entire ordeal, finally speaks up. "If you hurt any of them, I'll kill you," he growls. "Do you hear me? I'll kill you!"

"I look forward to watching you try," Dr. Grayson responds with a laugh. "Take them away," he orders with a wave of a hand.

My arms are abruptly yanked backward and I follow, but I don't make it easy for the thug who binds me and urges me forward. At the end of the hallway, our company pauses in front of two large metal double doors, a sign reading *Authorized Personnel Only* centered on the left one.

"I'm going to gander a guess you're authorized," I say to the man holding me hostage. He grunts and scans his bracelet. The door clicks open, and we step through. Immediately, I'm taken aback by what's inside. As the lights flicker on down the long room acknowledging our presence, cages and cages of what appear to be suffering animals lining the walls become visible. And the smell! Ammonia and some sort of super-strength, bleach-like cleaning agent. It stings my nostrils, but because my hands are bound, I can do nothing to avoid the pungent odor except breathe through my mouth, which makes me gag.

"Lovely, isn't it?" Abel says, and it's clear he's not as shocked by the scene before us as I am.

I don't realize I have stopped dead in my tracks until I feel the cold, hard metal of a gun pressed between my shoulder blades nudging me forward. The two men dragging Bill don't miss a beat but continue past the multitude of cages until they reach the back of the laboratory, stopping in front of the three large silver doors marking its end.

Above the door farthest to the left is a large red light, blinking at us like an eye. This is the door where the men dragging Bill's lifeless form stop. Fear swells up inside me like a giant wave. Whatever lies beyond those doors, I don't want any part of.

Helpless, I watch as the burlier of the two men carrying Bill raises an arm to the scanner that will, I now know, unlock the door, and before I can stop myself, I shout, "No!" as I tug and thrash my arms in vain.

Immediately, my cuffs are yanked backward with extreme force, and cruel, quiet laughter comes from just behind my left ear. My skin crawls. "Last I looked, you don't have a choice," the man behind me snarls, once again shoving his weapon in my back. "Now move!"

As we walk past the final rows of suffering, whimpering animals, I glance to Abel whose face has gone white as a sheet. Sensing my eyes boring into him, he turns and meets my gaze. I don't like what I read in his expression: fear, hopelessness, surrender. This is his world. How could he not have known what was going on right in front of his nose?

As though reading my thoughts, Abel whispers a cryptic message, "Jeb was right," he says. "I didn't know it. I should have, but I didn't. We're no better than those caged animals back there."

"What are you talking about?" I ask.

Abel doesn't answer. We have reached the large metal door at the end of the laboratory. Having been opened, it gapes wide like the mouth of a whale ready to swallow us whole. Beyond, it's almost too dark to make out what lies within, but as I squint my eyes, something solid materializes in the far back corner of the room. A bed maybe? Straining my ears, I think I hear the faint beeping of some type of monitor. Before I can make any sense of the space, however, the heel of my captor's boot pummels me from behind, and I am tossed into the cell with Abel right behind me. As the steel door closes us in, the only other sound besides the beeping of the machines and our heavy breathing is one of Dr. Grayson's men's sinister laugh that is abruptly cut in two when the door slams shut.

At first, I don't know what to do. I can't exactly see anything more than two inches from my face. Then I remember Bill, and fall to my knees, crawling awkwardly around the space of the room to find him and assess his current condition. Abel is also attempting to maneuver around the room, but he heads in the opposite direction.

Just as I bump into what I believe to be Bill's legs, the lights in the room blink on, and in the next few illuminated moments, two things become clear. One, Bill *isn't* dead, the rise and fall of his chest apparent now that I am so close to him. And two: the three of us are not alone in the room.

When I turn to inform Abel that Bill is, in fact, alive, I stop before I can even get the words past my lips. Abel is leaning over what I now see is some sort of hospital bed, his eyes wide with horror as he scans the body of the kid who is hooked up to so many wires it's difficult to tell where one starts and another begins. Because his hands are bound behind his back, he can do nothing else but stare at this boy who looks so frail and sickly.

Then Abel surprises me by putting his head to the boy's chest, and the look on his face is one of anguish. When Abel catches me looking at him, he whispers, "I told you he was right."

I stand with difficulty and shuffle over to Abel. "Who?" I ask. "Who is he?"

Abel shakes his head but doesn't answer my question. Instead he says, "Dr. Grayson doesn't care about the fate of the outside, Ryder. And he's just letting everyone here on the inside die. He doesn't care about anyone but himself."

"Abel, who *is* that?" I ask again.

"Does it matter?" he says, lifting his head, pain and anger in his voice.

"Does it matter?" I all but shout. "Does it matter? Of course it matters! He's he's—" I pause, searching for the right words, but they elude me. "Abel, what's wrong with him? Do you know? Who is he? Why is he here?"

Finally, Abel's eyes seem to clear, a look of resolution transforming his ashen face. "This," he tells me angrily, "is Dr. Grayson's experiment."

"His *what?*"

Abel sighs, either frustrated by my obvious confusion or saddened by it. "My guess is that those animals out there—they weren't enough for Dr. Grayson's specimen pool. So he went looking elsewhere. I guess to Dr. Grayson, the people outside The Community's walls—they're beneath him and thus expendable."

"Hold on a minute, Abel," I say, trying to wrap my head around it all. "Are you saying Dr. Grayson's been rounding up *humans*...from the outside...to experiment on?"

"That's exactly what I'm saying." Abel looks back to the pathetic excuse of a kid lying lifeless on the bed. "Just days ago, Jeb was a mostly healthy kid. He was friendly. He loved to tell stories. He didn't want *this*," Abel says, indicating the wires and machines surrounding Jeb. "He didn't deserve this."

"No one does," I say quietly.

From somewhere above the bed, alarms start sounding. Abel, startled, backs away from Jeb, nearly toppling over backward.

"What the hell is that?" I cry.

"I don't know! I don't know!" Abel inches back over to the bed to lean into Jeb's face. The alarms stop and start again, and Jeb flies to a semi-seated position, shackled by all the tubes, gasping for breath, a look of panicked horror plastered to his face which is streaked with purple, protruding veins. "Jeb!" Able cries. "Hey! It's me, Abel!"

Jeb grabs for Abel's shoulder, but his hand closes on a fistful of bedsheets instead. He gurgles, and bright red drool oozes out of the corner of his mouth.

"I think he's trying to say something," Abel says, his voice a combination of panic and hope. "Jeb, what is it?" he asks him. "What are you trying to say?"

This time, with Abel so close to him, Jeb reaches out, grabs Abel's shirt, and manages an utterance that sounds more like an animal's growl.

At first, I think he mutters through his clenched teeth, "He'll be—he'll be—"

So does Abel. "He'll be what? Jeb? He'll be what? Are you talking about Dr. Grayson?"

But hearing these words, Jeb thrashes in his bed, his head shaking from side to side as he tries once more to get the butchered words past his parched lips.

This time, however, there's no question what he says.

Abel recoils once again, and I can tell that he has heard his friend as clearly as I have.

"Kill me," Jeb begs. "Kill me, please."

23: CAT

I'm not sure how much time passes. I can't bring myself to speak to Claire. So I just stare at her, analyzing each feature of her face, down to the very small cluster of freckles that gather on the tip of her slender, yet slightly crooked nose. So much about her appearance, her hair, her skin tone, her blue eyes, is like mine. Yet I can't yet bring myself to admit that she is, indeed, my biological mother.

Because I know absolutely nothing about her.

Dr. Grayson left us in his grand boardroom alone. "To get to know each other," he said. He took a still-unconscious Wren with him. God knows where. Claire didn't even protest. She sat the way she sits now, staring out the window into The Community's commons as if every answer, every solution, is waiting for her out there. Neither of us wears an identification bracelet, Dr. Grayson having taken mine shortly after ushering all of his ladies into his office and locking us in. So the two of us are now stuck with nowhere to go.

I think I should feel some sense of comfort now that I am in the presence of the woman who brought me into this world. My mother. I want to *feel* something for this stranger who isn't supposed to be a stranger at all. But all I feel is lost. Just days ago, this place was my home. A place worth saving. And now? I don't know where I belong or where I'm meant to end up. Is any of it worth fighting for anymore?

Without realizing I'm doing it, I stand up and walk over to my father's desk and slowly sit down in his leather chair. I run my hands over the arms, pressing my palms into the fabric. I do this again and again before attempting to open the many drawers that accompany such an exquisite piece of furniture. They are, of course, all locked. I lean back in the chair and avert my eyes to the ceiling. How many times, I wonder, had my father done the same?

I look again to Claire, who continues to stare out the window. *Who am I more like? Her? Or Dr. Grayson?* I once thought—or wanted to think—I was like the woman who raised me. The woman I grew to love like my mother. Sienne. But now? I realize that couldn't be further from the truth. A lone tear finds its way down my cheek and drips onto the arm of my father's chair. I watch it, willing it to burn a hole into the leather, etch its existence forever in the fabric so my father will always be reminded of the pain he's caused.

Sensing Claire's attention shift, I raise my eyes once again to her, and our gazes lock for an uncomfortable moment.

What do you say to the woman who abandoned you and left you to a life of entrapment with a man she must have known was inhuman? *She* had left him after all, hadn't she? And taken her other daughter, my twin sister, with her.

I watch her chest rise and fall heavily with a sigh before she speaks. "I don't know where to start," she whispers, but it's unclear if she's talking to me directly or giving herself a feeble pep-talk.

Rising to my feet, I decide to help her out. "You could try the beginning," I suggest, and even though I don't mean for it to, my tone is more than a tad icy.

Claire nods her head. "Yes, the beginning," she says, but doesn't continue. Instead, she turns back to the window. This repeated act of submission from the one remaining adult I should be able to count on infuriates me.

"Look," I say a little too loudly for the small space we're in, "don't you think you owe it to me to explain *why*? Why you left me? Why you never came back? Why you chose *her* over me?" My hands form tight fists at my sides.

"Wren," she says so quietly, the name floats across the room in a whispered echo. For a moment I think she's gone mad.

"I'm not Wren," I remind her.

Claire leans her head against the pane of glass, giving the illusion that she might fall straight through to the ground below. She stays this way for a moment, making me antsy. When she does finally turn back to me, tears are streaming freely down her face. "I'm so sorry, Catherine," she says. "I've failed you both, and I'm so sorry." With this, she crumbles to her knees on the floor in a sobbing heap, her hands over her face.

It's odd the feeling that overcomes me in this moment. Seeing Claire like this, helpless and obviously suffering, awakens a yearning from somewhere deep within my heart. *She's your mother,* a voice inside my head says. *Go to her.* Yet for a second my feet stay rooted to the floor of Dr. Grayson's office.

When the battle within me becomes unbearable, however, I run to her and throw my arms around her shoulders, shocked that once I do, it doesn't feel awkward. It feels like home. Immediately, Claire turns to embrace me, too, and, through her sobs, attempts to answer my questions. "You have to understand, Catherine." Her hands stroke my hair. "I thought you were dead. He let me believe you were dead."

"It's ok," I tell her even though I don't believe it is. "It's ok."

My mother shakes her head. "No. No, it's not. It's so far from ok, Catherine, and what's worse is I can't do anything to change it."

When she says this, I pull back. "But you can!" I tell her, looking her square in the face. "*We* can. Stop Dr. Grayson, I mean. He's a human being, just like us. He's flawed. He has weaknesses, just like everyone else." Here I pause, gripping her hands. Because in this moment I realize something. There has to be a reason my father allowed Claire to walk out on him. There has to be a reason Claire is still alive today. "*You* make him weak," I whisper. "You've always made him weak."

My mother stares back at me but says nothing. She's looking at me with an expression of awe. I can't take it.

"Don't do that," I say.

"Do what?" my mother asks, sniffling slightly.

"Look at me like you're proud of me." She smiles through her tears, and the act lights up her whole face. *No wonder she makes him weak,* I think. Still, I know I don't deserve her praise. Not yet, anyway. "All my life," I tell her, "I allowed my father to manipulate me and the rest of us here in The Community. I let him poison us. I sat back and watched as he poisoned my mom—" I stop short.

Claire takes my face in her hands. "It's all right," she whispers. "There's no reason to feel guilty. Sienne was my best friend." Her face grows immensely sad with a memory, her eyes clouding over. "I betrayed her, but she never let me know it." A moment of silence passes between us. I wait for her to continue, not wanting to push her too far over the edge she seemed to be so precariously teetering over earlier. When her eyes grow clear again, she speaks with conviction. "Instead, she raised you as her own, and for that, I am eternally grateful. I think she's earned the title of your mom."

I nod my head, fighting back my tears.

Claire takes my hand as she gets to her feet. I follow suit. "So tell me," she says, tucking her hair behind her ears and setting her shoulders. "What do you have in mind?"

I inhale deeply. "First, we need to figure out a way to get out of this office. And then we need to figure out where Dr. Grayson has taken Abel and the others."

"Do you have any ideas?" she asks hopefully.

"I do," I say. "We don't have any prisons in The Community, but we do have a laboratory with some unusually menacing looking metal doors."

"I'm guessing that's precisely where he's taken your sister, too."

"Wren? What on earth for?" I ask, stunned. For most of my life, my father has been neglectful and quietly cruel to me. But he's never once threatened to physically harm me. Others, yes, but never his own daughter. "He couldn't possibly—" I start, but I can't finish the sentence because I do know what Dr. Grayson is capable of. I've witnessed his evils first hand.

"We need to find her. Quickly," my mother says, the smile on her face long gone.

I nod my head. "Then we need to find a way out of here, and unless you've got an identification cuff hidden up your sleeves, we're going to have to get creative."

"There might be another way," my mother says. "An old friend of mine knows I'm here. We've kept in touch. All these years, he's helped Wren and me without hesitation. He'll help us now."

I'm baffled. "Are you saying there's someone here in The Community who can help us?" And just as the words escape my mouth, I realize with certainty who she must be talking about. "Don? Don Waverly? You knew him, didn't you?" My mother nods. I laugh out loud. "Of course you did! You knew my mother—I mean Sienne. And they were childhood friends! Will he help us, do you think?" I'm so excited by this revelation that I forget for the moment that Don was with us only hours before at the hotel. *Strange*, I think as I realize he never actually made it to Dr. Grayson's office. Somewhere between the hotel and the office building, he vanished.

Where had he gone?

Seeing the change in my demeanor, my mother places a warm hand on my shoulder. "He'll help us, Catherine. I know he will."

Still, remembering the strange encounter with Don in the hotel lobby earlier, I can't fight the sense that something's off. "He was with us, though," I tell her quietly. "Back at the hotel. He was the one who told me about you. That you never would have left The Community unless you thought I was dead." And as soon as I say this, the wheels in my head begin turning rapidly as the color drains from my mother's face, her hands rushing to cover her mouth. "Wait, did you say you've been in touch since you left? But that means—"

"He knew," she finishes for me, shaking her head.

"He knew I was alive, and he never told you."

"Why?" My mother seems to be asking herself, the heavens, anyone who might have an answer. She slowly makes her way back over to the window where she places her open palms on the glass. "Why didn't he tell me?"

I approach my mother cautiously, thinking of any possible, painless reason. "Maybe he was afraid you'd come back," I offer.

My mother turns on her heels, fire in her eyes. "He *knew* I would come back! Catherine, he meant it when he told you I never would have left you had I known you were alive. What possible reason could he have had to keep me away all these years?"

"To protect you?"

My mother shakes her head. "I don't think this is about my protection," she says before growing quiet. She turns to stare back out into The Community. "It wasn't me," she whispers after a moment, a sad smile beginning at one corner of her mouth. "After all this time, it wasn't me. It was never me." She runs a hand through her thick blond hair, a movement that is so familiar, my breath catches in my throat.

"What do you mean, it was never you?" I ask. "Who are you talking about? Wren?"

My mother shakes off a memory that has seemingly wormed its way into her thoughts. She turns her attention back to me, her smile once again replaced by a look of seriousness. "It doesn't matter now, Catherine. What matters," she says, taking my hands in hers, "is that we find your sister before it's too late."

A quiet minute passes between us. Claire drops my hands. I can't read her expression, and even though I know she's trying to reassure me as only a mother would, the air between us reeks of defeat.

"We need to get out of here first," I remind her softly.

"Don's not coming," she replies quietly.

"We don't need him," I say.

My mother laughs once, but it is without humor. "We'll never get out of here," she tells me simply.

"Maybe you're right," I say, taking her hands once again in mine. "But we're not going to give up." When she doesn't immediately respond, I add, "We can't give up."

My mother laughs loudly again. "It's funny," she says softly, looking into my eyes. "In this moment you seem so much like Wren."

Her mention of my sister intensifies my desire to break free of this place. "Well, I'm not. And she's still out there. As is Abel, and Ryder, and Bill. And they all need our help."

Hearing the names, my mother inhales sharply.

"Look," I continue, scanning the room from door to window, "there has to be something we're missing, something that Dr. Grayson has overlooked—"

But before I can continue, there comes the muted sound of heightened voices from beyond the door to my right. Two shots are fired amidst the shouting and are followed immediately by the repeated sounds of doors opening and shutting with great force.

I look to my mother who stares back at me, her eyes as wide as mine. Together, we both turn to look at the large wooden door of Dr. Grayson's office, which appears to shudder with the *boom, boom, boom* of each slamming door.

Hesitantly, I approach the door with my mother only steps behind me. The noise from the hallway has lessened, but the voices continue.

"Try the door at the end!" someone shouts.

"Have your weapons ready," another replies.

Through the thick door, it's difficult to distinguish how many different people the voices belong to. But there is one that stands out among them all.

"Scan it!" an authoritative female voice calls, and almost immediately the red indicator light of the lock turns green, and the door is shoved inward, causing Claire and I to jump backward.

The group of people framed by Dr. Grayson's office door looks like a band of misfits: four men of varying ages wearing mismatched garments of filth and the girl in charge a petite, pale figure with fiery red hair. I don't recognize any of them. But Claire does.

"Oh my god! Alice!" she cries, making a move to hug her. "What on earth?"

But the girl shrugs her off gently, looking squarely at me. She hesitates for one awkward second, clearly stunned by what she sees, before plowing into my chest. "Wren!" she cries. "I can't believe you're all right!" Her arms continue to squeeze harder and harder until I'm stumbling backward into the wall of windows. Once her face is buried in my shoulder, the girl whispers, "I'm so sorry!" again and again. I'm too stunned to move. "I'm so sorry!" she says again, and I can tell that she's crying.

"Let her go! Alice, let her go," comes the commanding voice of my mother. "It's not Wren. Alice, she's not Wren."

The arms that bound me slacken, and the girl holding me inches back a few paces, her flame-red hair disheveled and matted to her cheeks. "She's not Wren?" she asks, confused.

My mother goes to the girl, takes her shoulders, and holds her at arm's length. She laughs. "She's not Wren. Her name is Catherine, and she's Wren's sister." By the way she talks, it is clear she knows this young woman with the fiery hair intimately, and I relax a bit, trying to make sense once again of the bizarre scene unfolding before me. "Her *twin* sister," she says with emphasis.

"Catherine?" the girl whispers as though trying it on for size before repeating, "Catherine?"

My mother hugs the girl to her. "I know it's a lot to take in! I can't believe you're here! How did you manage—"

I stop my mother here. "Can someone tell me what's going on?" I demand. Claire laughs once again, but this time, there is genuine happiness to the sound. She hugs the girl to her chest once more and then turns her around to face me, her arms resting atop the girl's shoulders.

"Catherine," Claire says gaily, as though proudly introducing an offspring to an adoring crowd, "meet Alice. Alice, meet my other daughter, Wren's sister, Catherine."

Tentatively we both reach out to shake each other's hand. Immediately I notice the identification bracelet encircling Alice's slender wrist.

"It's nice to meet you, Catherine," Alice says, but there's something about her tone that makes her words feel false. She turns back to my mother. "Well, Claire," she says resolutely, "We've come to bring you and the rest of our camp members back." Her sharp eyes scan the room once. "Any chance either of you know where we can find the others?"

Ignoring her question, I ask, "How did you get that?" nodding at her wrist.

Alice fingers the bracelet, twirling it slightly. "What, this?" she asks with a wry smile, turning to the four men who accompany her. My eyes widen as I see that they, too, all wear Community bracelets. "It's amazing what you can get just by asking," she replies, simultaneously lifting up the bottom of her shirt to reveal a shiny handgun.

My heart races. "You didn't hurt anyone, did you?" I ask, imagining young Sarah walking home by herself from clinical.

Alice's smile fades slightly. "Actually, we were ambushed," she says coolly. "Outside The Dome. The officers standing guard opened fire. We were defending ourselves." I don't like what I see reflected in her eyes. "Besides," Alice continues, "these bracelets just saved your life."

I don't question her further but file away a mental note reminding me not to trust this red-haired stranger. "Down the hall," I say, pointing to the end of the corridor, noticing for the first time two guards who lie awkwardly in a heap at the base of the laboratory door.

"What's that?" Alice asks.

I can't take my eyes off the two dead guards but manage to say, "I believe Dr. Grayson's keeping the others down the hall. In the laboratory at the end."

Alice's eyebrows lift. "Seriously? It's that easy?"

I'm appalled. *Killing should never be easy*, I want to tell her but instead say, "After you," urging Alice and her team to lead the way.

Alice signals to the group of men still framed by the door. "Come on, boys," she says commandingly. "Let's show these city folk how it's done."

Two of the men laugh, but the other pair wear a look of apprehension on their faces. With guns at the ready, the group of men shuffle down the length of the hallway and stop at the metal doors of the lab where one man calls back to us, "This the one?"

I nod and turn my attention to Alice.

"Well?" she asks. "What are we waiting for? Let's go get our boys."

I follow her and Claire, their strides strong and quick, watching Alice's wild hair bouncing in her wake. Before we reach the doors and begin the rescue of Abel, Ryder, and Bill, I can't help but wonder fleetingly, *Which one belongs to Alice?*

24: WREN

I wake for a brief moment, but I'm not actually aware that I am awake. A soft hum of machines accompanied by the beeping and chiming of monitors compete to lull me back into darkness, but I fight the urge by attempting to move my head from side to side.

I'm beneath a heavy, weighted blanket, it seems, and my feet are shackled to the bed. Except it's not exactly a bed. More like a table. I'm uncomfortable but not. I'm conscious, but I'm dreaming. I can't tell if I'm blindfolded or if the room is so dark I can't see through its oppressive thickness.

Then, from somewhere across the room, a door creaks open, and fear instantly smothers me like a pillow. I can't breathe. My entire body is racked with tremors. I fight to escape but can't move. My monitors go berserk.

"Easy," says a soft but chilling voice as a warm, strong hand grips my shoulder. "It'll be easier if you relax." Something is injected into my arm near my shoulder, and a slow, burning sensation creeps its way through my veins. Despite all attempts to stop it, I can't prevent the drug from slowing my heart and comforting my tense muscles.

"There you go," the voice croons. "Isn't that better? We wouldn't want to jeopardize the health of my patients now, would we?" The figure looming above me rubs a hand gingerly across my abdomen, and I cringe and tense against the touch. "That would prove such a waste. Hmm?"

Something about what he says confuses me, but then again, it could just be the drug taking hold of my mind. Either way, I can't do anything about the questions that swim through my head and make me dizzy. And as the effects of the medicine quickly overpower me, my eyelids close like two heavy metal doors shutting me in and locking out hope.

25: ABEL

After Jeb's short-lived but violent pleas for death, he gradually settled into a restless slumber, the monitors now back to a slow, monotonous, staccato song, letting us know he's still alive. The memory of his voice, however, full of panic and pain, haunts me.

Kill me. Kill me, please.

Both Ryder and I sit benumbed next to Bill who is now awake and slumped over with his head between his knees moaning every so often. When he finally came to from the drug-induced coma caused by whatever cocktail Dr. Grayson injected him with, Bill vomited all over the far corner of the room, leaving the sour scent lingering heavily in the air like a damp, toxic mist. I must be used to it by now because it no longer has a hold on my previously churning guts.

Beep. Beep. Beep.

I wait impatiently for the sound of the machines to drag out with each note getting farther and farther apart until they at last cease, but death, it seems, does not come to those who want it.

"Do you think they're ok?" Ryder asks me quietly, and although he doesn't mention them by name, I know who he's referring to.

"Do you want the truth?" I answer his question with my own.

When Ryder speaks again it is clear he doesn't. "He wouldn't hurt them, would he?" Again, even though he doesn't mention him by name, I know he's talking about Dr. Grayson.

"I would like to believe he wouldn't...." I let my sentence trail off before adding the 'but' I'd normally finish it off with.

Ryder takes a deep breath. "I would, too," he mutters.

Bill groans again. "What the hell did that guy shoot me with?" he complains. "A dinosaur tranquilizer?"

I nudge him awkwardly with my elbow, my chained hands tingling and on the verge of falling asleep. "Probably something stronger," I jest.

Bill moans again. "I need water," he says, smacking his dry lips.

"What we need is a miracle," Ryder responds.

As if on cue, there comes from somewhere on the opposite side of our prison walls the sound of something slamming hard against metal. At first, I think I must be imagining things, but Bill, hearing the sound, too, sits up a little too quickly but then immediately returns his head to his knees, cursing.

Ryder raises his eyebrows, and his look says, *"Could this be the miracle?"*

I get to my feet and press my ear against the cool metal of the door, listening. When Ryder comes up beside me and tries to speak, I *shush* him with a nudge of my shackled hand.

Faintly, I hear the sound of panicked animals chittering and chattering in their cages amidst another familiar sound that has me pressing my ear so hard into the door, it aches.

Voices.

My heart pounds against my chest, and I'm not sure what drives my heart rate up, fear, excitement, anxious anticipation, or a combination of all three.

I turn to Ryder. "I don't think it's Dr. Grayson," I say. "The voices sound too frantic."

I know the likelihood of it being Cat, Wren, or Claire is just about nonexistent, but still, I hope. I return my ear to the door. The voices have grown louder and more pronounced as what I hope to be our rescue party makes its way through the lab. They are too muffled to recognize as anything other than human, but the tone of the group is one of obvious excitement.

A moment passes, the voices become quiet. And for a second I fear the party has left. Abandoned us when we were so close to being freed.

But then the indicator light to the right of the door turns green, and the door to our prison is opened.

For whatever reason, I can't seem to bring myself to see who has unlocked and opened the door. Perhaps if I hold onto my hope for a moment longer, what I hope for might become true. Instead, I avert my gaze to Ryder whose expression tells me that what he sees framed in the doorway clearly shocks the hell out of him. But his shock is replaced with delight as our rescuers step over the threshold.

"Alice!" he cries. "Oh my god! And Claire! What on earth? How—" Ryder can't seem to finish his questions. He's staring now at the third person to make her way into the room.

I turn to follow his gaze and let out a sigh of relief. "Cat!" I cry out, making my way as quickly as I can over to her. She wraps me in a passionate embrace, her hands gripping my cuffed ones. When Cat lifts her face after a few seconds, she speaks over her shoulder to a red-haired girl who watches Ryder intently. "You got anything for these?" she asks the girl, jingling my chains.

The pretty red-head turns her attention away from Ryder who still stands motionlessly staring at Cat and me. "I've got something almost as good as a key," she says, a hint of dejection in her voice. "Henry, can you work your magic?"

A tall, gangly man steps into the fray and unzips a pack he wears around his waist. "Not a problem," he says, making his way over to Bill, who Claire is now tending to on the floor.

"Alice," Ryder says coolly, not turning his head, "where is Wren?"

A brief look of hurt creeps across Alice's face, but she regroups and makes her way over to him. She puts a hand on his shoulder, but he shrugs it away. Clearly, the two of them have some history. Alice lets her hand drop to her side before she turns away. "She wasn't with the others," she whispers. "I'm sorry."

I can't be certain, but it seems as though her apology is for something much greater than the moment.

"Sorry," Ryder repeats. "Sorry." Finally, and with some effort, he turns his attention to Claire. "Where is she?" he asks her.

Claire, who has Bill's newly-freed arms draped over her shoulders, attempts to come to a stand. Henry helps her get Bill to his feet. "I don't know," she grunts, beads of sweat glittering on her forehead. "We thought she might be with you."

"She's not," Ryder says coldly. "Did he take her? Does Dr. Grayson have her?"

Claire, still supporting Bill's large frame looks first at Ryder and then to Cat. There is evident pain in her blue eyes. "Yes," she whispers. "He took her."

"Why?" Ryder all but yells. "Why her? What does he want with her?"

Claire hesitates for a moment before answering him. "A test subject," she says simply.

My eyes go immediately to Jeb who still lies as still as a corpse on the bed in the corner.

"A test subject? Wren? But she's his daughter!"

Claire passes Bill over to Henry, who has just finished unlocking my cuffs. I rub my sore wrists to get the circulation going while I watch the moment of truth pass between Claire and Ryder. She places a hand on his cheek, and he lets her. "She's more than just his daughter, Ryder," she says softly. "She's his answer."

Ryder chokes on a sob. "His answer to what?" he pleads.

But Claire doesn't answer him, shaking her head instead. "Never mind, Ryder. We just need to find her, ok? We can worry about the rest later." She motions for Henry to finish with Ryder's cuffs, and he leaves Bill leaning against the wall to comply.

"The rest?" Ryder cries, not taking his eyes off Claire's as Henry works silently behind him.

Claire nods, her head tilted, eyebrows raised, waiting for Ryder to agree.

But Ryder has other ideas. "I'm sick and tired of being left in the dark. Someone, please tell me what the hell is going on!" He jerks his arms roughly as Henry frees them.

"Easy, man," I say, coming to Claire's defense.

Ryder turns his anger toward me. "What do you care?" he shouts. "You've got your girl! But Wren's still out there. She—"

"She needs our help, Ryder," Claire says seriously. "And she needs it *now*."

Ryder scowls for a minute more and then holds up his arms in surrender. "All right," he says. "Ok." But by the hitch in his voice, I can tell he's anything but fine with what Claire says.

"Ok," Claire repeats, smiling slightly and taking a step back to analyze the rest of the scene before her. When her eyes stop on the lifeless form of Jeb, they grow suddenly wide. "Who's that?" she asks.

"One of Dr. Grayson's unlucky test subjects," I tell her. *Kill me, please.* I swallow down the lump that's formed in my throat, not wanting to admit what I know to be true: that Jeb's closer to death than the Grim Reaper. That part of me thinks it might be best if we helped him along. Instead, I ask, "Do you know what Dr. Grayson's done to him?"

Claire walks over to Jeb's bed and checks out his monitors before putting a hand on his clammy forehead. The room is quiet as she does this. "Has he been like this the entire time?"

"He woke up once," I say, coming to Claire's side. "He's in pretty bad shape, isn't he?"

"There's no way to tell what Dr. Grayson's done to him," Claire says sadly. After a moment, however, she turns to address Alice, clearly having made a decision, her eyes alight with new fire. "We need to get Bill out of here," she tells Alice and her crew. "Can you handle that?"

Alice nods but looks to Ryder for approval. When he doesn't meet her gaze, she lowers her head and says quietly, "Yes, we have a boat. It's small, but it should work."

Claire turns back to Jeb. "Can you take him, too?"

Alice's grimace makes it clear she's not keen on the idea. "But he's sick, Claire! He's—"

"He's alive," Claire says simply, and before Alice can protest, she turns back to me and takes my hand. "He might not make it," she says softly.

Kill me, please. I nod with understanding. "We can still try," I tell her simply, not certain that Jeb would even want us to.

Claire closes her eyes to steady herself before addressing the rest of the room again. "Alice, I'm going to need you to get these men back across the river and back to camp."

"But what about Wren? I want to help—"

"You've done enough," Ryder says coldly.

"Ryder, please," Cat finally chimes in, clearly appalled by his reaction to the girl who just saved us all. "What the hell's the matter with you?"

"You want to know what's the matter with me?" Ryder growls. "I'll tell you what's the matter with me!" Here, however, he stops and decides not to finish what he's set out to say. Instead, he throws his hands up again and storms out of the laboratory.

Alice goes to stop him, but Claire steps into her path. "Don't," she says. "Let him go. He won't get far, and he needs to cool off."

Alice starts to open her mouth to protest, but then thinks better of it.

Cat walks over to me and lays a hand on my shoulder, and I know what she's going to say before she says it. "Let me go after him," she says, but she doesn't need my permission. She's made up her mind. "Take care of Jeb. And Bill. I'll go tame the beast."

Cat's blue eyes are trance-like, and despite not wanting to, I give in. "How do you do it?" I whisper, pulling her to my chest and burying my face in her hair.

"Do what?" she asks, her arms around my back.

"Make me believe that everything is going to be just fine?"

She doesn't answer at first, and I worry that I've upset her. But then she pulls back, and her face is serious. "Dr. Grayson's got science on his side, but he doesn't have what we have, Abel."

I tuck a loose strand of hair behind her ear. "And what is it that we have?"

"Family," Cat says simply. "We've got family."

Claire, having been watching us, comes over and lays a hand on Cat's shoulder, so we are for the moment connected. "And no one messes with my family," she says.

Cat takes one arm from around my waist and wraps Claire up into our embrace. "Not if they know what's good for them."

The three of us stand there for many minutes before breaking apart but not before I see the look of torture on Alice's face as she watches our tender moment from across the room. Part of me hurts for her because I know what it feels like to be an outsider. To feel like you don't belong. The other part of me, though, worries that Alice isn't exactly someone we want in our circle.

I kiss the top of Cat's head once more before she makes her way out of the laboratory in search for Ryder and turn my attention to Claire. "You really think we can get Jeb out of here?" I ask her.

"Sometimes you have to believe the impossible is possible," she says.

And there's something about the way she says this that makes me think she's witnessed this very thing before.

26: RYDER

That's it. I'm through with the charades. Everyone in the room seems content with Claire's ambiguity, but I am far from satisfied. I do know two things to be true, though. One, Wren is in danger. And two, I'm going to do everything in my power to save her.

And frankly, that's all I need to know.

Without uttering a word, I leave the mess of the laboratory behind and make my way hurriedly down the hallway stepping over the bodies of two dead guards. Once through the still-open stairwell door, I head down the many flights of stairs and out into the sunlight.

Once I'm standing in the fresh air of the square, I pause, breathing heavily. The last few hours feel like someone else's nightmare, and once I'm calm enough to take in my surroundings, I freeze.

People litter the square, and as they walk past me, they stare unblinkingly. I turn in a circle, but it's all the same. Men and women, young children. They all walk past me slowly and stare, their mouths agape. Some whisper. Many quicken their steps.

All at once, it strikes me how *normal* they look. Not alien. Each person walking by me could be any one member of my camp back home. Home. *This place is their home*, I think. And I've just invaded it.

Suddenly, Cat is beside me, taking my arm, and leading me down a narrow walkway. She waves off anyone who tries to speak to her. Once we're out of earshot, she screams at me in a whisper. "What the hell do you think you're doing?" When I don't immediately answer her, she softens her approach. "Look, Ryder. I know you want to find Wren. We all do. But heading up your own careless crusade is *not* the answer."

I can't look at her. When I do, all I see is Wren. And each time, I have to fight the urge to embrace her. To kiss her sweet mouth. My cheek stings, remembering Cat's hard slap from earlier. "She's out there somewhere," I say, my jaw clenched, staring off into the square, past the many people who continue to peer down the alleyway after us. "Dr. Grayson—"

"Ryder, if there's anything I know about my father, it's that he protects those who are important to him. And he's made it crystal clear that Wren is important to him. He's not going to do anything to hurt her."

"Do you honestly believe that?" I ask her.

"What other choice do we have?"

I take a deep breath and let it out slowly.

"Claire has convinced Alice to take Bill and the others back across the river," Cat tells me, taking a seat on the sidewalk and indicating I do the same. I hesitate but then take the spot beside her, careful not to sit too close. "I can't be sure, but I think you pissed her off pretty good."

"Who, Alice? I guess I didn't properly thank her for rescuing us," I mutter icily. I couldn't care less what Alice thinks in this moment. She's the catalyst to much of Wren's pain.

Cat shrugs beside me, clearly not looking for an explanation of the drama between Alice and me. "Claire and Abel are scouring the lab for any evidence that might tell us where Dr. Grayson's taken Wren. They'll meet us soon. What do you say I get us some water and some food and we come up with a plan over full stomachs?"

"I'm not hungry," I say, even though as I do, my empty stomach growls.

Cat sighs. "Maybe not, but you're no good to Wren if you're too dehydrated to help her."

I rub my eyes in frustration, a pounding headache forming behind each lid. "This community of yours, it's not so big that one could simply disappear, is it?"

"No," Cat says. "But Dr. Grayson has been hiding his experiments since its inception. What's one more deception? No one here believes he's up to anything wrong."

Referring to Wren as someone's experiment makes my stomach knot. "You and Abel do," I remind her.

She doesn't respond right away. "Dr. Grayson can make a temporary laboratory anywhere," she says, staring out into the square. "There aren't too many people he trusts, though."

"You can't think of anyone?" I ask.

"Oh, I can think of one," she says, "but I don't think Claire's going to like it."

"Not be cruel, Cat, but, frankly, I don't care if she likes it or not."

Cat nods, making a decision. "How's your balance?" she asks. "Because it might be a bumpy ride."

•　　•　　•　　•　　•

While we wait for Abel and Claire, Cat heads off into the square to grab us water and fresh bread, which is, to my disdain, quite tasteless, but I eat anyway remembering Cat's warning from earlier. Every so often, I steal a glance of the girl who looks and behaves so much like Wren, it's physically painful.

When Claire and Abel finally rejoin us, and Cat is fitted with the last of the stolen identification cuffs, we head to a small kiosk located a couple of blocks from Dr. Grayson's laboratory. Out of sight, I finger the cool metal of the gun given to me by Abel before leaving the alleyway while Cat and Abel speak quickly to an attendant who then outfits them with two round disks with handles that don't look they'd support a small child, let alone two grown adults.

"I told you it could get bumpy," Cat reminds me when she sees my look of confusion. "Claire and Abel, you can ride together. Ryder, you're with me."

When Abel attempts to protest the arrangements, Cat raises a hand to silence him. "It's difficult enough to maneuver these things when you know how," she tells him. "Imagine what will happen when you don't."

"Oh, all right," Abel acquiesces, helping Claire onto the bizarre contraption. "But I don't have to like it."

"After you," I say to Cat, holding out my arm to her. She rolls her eyes and gives me the look I've seen so many times before on her sister's face. It says, "*Don't forget who's in charge here.*" It's no use, I think. I can't separate the two in my mind, and my heart lurches slightly as I take a step away from the awkward-looking vehicle.

Once she's standing on the disk, she turns to look at me over her shoulder, her blond hair sweeping over her forehead, and once again my heart involuntarily leaps. "I'm steering," she says with a wink.

Of course you are, I think.

In seconds, we're all on the move, and about a mile into our travels, I understand Cat's earlier reference to a bumpy ride. Even though we move quite quickly and smoothly up the paved roads of the community, once we reach the outskirts of the town, the roads turn to cobblestone, and with the weight of two riders, I feel every hiccup.

We ride in silence until the lights within the community go out and we reach what appears to be the end of The Dome, it's seemingly ceaseless ceiling rising to the sky that is now sprinkled with stars. Standing ominously tall in front of the giant wall, marking the community's end like an armed guard, is a Gothic-style building with spires slicing high into the night.

This is where we stop.

"You've got to be kidding," I say into Cat's ear.

"All that's missing are the gargoyles, right?" she asks over her shoulder.

"What is this place?" I ask as I first dismount the vehicle followed by Cat who parks it in a nearby bush.

"There are three main buildings that mark our community's ends," she tells me. "Dr, Grayson's laboratory, his hotel, and this building."

"Which is?" I ask.

"Don Waverly's place," she says quietly, staring up at the dark windows.

"He lives here?" I don't notice when Abel and Claire come up behind us, but when Claire speaks, there is apprehension in her voice.

"He's one of Dr. Grayson's most trusted soldiers," Abel tells her.

"Oh, I know who he is," Claire says.

Abel raises an eyebrow. "Well, this is one of the oldest buildings in the city. If I had to guess, I'd say there's a passageway leading to the outside here."

"It would make sense," Claire says, following her daughter's gaze. "Don would need easy access to the outside."

"Why is that?" Abel asks her, but Claire doesn't answer him. She takes a few steps up the walkway before Cat grabs her arm.

"I don't think we should just barge in," Cat says.

Again with the charades. "Why not?" I interject. "We're armed. And we have the element of surprise on our side." I brush past Cat and turn to face Claire. "You know Dr. Grayson probably better than anyone," I remind her. "You know Don—"

Claire cuts me off. "But I don't know this place." She sighs. "Catherine's right. We need some sort of plan if this is going to work. Dr. Grayson might not realize we've escaped, but I bet he's got a plan in place just in case we did. We need to be two steps ahead of him." Claire looks deep in thought, searching the house. "She'll be somewhere he can keep an eye on her. But he'll want to be left alone. He doesn't like assistance of any kind. He'll want all the credit." Claire is talking to herself.

Credit for what? I wonder but keep my mouth shut.

"A basement maybe?" Cat whispers.

"Or the top floor?" Abel offers.

But Claire dismisses them both. "Dr. Grayson won't back himself into a corner," she tells us. "I'm guessing he'll have Wren somewhere he can escape quickly if he needs to."

"So we go around back," I say, ready to lead the pack. "Check for points of entry."

When no one argues, I nod and continue around the side of the eerily dark, ancient-looking house with Cat, Claire, and Abel in tow. Walking around the yard, staying so close to the building that I can reach out and touch its facade, I am reminded of the last time I searched a house for Wren. When Bill and I discovered an imprisoned Abel and the raider with a bullet in his brain. A chill creeps up my spine. Twice we were so close to finding Wren. But both times, Dr. Grayson had been two steps ahead.

Not this time.

We're standing in the rather small backyard when Cat breaks the thick silence that seems to accompany this world when the lights go out, and its people sleep. "Look," she whispers, pointing into the darkness at the great wall of The Dome. "Is that what I think it is?"

It's difficult to make out exactly what Cat's pointing at as the thick, opaque wall of their community obfuscates what lies beyond; however, if I were a betting man, I'd swear it's a bridge.

"It looks like a structure of some sort leading away from the house." Abel turns and follows its projected path straight to the wall of the large building. "It seems to lead underground. So there must be a basement." I can't be sure, but it sounds as though Abel's voice trembles slightly.

Again I find myself fingering the weapon at my back. Suddenly, filled with undeniable apprehension, I pull out the gun, check the chamber for bullets, and, seeing it is fully loaded, replace the safety and tuck it back into the waist of my pants. It wouldn't have surprised me to discover that Abel had given me an empty and useless weapon. After all, I had done the same to Bill.

I search the back of the house for signs of life. Of anything out of the ordinary. "Strange," I say, scanning the house again, "there don't seem to be any doors."

"Or windows," Claire adds.

"They're probably just hidden," Cat says, rubbing her hands gingerly over the wall of the house. "Check everywhere," she suggests. "Dr. Grayson will want to keep enemies out, but he'll also need a way to escape."

Sure enough, not five minutes later, Abel shouts, "I've got something! I think it's a scanner!" Cat, forgetting her own advice from moments ago, runs over with her bracelet ready to scan, but Abel stops her first, his grip around her arm. "Remember, we need to be smarter than him," he tells her.

By this time, the four of us are standing huddled around this supposed door that looks nothing like a door but instead like a wall of misplaced cinder blocks painted the same dark color as the house.

"Like you said," Abel continues talking to Cat, "he won't want to back himself into a corner. He could very well be right through this door."

I noisily pull my gun back out, and all three pairs of eyes turn in my direction as I cock the hammer. "So let's go get him," I say, my frustration mounting again. "I'll have no problem pulling the trigger."

Claire puts a hand gingerly on my arm. "Ryder," she says, and I don't like her motherly tone one bit, "there's a good chance we're going to need him alive."

"That's ridiculous!" I hiss. "You said it yourself. We need to be two steps ahead of Dr. Grayson. We are! We've escaped without him knowing, and now we've found our way inside. You're a doctor, too, Claire. Did you forget that? We don't need him!"

"We can't just go in shooting," Cat says quietly. "What if we hit Wren by mistake?"

I know she's right, but, still, I don't put away my gun.

"Let me go in first," Claire suggests. "Maybe if Dr. Grayson doesn't suspect we've all escaped, he'll lower his guard."

"I agree," Cat says. "If anyone can rattle Dr. Grayson, it's Claire."

"Well, I disagree!" Abel chimes in. "I'm not letting either of you put yourself in harm's way," he says, indicating Claire and Cat.

I can't help but appreciate Abel in this moment. "So it's settled," I say with a smirk, "I'll go first."

Claire, sensing she can't reason with me, turns her attention to Abel. "Listen, *if* our bracelets work, and we *can* get through this door, we should plan for the worst case scenario. If we all go in guns blazing and Dr. Grayson has a team of men waiting with weapons on the other side, we're all as good as dead. And what good would we be to Wren then?"

I'm more than tired of thinking this through. "We're wasting time," I say. "We don't even know that she's in there!"

"She's in there," Cat says not taking her eyes off Abel who stands shaking his head, and I know he's trying in vain to come up with a better option.

"There has to be another way," he whispers. Even blanketed by the heavy shadows of the house, I can see the uneasiness in his eyes.

Cat tenderly places a hand on Abel's arm. "She's my sister, Abel. And he's my father. Maybe Claire and I can talk some sense into Dr. Grayson." At this remark, I snort loudly. Cat frowns at me but begins to undo her bracelet. "Claire has one, too," she tells Abel, fitting the slender stollen cuff around his wrist. "Once we're inside, if you hear anything, *anything at all* that makes it seem like we're in danger, come after us."

I fidget. "This isn't a good idea," I grumble, but no one seems to care what I think anymore.

"Give us twenty minutes," Cat tells Abel and me. "If we're not out in twenty minutes, come in after us." She doesn't give him a chance to respond before turning to her mother and taking her hand. "You ready?" she asks Claire.

Claire nods, and with us all holding our breaths, Claire raises the dead guard's identification bracelet to the scanner. When the light above the screen quietly clicks to green, Cat pushes heavily on the door, and the two of them slip through a small crack and disappear into the house before Abel or I can stop them.

The sound of the door shutting slices through the night like a dagger to the chest, but because I'm not outfitted with my own all-access bracelet, all I can do is wait. And Abel seems quite content to do what Cat has asked him to do. *Give them twenty minutes*, I think. *That's it.* With each slow and tortuous passing minute, however, my frustration and anger build like a volcano on the brink of eruption, and by the time we're seconds away from following the girls inside, not even I am sure what I'll do once we go knocking down the door.

27: CAT

At first, it's nearly impossible to see. Immediately beyond the hidden door, the space is dark, and I feel my way along the cool walls slowly, carefully, until Claire gropes for my arm.

"We're in a hallway," she whispers.

I nod in agreement, fully realizing she can't see my gesture but too afraid to open my mouth.

"Let's see if we can find a light switch." But just as the words escape Claire's lips, the hallway is flooded in an eerie orange glow. Behind me, Claire cries out, but I hold my hand up to silence her.

"It's ok," I whisper, finding my voice after seeing we're alone. "Most of the buildings here are equipped with sensors." *And cameras*, I think, but I don't say this. Once my eyes have adjusted to the dim, not-quite-bright light of the space, I look around. To either side of me are cement walls, and I shudder realizing that even if something were to happen to Claire or me, Abel and Ryder probably wouldn't hear it. Not through these walls. I shake off the thought. At the end of the corridor, there is a large door with yet another scanner. "Come on," I say with false confidence and lead Claire down the hall as lights flicker off behind us.

At the door, we both hesitate, an unspoken truth hovering between us. When Claire finally speaks, it's without conviction. "You don't have to come with me, Cat," she says.

"Yes. I do."

"This is all my fault," she reminds me, but I disagree.

"You didn't cause this," I tell her softly. "You did what any mother would have done." I place a hand tenderly on her shoulder. "What Dr. Grayson's doing, what he's done...if anyone's to blame, Claire, it's him."

"When this is all over," Claire whispers, taking my hands, "I plan to make it up to you and your sister, ok?"

"Deal," I say, forcing a smile. "Now let's go get Wren."

Claire lifts her bracelet to the scanner, and once the light blinks green, we push it open. This time when the darkness greets us, there are faint sounds to accompany it. It takes another disorienting moment to figure out what I'm hearing.

"Is that?" Claire asks.

"It sounds like hospital monitors." Lights flicker on above us, and immediately the large, dark, rectangular window that lines the far wall of the room gets my attention. "There!" I say pointing in its direction before jogging over to peer through the glass. "Damn it," I whisper, trying, again and again, to squint through the thick glass. Wren's in there. I know it. I can't see her, but I can feel her presence with every fiber of my being. It's uncanny and unsettling. "We need to find a way in," I say.

To my left, Claire is analyzing the dark window as well. "I wonder," she whispers, fear in her voice. "We can't see through it, but—"

Before Claire can continue, however, the veil is lifted, and the scene beyond the glass illuminates as if by the hand of some unseen magician. Claire gasps, but I am so shocked by what I see, I don't make any sound at all. Because on the opposite side of the glass lies Wren, her body shackled to a table, tubes running in so many different directions, that I can't begin to count them. A heavy silver blanket is pulled to her chin, and her wavy blond hair hangs off the end of the table. Her eyes are closed. She looks as though she's suspended in midair. But it's not Wren's appearance that makes my stomach drop to my feet. It's the figure sitting casually beside her, analyzing a chart in his hands.

"I can see you," Dr. Grayson croons, not bothering to look up from his notes.

Claire begins pounding on the glass, the harsh sound startling me. "Scott!" she cries, "let me in!" *Boom, boom, boom!* "Let me in to see my daughter!"

Dr. Grayson carefully places the clipboard on a table to his left and folds his hands in his lap looking up slowly. *He's enjoying this*, I think appalled. "Or what, Claire? You'll run away again? Or will you kill me this time?"

"Scott, please," Claire begs. "Please, just let me see her. Let me see that she's all right."

Instead of answering her, though, Dr. Grayson looks not at us, but *past* us, and nods. Immediately, I turn, on guard, but I don't carry a weapon, so there's nothing I can do to stop the lone figure who emerges from the shadows holding a gun in our direction.

"Don," my mother whispers, her voice heavy with defeat now, her hands up in surrender. "Don, you don't have to do this. Think about Sienne," she pleads. "This isn't what she'd want, and you know it."

"What I *know* is that she wanted you to suffer as much as you made her suffer," Don replies icily.

It's so uncharacteristic, the tone Don holds when speaking to Claire, I can't believe it's the same man I've grown up with. I also can't believe that the woman who raised me could ever have wanted anyone to suffer. Not for any reason. I take a small step toward Don. "And what about me?" I ask. "And her?" I point in Wren's direction. "Would my mother have wanted that?"

For a fleeting moment, Don's arm wavers slightly, his eyes on mine. But the moment passes as quickly as it came, his angry eyes back on Claire. "She wasn't your mother," he says through gritted teeth. "Right, Claire?"

"Don," Claire pleads again, "it was a mistake! I was young and foolish! The world was dying, and Scott—"

Don laughs. "Please! Don't you think I know? I was there, too, Claire. I saw how the two of you behaved around him! Like smitten kittens. How could you resist? It didn't matter that he chose Sienne!" Don seems temporarily lost in his painful memories, but with one quick glance through the window, he sets his shoulders and shuts his mouth.

I turn my head to see Dr. Grayson watching us like we're characters on an old sitcom, a strange smile on his face. When he recognizes that all of our eyes are now on him, the spell breaks and he gets to his feet and joins us in the rather spacious foyer.

For a moment, no one speaks. Don's weapon lowers slightly, then resumes its position. For a lingering few seconds, Dr. Grayson stares at Claire whose chest heaves rapidly. He raises a hand like he's going to strike her, but instead places it delicately on her cheek. Claire turns away and breaks the silence, "What's wrong with her, Scott?"

At first, Dr. Grayson doesn't answer but takes Claire's hand instead, twirling the stolen identification cuff around her wrist looking impressed. "A wall patrolman, then?" he asks but doesn't wait for an answer before dropping her hand and crossing his arms over his chest, a smug expression on his face. "What's the matter, Claire? Are you feeling guilty?"

"Damn it, Scott!" Claire shouts, pounding on his arms. Dr. Grayson doesn't flinch. "What did you do to her?"

"Don't you mean, what did *you* do?"

I'm not about to be roped into an ex-lover's quarrel, so I interject, repeating Claire's question. "What's wrong with her?" I ask.

Dr. Grayson looks at me as though noticing me for the first time, his lips curling into a crooked smile. "Glad to see you and your mother are making up for lost time."

I clench my fists with rage. "No more charades," I tell him. "I think you owe us an explanation."

Dr. Grayson laughs. "Oh, you do, do you? Think I owe you an explanation?"

I nod.

He turns to look first at Claire and then at Don, whom he nonverbally instructs to lower his weapon. Don hesitates but slowly brings his arms down. "Let's get one thing clear, Catherine," Dr. Grayson says, turning his attention to me. "I don't owe you anything. I gave you life. I gave you a second chance. And all you did was disappoint me."

His words hurt, but the pain only enrages me further. Despite how much I want to scream, however, I stay silent and wait for him to continue.

He looks through the glass at Wren, still unconscious on the table, the monitors still indicating her vitals. "Your sister, on the other hand," and as he says this, he pushes by me and makes his way over to the window where he places a palm on its surface, "will prove to be much more useful."

Claire joins Dr. Grayson at the window, hesitantly laying a hand on his shoulder. "Scott," she whispers so quietly I almost can't hear what she says next, "you don't need her. Take me instead, ok? I can give you what you need. You know I can."

Dr. Grayson doesn't take his eyes from Wren. "Oh, Claire. That's sweet of you. Really. But I don't *want* you," he says.

The pain in Claire's voice is apparent when she replies, "But you need me."

Dr. Grayson considers this for a second before shaking his head. "I *needed* you, Claire. But whether you realize it or not, you've given me everything that's required to proceed."

"Scott, for heaven's sake, she's your *daughter*," Claire says, tears glistening on her cheeks as she turns to look at him. "Please."

Dr. Grayson steps to the right, letting Claire's hand fall from his shoulder. "Don't worry your pretty little face, Claire," Dr. Grayson says, and I know by his tone that he's about to reveal something he's proud of. Some secret he was hoping we might guess but haven't yet. This is still a game to him. "I have every intention of keeping Corrine alive and healthy."

Claire's eyes go wide. "She's ok, then?" she asks.

Dr. Grayson's smile grows wide. "Of course she is."

"But then—"

"What's the catch?" I ask before I can stop myself, breaking into the conversation and stepping between Claire and Dr. Grayson. Behind me, I hear Don shift his weight as he follows closely behind me.

Dr. Grayson laughs again. "Catherine, my dear, you know me so well! But this time there is no catch. You see, Corrine is carrying something of great interest to me. Something I believe will be *much* more valuable than you or your mother." He narrows his eyes, urging me to understand. I look to Claire and then to Don, who seems poised and ready to draw his weapon on demand, and I remember with distinct clarity something Don told me back at the hotel.

"Wren was sick."

Claire's sharp intake of air confirms my suspicions.

"You cured her, then?" I ask, and I'm not sure who my question is directed to, Claire or Dr. Grayson. When neither answers, I continue, "You cured her, and then, what? *Forgot* how you did it?" Because why else would we still be searching for a cure that's already been discovered? Why else would Dr. Grayson just allow his people to die?

Dr. Grayson laughs.

"You need her blood, then?" I say grasping at straws. "To continue your research, you need Wren's blood." But even as I say this, I know it can't be that simple.

"Her blood is useful, yes," Dr. Grayson says, "but that's not what I'm most interested in." When I say nothing in response, Dr. Grayson continues. "In fact, once she delivers what I need, I'll let her go," he says, each word tumbling out slowly.

But when he pauses ever-so-slightly on the word *delivers* something in my brain triggers. Thousands of neurons firing at all cylinders. I blink my eyes hard. Once. Twice. *But it can't be*, I think. *It's not possible*. I shift my eyes to Claire, then back to Dr. Grayson and repeat. All my life, I have lived under the impression that *every* survivor was given the vaccine, the same mandated vaccine given to every member of The Community to thwart off the Virus. No one could survive without it. But I was also led to believe there were no survivors on the outside.

"Wren was never given the vaccine," I whisper.

"It wouldn't have worked on her," Claire says, her blue eyes a deep pool of confusion and sadness. "She was already sick."

My head swirls with questions and possibilities, pieces of a puzzle trying to pull itself together. "But that means—" I can't finish my thought because it's just so preposterous.

"What?" Claire demands. "What does that mean?"

She doesn't know, I think. Why would she, though? Claire wasn't here to suffer through the side effects of the vaccine. How could she know that here in The Community, we only have one final class of students left? One. And they are 12 and 13 years old. There are no children born here, and it isn't for lack of trying. Simply put, babies weren't conceived within The Community *not* because the people here didn't want to have children. Its women *couldn't* have children.

The vaccine made it that way.

Suddenly, my stomach grows sick with rage. "What did you do to her?"

Dr. Grayson laughs again. "You're just like your mother," he says. "When are the two of you going to realize that *I* haven't done anything to Corrine."

"Then how?" I whisper.

"Does it matter?" Dr. Grayson's eyes are alight with fire. "To have Corrine is one thing." Again, he turns his back to us, his eyes once more focused on Wren, still sleeping, her monitors alive with activity. "But to have her child—"

That's it. I snap. Somewhere in my mind, a light switch flips, and I'm suddenly blind with rage. Behind me, Don gasps, clearly as shocked by Dr. Grayson's revelation as I am, and I know this is the moment I need. I pivot on my heels and crash into Don, sending him and his weapon flying. Before he can react, I dive, arms out, sliding across the floor toward the gun. In mere seconds, it's in my hands, and I'm firing at Dr. Grayson. My father. *I'm going to kill my own father*, I think.

When at least one of the bullets reaches its target, Dr. Grayson jerks back, slumping heavily against the window. His face does not contort with pain, however. His expression, instead, is a bizarre combination of surprise and pride. And just before his eyes close, he meets my gaze, smiles his crooked smile, and collapses to the floor.

What happens next isn't exactly clear. The sound of my heart beating like a battering ram in my chest is all I hear, my eyes welling and blurring with tears of rage. Or regret. I must have dropped the weapon after emptying its chamber because it's no longer in my hand. Claire is mouthing something to me from across the room, but I can't hear what she says. Her eyes are frantic, and she's cradling Dr. Grayson's head in her arms. *Why is she yelling at me?*

Suddenly, I am yanked to my feet and realize with horror that I have forgotten all about Don, who begins dragging me to the door where Dr. Grayson emerged from earlier. The shock doesn't last, though, but instead morphs into what I recognize as relief. *What does it matter now?* I think as I relax against Don's stronghold. It's over. Dr. Grayson's dead. He won't be experimenting on anyone ever again. Wren is safe. We are all safe.

Don says something in my ear as he bends to pick up Dr. Grayson's discarded gun on our way out of the room. It sounds something like, "You've made a mess of everything," but that can't be right because I've just freed us all from the one man who was keeping us all prisoners.

Claire gets to her feet and is pounding on Don's back as he continues to drag me from the room, but he doesn't falter. I want to tell Claire that it's ok. That I'm not afraid of Don. He's just doing what he was brainwashed to believe is right. We can change his mind. He'll let us all go. Everything will be fine now.

But I can't speak. I can't say anything.

And when the doors to the foyer are all but kicked in, and Able and Ryder fill the space. I think my relief can't possibly swell any larger. Except there's no relief written in Ryder's expression. He's staring past us into the window—at Wren's lifeless form—with his weapon pointed in our direction.

I don't blame him for what happens next. It's strange. The power of rage. How it comes from a place of love so pure but then twists and transforms into something wicked that nothing on this earth can control. It's the same emotion that drove me to murder my father. It's the same emotion that now drives Ryder to react without thought.

So when the bullet meant for Don hits me instead, and I crash to the floor with Don and Claire right behind me, I'm not surprised. Only sad I couldn't do more to stop it.

Because I was once again so close to finally meeting my sister. And now, as my consciousness fades in and out, a slowly abating tide, I fear I never will.

28: ABEL

The drone of the van's engine is what I concentrate on. That and Cat's shallow breathing. Everything else I try to ignore. It's no small feat.

After Ryder's cavalier and reckless attack...after watching as Cat took the bullet meant for Don and collapsed as though in slow motion to the floor...I could have easily lost it. I could have easily done something I would inevitably have regretted. Instead, I put all my efforts into getting us all the hell out of The Community once and for all.

Subduing Don was easy. He may have been fine with Dr. Grayson's unethical experiments, but he never wanted the girls to *die*. So in his state of despair, I managed to convince him to turn over the keys to his vehicle—kept in an impressive underground garage—and let us go.

Through her tears, Claire told him again and again, "It's what Sienne would want, Don." He didn't seem to be in the mood to argue.

Now, with Wren and Cat loaded carefully into the rear of the white van and Ryder driving alone in the front cab, we make the thirty-minute ride across the river and down the old highway in silence, heading toward the safety (*hopefully*) of Claire's camp.

Turns out Cat didn't actually kill Dr. Grayson. Whatever tranquilizer was fired into Bill was also administered to Dr. Grayson—multiplied by two or three more doses. He's going to feel quite rough when he awakens, but he'll be alive. Had Ryder not been suffering from debilitating grief, he might have tried to alleviate that point. But I just couldn't let Cat live with that guilt.

Now, across the river with the lights of The Community growing dim behind us, I tenderly stroke Cat's cheek with my index finger. She and Wren, lying side by side, look like identical sleeping angels, a halo of golden hair splayed out around their faces.

"She'll be all right," Claire tells me softly. Again, I try to focus my concentration on the static noise of the engine cutting through the night, but Claire's not done talking. "This is all my fault," she admits sadly.

I don't have the heart to disagree but unenthusiastically add, "I think Dr. Grayson had a large hand in this mess, too."

She nods. "Yes, but I was the one who gave him what he was searching for. And I knew what he would do with it."

"And what exactly was he looking for if not the cure for the Virus?" I ask, keeping my eyes on Cat's steadily rising and falling chest.

"His answer to immortality."

Immortality? "I don't understand," I say, now fully committed to the conversation. "Wouldn't finding the cure be enough for that? He would have been a hero."

"That's not the kind of immortality he's seeking," she says.

Something about this conversation reminds me of a prior one between Cat and me. "Wait a minute," I say, Claire turning to look at me. "Cat mentioned something about a pet mouse—a Mr. Something."

"Mr. Jingles," Claire reminds me and then sighs a long, heavy sigh.

"Claire, I think it's time you started from the beginning," I say, turning my gaze to her. When she doesn't immediately respond, I prod, "For Cat and Wren."

"For Cat and Wren," she repeats. And then a faraway look glosses over her face.

"Tell me what happened," I gently demand.

Claire turns to look at me, and whether it's my softening expression or her desire to finally clear her conscience, she nods. "During the onset of the outbreak, we discovered what we believed was a possible vaccine." She looks back to her daughters. "But we didn't have the proper time to conduct trials. So many people were dying. Everyone was in a panic. There were riots and violence in every street. Their father," Claire pauses briefly, "he was well-known and admired. He knew people. Important people. He convinced the right people at the right time to build a sort of quarantine, test the drug on willing participants. But it took too long. Once the project was complete, there weren't many viable survivors left. There also wasn't enough of the drug to reach everyone. So Scott—I mean Dr. Grayson—he took matters into his own hands and thus The Community was born."

"And only the rich and wealthy and important were allowed in," I mutter bitterly, thinking of my parents.

"He meant well," Claire says. "He was just trying to ensure the best possible outcome for our dying society."

"You're not seriously defending him!" I say, appalled.

"I suppose I am," she replies quietly. "But just imagine what you would have done given the same situation. On one hand," here she lifts her left hand for emphasis, "there's a drug that seemingly protects you from the Virus. Sure, the side effects are uncertain, but it *appears* to work. On the other hand, you could take the gamble that so many of your closest friends and family members have already lost and try to outrun the Virus' course. But the side effect of that option is almost certainly death. When faced with such a decision, taking a chance on a drug that buys you more time here on Earth doesn't seem like a terrible option. Dr. Grayson was the one doctor who could offer people that option."

"But the vaccine *wasn't* an option," I remind Claire.

She sighs heavily. "That is where Dr. Grayson went wrong."

I shake my head, still finding it difficult to believe anyone would support what Dr. Grayson has done: singled out the rich, powerful, and intelligent to live in his temporary haven while the rest of the outside world was sentenced to death. A tense moment passes between us before I speak again. "This still doesn't explain why Dr. Grayson needs Wren. It also doesn't explain what happened to Mr. Jingles."

Claire sighs again. "The girls were too young for the vaccine. I wouldn't allow it—not without proper testing. What kind of mother would I be if I allowed my daughters to be injected with a drug that could very well turn out to be poison?" She covers her face with her hands and moans. "But then Wren got sick. And Scott was busy with his project. He didn't even notice."

"Didn't notice or didn't care?"

Claire shakes her head, her face still buried. "He didn't notice that Sienne and I—we were still looking for a better alternative. She and I, we predicted the vaccine would be temporary. And it only helped those who hadn't yet started showing symptoms of the Virus. We were determined to find something more permanent. Something that would also help someone already suffering."

"Someone like Wren."

"Yes, I was desperate to help Wren."

"What did you do, Claire? What did you do to Wren?"

Claire looks at the ceiling of the van, moaning again softly. "Sienne was the one to discover it. A drug that miraculously *killed* the Virus. Halted it in its tracks in a matter of hours. I was ecstatic. I couldn't believe it. But there he was, in his tiny cage, this little mouse who had survived the Virus! I could save Wren. We could save *everyone*."

"Except?"

"Except Sienne wouldn't let me. She said it was too soon to know the outcome. That it appeared the drug might do more than just stop the Virus. That until we knew more, it was unethical to move forward with any type of human trial."

"But you gave it to Wren anyway," I say.

"I went to Scott. I told him what Sienne had discovered. At first, he was outraged that we'd gone behind his back, continued with the project and not included him, but once he cooled off, he was excited. Hopeful even. We both were willing to give the drug a chance if it could save our daughter. But on our way back to the laboratory to try to convince Sienne—"

"There was a bombing," I finish for her. "Don told us the story. You thought Sienne and Cat were inside."

"I thought I had lost them both. My best friend and my daughter." She turns to look back at me, and I recognize the despair on her face. I know what it feels like to think you've lost someone you love. "We lost everything that night. All of our research. All of our lives' work went up in flames and smoke in an instant. I went mad. I wasn't thinking. I ran across town covered in soot and ash to the hospital where Wren was quarantined. I didn't care if I got sick. I went straight to her room and climbed under the covers with her small, ravaged body." Claire begins to cry freely. "I told myself I'd rather die of the Virus then lose them both."

"But you didn't lose them," I remind her.

"No," Claire whispers. "But I thought I had." She turns back to Wren. "All night, I watched her sleep. My beautiful baby girl." Claire strokes her daughter's face tenderly. "I imagined that the world was thriving again, and the Virus had never been. That *both* my girls were alive and well. I spoke to her of the ocean. Of the future we would have. With every word, I knew I was lying. But I kept spinning stories late into the night and early the next morning. She didn't once open her eyes." Again, Claire covers her face for a moment and wipes away her tears, sniffling. "In my despair, I completely forgot that I had taken a vial of Sienne's drug with me to see Scott. In case he needed proof of what we had accomplished."

"You used it on Wren," I say once more.

Claire nods.

"You saved her life," I remind her.

"No, I didn't," she says, and her voice is so sad my own heart breaks. "I stole it from her."

•　　•　　•　　•　　•

When Ryder pulls the van into camp, everyone seems to be waiting. The fiery redhead, Alice, runs over to embrace Ryder almost as soon as his first step from the vehicle reaches the soil, but he clearly has no time for it. He marches robotically to the back and throws open the double doors where inside Claire and I sit in silence, staring at opposite walls of the van.

Ryder and I don't speak to each other as we carry the girls up the driveway to Claire and Wren's garage, which is open and apparently serves as the camp's medical facility. I get the sense that Ryder is acutely aware of how I feel seeing how he was the one who shot my girlfriend.

There are still so many questions I want to ask Claire, but the girls need our attention now, so all night, Ryder, Claire, and I watch over them in silence. Bill, back to full health, checks in on us periodically, bringing us food and water. I can't be sure, but I think I smell the sour stench of alcohol on his breath.

Claire is a wonder. Once she's got Cat and Wren flooded with IV fluids and other medicines, she meticulously addresses Cat's wound. The bullet, I am told, went clean through her shoulder.

"She'll be fine," Claire assures us all.

And Wren?

There's no telling. She's the only one of her kind—the only one given the miraculous cure that might just have the power to halt not just the Virus but death itself. But at what cost? Claire doesn't say.

Ryder, no surprise, isn't handling the news of the baby well. At first, he glares at me in a way that makes me think he'll kill me in my sleep. If I were to ever actually sleep. After some thoughtful deliberation, I decide it's best not to tell him or the others about the raider. I put myself in Ryder's shoes. In Claire's. And while I'm not entirely sure what would be worse...assuming the baby is mine or *knowing* how it really happened...I opt for the road of uncertainty.

Sometime in the early afternoon of the second day back in camp, Cat opens her eyes. Ryder is "on a walk" and Claire has gone to get some much-needed sleep, so for the time being, we are alone. I don't notice at first that she's awake, and when she reaches for my hand, I nearly jump out of my skin.

"Cat!" I cry. "You're awake!"

Her smile nearly turns me into a pile of sap. "Yeah, I guess I am," she says, gently analyzing the gauze that covers her shoulder. "Ryder shot me," she continues, but there is no trace of anger or resentment in her tone. If anything, she sounds like she's messing with me.

"How do you feel?" I ask, squeezing her hand gently.

Her smile doesn't falter. "Like I've been shot," she says, but then her face grows serious. "Where are we? How's Wren? Is my father...is he dead?"

Only one of her questions is easy to answer. "We're in Claire's camp. We're safe. For now."

"And Wren?"

I nod in her sister's direction. With effort, Cat turns her head. She drops my hand to reach for her sister's.

"Do we know what's wrong with her?"

I shake my head, but Cat doesn't see me. My silence is her answer.

"And the baby?"

"We won't know anything until it's born." I give Cat a moment to process it all before I continue. "Your mother seems to think that Wren's in a stress-induced coma...that the...that everything...every trauma that she's recently been through finally caught up with her, and she simply couldn't cope any longer."

Cat uses her other hand to wipe away her tears. "Well, we have time now, right? We're in good hands with Claire. We're safe. Right?" Cat turns to look at me, her eyes pleading. And I can't help it. I can't lie to her. I never could.

"Cat," I say gently. "Dr. Grayson's alive. The weapon you fired was filled with tranquilizers. Not bullets." Again, I let this information settle before I continue. I'm not entirely sure how fragile Cat is right now. "We can only stay here as long as he's willing to let us."

If Cat's shocked by this revelation, she doesn't show it. Instead, she sits up in her bed, grimacing from the pain. "Well, that's not going to work," she tells me resolutely.

"It's the only thing for us to do."

"What? Run?" Cat looks again to her sister. "That didn't work so well the last time, did it, though?"

Her comment stings. "What do you suggest we do then?" I ask her, masking the hurt in my voice.

"We fight," she says matter-of-factly, still looking at her sister who, despite everything she's been through, looks to be at peace. "We keep fighting. For Wren," she whispers, "and for us." When she turns back to face me, her deep blue eyes shining with tears, something inside me ignites a warmth beginning in my stomach and weaving its way straight to my heart.

Hope.

"We keep fighting," I repeat because I cannot bear to break her heart. And because if Cat believes we can defeat Dr. Grayson—her father—in battle, then who am I to convince her otherwise?

29: WREN

I hear everything they say. Claire, Ryder, Abel, and Bill. My sister, Cat. Every word. Every sigh. Every intake of breath. I feel every gentle kiss from Ryder, every squeeze of the hand. I know what's happening to my body. I know that for reasons the universe can't possibly explain to me, I am carrying another life inside of me, a life that might prove vital to the rest of our existence.

Still, I say nothing in response. I can't seem to will my body to move, trapped by some invisible force that seems to know me better than I know myself. Fear keeps me a willing prisoner. In my current state, I am not in pain. I am not suffering. Once fully awake, however, I know I will be forced to confront my reality. And, simply put, I'm not sure I would survive it.

So I remain numb to it all, content with my decision to lie dormant.

But when Cat and I are finally alone, the others presumably having gone to sleep, and she speaks to me, a piece of my resolve shatters.

She tells me about her childhood. About Sienne. How she wishes I could have been a part of it all. How I *should* have been a part of it all. She tells me about her first kiss with Abel, how she knew she loved him from the time they were children. It makes me think of Ryder. And I want to ask her how she finds it possible to feel anything even *resembling* love in a world so jaded. I want to ask her how she finds herself capable of believing there is still good in people when I've seen so much bad. But I don't. Because when she speaks, her voice is light and happy. Hopeful even. And who am I to take that from her?

"Can you hear me, Wren?" my sister asks me after a while, laying her head softly on my chest. "Can you hear anything I'm saying? Anything at all?"

The longing—the hope in her voice—makes my heart ache. I want to tell her that I can. I want to shout, "I can hear you, Cat! I can!" I want to tell her that if anyone has the power to set me free, it's her. That she should never,

ever give up. Not on me, not on our families, not on our world. That it might be worth the fight after all.

But I can't. Not yet. Because I'm not ready.

I'm not sure I'll ever be ready.

But I can hope.

I can hope.

EPILOGUE

No one suspected what I was up to. No one believed that sweet, forgiving Sienne could even be capable of such mass destruction.

But I knew what Claire was going to do even before she did. And I wasn't going to stand back and allow it. Of course, I let her believe I had forgiven her. "It was a one-night stand," she told me through her tears. "It was a mistake. It didn't mean anything."

But it meant something to me and my barren and imperfect womb.

With my husband, she had conceived not one but two children. Two perfectly healthy and beautiful girls. Anyone who met them couldn't help but love them. I loved them. Even though every day they served as living, breathing reminders of the ultimate betrayal.

When Corrine got sick, a small, dark, shallow corner of my heart was happy. Finally, I thought, Claire would suffer as I had suffered. But the larger part of my heart hurt. Deeply. It wasn't Corrine's fault her father was unfaithful. It wasn't the little girl's fault her mother couldn't resist the charms of Dr. Scott Grayson.

So together, Claire and I fought to find a cure that would save Corrine. Neither of us slept. Neither of us gave up until the early morning hours when the impossible became possible. The idea came to me in a dream after I had unwillingly drifted off to sleep atop a pile of paperwork, a photograph of the twins in my hand. But upon waking the idea stayed with me, a persistent, beguiling voice daring me, tempting me. What if? What if?

Claire's two little girls, Catherine and Corrine, were my inspiration. The very existence of identical twins was a miracle of nature. A tiny little embryo with the power to divide in half to create two of the same.

The idea made me giddy with excitement. With hope. And because my desire to save Corrine—not to mention a rapidly dying world—was so immense, and because I am a scientist searching always for undiscovered possibilities, I didn't think about the potential moral and ethical dilemmas I would dredge up if my idea worked.

And it did work.

But at what cost?

Killing two to save one.

Because in order to cure three-year-old Corrine, a doctor would first need two embryos. But not just any two embryos. Two embryos having just gone through the miraculous divide into twins. At the precise moment, a doctor would then need to extract the stem cells of these embryos to create the serum that could finally be injected into the dying patient where the drug would then attack and replace her cells with newer healthier ones. Over and over and over again.

Which, if my theory was correct, would mean that not only would little Corrine survive the Virus. She would also survive death.

Of course, I shared my discovery with Claire. And of course, she demanded we take the information and the serum straight to Scott. But I couldn't ignore the feeling of guilt that began tugging and gnawing at my heart the moment I destroyed the perfectly healthy set of embryos required to make this miracle drug possible.

Mice are one thing, but human life? Who are we to play God? I asked Claire.

But she wouldn't listen to me. Corrine was dying, she screamed. What was the issue?

Murder? I suggested.

When Claire ran from the room sobbing and unwilling to hear me out, I went to the one person I knew would listen. The one person in the remaining world who would do anything I asked of him. The one person who, through it all, had remained loyal. I went to Don and asked him to destroy the lab, the last place all of us, Claire, Scott, the girls, me, called home.

Then I took young Catherine's hand in mine, and we went to the amusement park for the afternoon where we smiled and enjoyed the day despite the threat of the Virus. Despite the fact that Corrine would die.

I didn't know Claire would run. I didn't know she would take a vial of the serum with her when she did. I didn't know she would take a gamble with her daughter's life. I didn't know that I would never forgive myself for *believing I had destroyed the one hope our society had left, for thinking I had wasted the lives of two perfectly healthy embryos.*

    I didn't know.
    I didn't know.
    I didn't know.
    I didn't know.

believing I had destroyed the one hope our society had left, for thinking I had wasted the lives of two perfectly healthy embryos.

ACKNOWLEDGEMENTS

This book was a journey that initially began as a novel-length horror story drafted during the summer I turned fourteen. Since then, it has been many things: a handwritten sketch in a classroom journal, a short story about a miraculous anti-aging drug gone wrong, a few wispy chapters spit out during my first shared venture through Nanowrimo. Add six years, one very frightening *Time Magazine* news article about antibiotic resistance, countless revisions, and one summer where I all but neglected my children, and the dream of finishing my first novel *Resistant* was finally realized.

A special and heartfelt thank you to Alice Warnick whose comments, questions, insights, and falling-out-of-the-desk stories while reading the initial manuscript kept me on my toes and eager to keep the story alive. Thirsty young readers are the reason I write, and you, Alice, are at the front of the pack.

Thank you to my wonderful students who never stopped encouraging me to finish the story I am so passionate about, especially those in my creative writing club who read and "reviewed" the earlier chapters. I hope I have been as much of an inspiration to you all as you all have been to me.

Thank you to my English teachers who instilled in me a love of literature and writing. I am especially grateful to Donna Butler, my eighth-grade teacher. You lit the match that ignited the writing fire within me with your novelette assignment, which, by the way, I still have tucked away in my bedroom closet. I am also indebted to my fabulous twelfth-grade creative writing teacher Julie Givler who continued to stoke the fire with inspiring prompts, music, and magical trips to places like Hollywood Cemetery where our one task as students was simply *to write*.

Thank you to my family. To my literature-hungry daughter, I can't express through words how much I relished your breath on my cheek as you read over my shoulder while I wrote. To Holden and Rylan, my energetic boys, thank you for not destroying the house or each other while I "worked from home." And to my husband who gave me the support and time I needed, thank you, thank you, *thank you*.

And to Judy Poore—this book is because you believed. You were the first to read the initial chapters, and it was your enthusiasm for Cat, Wren and their story that encouraged me to keep writing. Without your continued guidance and support throughout the process, *Resistant* would still be just a few unfinished pages, a story left untold. Simply put, you were a light when the struggle of writing often became dark. The phrase 'thank you' is nowhere near adequate.

Finally, to Erin, my other half: You and I both know there's a unique bond shared between identical twins that *only* identical twins can understand. We finish each other's thoughts. We know each other's deepest, darkest, truest feelings and secrets. We celebrate each other's successes. We suffer through each other's heartbreaks. Without you, I would be lost. Truly. This book is for you and all the ways we complete each other—even from across the miles.

NOTE FROM THE AUTHOR

Word-of-mouth is crucial for any author to succeed. If you enjoyed the book, please leave a review online—anywhere you are able. Even if it's just a sentence or two. It would make all the difference and would be very much appreciated.

Thanks!
Erika

ABOUT THE AUTHOR

Erika Modrak graduated from the University of Virginia with a degree in English literature. Her debut novel, *Resistant*, was written while teaching English and creative writing to middle-school teens, many of whom she credits for the novel's completion. She lives with her husband and three children in Virginia.

Thank you so much for reading one of our **Sci-Fi** novels.

If you enjoyed our book, please check out our recommended title for
your next great read!

People of Metal by Robert Snyder

The well-intentioned leaders of China and the U.S. form a grand
partnership to create human robots for every human vocation in
every country in the world. The human robots proliferate, economic
output soars, and the entire world prospers. It's a new Golden Age.
But there are unintended consequences—consequences that will
place biological humanity on a road to extinction. Ultimately, it will
fall to the human robots themselves to rescue biological humanity
and restore its civilization.

View other Black Rose Writing titles at
www.blackrosewriting.com/books and use promo code
PRINT to receive a **20% discount** when purchasing.